Dear Reader,

In 2012 I was forty years old. I was an author who had topped
bestseller lists in six countries, I'd just moved into my dream
house and achieved most of my life goals but felt so miserable
that I tried to kill myself.

I wound up spending three months in a psychiatric hospital.
I met my characters Georgia and Julius there, or at least
troubled but brilliant teenagers who were very much like them.

In group therapy I listened to their stories of adult betrayal,
crippling academic expectations and, above all else, the
way these young adults wanted to be good people but didn't
know how.

When I left hospital I wanted to write about my experience and
the people I'd met, but it took me five years to figure out how to
find a way. The result is Arctic Zoo, a book about two teens who
meet in a mental health unit and want to make a difference in a
world where there are a lot more questions than answers.

I hope you enjoy reading it!

Robert Muchamore

ARCTIC ZOO

ROBERT MUCHAMORE
ARCTIC ZOO

Special thanks to the Inclusive Minds network of Inclusion Ambassadors for their input.

First published in Great Britain in 2019 by
HOT KEY BOOKS
80–81 Wimpole St, London W1G 9RE
www.hotkeybooks.com

A CIP catalogue record for this book is available from the British Library.

HB ISBN: 978-1-4714-0764-2
TPB ISBN 978-1-4714–0832-8
also available as an ebook

1

Designed by Perfect Bound Ltd
Printed and bound in Great Britain by Clays Ltd, Elcograf S.p.A.

Hot Key Books is an imprint of Bonnier Books UK
www.bonnierbooks.co.uk

PART ONE

PART ONE

Walter J Freeman Adolescent Mental Health Unit – East Grinstead, UK

Georgia Pack tilted on the back legs of a plastic stacking chair, curling socked toes into the therapy room's grungy turquoise carpet. Her eyes scanned the ceiling tiles as she tuned out, letting Henry's voice merge with the rattling air con.

Georgia was fifteen and she'd been on the unit long enough to know things. Like the knack for opening the jammed dryer in the laundry room and that Monday night's Quorn Bolognese was best avoided. On weekdays, patients who weren't psychotic or sedated had group therapy. Georgia shared the circle of chairs with four fellow teens and a slight Indian therapist named Tanvi.

Henry dominated the therapy session. Seventeen and pretty. Floppy hair, stout legs. Canterbury training pants tucked into striped rugby socks. His posh accent and machine-gun laugh were everywhere on the unit, carrying up stairwells and booming in the dining room. Georgia even heard blasts of Henry from the smokers' patio if she opened the window in her room to shift the unit's hot, dead air.

At thirteen, Ross was the youngest patient in the unit. He sat fidgeting with a stick of lip balm and nodding approval at every word out of Henry's mouth. Laura was a shy new arrival, with elastic bandage up the arm she'd gouged when she tried to kill herself three nights earlier. The last patient in the group was Georgia's friend Alex. Broad-shouldered, with the number nine peeling off the back of an old Newcastle United shirt.

Georgia knew something was up with Alex. She liked to spar with Henry in group, but today her friend had let him grind on, ignoring obvious chances to swat his ego.

'Our au pair drove all the bloody way from Hertfordshire with my Xbox,' Henry ranted, growing more irate with every sentence. 'I set up a death match with my buddies in the rec room. Then Keith the nurse strides in. Sees my HDMI lead going from the Xbox to the telly on the wall and tells us it's too long.

'I know we're not allowed to have long cables so us loons can't neck ourselves. But he wanted to take it right there, with the three of us mid-tournament. I said I'd hand the cable in at the nurses' station when we'd finished playing and get our au pair to bring a shorter cable . . .'

Tanvi the therapist made a stop-talking gesture. Then spoke with a lisp that made *sss* come out like *thh*.

'This is where you lost your temper and there was an incident?'

'I hardly *lotht* my temper,' Henry mocked, sitting up defensively and tucking his feet under the chair. 'Keith tried to yank my Xbox cable. I pushed him away and he tripped on the stack of board games. Keith charged back to the nurses' station and made a tiny incident into this huge thing. The night manager came out, saying she was locking the rec room, and made us all go back to our rooms . . .'

'Let's pause there,' Tanvi interrupted. 'Henry has issues with impulse control and this is a good opportunity to discuss techniques that could have stopped a situation from escalating.'

Georgia cringed at Tanvi calling Henry's problem impulse control. 'Nasty thug' felt more truthful.

4

Henry's story was known around the unit. He'd been dumped by his boarding-school girlfriend. A couple of months later, he'd seen her kissing a music student at a house party. Henry sucker-punched the student, shoved him down a flight of stairs and stomped his head into a four-day coma.

Any ordinary brat would have bounced to jail, but Henry's daddy found a fancy lawyer, who paid an even fancier psychiatrist to write a report, claiming that Henry had cognitive issues and had been suffering from depression, which led to his outburst of 'uncharacteristic behaviour'.

So Henry got to spend nine months at the Freeman Unit, bleating about his Xbox getting confiscated, instead of three years in young offenders with lads whose parents didn't own three houses and a sixteen-metre racing yacht.

'What behavioural technique could Henry have used to help control his anger?' Tanvi asked the five patients.

Ross broke a moment's silence. 'That thought, feeling, behaviour, triangle thingy?' he guessed, keen to please.

Tanvi shook her head. 'The cognitive triangle is used to understand how our feelings affect our behaviour. I'm talking about a specific technique that I mentioned earlier in this session...'

Ross blurted when he got it. 'Transposition. Like, when before reacting, you try to put yourself in the other person's shoes.'

'Brilliant, Ross,' Tanvi said brightly. 'Henry, instead of jumping straight to anger, try to imagine Keith's position. When a nurse in a mental health facility walks into a room and sees a length of cable that a patient might use to harm themselves, what might they be thinking?'

'Keith is only a student nurse,' Ross said, lapping up the

5

therapist's approval. 'He's probably scared about losing his job or getting in trouble with management.'

Georgia nodded supportively. 'The nurses work twelve-hour shifts. Keith was probably wiped by the time he came in and saw Henry playing video games . . .'

Georgia had eight million Instagram followers and a face that had been on magazine covers. Henry couldn't look down on her so focused his resentment on Ross.

'Why are you against me?' Henry growled menacingly.

'Henry,' Tanvi said sternly. Therapists were supposed to stay neutral, but she couldn't completely hide her irritation. 'I'm trying to help you deal with anger issues. Please tell me something Keith might have been thinking during the confrontation?'

Henry didn't want to play. He folded his arms and his voice went high.

'God!' he blurted, knee bouncing and knuckles turning white. 'I feel like everyone in this room is attacking me!'

Tanvi was about to speak, but Alex finally broke the silence.

'You're a total drama queen, Henry,' Alex blurted. 'Your stupid voice has been drilling into my head for most of the last hour. Nothing is *ever* your fault. Your au pair brought the wrong clothes, some of the night staff don't let you have pizza delivered, your Xbox, blah, blah, blah . . . And the second someone disagrees or challenges, you claim we're attacking you.'

Tanvi made a simmer-down gesture to Alex. 'It's good to finally hear you contribute, Alex, but you know the group rules. Remain fully in your seat and make sure comments are constructive, not abusive.'

Alex moaned with exasperation. 'Henry almost stamped a

guy to death. In the six weeks since I got here, I've heard him verbally bully younger patients, like Ross. He's yelled at nurses and lobbed scrambled eggs at kitchen staff. The point of group therapy is to talk through your problems. But how can that work with a person who can't handle the slightest suggestion that something might be his own fault?'

Henry looked at Tanvi, clutching his chest like he'd been shot. 'Are you going to let her attack me like that?'

Tanvi paused for a deep breath, stressed but projecting calm. 'Alex's tone could be less aggressive, but she's raised an interesting point about how we need to examine ourselves honestly to benefit from group therapy.'

'I'm stuck in this place, aren't I?' Henry spat. 'I got expelled from one of the best schools in the country. Am I not being punished?'

Alex tutted and grabbed her hair. 'I've been in young offenders. This place is a Holiday Inn by comparison.'

'Why should I justify myself to a girl who smoked crack when she was twelve?' Henry blurted.

Georgia shot up and yelled, 'That's out of order, Henry.'

Tanvi made two sharp claps, asserting herself before her group got out of control.

'Cool heads,' she said firmly. 'Abuse is never acceptable during group work. Settle in your chairs . . . We only have a few minutes of the session left. Let's take out the sting with some breathing exercises.'

'I can't be in a room with that knobhead,' Alex spat, hooking her fingertips inside the wrecked pair of New Balance under her chair and making for the door. 'Sorry . . .'

'We all agreed to abide by the group rules,' Tanvi pleaded. 'That includes staying in the room for the full hour.'

Georgia glowered at Henry, now wearing a triumphant smirk. She didn't want to stay in the therapy room when she heard Alex smash her palm against the vending machine in the lounge outside. But, unlike Henry, the expensive psychiatrist had yet to write her report on Georgia. She had to toe the line if she wanted to stay out of prison . . .

'This session is almost over,' Tanvi said, gesturing Georgia towards the door. 'Alex probably needs you more than we do.'

The deserted lounge area had a dozen sofas arranged in rows. Patients did group or addiction therapy in rooms that branched off either side. The coffee and snack machines were against the wall by the main doors and Alex pounded the machine again as Georgia closed in.

'Henry sucks!' Alex said, eyes glazing as Georgia gave her a hug.

Georgia knew that something more than Henry was bugging her friend.

'You were so quiet in there,' Georgia said.

Alex shrugged as she jabbed the button for hot chocolate. 'You didn't have to run out after me. You've got your sentencing coming up.'

'At least we beat the queue for drinks,' Georgia said.

When the clock hit four, the unit's teenaged patients would stream out of therapy rooms, checking phones and forming a queue for hot drinks, chocolate bars and McCoy's crinkle-cut crisps. The Henry types would sprawl over the lounge, flirting and yapping until the kitchen opened for dinner, while the shy and desperate hid in their rooms.

'My stepdad spoke to his insurance company,' Alex confessed reluctantly as her drink spattered into a cardboard cup. 'They won't extend my stay here beyond forty-five days.

He can't afford to pay himself. With my drugs and psychiatrist bills, it's a thousand quid a day.'

'Sucks here anyway,' Georgia said, trying to smile but hating that so many kids left the unit when insurance money ran out, instead of when they'd got better. 'What happened to that NHS programme you applied to?'

Alex sighed. 'Dad drove me up for an assessment, but there's eighty people on the waiting list and I'm low priority since I've never tried suicide and I don't present a danger to the public . . .'

'They'd let you in if you stabbed Henry,' Georgia joked darkly as she pushed the button for a caramel latte.

Before Alex could react, the double doors by the snack machine flew open. One door crashed the wall loudly as a wailing, half-dressed figure burst through.

'I am not to be touched!' the runner shouted desperately.

The runner had evidently been dragged out of school, wearing the bottom half of his PE kit and a deckchair-striped school blazer over a bare chest. As he reached a dead end at the far side of the lounge, a burly Spanish nurse named Carlos and the two green-uniformed paramedics charged through the doors in pursuit.

'Julius, calm down, mate,' one of the paramedics begged in cockney. 'They're all right here.'

'Remember our chat in the ambulance?' the other one added. 'There's nothing to fear.'

Arrivals on the unit were often dramatic. Georgia had seen bodies flopped into their rooms under sedation, sobbers grasping parents, kids withdrawing from heroin wheeled to the addiction ward with puke buckets between their knees. Most common were teens who'd attempted suicide, fresh from the casualty department with neck braces or bloody bandages.

9

But overpowering the admissions staff and doing a runner was something new. Julius's shocked white eyes contrasted with his sweat-beaded black head, as he glanced frantically for an escape route.

'Move aside,' Julius roared, as Carlos stepped closer. 'I cannot be here.'

Julius decided his best chance was back the way he'd come, hurdling sofas and running along cushions.

Hot chocolate splashed Alex's jeans as she backed up to the wall. Julius's head almost touched the ceiling as he vaulted between sofas, but Carlos had a plan. The burly nurse didn't fancy tackling a giant, so he grabbed the base of a sofa, tilting it enough for Julius to lose balance.

The enormous teenager became a falling tree, and a coffee table splintered under his weight.

While the paramedics moved cautiously between the furniture, Carlos was fearless, straddling the toppled sofa, then sticking a needle through Julius's PE shorts.

Julius still had some fight, despite the sedative in his blood and a gory spear of the coffee table pushed through his cheek.

'Big ones can take another,' the cockney paramedic suggested as he threw Carlos another syringe.

Julius managed a rabbit kick as Carlos pulled down his shorts, but the second needle sent him straight to fairyland.

'I'm not paid enough for this . . .' Carlos moaned, holding his back as he straightened up.

Now they felt safe, Alex and Georgia stepped around the sofas to get a better look. Julius was a beached whale, splayed over the collapsed table, with the syringes in his arse still swaying from side to side.

ONE

One Year Earlier: St Gilda's High School – Akure, Nigeria

The bell had already signalled the end of school. Boys spilled into crisply air-conditioned hallways in white shirts and grey shorts, stripping ties as they headed for home.

Julius Adebisi was a fourteen-year-old in a hurry, but his class remained trapped behind desks. Their form teacher peered over gold-rimmed sunglasses, speaking with the deliberate authority of a former army officer.

'While I am not averse to members of form 9C using this classroom for study during the lunch period, I do not find it acceptable if I return here to find food wrappings about the place, obscenities on my whiteboard and general disarray of the chairs and tables. If this happens again, my classroom will be locked. Is that understood?'

A lukewarm groan of *yes, sir* swept the room.

Julius jiggled his black shoe as the teacher paused. *Come on, come on, come on...*

'Class dismissed.'

Chairs grated the floor. Julius hooked an overstuffed

backpack on one shoulder and grabbed the battered shortboard propped against his desk.

'Coming through. Major hurry!' Julius shouted.

He was the biggest kid in 9C. But he wasn't the strongest and at least one tough guy didn't like being shoved.

'Sorry!'

Most classes had been dismissed at the bell. But while the hallway had mostly emptied, there was a scrum by the doors at the far end and Julius thought it would be quicker to go out the back way. He almost dropped his board as he barged a door, exiting the school playing fields.

St Gilda's grounds were immaculate. Bright blue tennis courts and six all-weather pitches, the largest surrounded by an athletics track. Beyond the track was a shaded grandstand with green and orange seats and a podium used for graduations.

But donations from wealthy parents couldn't control Akure's air. It was thirty-two degrees and it hadn't rained for a couple of days. With nothing to flush the open sewers in the city's slum areas, the afternoon breeze brought a strong kick of garbage and human shit.

Julius jogged through the heat haze around the building housing the school's diesel generators, then through soccer players walking down from the girls' school. He thought he'd probably left things too late when he glanced around the school's main building into a jostling parking lot.

Kids – especially the little green polo shirts from St Gilda's elementary school – streamed between parked cars. It was all fancy metal, German or Japanese. A few mothers in SUVs, but mostly chauffeurs, who broke the monotony of their jobs by arriving early and leaning on their dark saloons, gossiping as they ignored *No Smoking* signs.

Julius hurried behind a line of giant palms at the back of the lot. His eye caught Simeon, one of the half-dozen driver/bodyguards employed by his mother. Luckily, Simeon faced away, one hand in his jacket, chatting to an older driver in a garishly brocaded shirt.

He had to slow down on a stepped path, dodging green-shirted terrors running the other way. The elementary school was inside St Gilda's original, 1930s schoolhouse. Outside, kids swung and clambered through a play area dominated by two wooden turrets, with a queue for the zip line spanning between them.

'Gabriel,' Julius gasped, relieved to catch his ten-year-old brother before he got to the waiting Mercedes.

Gabe – as he preferred to be called – was still young enough to spend lunch hour tearing around, and had scuffed shoes and dirty knees to prove it.

'Why are you up here?' Gabe asked suspiciously as he backed away from a group of classmates.

Gabe was infuriatingly cool. While Julius loomed over his peers and felt crippled every time a word came out of his mouth, Gabe was a smooth-talker who had half the girls in his year crushing on him. He was the star striker for St Gilda's U11 soccer team, and a cheeky smile or flick of an eyebrow got Gabe out of troubles that would have had Julius grounded for life.

'Need a favour,' Julius said, catching his breath and wary of his old third-form teacher standing in the elementary school's doorway. She was a sweetheart, but he'd never get rid of her if she came to reminisce.

'What's in this for baby brother?' Gabe asked, rubbing his palms.

Julius tutted. 'Tell Simeon that I'm working on an after-school project. And that he doesn't need to come back and pick me up later, because I've arranged a ride with a friend.'

Gabe looked incredulous. 'You don't have any friends.'

The jab was close enough to the truth to hurt.

'I'm in a rush,' Julius said irritably. 'Can you *please* not be an obstacle for once?'

'Simeon will interrogate me,' Gabe snapped back. 'He's more scared of Mum than we are.'

'Be vague,' Julius explained. 'If I say drama club, or detention, Simeon might try and find me to check before he takes you home. But he can't search every building on campus if he doesn't know where I am.'

'What if he calls you?' Gabe asked.

'I forgot to turn my phone back on after class . . .'

'Ten thousand naira,' Gabe suggested.

Julius tutted. 'You're not getting paid. I've covered your ass a million times.'

'Finally got a girlfriend to sneak around with?' Gabe teased. 'I've had four – you're starting to look bad.'

'You're ten. You wouldn't know what to do with a girl if you got one.'

'Price might rise if you keep that up,' Gabe said. 'And I'm not covering if I don't know what this thing is.'

Julius drummed fingers on his board.

'I know a guy,' he began reluctantly. 'He's taking me to a skating spot he's found. It's supposed to be legendary, with ramps, drops and all sorts.'

Gabe looked wary, moving further from his friends and lowering his voice. 'There's kidnappers *everywhere*. Uncle is state governor. Mum says we've got targets.'

'Mummy says,' Julius squeaked, mocking Gabe's unbroken

voice. 'I've got regular clothes in my bag. I'll just be another kid on the street. And nothing happens any more. When did you last hear of an actual kidnapping?'

'You'd better not get caught,' Gabe warned, smiling devilishly at the prospect. 'Mum will have one of the bodyguards take you in the garage for a beating.'

'That's my problem, brother. Simeon will be up here looking for you soon. Are you going to help me or not?'

'Still got that New York Islanders cap? I always liked that . . .' Julius tutted. 'OK. It's yours, you thief.'

Gabe cracked one of his winning smiles as the brothers sealed the deal with a fist bump. 'And if Mum won't pay your kidnappers, I can have your big bedroom . . .'

TWO

Disused Mr Carpet warehouse – Leighton Buzzard, UK

Drone racing used to be fun. Georgia was Daddy's girl, legs swinging off a table, drinking Coke while her crew changed propellers, debated software updates and huddled over her quadcopter like surgeons. Entire days went by, waiting for races that lasted minutes. Georgia would bring her tablet, playing games or churning through entire seasons of *Friends* and *Brooklyn-Nine-Nine*.

Georgia was talented too. UK Open Specification champion at under nine and under ten. Runner-up in the European under-eighteens when she was only eleven. Back then, she practised flying most days after school, and the tournaments gobbled every alternate weekend during the season.

But Georgia was fourteen now, and over it. She hated the kitschy retro bowling shirts the team wore, with *Drone Pack* embroidered on the back. She'd evolved from sitcoms to *Game of Thrones* or *Rick and Morty*, but unlimited screen time no longer compensated for long drives, fast food and trying to do homework in budget hotel rooms while her dad watched football.

The worst thing about drone races was the men. From the geeky boy pilots who eyed Georgia up, to Steve, Drone Pack's bearded technician. He always knew best, even though she was the team's best pilot and understood the technical stuff as well as he did.

Georgia broke her dad's heart when she'd used starting GCSEs as an excuse to get out of a twelve-round season in the UK Drone Racing League. But he'd talked her into a one-off appearance, at the qualifying rounds of the Rage Cola Classic during half-term week.

Drone racing had grown massively since Georgia had started. The courses she'd raced when she was nine were set up by middle-aged hobbyists, who hired school gyms and car parks and made the gates drones flew through out of garden wire and swimming floats, anchored down with concrete blocks or beer kegs.

Rage Cola had spent big money, filling the disused carpet warehouse with professionally built air gates, lit with coloured LED strips. There were huge banks of lights, a laser tunnel, cameras covering every angle of the course and even smoke machines for the following day's final, which would be live-streamed on the Rage Cola website, with highlights on satellite TV.

'Feelin' the buzz?' Georgia's dad – John Pack – asked, as he sat on a tabletop next to his youngest daughter's outstretched Nikes.

'I guess,' she answered, yawning as she looked up from her phone.

John tapped his watch. 'Fifteen minutes till your final qualifier.'

Georgia was carefully balancing the way she acted around her dad. He'd had a crap year, with Georgia's mum walking out, his older daughter having work and debt problems and his survey drone company losing its biggest contract.

She'd agreed to fly the Rage Classic because she hoped it would cheer her dad up. But since saying she'd take part, he'd not stopped going on about how the event might rekindle her interest in flying. So, Georgia had to make clear today wasn't her idea of fun, while not being a total shit and spoiling her father's weekend.

'Steve replaced the wiring to the motor that kept dropping in your first qualifier,' John said. 'He's not happy with the power distribution board either. We don't have a spare, so your Uncle Phil is trying to beg or borrow from another team.'

Georgia wasn't concerned. Her quadcopter could go from zero to a hundred kilometres per hour in four seconds. She'd had a big crash in free practice and it would have seemed odder if there wasn't some last-minute mechanical drama.

'Has Steve taken back forward trim, like I asked?' Georgia said.

The more a drone tilted forward in flight, the faster it would go in a straight line, but a flatter profile would make it more stable and manoeuvrable.

John shook his head. 'Steve says . . .'

'He *never* does what I ask,' Georgia interrupted furiously. 'If Steve knows so much about flying, how come *he* didn't make it out of the first qualifying round?'

'He's always been a better technician than a pilot, Georgia.'

'The quad feels horrible in the twisty section through the trucks. I barely scraped into the third qualifying round. My best lap was two-point-three seconds off that Van Hooten bloke.'

'The Dutchman?' John said, laughing. 'He's a former European champion. Just won the $100,000 prize in the Abu Dhabi Drone Prix. The only reason he's not an automatic entry for tomorrow's final is his team lost all their ranking points for using illegal battery packs.'

'I know I don't practise any more,' Georgia said, feeling some of the passion of her younger self, who'd sob the whole drive home if she didn't win, 'but I'm not two-point-three seconds slower than *anyone*.'

John cracked a huge smile. 'Cookie, since you're so sure, I'll get him to make the change.'

Georgia smirked. It was ages since her dad had called her Cookie and she found it adorable.

'I know we usually fly with more tilt,' Georgia explained, 'but the motors are zippier than they used to be and the coloured lights we've had to fit for TV coverage alter forward balance.'

Georgia hoped she hadn't shown too much enthusiasm as she watched her dad cross to Steve and the drone, which was surrounded by tools at a folding table a few metres away. She checked the time on her phone and decided she had time to stroll to the ladies'.

Seventy teams and two hundred and fifty-six hopeful pilots had entered the qualifying tournament that morning. Georgia was one of thirty-two who'd survived two qualifying rounds. Only eight would get to join some of the best pilots in the world for the following day's final, where there was a £10,000 prize pool and places in the million-dollar Rage World Classic, held in San Francisco at the end of the year.

There was a lot of empty space and litter around the team concourse, since teams with no pilots left in the competition had already headed home. As she crossed the warehouse, Georgia noticed that most of the remaining teams had fancy rolling tool cabinets, better uniforms and swankier laptops than Drone Pack.

John, Steve and Georgia's Uncle Phil were still arguing over the trim changes when she got back.

'She's two seconds off the top runners,' Phil – a younger version of Georgia's dad – was saying. 'What's the worst that can happen?'

'I say we chance it,' John agreed, not seeing his daughter approach.

'Why is this a debate?' Georgia asked sharply, making her dad jump. 'I bet the best pilots on the other teams get their drones set up how they want.'

Georgia forced herself between Steve and her uncle, then grabbed a laptop, wired to the drone she was due to fly in less than six minutes. She expertly opened a window for the drone's operating software, clicked on a box and started typing numbers into a series of trim-setting boxes.

The three men saw Georgia was close to boiling over. They cast wary glances and feared she'd snap Steve's finger when he jabbed it towards the screen.

'What?' Georgia growled.

'You missed a decimal point,' Steve said. 'Unless you want to fly a spinning top . . .'

'Right . . .' Georgia said, inserting the point, then clicking an upload box to send the revised settings to the drone. 'How am I for time?'

Pilots had to have their drones at the launch line two minutes before the race. Georgia hooked her control set around her neck and grabbed her first-person-view goggles as her dad plugged a battery into the drone.

Georgia was the last of the eight pilots to arrive but was fine because an air gate was being fixed after a crash in the previous race. While John stepped over a low barrier to put his daughter's quad on the launch line, Georgia had her ID badge scanned by a steward, before going four steps up to a podium.

She was still irritated by the argument over trim changes and tried to get her head in the zone by reciting carefully memorised course directions under her breath.

'Launch, hard forward, gate one – full power, three seconds, gate two – sharp left, laser tunnel, gates three, four – climb and right, gate five, sharp left tilt, through the double doors into loading bay – climb to ceiling, gate six, full power for seven seconds – gate seven . . .'

'Excuse me,' a cameraman interrupted, almost getting Georgia's toes as he filmed Niels van Hooten.

The exuberant Dutch pilot jumped onto the stage, with a smug grin and a bright orange boiler suit covered with sponsor patches. He waved to a crowd of thirty, with his FPV headset balanced atop waves of greying hair.

If Georgia still cared enough to read her dad's issue of *Drone Monthly*, she'd have known Van Hooten and his team's disqualification had been the scandal of the season in the racing community.

'What does it feel like having to go through three qualifying rounds to reach a final your big rivals have qualified for automatically?' a scrawny guy holding a voice recorder in Van Hooten's face asked.

'I practise every day,' Van Hooten told the recorder. His English was confident, but not his first language. 'Racing is the best practice there is.'

'But there's a chance of a crash or a mechanical failure during a qualifier,' the interviewer pointed out.

'I may get struck by lightning when I go jogging,' Van Hooten said dismissively. 'But I live my life. What good is it to lie awake at night worrying about your own shadow?'

As one of the race stewards hustled the interviewer off stage, a green signal light came on, indicating that the damaged gate was fixed and the course ready to race. As the slowest qualifier, Georgia had to cross the stage to a marked space on the far side. Van Hooten was in her way, shaking hands with another qualifier.

'Ronnie, you massive vagina!' Van Hooten tooted. 'I might let you have second!'

When he saw Georgia, Van Hooten's booming laugh erupted again. 'I am aghast! You must be the most beautiful Rage Cola girl I've ever seen.'

'I'm not a . . .' Georgia said, but tailed off when she figured him out.

The headset and control unit made it obvious Georgia was a pilot. Van Hooten was trying to wind her up.

'You staying in town tonight, beautiful?' he continued. 'Can I buy you a cocktail?'

'I'm fourteen, pervert,' Georgia growled, loud enough for plenty of people to hear.

Van Hooten was only flustered for an instant. 'Hey, Ackroyd,' he said, smacking another contestant on the back. 'She's fourteen, but that doesn't usually stop you, does it?'

Georgia shuddered. *What a dirtbag . . .* There wasn't much of a crowd for a qualifying tournament on a weekday, but Georgia still felt self-conscious. The youngest pilot on stage. The only girl. She imagined eyes crawling up her back.

All those creeps looking at my arse.

'Pilots, one minute,' a race steward shouted as a bank of red lights began flashing over gate one, twenty metres in front of the launch line.

Georgia realised how skilfully Van Hooten had messed with her head. She hadn't switched on her control unit, or properly adjusted the controller strapped around her neck. She'd forgotten to check the batteries on her FPV goggles and it was now too late to change them if they were low.

Just breathe ... The meter inside the goggles said they were good for sixty-three minutes, and the race would last less than six. Drone battery was one hundred per cent, video signal a full five bars, no diagnostic warning lights ...

'Knock 'em dead, Georgia,' John shouted, making her even more embarrassed.

Georgia felt weirdly sentimental about her dad as she pushed down her headset and moved into another world. Now she saw through the drone's eye, face sweating, thumbs on the control sticks. Five red lights about to turn green ...

THREE

As Gabe ran down the stepped path to meet Simeon the bodyguard, Julius rushed back to high school to change out of uniform.

He emerged from the driest-floored toilet cubicle he'd been able to find in market-stall sunglasses, a long-sleeve no-brand T-shirt, cargo shorts with a torn pocket and Vans with soles worn smooth. He'd bought a ton of fancy skateboarder clothes on his last trip to London, but wearing good stuff in the city was like having a *Please rob me* sign around your neck.

Julius's locker was in the ninth-form common room way across school, so he dumped his backpack on top of a fire extinguisher cupboard. If it wasn't there in the morning, he'd only lose a sweaty uniform and a pencil case.

The playing fields were now filled with after-school matches and training. Julius got a *what-are-you-up-to* look from one of the games masters as he jogged between two pitches. Boys weren't allowed near the girls' high school and Julius's face felt hot as he passed a classroom filled with aproned girls doing pottery.

Beyond that was the girls' school parking lot. End-of-school traffic had thinned, but bored drivers chattered and stared at smartphones, waiting on detentions and after-school tuition. Julius saw a million things that might go wrong: a hand on his shoulder, a teacher's shout from a first-floor window, a group of girls asking why he was here, CCTV . . .

'Thought you weren't coming,' Damola said, snapping his train of thought.

Julius had made it through the gate, out of St Gilda's spotless grounds into a dust-blown street. Opposite the school's razor-wire fence were tin-roofed shops, a busy cafe and a truck driver getting honked by traffic as he unloaded bottles of cooking gas. Julius knew the street, but only from inside a Mercedes.

Sixteen-year-old Damola – known as Duke – stood by his beat-up scooter. It was a Chinese-made clone of the classic Honda Super Cub. Cheap to buy, easy to fix and as common as flies on Akure's streets.

'Gabe made things difficult,' Julius explained, glancing about nervously. 'Are we safe here?'

'You're an utter wreck!' Duke said, opening a smile filled with perfect teeth. 'Dripping sweat. Voice trembling!'

Duke was average height, with slender limbs but broad shoulders. He had two studs in one ear, and wild hair with a patchy bleach job that had earned him a warning letter from St Gilda's.

'I've never ditched my driver before,' Julius explained sheepishly. 'Are my clothes OK?'

'I wouldn't rob you,' Duke said, glancing at the cafe across the street. 'But some of our teachers drink beer in that bar, so better get moving.'

Julius nodded. 'Your uncle letting you have a bike is cool!'

'He works in Lagos half the time, so there's no choice,' Duke explained. 'And it can be liberating, but I wish we were rich enough for a Benz and a driver every time rain hits. Have you been on a scooter before?'

'Heaps,' Julius said, which was an exaggeration. 'My cousins have them, back in my grandparents' village.'

Julius squeezed on the back half of the seat, arms around Duke's waist, stomach squashed against the bright orange skateboard deck poking out of Duke's army-issue backpack.

'Lord Almighty, you're heavy!' Duke laughed, having to go full throttle to get the bike moving. 'If we get a steep hill, you might have to push!'

It had been a couple of years since Julius had been on a scooter. He liked the sense of freedom and the rush of wind through sweaty hair. But a couple of streets was enough to remind him about grit in your eye and potholes trying to throw you off your seat.

Duke sped north, choking on fumes as they zipped between clogged traffic on the four-lane beltway around the town centre.

A chunky traffic cop waved the bike to the side of the road as they exited a junction. The officer noisily sucked air between his teeth and suggested that Duke's front tire had *insufficient tread*. To nobody's surprise, the problem disappeared the instant Duke palmed him a ₦200 note.

'Drive safely, young fellow!' the cop said politely as they pulled off.

They wound up on hilly ground in the Old Town, a couple of kilometres from Akure's centre. Over the last stretch, they'd passed several grand houses and an abandoned colonial-era governor's mansion.

The city's wealthiest citizens now preferred life behind high walls, in guard-gated communities at the south end of the beltway. But despite a drop in status, Old Town remained one of the nicest parts of Akure. The kind of place where a doctor or senior union official might live.

'Is this your area?' Julius asked, shading his eyes from late-afternoon sun.

One side of the street was level with rooftops of houses below. The other had a rocky embankment, topped by a crumbling latticed-brick wall. The high ground gave a view over lines of modest houses with Korean SUVs and rusty satellite dishes.

'My apartment block is the other side of the hill,' Duke explained. 'You'll see it when we get inside.'

Duke glanced about to check nobody was around, then rolled his scooter behind a mound of rocks, tilted it carefully on its side and shifted a graffitied sheet of wood over the top. It was clearly something he'd done before.

'Now the tricky part,' Duke said, taking a run, before starting to scramble up the steep embankment.

'What's inside?' Julius asked.

'Paradise,' Duke teased, one skinny arm hooked through the latticed bricks, the other aiming down to grab Julius's board. 'Don't you trust me?

His friend wasn't expecting an answer, but Julius pondered the question.

Duke was in form eleven, so they didn't share any classes. He often walked around St Gilda's with a plastic tube containing drawings over his shoulder. Combining that with pierced ears and big hair was enough to get the wrong sort of attention in an all-boys high school.

The first time they'd ever spoken, Julius found Duke under a stairwell, claiming to be fine after three lads had beat the shit out of him. Duke could barely walk and his eye was closing, but he refused to go to the nurse's office. Julius had fetched a wodge of wet tissue to wash blood off Duke's face. Then they'd spoken about how hard St Gilda's sucked, and their friendship was sealed when Duke noticed the storm-trooper-on-a-skateboard sticker on the back of Julius's iPhone.

'Death or glory!' Julius boomed, steeling himself for the rocky slope.

He took a longer run-up than Duke. The Vans, with grips worn smooth, made bad climbing shoes. But after a downed knee and a flurry of tumbling pebbles, Julius got far enough to grasp Duke's hand and take a pull.

The teenagers shuffled along the wall, then swung legs over where it had mostly collapsed. The wind carried a vile, vomit-like smell as the boys jumped down onto a footpath that had cracked and subsided, spawning plants that went up to their waist.

'What in the Lord's name is *that*?' Julius complained, shielding his nose with an arm.

'Snow leopard shit,' Duke explained.

Julius glanced about, confused by rusted metal fences and mildewed concrete buildings daubed with graffiti. 'There are leopards here?'

Duke laughed. 'Not *right* here. They're in cages on the other side of the revolving restaurant . . .'

Julius realised where he was.

'Arctic Zoo,' he blurted. 'I was supposed to come here on a trip when I was in nursery class. But the place closed down.'

The story of Arctic Zoo was a local legend. Nigeria spent most of the 1980s ruled by military dictators. General Sebastian Edochie was put in charge of Ondo State. He quickly grew bored with everyday problems, like clean water or the seventy per cent of Ondo's children who didn't get enough food, and decided that what Akure really needed was a zoo. And since Nigeria already had plenty of gorillas, giraffes, hippos and big cats, Edochie decided people would only visit if he filled his zoo with creatures from cold places.

A famous Danish architect created austere pens with hexagonal pools and swooping concrete pedestals. His design also included an education centre and a squat tower, topped by a revolving restaurant that gave hilltop views over Akure. A French company engineered a complex water-cooling system to keep animals comfortable and South African gamekeepers travelled the globe, buying or catching polar bears, Siberian tigers, white wolves, snow leopards, muskox and reindeer.

The zoo was a disaster. A fresh military coup meant General Edochie fled Nigeria before Arctic Zoo opened. The revolving restaurant only worked for two weeks, cage bars warped in the heat, concrete pedestals were dangerously slippery and the cooling system had no back-up generators to cover frequent power cuts.

Most of Akure's population were curious, but few could afford Arctic Zoo's entry fee. Penguins died of heat stroke, muskox caught bovine malaria and when the food budget ran low, underfed white tigers scoffed a couple of zookeepers.

The only people who did well out of Arctic Zoo were General Edochie's son-in-law, who embezzled several million dollars from the construction budget, and the Danish architect, who won a World Architecture Association gold medal for the zoo's *outstanding and innovative* design.

'How come there are still animals here?' Julius asked.

'Not many job opportunities for out-of-work zookeepers, so a few staff stuck around after the state stopped paying their salaries,' Duke explained, as he started a brisk walk, occasionally using his board to swipe a big plant out of the way. 'The original animals are dead or on their last legs, but leopards breed easily and there are plenty of fools who'll buy a big furry cat as a pet. They also take animals into schools or kids' parties and locals donate food or money, because the zookeepers are all that's stopping this land from turning into a giant squatter camp.'

'It's close to the city centre,' Julius said thoughtfully. 'Some rich property developer must buy it eventually.'

'Which one?' Duke teased. 'A shopping mall for your uncle, or a new church for your mother?'

'That's not even a joke . . .' Julius sighed, but his mood brightened as the boys reached a fork in the path.

A vista had opened over an empty penguin pool, more than eighty metres long. The surroundings were shabby, but the toughened concrete that formed the basin remained eggshell smooth. And while penguin feet had struggled on slippery ramps leading to hexagonal platforms, they looked like a skateboarder's dream.

'I came here sketching cages and wrecked buildings,' Duke explained as he led the way through an empty doorframe marked *staff only*. 'When I discovered this place, there was a lot of debris in the bottom. I found an old rake and scraped most of it into one pile. But you have to ride with your eyes open.'

Julius smiled ear to ear as he stood with the sun on his neck and toes over the edge of a six-metre drop.

'Start at the shallow end,' Duke suggested.

FOUR

The quickest possible start was a full-throttle climb from the launch line and a skim over the lowest part of the first gate. But if all eight pilots aimed their quadcopters at the same spot, the result would be a holocaust of flashing lights and broken props. Georgia had seen plenty of starts like that, but she'd also seen ones where everyone played safe, except the guy who won the game of chicken and stormed into a massive lead.

In the event, Georgia needn't have worried. Her new trim settings caught her out, sending her quad lurching to the left. Full power saved her from an embarrassing scrape with the floor but left her too high with no forward momentum.

Van Hooten's orange-lit drone took the lead, with a good angle off the ground and a cautious passage through the centre of gate one.

Georgia was far enough back to see the purple-lit drone clip the gate, flip upwards and smash into the light-green one. The two drones clattered to the floor, light green dead on impact, the pilot of purple trying a relaunch, but getting nowhere with a broken prop. Pink had avoided the carnage by ducking under the gate, but that would add a five-second penalty to the pilot's time. Disqualification if he missed two more.

Georgia went high through gates one and two and entered the laser tunnel sixth out of six runners, needing first or second to make the next day's final. Footage of drones in the brightly lit laser tunnel made spectacular video, but pilots loathed glare that made it easy to drift into the tunnel wall or clatter a rival.

Over the next few gates, Georgia dropped back until it felt like she was in solo practice. She glimpsed the four drones fighting for second on longer straights, with Van Hooten out of sight in the lead.

But Georgia had been flying drones since she was seven and she'd learned a lot about her rival pilots. Most saw themselves as gladiators, bragging about their quad's top speed and overestimating their ability to consistently throw unstable craft through the bendy bits.

By age ten, Georgia regularly chewed up teen boys, whose quads were blindingly fast but had the steering finesse of a house brick. The pilots in this race weren't kids, but Georgia was getting a feel for the trim adjustments she'd made and hoped to make up ground as the course entered its most difficult section.

Gate eleven was a skylight in the warehouse roof. The best-funded drone teams used military-spec camera arrays that gave a stable image from night vision to blinding sunlight. The camera on Georgia's drone cost £35 and left her blind for a quarter-second as its sensor adjusted to daylight.

There were two tight gates on the factory roof, followed by a three-storey drop to ground level. From here, the course went through four juggernaut trailers parked in a W-shape. Each truck was entered at the rear, but the exits varied. Some in the side, some the roof and the tightest of all through a narrow blue tunnel.

Georgia moved nearer the pack through the first three trucks and was close enough to witness the red drone smash into the inside of the fourth truck, disintegrating with such force that it had to be signal dropout, not pilot error.

Georgia was third behind deep-blue as they exited the last trailer, falling back to fourth through five gates arranged in a giant arc. The quads hit 130kph on a straight run back into the warehouse through giant hangar doors, slowing for the entrance to a second laser tunnel, then whizzing in front of the pilots' stage and across the launch line for lap two.

Georgia had found her rhythm, losing less in the opening section and gaining more through the trucks. Lap two closed with her running third out of five, a couple of metres behind deep-blue. Pink was close behind, but Georgia had seen it take a time penalty for missing the first gate, so he'd have to finish over five seconds ahead to beat her.

Flying required complete concentration, but Georgia heard a sensation. Shouts and gasps from the audience, watching the banks of screens over the stage. She didn't know why until she exited the laser tunnel at the start of the final lap and glimpsed Van Hooten's orange quad floundering beneath her. With a twelve-second lead and the best quad in the race, the Dutchman had made a rookie mistake and clipped the tunnel exit.

Van Hooten seemed undamaged. He launched from the ground, closing on Georgia and deep-blue. Georgia led the race briefly but lost ground over the factory roof. She could only see straight ahead, so she didn't know who hit her rear and made her skim close to the truck wall.

Georgia was faster than deep-blue and pink through the

trucks, but she couldn't gain on Van Hooten and her quad was pulling right, probably from minor propeller damage when she'd been whacked.

Van Hooten's orange quad started pulling away, through the wide arc gates and hangar doors. Georgia didn't mind when deep-blue overtook on her outside to finish in second place. Third was good enough to prove her point about not being two seconds a lap slower than anyone. Her dad would spend the drive home bragging that she'd have made the final if she'd not lost time on the start, and Georgia would get to sleep in her own bed and finish the history assignment she had to hand in on Monday.

'I love you so much,' John shouted, jumping on stage and hugging his daughter the instant she landed the quad.

Georgia pushed up her sweaty goggles as he gave her a kiss and lifted her off the ground. Van Hooten had stormed across to the stewards' area, in a foul mood about something.

'Think how good she'd be if she still practised,' Phil said, slapping his niece on the back. 'That was amazing!'

Georgia got a voice recorder shoved in her face. The blogger who'd interviewed Van Hooten before the race.

'Georgia Pack, you've been off the radar since you finished runner-up in the European under-eighteens a few years back, but you'll be the youngest pilot in tomorrow's final, finishing second today. What does that feel like?'

'Third,' Georgia corrected, pushing her dad away, so she could look at the timing screens over the stage.

2nd Place Georgia Pack (UK, Junior)
Time 4:51.72
Penalties 0:00.00
Total 4:51.72

'I don't get it . . .' Georgia said, scanning the screens.

'Van Hooten copped a penalty,' John explained. 'He missed gate three after he spun exiting the laser tunnel. Why did you think we're all jumping up and down and Van Hooten's raging at the stewards?'

Now Georgia's head was in a tangle. Sticking it to Van Hooten felt great and she hadn't seen her dad this happy since before her mum walked out. But it also meant another night of her dad's snoring at the Premier Inn, and having to work on her history project over the weekend.

'Hey, Van Hooten,' John carped across the stage. 'Do you still want to take my underage daughter for a drink at your hotel? Or will you be skulking home to your windmill in your little clogs and sticking a tulip up your arse?'

Van Hooten's face snapped around, radish red, as folks by the stage laughed.

'What's it like getting beat by a fourteen-year-old girl?' Uncle Phil added, making a dickhead gesture.

'This is absolute crap!' Van Hooten fumed, booting one of the stewards' plastic chairs. 'This isn't a proper course. It's a television stage, designed by idiots.'

The Dutchman seemed keen to thump someone but got shepherded away by a couple of guys from his team.

Georgia did another short interview, with a bloke from *Drone Racer* magazine, then the event photographer made her feel awkward, telling her to put on a Rage Cola baseball cap, then lining her up with the pilot of deep-blue and taking pictures as each held one end of a sign with *FINALIST* written on it.

'Eyes down my lens. Nice big smile! Come on, Georgia, a smile never killed anyone . . .'

Back at their table in the team concourse, John took a selfie with Georgia holding her drone and posted it to his Facebook and the @DronePack Twitter account: Tearful dad with my No1 Pilot. Qualified for final of Rage Cola Classic!!!

'Don't you *dare* tag me,' Georgia warned. 'I get enough stick for being a geek without everyone at school knowing I spent half-term wearing this atrocious bowling shirt.'

'Gotta love teenagers,' John laughed, looking at his brother and shaking his head. 'When Georgia won her first league race, she took her trophy into primary school and was made up when the headmistress asked her to fly in morning assembly.'

'Dad!' Georgia moaned, covering her face. 'Embarrassing me isn't compulsory.'

'Does that mean you don't want me to forward the nice pic with Daddykins for your Instagram?'

'For all of my seven followers?' Georgia asked grumpily.

As Steve, John and Phil started packing up for the day, Georgia remembered she'd turned her phone off before the race. After booting up, she got a ping from Messenger and took a couple of seconds to recognise the face. It was Tasha from primary school, but she'd gone punk since Georgia last saw her.

Georgia opened the message.

I know it's been ages and wish I'd done more to stay in touch. You poss remember, my mum is an x-ray technician at Park Hospital where your sister worked. She heard what happened to Sophie this morning and came home crying. I'm sad too and wanted to say, am still your friend and here for you any way I can be.

After that came a bunch of kisses and heart emojis.

Georgia's twenty-four-year-old sister, Sophie, was a junior doctor at Park Hospital. She'd been suspended two months earlier, after a patient received a fatal dose of medication. Since

Tasha's mum worked at the same hospital, Georgia's best guess was that she'd heard bad news about the investigation before anyone else.

But Tasha's mum barely knew Sophie. So why would she come home in tears?

Sophie lived with her phone in her hands, so Georgia closed Tasha's message and switched to her last messenger conversation with her sister.

Sophie Pack. Last online sixteen hours ago.

That seemed *very* wrong.

Georgia called Sophie, but got no answer on Facebook and her mobile went to voicemail. Georgia had been with her dad all day, so there was no way he'd know anything. She scrolled down to *Mum Mobile* in her phonebook and shuddered.

Georgia hadn't spoken to her mum in weeks. Their last conversation ended with, '*You'd take your father's side no matter what I said or did. You've always been daddy's girl*,' before she'd stormed off to her car.

But Tasha's weird message and Sophie not being online for sixteen hours was scarier than the prospect of speaking to her mum.

She answered right away. 'Georgia, honey?' Rachel Pack said, sounding tense but weirdly gentle. 'How's it going up there?'

Georgia ignored the question. 'Mum, I'm worried about Sophie. Do you remember my old friend Tasha? I got this weird message about Sophie, and she's not been online since late last night...'

'I was waiting for you at home,' Georgia's mum explained. 'I still have my house key. I didn't want to tell you over the phone, but I guess you can't keep news off the internet.'

'Tell me what?' Georgia asked, her free hand making a tense fist.

'You'd better put your dad on.'

'Mum, what the *bloody hell* happened?' Georgia demanded, loud enough for her dad and uncle to look around.

'Honey . . .' she answered, her voice wavering.

'Dad's busy,' Georgia said firmly. 'I'm not a kid any more.'

There was a pause. Georgia felt tears in her eyes, knowing it was terrible. John came over and asked what was happening, but Georgia shushed him.

'Mum, are you there?'

'Georgia . . .' she finally croaked. 'Zac came home from his shift early this morning. He found Sophie under the stairs in their flat . . . Your sister . . . She . . . I didn't want to do this on the phone . . . She hanged herself. Zac cut her down, but it was already too late.'

FIVE

Duke saw something comical in his friend Julius. Overfed, way too tall and tortured by shyness, he had a way of glancing about when he walked St Gilda's hallways, as if he was scared he'd step on someone smaller.

Duke had never seen Julius ride. Nerves at the school gate and the clumsy scramble up the rocks made Duke wonder if his friend's enthusiasm for skateboarding would be undermined by his basic lack of coordination.

But Julius had worked hard, wearing the soles of his Vans flat. He could handle drops, grind the sides of the penguin pool's hexagonal plinths, ollie kerbs and land a 360 flip. For Duke, seeing Julius skate was like going to a family party and seeing your grandma start breakdancing.

Duke gave up after half an hour, stripping off his shirt and lying against a gently angled section of the concrete bowl. Julius kept going, gaining confidence until he was dropping off the sloped wall at the deepest part of the pool.

Duke made some video clips and was recording when Julius drew blood. He'd swerved between two hexagonal penguin platforms, then veered to avoid a plastic bag floating on the hilltop breeze. The correction sent him towards a rusted pool filter and a front wheel wedged in its rusted grate.

Julius stumbled over the nose of his board, making three desperate steps before scraping down on his right knee and elbow.

'Shit!' Duke gulped, ditching his phone as he ran to help. 'You OK?'

'I've survived worse.'

The cut knee wasn't much, but the blood looked dramatic, streaking down to stain the top of Julius's sock. He managed a wry smile as he kicked up his board and limped towards Duke. 'Knee's wrecked, so I guess that's enough for today . . .'

Duke handed over his water bottle. After a drink, Julius peeled his sweaty T-shirt over his head and settled next to his friend on the smooth concrete

'See why I always wear long sleeves for skating?' Julius said, holding out the arm to show a rip in the elbow, then using the shirt to mop the worst of the blood off his lower leg

As he caught his breath, Julius held the balled shirt over his knee and leaned across Duke, who'd turned his phone sideways and set the crash to replay in super-slow-motion.

'I got nice footage of you dropping off the deep end too,' Duke said. 'That ride is too steep for me.'

'Practise,' Julius suggested. 'Been skating since I was seven, but I took lessons with a pro when I was in London last summer. I'd watched all the trick vids on YouTube, but having someone watch you ride and explain what you're getting wrong made *so* much difference.'

Duke looked impressed. 'You've been to a proper skatepark?'

Julius nodded. 'Huge indoor one in Berlin, and a couple in London.'

'There was talk about building a skatepark in Lagos,' Duke said. 'But I'll believe it when I see it.'

The weeds growing high above the pathways made the pool seem isolated. Julius liked the sense that they could sit here for hours without seeing another soul.

'It was really cool showing me this place,' Julius said, feeling he ought to offer something in return. 'We should meet up Saturday night. My brothers are having their birthday party.'

'How many siblings you got?' Duke asked.

'Three brothers. Kehinde and Taiwo are turning seventeen. Gabe's ten.'

Duke laughed uneasily. He knew Julius had brothers but hadn't realised they were two of the biggest thugs in the school.

'We're not friendly,' Duke said. 'They hang with that nasty piece of work, Collins.'

'Collins is my cousin,' Julius said. 'The governor's son.'

'No disrespect,' Duke said awkwardly.

'Rip my family all you like!' Julius laughed, waving hands like he was batting off flies. 'My childhood memories are big brothers and cousins ganging up, chasing me with sticks or rubbing their butts on my face. The party is at this punky club place called Dog Head. It's a private party, so we can drink and stuff.'

Duke made a *don't be dumb* face. 'Julius, the last interaction I had with your cousin, Collins pulled a knife. Said he'd cut my throat if I ever looked at him again. So, thanks, but better to give that a miss.'

'Pity,' Julius said, burying his head in his hands. 'Everyone's jealous because I'm rich. But my family pisses me off. I can't go anywhere without a bodyguard. It's like prison.'

'Comfortable prison,' Duke pointed out. 'Marble floors, big-screen TVs. No uncle who comes home and turns off the air con to save diesel.'

The boys had squeezed close to watch the videos and when Julius took his hands off his face and looked up, their noses almost touched.

Duke's eyes seemed sadder from close up. Julius wondered what it must be like, waking up every day knowing people were going to punch, kick and call you a homo. If he'd found himself in the same position, Julius was sure he'd have ditched the earrings, chopped his hair and tried to make himself invisible. He admired Duke's defiance, but it was also infuriating.

Duke kept staring back. Like the pause in a movie, before they kiss.

'Getting achy,' Julius said, knee buckling as he shot to his feet. 'Better walk it off.'

'We could go see the snow leopards,' Duke suggested.

They left shirts and boards and strode along more overgrown paths, uphill towards the tower. Julius was fascinated by a faded billboard above the restaurant entrance. It showed a family eating fancy food from an orange tablecloth. Dad smoked a cigar, the kids wore shirts with giant collars and a bow-tied waiter carved meat from a rib joint: *Dine with us at Antarctica Revolving Restaurant – Akure's best views and finest food*.

'Views of what?' Julius joked as Duke kept strolling. 'The army barracks? Slum fires? Moonlight twinkling on that big lake of turds?

'Such a cynic!' Duke said, laughing. 'Where is your Sunshine State pride?'

The next stretch was down the other side of the hill, through a huge abandoned enclosure. Its zinc roof panels had been stolen for scrap, and clumps of fungi had spawned on the exposed beams.

Julius thought he saw something move in a cage to one side.

'That's Eddie,' Duke explained, as Julius squinted between rusted bars. 'He was born here, just after the zoo opened.'

The aroma was urine and bleach and a perished tyre swung from frayed rope. Julius sighted the scrawny polar bear in deep shadow. Trying to cool himself by lying in a puddle drizzling from a green hose.

When Eddie moved into a triangle of sunlight, Julius noticed bloody sores around his feet and a mound where his right eye should have been.

'They sold the other polar bears to a zoo in the Middle East,' Duke said. 'Nobody wanted Eddie, because his gammy eye scares kids.'

The big cats were further downhill. After so much decay, Julius was surprised to find a row of small but clean pens, with fresh paint on the bars and security cameras in the ceiling. The boys stopped by a cage with five pointy-eared lynx cubs, so tiny they'd yet to open their eyes.

'Cute,' Julius said, catching a wary glance from the cubs' mother as he dropped down on haunches for a closer look. 'What would one of these cost?'

Duke shrugged. 'Not cheap, that's for sure. With big cats, most owners want cubs. When they get big, the zoo takes them back and zaps them. White lynx and leopard fur is big money. Teeth, balls and claws go for Chinese medicine. The best cuts are sold as bushmeat, and Eddie eats whatever's left over.'

'That's messed up,' Julius said, shaking his head as he imagined this future for a baby lynx breaking into a super-cute yawn.

'How's it worse than eating cow or pig?' Duke asked.

Further down, Julius looked in cages wriggling with snow leopard cubs and a single adult Siberian tiger.

A beatbox was blaring Breez 99 FM. Duke located its owner in a bare-concrete room. The room fizzed with flies as plastic-gloved hands dug offal out of a drum and dropped it into a line of feeding bowls.

'Skater boy!' a zookeeper shouted over his radio. 'Who is this friend with the bloody leg?'

'George, this is Julius,' Duke introduced as he peeled a pair of ₦200 notes from his pocket. He was wary of touching the keeper's gory glove as he handed them over.

There was an awkward pause, until George glowered at Julius.

'This place isn't cheap to run,' he noted forcefully. 'Meat costs money.'

Julius realised he was expected to pay something for the right to skate. The etiquette for bribes was for hands to work while faces pretend nothing is happening.

Two hundred naira was less than the price of a Coke. People kept low-value notes rolled up in front pockets or handbags, ready to slip into the hands of cops, thugs, government officials and anyone else who had a little power over your existence. There was never a thank-you or any other direct acknowledge-ment, though you'd soon know if you hadn't paid the going rate.

Julius had nothing in the front of his shorts and grew flustered as he dug a wallet from his back pocket. His smallest note was a thousand and he blurted, 'I hope that's not too much,' as he handed it over.

The zookeeper pushed the ₦1,000 into his bloody apron,

then looked at Duke and erupted in a volcanic laugh. 'What the hell is this fellow?'

'His family are big men,' Duke said, laughing as Julius felt mortified. 'He's not used to dealing with little people like us.'

'Is that right? Julius, you're a big man?' George teased. 'Get that wallet out in front of people, it can get snatched from your hand in one heartbeat.'

Julius got more embarrassed and Duke kept laughing as they stepped back into sunlight.

'It wasn't *that* bad,' Julius protested.

'Sorry,' Duke said, with a grin that showed he wasn't. 'It's wrong to laugh at the social awkwardness of the rich and extremely fortunate.'

'Screw you,' Julius said, before launching a gentle kick at his friend's butt.

Duke dodged the flying sneaker, then randomly broke into a sprint back up towards the tower.

Julius couldn't go beyond a fast limp with his gashed knee. As Duke vanished into the weeds, Julius's mind went back to when they'd been staring at each other.

Why did I freak out and stand up when I wanted him to kiss me so much?

SIX

Georgia dropped teabags in four mugs, spooned two sugars and instant coffee in another, then waited as the first steam wafted from the kettle spout. They were all talking in the living room: Mum, Dad, Uncle Phil, Nan, Auntie Michelle and the widow from next door who'd come knocking with a tin of rock cakes.

It turned out they'd been lying to Georgia. She'd known about Sophie being suspended from work, but everyone was like, *There'll be an investigation – Sophie made an honest mistake, but they have to follow procedures before she goes back to work.* But now her mum was riding a guilt trip and truth was spewing forth. *We should have done more... Helped Sophie with her debts. Paid for Sophie to see a private psychiatrist instead of waiting six weeks... Gone over there to make sure Sophie was eating properly... The pills the GP put her on made her drowsy all the time and she should have come back to live with me after she took the overdose.*

Georgia had messaged her sister every day. She'd thought they were tight, but apparently, she knew nothing.

Just a kid...

As Georgia filled the mugs with boiling water, she relived an incident six weeks back. Sophie didn't answer any messages for a day and a half. Afterwards, Sophie said her phone had been stolen. But the next time Georgia saw her sister, she could tell Sophie had the same phone from the crack in the screen.

At the time, Georgia thought it was weird that Sophie hadn't mentioned getting her phone back. But now Georgia connected the dots. Sophie wasn't answering her messages on the same day her dad suddenly had a *really important meeting* and Auntie Michelle came round to make dinner . . .

Georgia finished making the drinks, found half a pack of chocolate digestives and had to look in four cupboards to find the big tray to carry it all through.

'Thank you, angel,' Georgia's nan said as she took her mug.

Georgia's mum was in the armchair by the living room window, the floor around her dotted with make-up-smeared tissues.

Her dad was the practical one. He had his iPad out, looking up how to obtain a death certificate, while Uncle Phil watched over him from the arm of the sofa.

Georgia felt deceived and couldn't stand the little room packed out with family. They'd protected her from the truth because they cared, but it also showed that they thought of her as a child. Georgia imagined text messages and late-night phone calls. Everyone talking about *what Georgia should know* and *how she's already been through enough this year with the divorce.*

'Where are you off to now, Cookie?' Georgia's dad asked, thumping an empty spot on the sofa. 'Come sit by your old man.'

'We were up at five to get to the Rage Classic,' Georgia said. 'My head's banging. I'm going up to my room for some peace.'

'I made rock cakes,' the neighbour lady said, pointing to the tin, which nobody had touched.

'Are you sure you want to be on your own?' Aunt Michelle asked. 'I could come and sit with you.'

The idea of her aunt propped at the end of the bed boosted Georgia's sense that everyone thought she was a kid. She felt a heave of anger and imagined herself screaming out, *I'm fourteen not four.*

But Georgia wasn't a drama queen. She left that to her mum.

'I probably won't be back down,' Georgia said drily. 'I'll say goodnight to everyone now.'

She was a sweaty mess under the Drone Pack bowling shirt. She brushed her teeth and showered. Georgia's duvet was in a mound, because her dad had been yelling that *Everyone has been waiting down here for ten minutes* when she'd left her room that morning.

Apart from the consequences of this hasty exit, the room was immaculate. Footwear lined up under the bed, schoolbooks clamped between bookends and a wipeable planner board behind the desk, marked with key dates, like holidays, homework deadlines and the Geography field trip.

There was a pair of display cabinets on one wall. The larger one was full of drone-racing trophies and mangled remains of several quads she'd wrecked during years of racing. The smaller cabinet contained a couple of cheap plastic trophies and a row of medals on coloured ribbons won at swimming club.

Beneath the cabinets were piles of stationery. While some kids collect action figures or keychains, Georgia had a thing for stationery. When relatives first caught on, every birthday and Christmas became a mass of coloured Post-its, glitter pens and novelty erasers. Over time, her tastes had gone upscale. Nuuna notebooks, Blackwing pencils, MT Scrapbooking tape and handmade Japanese writing paper.

Georgia dug out a set of flannel pyjamas with seahorses on. She hadn't worn them in ages and the arms were too short, but there was something comforting about the thick cotton, covered with lint baubles that she could pick at for hours.

She combed her hair in front of her mirrored wardrobe and the pyjamas reminded her of old Christmas-morning pictures. Georgia going bonkers, tearing through presents. Sophie, nine years older, with a smile for the camera, but eyes suggesting she'd have preferred an extra hour in bed . . .

Georgia's Venetian blind wasn't fully closed and she got dazzled by headlights onto the front drive. Uncle Phil and Auntie Michelle were already in their car, and Georgia's nan gave her dad a big hug, then a more stilted one to her former daughter-in-law.

As the Prius reversed out, Georgia heard her parents in the hallway. Her mum had already said she was *too exhausted for an hour-and-a-half's drive home* and was going to stay the night. But the only spare bed was in Sophie's old room and she couldn't stomach sleeping in there.

For a horrible moment, Georgia thought her parents were going to share their old bed, but she heard her dad say he'd get some bedding and her mum saying *the sofa is fine, because it's only one night* and *it's not like I'm going to sleep anyway.*

John came up to get bedding from the boiler cupboard. Instead of going straight back down, she heard him creep up to her door. Georgia loved her dad, but she couldn't face more cheesy life-goes-on, arm-around-the-back stuff, so was relieved when she heard him start down the stairs.

'Think Georgia's settled,' John said, in one of those whispers that carries more than a normal voice.

Georgia remembered reading that having your kid die is the most emotionally devastating thing that can happen to anyone, but she was too angry about all the secrets to feel sympathy.

Despite being awake since five, sleep felt unlikely. Georgia was satisfied with her choice of comfy old pyjamas and felt the next step down this road was to get her laptop and snuggle under the covers, watching something brainless that she'd seen at least three times before. But not *Friends*, because she watched that with Sophie when she was little and that would *wreck* her.

I'll never hear Sophie's voice again...

Georgia blotted tears as she stepped close to the window and fished out the cord for her phone charger that had dropped behind her bedside drawer unit. She'd normally check her phone before putting it on charge, but couldn't face social media. Sophie had a zillion friends and Georgia could imagine the bland sentiments and tearful emojis from obscure cousins, med-school acquaintances and girlz she'd met once at a hen party in Tonbridge...

As Georgia snapped in her charging lead, she noticed movement on the driveway. She peeked through her blind as a stocky male figure headed for the front door, then changed heart and darted sideways towards the bin store. She'd only caught the figure's outline but felt sure who it was.

After pushing feet into a pair of tatty Chucks, Georgia moved swiftly downstairs to the front door, half expecting the bell to ring before she got there. Her parents were busy pulling a cover over the spare duvet in the living room and didn't see their daughter step into the dark.

'Zac, is that you?' Georgia asked, shivering as night air hit still-damp hair.

As the gravel crunched under her sneaker, she swiped her dad's keys from a shelf over a radiator, then quietly pulled the front door shut.

'Zac?' she repeated, wanting him to hear but not be so loud that her parents did too.

She was starting to wonder if her mind had played a trick when Sophie's boyfriend stepped out from behind three wheelie bins, giving a limp wave.

'You saw,' he said weakly.

It was the most un-Zac thing Georgia had ever heard Zac say.

Georgia loved her big sister, but Sophie was a tough act to follow. Top exam grades, Cambridge University, bachelor of medicine – first with honours, of course. And Zac Li was her long-term companion and perfect action-figure of a boyfriend.

A Hong Kong-born hunk. By day, Zac was a life-saving, motorbike-riding paramedic, in black boots and dark green NHS uniform. By night, he wore chunky knits and skinny jeans and was handsome enough to have stepped out of a menswear catalogue.

'Are you coming inside?' Georgia asked.

Zac took broken steps on the driveway gravel. He wore his motorbike boots and dark green work trousers with an OBEY baseball cap and a red Socialist Worker's Party T-shirt with *Smash Capitalism* and a picture of Big Ben snapped in half.

'Have you been drinking?' Georgia asked.

'I came by earlier,' Zac explained. 'But the lights were on and I could see cars on the drive. Your whole family was inside, and I couldn't face them . . .'

'You would have been welcome,' Georgia said warmly, then

shrugged. 'They were doing my head in, if I'm honest.'

'I wandered to the pub down by the housing estate . . .'

'The Old Bulldog,' Georgia said, alarmed. 'You're taking your life in your hands. A year-thirteen from my school got stabbed in there.'

'Thumped some fascist in a suit,' Zac admitted drunkenly, stretching out his T-shirt. 'Didn't take kindly to this. Then I strolled the canal before coming back here.'

Georgia half smiled. 'I thought you were a pacifist.'

'He swung first,' Zac said.

He stepped out from the bins into the light coming between the living-room curtains. Georgia saw the eyes of someone who'd been crying all day.

'I don't know what to say,' Georgia shrugged. 'Nothing's gonna make this better, is it?'

'You're starting to look *so* much like your sister.'

'A lot of people don't notice because of the age gap,' Georgia said. 'But we are alike if you see pictures of us at the same age.'

Zac put his arms out and Georgia collapsed against his chest. She'd had a crush on her sister's boyfriend the whole four years they'd been going out. Zac's smell was staler than usual, but Georgia still loved it.

'I tried everything to make your sister happy,' Zac said. 'Maxed my Mastercard and booked a holiday, but she refused to go. She was *so* depressed. Wasn't eating, wore the same clothes for days on end . . .'

'Nobody told me,' Georgia said bitterly as the hug came apart. 'I'm so pissed off. I was messaging Sophie, complaining about how much homework I had. And bitching about the big row I had with Mum. I *never* would have mentioned that stuff if Mum and Dad told me she was depressed.'

Zac shook his head. 'Don't blame your parents. Sophie didn't want you to worry. She was going mad because everyone kept asking the same questions. Asking how she was doing. Asking how her meds were working. You were the one person who didn't keep going on about it.

'But things kept getting worse. Your dad and I both thought you had a right to know when Sophie took the overdose, but Sophie erupted when your dad said he was taking you to visit her in hospital.'

Georgia felt like she'd been shot. The anger towards her parents had focused her mind. But it wasn't their fault, which just left grief.

'Why would she do it?' Georgia yelled furiously. 'She did one thing wrong in her whole life. In a new job, when she was exhausted at the end of a fourteen-hour shift. It's not fair.'

'It's not,' Zac said as the front door swung open. 'I won't be letting this drop. The hospital wanted a scapegoat and Sophie was an easy mark.'

'Georgia?' John asked, then saw Zac and his daughter. 'Zac! I wondered where you were. I left messages on your phone.'

'Hello, Mr Pack,' Zac said. Then awkwardly added, 'John.'

Georgia had never heard her dad say anything bad about Zac, but they had zilch in common.

John Pack ran a small business, wore the V-neck sweaters his mum bought him for Christmas and liked watching a bit of football on the telly. Zac Li was half his age and a left-wing activist who proudly boasted that he'd egged three prime ministers and spent his teens leading a pro-democracy campaign in his native Hong Kong.

But both men adored Sophie, and nothing was held back as they hugged and slapped each other on the back.

'There was nothing I could do, John,' Zac said. 'She was dead when I got home.'

'Come inside and sit down,' John said firmly. 'Your knuckles are bloody. Have you been in a fight?'

'Scraped them at work, carrying a patient downstairs,' Zac lied, staring at his hand like he was seeing the wound for the first time. 'I'm walking home.'

'Well, at least let me fix you an Uber. It's six miles.'

'You'll see me in a coffin before you see me in an Uber,' Zac said, narrowing his eyes.

Hating big corporations was part of Zac's left-wing thing. Georgia remembered Sophie's mischievous laugh as she told an anecdote about buying Zac's birthday gift from Amazon and having to bury the packaging at the bottom of the bin before he got home from work.

'I can find another cab company,' John said.

'And you found her in the flat,' Georgia added. 'Do you *really* want to sleep there tonight?'

But Zac had stopped listening. He was focused on retrieving a battered canvas bag that he'd left by the bins.

'Sophie said these are the ones you like,' Zac explained as he took out a shrink-wrapped box of Jirafu notepaper, embossed with the logo for the Tokyo 2020 Olympics.

Jirafu was Georgia's favourite stationery brand. She tried to collect all the different pads they released each year, but the Tokyo 2020 ones were gifted to members of the Olympic Committee and had never been sold to the public.

'Do you know how she got them?' Georgia asked, turning the packet over in wonder. 'I always look on eBay. Everyone on the Jirafu fan site wants these!'

'She said you'd be excited,' Zac said, clearly bemused by

Georgia's stationery obsession. 'I also found these on her desk.' Zac's hand trembled as he held three envelopes with Sophie's writing on the outside. One *To Mum*, one *To Daddy*, and one marked *To Georgia*.

SEVEN

The after-school adventure seemed dreamlike now that Julius was back under guard. He sat at the desk in his bedroom, curtains drawn, schoolbooks spread and his face lit by a Wikipedia page on his laptop screen.

He'd stripped down to undershorts, but stayed hot. He kept reading the same line from a textbook, *In a ray diagram, the mirror is drawn as a straight line with thick hatchings . . .* The words bounced off a brain that was still at the penguin pool, watching Duke glide on his neon deck. *The light rays are drawn with straight lines, with arrowheads that show the direction of . . .*

Julius groaned and wheeled his chair back. He stared at the silent vents of the air conditioning and decided to blame his lack of concentration on the heat.

Gabe had a friend in the house, shooting Nerf guns along a shadowy hallway as Julius stepped out of his room and headed downstairs sprayed with foam darts. He stopped to look out of the landing window. Two bored soldiers guarded the front gate from white plastic chairs, while an array of generator parts were spread over the tiled driveway. An orange-overalled engineer stared at them, his clueless air suggesting little chance of power being restored any time soon.

Julius carried on down to a large kitchen on the ground floor. The wipe-down walls, functional steel benches and large commercial appliances clearly belonging to people whose staff did the cooking.

'When's the power coming back?' Julius asked, moving towards the stove and feeling his stomach growl as he lifted the lid on bubbling pepper soup.

Orisa hopped across the floor and smacked Julius's hand away. 'Leave my food until it is ready!'

Orisa was a small, pretty woman in her mid-thirties. She was a distant cousin, sent from Julius's grandparents' village when his twin brothers were born seventeen years earlier. And while other household staff got hired and fired, Orisa was family and not to be messed with.

'Would you like a cold drink?' she asked brightly. 'Pepsi?'

'Sounds good,' Julius agreed, then tapped his stomach. 'Diet, if we have it.'

'Your mother is home, so we will all eat together in an hour,' Orisa said as she part-filled a glass from an ice dispenser and pulled a large Coke bottle from the fridge. 'And you have wardrobes filled with clothes, so why must this house be full of boys in their underwear?'

Julius nodded thanks for his drink and changed the subject. 'So, when *is* the power coming back on?'

'We have solar power,' Orisa said, pointing to the roof. 'My kitchen is fine.'

'Real power,' Julius said, between gulps of Coke. 'Cold-blast-of-air-conditioning-shooting-up-the-legs-of-my-shorts power.'

Orisa smiled. 'You won't get your balls cooled unless the

mains electricity is switched on later. The diesel generator needs parts from China. It will be two days, at least.'

Julius tutted. 'Can't we check into a hotel?'

'Don't be soft,' Orisa said as she picked a wooden spoon off a countertop and gave Julius a good-natured thwack on the upper arm. 'When I was your age, I'd never *seen* an air-conditioning unit.'

'Life was hard,' Julius moaned sarcastically. 'The Adebisi family lived in dirt holes. There was only cow dung to eat, and we all died of malaria six months before we were born . . .'

This earned him a harder whack with the spoon. 'Would you dare with that cheek in front of your mother?' Orisa asked, throwing down the spoon and making *get out* gestures, but smiling. 'Leave my kitchen. And wear some blasted clothes!'

Julius grabbed his Coke and moved back to the staircase. A Nerf dart skimmed his head as he wondered where to go next. The thought of sitting in the outdoor courtyard by the pool was enticing, but the twins were there, blaring death metal, and the physics assignment was going nowhere.

'BANZAI NINJA!' Gabe screamed, vaulting over a bannister as his friend came down the stairs after him with a fully loaded Nerf.

Julius wanted to be ten as he sighed and turned up the stairs. Then he wished the ground would gobble him as he neared the top step and saw Simeon come out of his mother's office. The heavily built driver had a thick bundle of ₦1,000 notes and the expression of a boy who'd wet himself.

'Your ma would like to see you straight away,' Simeon said, almost tearful. 'I just received a week's severance pay.'

'Why?'

'I have three kids at home,' Simeon told Julius bitterly. 'I hope your escapade was worth my livelihood.'

Julius felt sick as Simeon banged down the stairs. For half a second, he planned to storm his mother's office and yell at her. But that would need suicidal bravery, so he bolted for his room, sick with angst as he leapt into clean shorts and tugged a Ralph Lauren polo over his head.

'Julius, where have you run to?' he heard his mother shout. 'When I ask to see you, I mean right *now!*'

'Coming, Ma,' Julius yelled back.

I am so screwed...

Julius drained his Coke, then skidded as he charged down the hall to his mother's office. Gabe watched the unfolding drama through stair rails and the ten-year-old made a noose gesture as Julius aimed a knock.

'Come,' his mother blasted. 'Get here, be still in this chair!'

Julius felt chilled air from a ceiling-mounted unit. Apparently, the solar panels were generating enough energy to keep the most important person in the house cool . . . After settling in the chair, Julius's eyes were drawn towards the centre of his mother's elaborately carved desk: house keys, a Mercedes plipper and Simeon's ID badges for the governor's mansion and state parliament.

Bunmi Adebisi shared her middle son's height and looming posture. A pink-and-gold gele and floor-length dress of the same fabric gave her the air of a vast flamingo as she settled into a throne-like chair, then took big gulps from a glass of Guinness.

Julius's mother wore similar traditional clothes in photographs on the wall behind. They showed her posing alongside Nollywood actors, footballers and army chiefs. Pride of place went to a photo taken at the Nigerian Embassy in London, in which Bunmi wore a patriotic green and yellow headdress and towered over then-Presidents, Jonathan of Nigeria and Obama of the United States. The photos were full of smiles but reminded anyone who came that they were dealing with a serious and well-connected person.

'My son,' Bunmi began as she topped up her Guinness from a large bottle. 'What is this nonsense with the school today? Giving Simeon the slip when I pay him to protect you.'

She knew something if she'd fired Simeon. But Julius still began with a vague lie. 'I had an after-school meeting, in the library. My friend's father drove me home.'

'Really, really?' she said, leaning forward and locking chunky-ringed fingers together. 'Then why am I hearing other things, from your brother?'

Gabe, you little …

'A boy who knows Kehinde and Taiwo saw you by the girls' college. He says you rode away on a scooter with a notorious homosexual.'

'That's craziness,' Julius insisted, sensing big trouble but pleased it wasn't Gabe that had snitched.

'Taiwo said you're spending all your breaks with this boy, Damola Balogun.'

Duke's real name sounded peculiar from his mother's mouth.

'Ma, he's no queer,' Julius scoffed. 'Collins and the twins push Duke around and *call* him gay. But they're shitheads. In their opinion, half the kids in school are queer.'

'I hear this Damola has bleached hair and earrings.'

Julius tutted. 'That doesn't mean he's gay.'

'And he walks like a girl?'

'Ma, I don't know what that means.'

'You know what it means – with precision!' Bunmi snapped,

banging furiously on her desk. 'Don't act the fool with me. You are not stupid. You can *always* tell these homosexual types.'

Julius raised his voice and tried to push her off-topic. 'Why did you fire Simeon? I just told Gabe to give him a message. What was Simeon *supposed* to do?'

But his mother saw through the ruse. 'Who I employ is never your business. Focus on the matter I am discussing.'

'I'm fourteen,' Julius protested. 'I have *no* freedom.'

'You can socialise, but always with a driver. We are a high-status family. You have a target on your back. I did not make this world full of robbers and kidnappers. But that is how it is.'

'I wore old clothes,' Julius said. 'I'm nobody, anonymous.'

Bunmi wagged her finger furiously. 'Have you any sexual feelings for this Damola?'

'No,' Julius lied, cheeks hot enough to cook an egg. 'Duke is a cool guy. We're big friends. He's got a scooter. I wanted to take a ride around the city and hang out. Kehinde and Taiwo are *always* off chasing girls. They've skipped school and dropped their drivers a heap of times.'

'The twins are punished for high jinks,' Bunmi dismissed. 'This type of boy is a bigger concern. You have always been the lonely type. Adebisi is a family with a reputation to uphold. My ministry has a congregation of more than a quarter million. Your uncle is state governor and his re-election is less than one year away. People are always looking for chinks in the Adebisi armour, seeking ways to damage us. Cavorting homosexually could make a massive eruption of scandal.'

'He's a mate,' Julius shouted. 'I went on his bike. I didn't tell Simeon, because I didn't want a four-tonne black Mercedes on my tail. You're being ridiculous!'

'Am I?' Bunmi asked. 'You are too young to understand

these queer people. Before you know it, he tells you his way of what is acceptable, your moral compass is set spinning and you have become a fully fledged homosexual. People like this have no wife or children. They die alone and burn in hell.'

'You don't catch being gay,' Julius said, exasperated. 'It's not the flu! And don't preach to me. I'm not one of the gullible idiots at your ministry, yelling *halleluiah* and paying twenty thousand naira to read *Hot Prayers to Achieve Prosperity*, or whatever pamphlet you're pushing this month.'

'Do not antagonise me further,' Bunmi warned, rising up behind her desk. 'How many boys are in your school?'

Julius looked baffled. 'A thousand? Maybe twelve hundred.'

'Then this is simple, Julius. Twelve hundred boys to make friends with. Steer clear of this single one.'

'Duke is my friend,' Julius insisted.

'Kehinde, Taiwo and all of your cousins will be asked to look out,' Bunmi said. 'If I find that you have been associating with this homosexual boy, I will have Orisa pack your bags and send you directly to the Army Boys Academy in Nasarawa.'

'You can't!' Julius blurted.

'Are my instructions abundantly clear? I wont repeat myself again.'

Julius eyed his mother defiantly. But she didn't make empty threats and Army Boys Academy would shave his head, stick him in camouflage and make a soldier out of him, whether he liked it or not.

'I didn't give birth to a deaf child,' Bunmi stated. 'Answer or shall I find a man to knock the wax in your ears loose?'

'I guess you win, like you always do,' Julius said, slow and hateful. 'Take away my only friend, make me miserable. What do you care? It's not as if you're my mother, or anything.'

EIGHT

Hey Georgia,

I'm writing four letters, but honestly, this one to you is way the hardest. When I think about killing myself, I know it will hurt Mum, Dad and Zac, but they're adults. You're the kid sister, who I looked out for and never wanted to hurt.

You're going to ask why I'm doing this. They'll roll out all the clichés – Sophie was a bright girl, Sophie had her whole life ahead of her, it's all such a waste. She had a good family and an amazing boyfriend. Everything to live for.

It's like I've been on an express train my whole life. Storming the best grades in school. GCSEs, A-levels, good university. Be nice, be popular. Find a cool boyfriend. Get a first. Get a placement at a good training hospital.

Then, one night, you're screaming and crying. There's a guy who's dead because you got mixed up. Dosed a patient with five hundred instead of fifty, when I had a snotty cold and my eyes were so tired I could barely read the tiny print in the *Handbook of Clinical Medicine*.

And then I was off the express train. Sat in our flat, borrowing money and wearing Zac's hoodie. Daytime TV and microwave meals. Everything I've done or could do feels so pointless.

Reaching for the remote sucks all my energy. And everyone is full of advice: yoga, meditation, read this book, see the world, take meds, take this herbal thing instead of meds, get a dog, get a therapist, get religion.

I live in my head and my head is a torture chamber now. As much as I love everyone, my life has to stop because everything hurts too much.

But the thing that scares me most, G, is that you are so like me. You want to be best at everything. You're talking about doing medicine or maths at uni. You do the same stuff I used to do to stop Mum and Dad from killing each other. And, let's be honest, you've even got a little crush on Zac :-)

PLEASE, think before you go on blindly like I did. Mum, Dad, Nan, school and everyone else will shower you with praise for working hard and aiming high. But at some point you need to stop. Ask yourself who Georgia is and what YOU really want to do.

In the end, I drove myself so hard for so long that I literally couldn't see straight and wound up killing a thirty-eight-year-old boiler engineer with a pregnant girlfriend.

There's nothing wrong with being great, but above all, be happy.

Massive love.

Sophie
xxx

Georgia had read the note a hundred times. She accidentally smudged butter on it, after which she photographed the letter on her phone and put the original in the envelope at the bottom of her desk, with her swimming certificates.

And she couldn't do her history project. Georgia got out three different coloured Uni-ball pens and a new Rhodia pad to make reading notes. But the whole thing felt ridiculous.

Who gives a damn about Ancient Egyptian medicine?

Read it, remember it, write about it. And the next year you forget the lot and learn other random stuff to jump through the next set of hoops . . . It *had* all made sense. It *had* all been leading to something. Georgia had never known precisely what the something was, but she'd believed hard work and A-stars would take her to better places than the kids who got Bs and Cs and who didn't volunteer, helping grannies in and out of the pool at the Old Ducks Aqua Club.

Dr Sophie Pack proved the argument, with her yellow Audi and the boyfriend who smelled like heaven. But the proof had agreed to donate her body to science when she started med school, so now Sophie had been stripped of heart valves, corneas and other useful tissues, and was lying in deep freeze, waiting to be a practice dummy for trainee surgeons.

Nothing had meaning as Georgia took the lid off her pen and doodled a giant nuclear mushroom cloud, with a bunch of little stick figures running away. Then she gave them speech bubbles. One asked, *'What's the meaning of life?'* while another said, *'Honey, I have to go back – I think I left the iron on.'*

Then Georgia sat facepalmed, hearing the washing machine and her parents bickering, until her dad yelled, 'Food down here if you want it.'

He'd heated Bolognese out of the freezer and was tipping spaghetti in pasta bowls as Georgia walked in.

'Hitting the books, Cookie?' John asked brightly.

'History,' Georgia answered.

Georgia's mum had spent Thursday and Friday nights on the sofa. Georgia understood that she didn't want to go back to her flat and be alone, but having her around didn't make life easy. She was a natural-born moaner, from the couch jarring her back to the inferior taste of Lidl coffee.

'Has anyone spoken to Zac today?' Georgia asked as she twirled her Bolognese around a fork.

'He's working,' John said, throwing down a dishcloth and settling at the table.

'Already?' Georgia said, surprised. 'Doesn't he get compassionate leave?'

John nodded. 'They're short-staffed, and Zac said he'd rather work than sit around brooding.'

After two days stuck at home, Georgia could understand.

'Zac texted last night, saying his mum was trying to book a flight from Hong Kong,' Georgia told her dad. 'I hope she does, because you know . . . He's alone in the flat where Sophie . . .'

Georgia didn't finish because her mum had pushed her pasta bowl away, shaking her head.

'How much salt did you put in this sauce?'

John sighed. 'It's from a jar, the same one we've always bought.'

'Well, you added *something*.'

Georgia shovelled in another mouthful. Her dad's defrosted Bolognese would never win culinary prizes, but it wasn't offensive.

'Rachel, if I'd known you were staying, I'd have added cyanide,' John said, giving Georgia a cheeky eyebrow flick.

'Mature . . .' Rachel said.

'Tastes fine to me and Georgia's tucking it down,' John noted.

'Big surprise,' Rachel said, holding her arms wide open. 'Hold the front page. Daddy's girl takes Daddy's side.'

Georgia baulked.

'What the . . . !' Georgia gasped, so furious that a half-chewed piece of spaghetti flew out of her mouth. 'Quietly eating dinner is taking sides now?'

'Nothing I say is ever right,' Rachel said, folding her arms.

Georgia had heard that line a thousand times and it made something snap.

'Fine,' Georgia growled, tilting her pasta bowl towards her mother. 'Here's a compromise. I've eaten half, you can scoop the other half in the bin and then I've made you both equally unhappy.'

Georgia sent her bowl spinning into the middle of the table. She couldn't stand the thought of going back to her lonely room, or staying here listening to her parents fight over nothing. She grabbed a bomber jacket off the rack by the front door, patting to make sure her keys were in the pocket as she whipped it up her arms.

'Georgia, where are you going?' John asked anxiously as he rushed into the hall. 'It's getting dark.'

'I can't spend another second in this house,' Georgia yelled, trembling with anger as her dad blocked the front door.

'Cookie, you're upset, but you can't wander the streets on a Saturday night.'

'I'm not your bloody Cookie!' Georgia shouted, knowing she'd never outmuscle her dad and wondering if she could make a dash for the back door. She zipped the jacket, but this defiant gesture was spoiled by the realisation that she only had slipper socks on her feet.

'Calm down,' John soothed. 'We all feel rotten at the moment. If you're fed up being cooped in the house, we could go for a drive. Buy ice cream for dessert. Or maybe there's something on at Cineworld.'

'Dad, just . . .' Georgia grunted with frustration, then surprised herself with blurred vision and a powerful voice. 'Get out of my way!'

'You know that's not going to happen,' John said firmly.

'I hate this stupid family,' Georgia screamed, knowing she was being a massive teenage cliché as she spun and stomped upstairs.

She slammed her bedroom door, hoping her dad would assume she was staying there. Then grabbed her wallet off her desk, slid on a pair of flats and checked her hair in the mirror. After standing by the door to make sure nobody followed her up, Georgia opened it quietly, stepped into Sophie's old room and turned a handle to open a window.

The window was at the same height as the one in her own room, but the bin store directly beneath halved the drop. Rotten timber creaked alarmingly as she lowered herself out, forcing her to abandon stealth and leap noisily into the gravel driveway.

NINE

Ondo State Governor's Mansion – Akure, Nigeria

Julius had grown several centimetres since the tailor had fitted his dark suit. He felt weighed down as he sat in the corner of an icy-chilled, marble-floored ballroom. The space was lavishly finished, with windows made from Chinese coloured glass, chandeliers from Italy and walls hung with six-metre-high tapestries, designed by a major Nigerian artist and woven on computerised looms in Guangzhou.

It was close to 7.30 p.m. Along with more than thirty members of Julius's family, drinks and nibbles were being served to some of the most important figures in Ondo state. The reception was an election fundraiser for Julius's uncle, SJ Adebisi. As governor of Ondo, SJ was supposed to be the centre of attention. But Julius watched wryly as people who mattered shook the governor's hand when they arrived but quickly moved towards his mother.

Julius watched his mother's giant purple headdress wobble above the gathering as she greeted the chief of Ondo State police, the leader of the local transport union and the chief executive of UNICEF in West Africa. Bunmi's biggest smiles came for the grey-suited men from the Chinese Development

Bank. The Chinese had funded billions of dollars' worth of projects in Ondo State, including twenty million for the elaborate governor's mansion in which they now stood.

Julius was angry and miserable about his mother banning him from seeing Duke, but it was hard not to feel some pride as he watched her work the room.

Bunmi was the daughter of an army colonel, a big man in a village where most families laboured on cocoa plantations. She began selling textiles around local villages when she was in her mid-teens. At the time, fabrics used for traditional Yórùba clothing were made locally, and cheaper imported fabrics were banned.

Bunmi used her father's military connections to set up a smuggling operation, using Nigerian Army trucks to bring Chinese fabric from neighbouring Cameroon. Cheap smuggled fabric turned Bunmi into one of the biggest cloth distributors in southern Nigeria and she used a chunk of her profits to buy an abandoned cinema and turn it into the slickly marketed *Healing Prayer Church (HPC)*.

HPC hired handsome men to preach an upbeat mix of Christianity, with some superstition thrown in. The community promised wealth and success, especially if you purchased Hot Prayer books and necklaces, paid a priest to bless your home or bought sacred charms for your car, sports team or your child's school backpack.

HPC now had eleven worship centres, Nigeria's second most popular religious radio station and three services per week on government TV channels that were constitutionally banned from religious programming.

After business and religion, Bunmi decided to conquer politics. But a physically overbearing, never-married female, who'd fathered four sons by three different fathers, made an awkward political candidate. Instead, she groomed her youngest brother, SJ. First winning a term in the state assembly, then deposing two-term state governor Rotimi Rotimi.

Julius saw that his family was being herded by Teddy Mac, the Chicago-born political technologist who ran his uncle's political campaigns. Teddy's ink-blue suit and pointy shoes contrasted with the looser local styles, while his zippy can-do attitude and grind-you-down persistence got under Julius's skin.

'Someone's been growing,' Teddy said cheerfully, eyeing Julius's cuffs. 'Where's your cute little brother? He *has* to be in the pictures.'

Gabe was located, with ketchup on his tie. As Orisa rushed him to a bathroom to sponge it off, Julius followed a gaggle of uncles and cousins out of the ballroom and onto sweeping marble steps in front of the mansion.

Most Nigerian voters agreed that a successful person should look after their extended family, so photographs of political candidates surrounded by prosperous-looking relatives featured in every campaign. Voters awarded bonus points if the entourage included sweet kids and grey-haired grandmas. Gold jewellery and designer clothing were also popular, but never to be overdone, in case voters thought you'd skimmed too much from the state coffers.

No expense had been spared on the photo shoot. The water features in front of the mansion had been drained so that lights could be set up in the fountain bowls. There was a carefully disguised platform to make the governor look taller and a quarter-hour passed while Teddy and two photographic assistants shuffled bodies.

Kids fidgeted and SJ's wives bickered over which two got to stand next to him. At the previous election, Julius was ten and cute enough for a spot up front. Now, the looming teen was relegated behind rural cousins and great-uncles, who'd got bussed in for a new suit and dinner at the mansion.

It was past eight when the photographer called a wrap. Bodies began dispersing over the steps. Oldies filtered inside for a sit-down dinner, kids were scooped up by nannies and housekeepers to be put to bed. Julius found himself uncomfortable amidst his twin brothers and a bunch of cousins in their teens or early twenties.

'You partying at Dog Head, little brother?' Taiwo asked, wrapping a meaty arm around Julius and dragging him down a couple of steps.

'I'm tired,' Julius said, wishing he'd escaped inside with the olds.

He'd never been to Dog Head. Everyone said it was a cool venue, but the twins and their cronies were meathead bullies at school. Add booze, girls and local punk bands and Julius reckoned it would be a miracle if everyone lived till sunrise.

Taiwo, identical twin Kehinde and their ever-present cousin Collins formed an intimidating triangle.

'I would take great offence!' Collins told the twins mockingly. 'Brother won't attend your birthday celebration. Does Master Julius not like you?'

Taiwo moved his arm up to crunch Julius's neck. 'Collins isn't right, is he?' Taiwo laughed. 'I'm quite certain that you love your big brothers.'

'Get off,' Julius croaked. He was taller than the twins, but they were three years older and strong as hell. 'I can hardly come to Dog Head in a suit.'

72

'Lucky for you, Ma doesn't want you moping around another night with your sour horse face,' Kehinde revealed, as Taiwo finally let go. 'She made Orisa pack clothes for all of us.'

Julius knew he was going if his mum was on the twins' side. He figured his best strategy was to appear briefly, then tell a family driver he felt sick and needed to go home.

Orisa had stuffed a bunch of clothes in a wheeled Samsonite and Julius was happy with skinny jeans and an embroidered Volcom shirt in army green. He was in a mood for hating things and started picking on Dog Head because it was done out like a dive bar, with graffiti and layers of peeling paint, although it was on the upper floor of a mall that had opened barely a year earlier.

The twins' party was in a VIP area on the club's mezzanine level. Julius was pleased to see a ton of Adebisi bodyguards on hand in case of trouble. He grabbed a beer out of an ice bucket and tried to make himself invisible, standing with his back to a post, as the twins brayed and bumped fists with school friends. They were the kind of loud, beefy guys Julius avoided, and also the type of girls who hung out with them.

'Hey, stranger,' a girl with a country accent yelled over deafening bass and drums. 'You too good for us now, Julius?'

There were two of them, fifteen and seventeen, dressed for a formal photo, not a club. Lights were flashing and they'd grown since Julius last saw them, so it took a second to recognise two favourite cousins, Blessing and Pru.

'Too good for what?' Julius shouted.

'When did you last come back to the village?' Pru, the older one, asked.

'I went to London the last two summers,' Julius admitted. 'What's happening back there?'

Blessing's teeth caught the flashing lights. 'In the village?' she asked.

'Nothing,' Prudence said, grinning. 'Nothing ever happens. I'm starting university in Lagos soon.'

The band was playing a loud bit and Julius cupped his ear. 'Pardon?'

'University,' Prudence shouted.

'Ahh, that's good!' Julius shouted.

The trio drank beers and shouted themselves hoarse, remembering stuff they'd done together at the family village in olden days. Julius had cheered up by the time his cousins dragged him out of the private area and headed close to the stage to dance. It was a crazy scene, with shirtless guys, flying sweat and the floor slippery with spilled bear. But when the lights went up for a change of band, Adebisi security fished the trio out of the crowd.

'Stay in the private party,' a slab of a guard said bitterly. 'You're fourteen. Are you trying to get another one of us fired?'

Pru and Blessing acted stroppy as they got chaperoned back to the mezzanine, but Julius felt guilty about Simeon and made no fuss.

He grabbed a third beer and found himself stood among more cousins. They looked as out of place as they felt, clustered together sipping beers as the birthday boys and their rich-kid St Gilda's pals kissed girls and ordered expensive drinks and food platters.

A two-tier birthday cake fizzed with sparklers, after which most of the cousins had to leave for an overnight bus ride back to the village. Julius hugged a bunch of relatives and his phone said 22:43 as he came back from the bathroom, a touch drunk. He reckoned he'd stayed long enough to show good faith and asked a white-haired driver called Abeo to take him home.

Weirdly, Abeo crossed the mezzanine and spoke to Luke Adebisi. The governor's oldest son was a burly twenty-year-old, who'd graduated from St Gilda's with grades good enough for an American college. But Luke dropped out after two terms, preferring a lucrative and not-too-demanding job as a Youth Issues Advisor, in his father's administration, and a mounting reputation as a party boy.

Julius got a bad vibe as Luke's gold-festooned hand beckoned him.

'Come on, come on, come on, come on!' Luke said, sounding oddly like a turkey gobble.

Julius hesitated.

'What are you afraid of, my cousin?' Luke asked, cracking a big grin as Kehinde, Taiwo and Collins enclosed Julius, with their St Gilda's cronies sliding out of a booth to watch.

Julius got the sense that everyone but him knew what was going on. His heart quickened as he glanced about, hoping one of the family drivers would rescue him. Instead, a gap opened in the circle and a girl was shoved through, hard enough to stumble on her high heels.

No older than eighteen, with a curvy figure, silver nails and a strapless metallic dress. She was clad like rich St Gilda's girls, but crooked teeth and missing incisors suggested she'd grown up too poor to afford a dentist.

'Bella, this is my cousin, Julius,' Luke told the girl as he rested his rings on her bare shoulder. 'He's not what you'd call a lady's man.'

'People are saying he's a homo,' Taiwo said, before adding firmly, 'but we don't have that in our family. He just needs to be shown a few things . . .'

Julius felt his face heat up as Bella stepped closer. Even with her silver heels, the top of her head didn't reach his neck.

Why didn't I leave with the cousins? Something messed up was always gonna happen if I stuck around too long...

'Give her a nice kiss,' Luke said firmly.

A couple of lads in the outer circle had their camera phones out.

Julius thought about running, but the circle was tight, so he leaned forward and kissed Bella nervously on the lips. Her breath smelled vinegary and nothing stirred. Not the way it stirred when Julius watched Duke glide on his skateboard.

'What was that?' Collins sneered, grabbing Julius's hand and placing it on Bella's butt. 'Kiss her properly.'

Julius was trapped. The beers had made his head thick and Bella's smell made him queasy, but if he didn't prove himself he'd be labelled queer and spend his last three years at St Gilda's being bullied as mercilessly as Duke.

Julius dug awkward fingers into Bella's buttock and she made a heaving sound as she pushed against him. Luke must have paid her.

'Get in!' Taiwo jeered.

Julius caught Bella's breath again and found it unbearable. She was expecting a kiss and he tried to imagine it as something short but painless, like a trip to the dentist. But how many guys had a girl like this been with, and what might she have caught from them?

'I'll do anything you want,' the girl said, full of longing. 'I've got a room out back ...'

Julius imagined a space with a dirty mattress and a smell of body spray as Bella cupped his balls.

'Please,' Julius stumbled, taking a step back but dragging

Bella with him.

The circle closed in, reinforced by St Gilda's girls keen to see the action.

'Kiss her,' Collins demanded. 'Don't show our family up."

But Julius decided he'd rather get stomped by every guy in the circle than let himself be humiliated.

'I'll find my own women,' Julius shouted as he gave Bella a slight shove. 'No disrespect.'

The circle erupted in outrage as Bella flung herself back in a dive worthy of the English Premier League.

A furious Collins went on tiptoes and got right up in Julius's face.

'You're a shame on this family, Julius. You're no cousin of mine . . .'

Collins was a monster. Julius knew his hardest punch would just make an excuse for his cousin to beat him bloody. But Julius had a moment of drunk inspiration, grabbing the back of his cousin's head and sinking teeth into Collins's nose.

Collins escaped easily, but the blood streaming over his top lip and into his mouth bought Julius time, as guys backed off and someone screamed.

Julius half expected to wake from a dream as he stumbled back. Pulsing blue lights showed Collins bleeding, Bella being helped off the floor and several phones filming. But the mushroom of flesh in his mouth was real, and so was cousin Luke's enormous fist, covered in gold rings and coming straight towards his face . . .

TEN

Georgia strode briskly, hands in pockets to keep warm. She walked long enough for her nose to start feeling numb. At first, she was scared her phone might ring, but after an hour she was offended that it hadn't. Presumably, John thought she was in her room and had decided to let her stew.

She dared herself to walk through the Isaac Newton Estate in the dark. She almost wanted something bad to happen to stall the dark thoughts circling her head. But the estate was more cosy than daunting. Kids on pre-bedtime bike rides with parents keeping an eye out from balconies, TVs flickering and bodies shifting inside steamed-up kitchens.

Georgia choked up when she realised she'd unconsciously found the way to her old primary school. She'd been a proud but heartbroken nine-year-old when her big sister had left for university.

Sophie had surprised Georgia by coming to collect her when she got home for Christmas holidays. Georgia remembered whipping her coat off her hook in the year-four cloakroom and belting out to hug a student edition of her sister, with dyed hair, new glasses and a whiff of cumin and joss sticks.

As she walked on, Georgia saw people entering church for evening service. She could see herself on a pew watching candles flicker but still felt tearful from seeing her old school and worried that the greeters handing out hymn books in their bright yellow sweatshirts would ask her business.

Georgia's heels were painful by the time she got to the town centre. She wished she'd put on her comfy Nike Frees as she queued for a latte and a pain au chocolat in Costa Coffee at the mainline station.

She people-watched as the mug warmed her hands. Couples meeting for date night, two fat men in fluorescent Network Rail vests arguing in Polish. Most touching was a lonely old guy, who counted out coins for the cheapest filter coffee and tried to make conversation with disinterested staff. Trembling hands sent his coffee dribbling and a woman with twins in a buggy shot up to help him find a seat.

When Georgia heard a message ping, she slid out her phone, imagining a stiffly phrased text from her dad, calling her irresponsible and offering to pick her up in the car. But Georgia's screen had no message icon. The woman at the table behind had set the same sound.

Georgia watched her reflection in Costa's plate glass. The woman flicked back bleached hair and smiled as she tapped her phone at hyper-speed. *Bing* – a reply. *Bing* – another message. *Bing, bing* . . . Then her friend arrived. Georgia noticed they had the same build and both wore striped tights as they hugged and cooed.

'It's been ages, sis . . . My God, I love your hair!'

I used to have a sister . . .

When they were gone, Georgia stared at the dead milk foam around the inside of her cup, and thought about how hardly anyone ever messaged her. She wasn't disliked, and knew plenty of boys were after her, but Georgia had always found schoolwork and hobbies more interesting than the gossip and overblown dramas around which her fellow teens built friendships. Or, as they put it, Georgia was a geek.

Georgia felt a chill of dread. She'd doubted her life choices a thousand times since reading Sophie's letter. It was like being locked in a room, forced to listen to the same song, over and over. And your brain doesn't have an off switch.

You're just like me. Don't end up the same ... Be happy.

But how can I be happy, Sophie Pack? Georgia asked furiously. *If you knew, you'd still be here ...*

'Georgia?' someone asked, startling her out of thought.

Georgia caught her mug with her cuff, making it clatter as she turned round and saw Maya Norris from school. She wore black leggings, a furry jumper and too much make-up.

Maya and Georgia had spent seven years in the same class at primary school, during which they'd been friendly, but never friends. Now in year ten, they only shared one top-level maths set and fell on opposite sides of a social divide.

Kids like Maya came from the estates and their parents worked at the airport or the Amazon warehouse. Estate kids tended not to hang with slightly posher kids like Georgia, who lived in semi-detached houses and mostly had parents who commuted to better-paid jobs in London.

'I didn't want to stick my nose in,' Maya began. 'But I heard what happened and I saw you through the glass, looking sad.'

Georgia smiled. 'My sister's in our school admissions brochure, as a shining example of an ex-pupil.'

'Guess they'll have to reprint,' Maya said, pointing at the empty chair opposite. 'Can I?'

Georgia felt strangely refreshed, realising how much she needed to talk to someone other than family. 'My parents were at each other all day,' she explained, making mouths with both hands. 'I had to get out before my head exploded.'

'You're alone?'

'Sure,' Georgia said, trying to make out it wasn't a big deal.

'It's dodgy round the station, especially after eleven when the Railway Arms kicks out,' Maya warned.

'You're alone,' Georgia noted.

'Came out with Rolf Santos,' Maya explained. 'He said he'd treat me to Cineworld and Nando's. But he rocked up a half-hour late, saying there's no time to go to the cashpoint. So I shell out twenty-two quid for tickets and popcorn. After, we stop at the ATM and he gives me some shit about the magnetic stripe on his card not working. *You pay for Nando's and I swear I'll pay you back*. But that scrounger never paid back nothing, so I was outta there!'

Georgia only knew Rolf by reputation. He was a handsome, cocoa-skinned Venezuelan. He looked fine in football shorts but was part of a sleazy clique of year-twelve boys who relentlessly hit on younger girls, and Georgia felt disappointed that someone as smart as Maya had given in.

'Sounds a dick,' Georgia noted.

'All guys are dicks,' Maya replied knowingly.

'You want a coffee or something?' Georgia asked hopefully as she held up a fiver. 'I *do* have money.'

Maya checked the time on her phone before shaking her head. 'There's a bus from the terminal at ten twenty-two. The one after that isn't until ten fifty and that's when the creeps start coming out of the woodwork. You live two stops after me, but I'll take you home. I don't mind walking back.'

Georgia looked surprised. 'You know where I live?'

Maya put on a sinister accent and tapped her finger on the table. 'I know where you live, Miss Pack.' Then back in her normal voice, with a wry smile, 'Your birthday party, years two, three and four . . .'

'Oh God!' Georgia said, facepalming. 'Totally forgot you came to my house in those days! My head's not straight right now. And I *always* liked you, but you always had your little clique of . . .' Georgia almost said *estate girls*, but that was awful and she settled on *pals*.

'Gotta admit, I hated you,' Maya said, smirking. 'I'd work my arse off and get seventy-five. You'd get ninety-seven and not break a sweat.'

'Really?' Georgia gawped.

'I was nine and jealous as heck-a-doo. One time, me and Amber stole your furry pencil case and dropped it behind a radiator. But I'm over it. You're smart. Be proud of that.'

'My furry pencil case,' Georgia said, banging on the table and realising she was laughing properly for the first time since Sophie had died. 'I'd forgotten that. My mum went on for hours, and for about two years after, every time I wanted something expensive, Mum was like, *Not until you've learned to look after your things. Look what happened to your good pencil case.*'

'It's probably still there,' Maya laughed. 'We could break in and grab it.'

Georgia laughed, glad to have lighter thoughts in her head.

Maya checked the time on her phone. 'We need to scram if we're riding this bus. If you can't face the 'rents, you can come to mine. Go to my room and play tunes or something . . .'

'Should probably go home,' Georgia sighed, her chair grating as she stood up. 'Dad's a good guy and he's got enough on his plate.'

The bus stop was a hundred metres away, in a one-way street that ran between the station and the slab-sided leisure centre that contained Cineworld, Ultra Bowl and the council swimming pool. They hadn't got out of the station concourse when Rolf jogged in front of them.

The athletic seventeen-year-old was holding two packets of chips, one open, one wrapped. And based on his wobbly gait, Georgia reckoned he'd spiced his Cineworld soft drink with booze.

'Got you chips,' Rolf said, stepping closer to Maya. 'I'm *really* sorry about the money. I'll pay you back, I swear.'

Rolf had caught Georgia's eye on several Wednesday mornings when she sat in the Chemistry lab eyeing year-eleven PE on the all-weather pitch. He looked even better in tight jeans and his Saturday-night shirt, with sleeves rolled over chunky biceps.

Maya was less impressed, stepping aside and hissing. 'I don't want your chips, or your vodka breath.'

'It's our special night,' Rolf said, then aimed a hand at Georgia. 'And where did super-geek come from?'

'She's an old friend,' Maya said, getting impatient as she saw the double-decker turn in at the end of the street.

'Clint's having a party,' Rolf said, backing up, then stepping in front of Maya again. 'Come on, baby.'

'Get out of my way.'

Anger flashed over Rolf's face. He grabbed Maya's arm and yanked it powerfully enough to make her head snap around.

'Hey,' Georgia shouted. 'No!'

'You were all over me in the cinema, and now you act like I'm shit,' Rolf growled.

'Your breath stinks,' Maya said, wafting a hand. 'I'm too young to work. I'm one of five kids. Your jumbo popcorn and VIP seat was *my* lunch money for next week.'

'Let go of her arm,' Georgia said firmly.

Maya tried to break loose, but Rolf dug a thumb into her bicep, making her face twist in pain.

'Say you'll come to the party,' Rolf snarled. 'What you gonna do? Sit in your room at ten o'clock?'

'Let her go,' Georgia growled.

Rolf cracked a confident smile. 'Or what, geek?'

Georgia shoved herself between Maya and Rolf to separate them, then surprised Rolf with a palm-under-the-chin move she'd learned when a self-defence instructor came into PE class. Rolf hadn't expected Georgia to act forcefully, and Maya laughed as he stumbled drunkenly and wound up on his bum.

'We can make it,' Maya said, eyeing the last passengers boarding the bus, while Rolf stayed down, grasping his back.

Georgia ran full pelt, but Maya was in heels. Georgia leapt aboard behind the last person in the queue, then enraged the driver by blocking the door.

'My friend's coming,' Georgia gasped.

'I've got a timetable,' the driver shouted. 'In or out.'

Georgia held her nerve until Maya charged aboard. They blipped their under-sixteen passes and walked to empty seats at the back of the bus.

'Had to grab these,' Maya said breathlessly as she planted the chips Rolf had bought her into Georgia's lap. Hot to touch and the paper opaque with grease. 'I'm bloody starving.'

ELEVEN

Outside school, Duke spent most of his time alone in his uncle's book-lined apartment. It was past midnight. Duke had the balcony doors open and a south breeze drew country air through the insect screens. The TV flickered in silence as bass rumbled from a party in an apartment two floors down.

For the past two hours, Duke had sat at a big draughtsman's desk in the apartment's living area, trying to sketch from memory. He'd taken a mid-afternoon walk to a nearby street market, and while sitting at a street counter eating chicken thighs and jollof rice, a small beggar girl had approached. Her eyes huge and beautiful, but her pencil-thin limbs scarred with eczema.

Duke had grown frustrated, using pencil strokes to try capturing the lacy translucence of her peeling skin and the bloody sheen of an angry sore in her elbow joint. But it was a contented frustration, taking his mind away from real life and gobbling lonely hours.

When Duke's mobile rang, he'd been sitting for so long that his calf muscle had gone dead. He feared he'd miss the call as he dragged his leg across the tiled floor. He lived with his

Uncle Remi, a controversial journalist with plenty of enemies. Late calls always pricked Duke with the fear that Remi had been kidnapped, or killed. So Julius came as a relief, though he seemed desperately upset.

'Did I wake you?' Julius asked.

'I was drawing,' Duke said gently. 'You sound terrible . . .'

'I . . .' Julius began, then choked. 'I'm sorry I didn't call before. But my ma says I can't ever see you or talk to you.'

'Your brothers took the trouble to inform me at school,' Duke said wryly. 'Collins emphasised with a knee in the stomach.'

'Sorry,' Julius sniffed. 'I *hate* my family. You know I'm nothing like them.'

'For sure,' Duke said.

'My mother will check my calls,' Julius said. 'So I dug out my old Samsung and snuck in my mother's office. She keeps prepaid SIM cards, for when she calls certain people.'

'Wasn't it your brother's party tonight?' Duke asked.

'It was OK at first, catching up with country cousins. But my cousin Luke paid this girl to come on to me. Straighten me out, as they put it . . .'

'Like, a whore?' Duke asked.

'They were telling me to kiss her. Making me put my hands on her ass and trying to get me to go in this room with her. When I pushed back, Collins got up in my face. I lost it. Grabbed the back of his head and bit the tip off his nose.'

Duke thumped the tabletop with delight and beamed. 'Say that a-*gain*?'

'I was drunk. And his nose was there, and . . .'

Duke smiled. 'You bit it off?'

'A whole chunk. It was in my mouth.'

'Like, how big?'

'The fleshy tip. The size of a butter mint.'

'Julius, you beautiful man!' Duke howled. 'I cannot imagine a human more deserving! It must have bled like an absolute bastard!'

'I didn't see,' Julius said. 'Luke punched me to the ground. I've got a big gash down my cheek from his gold rings, and my jaw feels like it's set in cement. Luckily, our bodyguards piled in before I got a proper beating.

'My mother's campaign hotshot, Teddy, was at the club. He's this creepy American, who claims he worked with Obama. He made sure nobody left the VIP area until they'd deleted all the videos from their smartphones. They found a doc, who squirted glue in my cut. Collins got taken to the heliport. He's got to see a plastic surgeon in Lagos.'

'Quite the night,' Duke noted. 'Where are you at now?'

'Home. In my shower cubicle so nobody can hear us talk. I don't know what's going to happen. I thought I'd booked my ticket for military school, but Mother sort of took my side. She screamed at the twins for being in on the prank and *flaunting Julius's defect in public*.

'When my uncle called in a rage, Ma told him I'd stood up for my dignity in the face of humiliation and done nothing to be ashamed of. But she's always like that. She can rip into us, but any outsider who says something bad about her boys is in trouble.'

'Maternal instinct,' Duke said thoughtfully. 'My ma is the same.'

'School will be unbearable once everyone hears what happened.'

'A lot of people hate Collins,' Duke pointed out.

'But *everyone* hates queers,' Julius sighed. 'And you've got enough problems, without me calling you at all hours.'

'It's no problem,' Duke said firmly. 'My uncle's a good guy, but I'm lucky if he's home two nights a week. I'm a lonely soul and your friendship means a lot to me.'

Julius sighed, then managed to sound more upbeat. 'Skating at Arctic Zoo was the best afternoon ever, but everything that's happened since . . .'

'We'll ride the penguin pool again or die in the attempt!' Duke announced with a defiant laugh. 'Just one question.'

'What?'

'After you smashed up your knee, I thought something was about to happen. But when I made my move, you sprang away . . .'

'I-it's . . .' Julius stuttered. 'The whole world tells me the thing I want most is wrong.'

'The world can lick my salty ballsack,' Duke said. 'We'll put our heads together and get through this.'

PART TWO

TWO WEEKS LATER

TWELVE

It was a few minutes after ten as Julius peeked between heavy bedroom curtains, watching Orisa load empty shopping bags in the trunk of a black Lexus. The boot shut electronically as the dark-suited driver opened the rear door, giving a polite nod as Orisa slipped inside.

The twins had been out partying and were unlikely to surface before noon. Gabe was at Saturday-morning soccer practice and Bunmi had an early meeting at the governor's mansion. That left a security guard and a maid in the house, plus two soldiers on the front gate.

The diesel generators were in good form and the house felt wonderfully cool as Julius grabbed a well-stuffed and knotted black bin liner off his bedroom floor and moved swiftly downstairs to the kitchen.

The maid was vacuuming in the living area, but the kitchen was eerily empty, with everything stacked away and Orisa's house sandals and apron folded by the rear door.

Between the kitchen and the back exit was a windowless laundry room. A large Samsung washer was spinning, rattling the baskets of old toys, stacks of plates and the oversized pots Orisa used for family gatherings.

Julius slid his arm behind a bag of Gabe's outgrown clothes and pulled out a flat green cap and tattered Nigerian army combat jacket. He'd bought these for ₦10,000 from one of the terminally bored soldiers who guarded the front gate.

The black bag gave Julius reason to visit the big trash containers in the courtyard behind the kitchen. The army cap and jacket meant he'd be mistaken for one of the soldiers on guard, if the guard in the CCTV room didn't look hard.

Julius got a blast of heat and a faint whiff of trash as he turned the knob on the back door and stepped outside onto dusty tiles. He'd been fascinated by the matrix of screens in the security room when he was younger, and still remembered the camera positions.

After six swift strides, Julius ducked into a blind spot between the perimeter wall and a huge wheeled trash container. He ripped open the black bag, revealing a backpack with his skateboard poking out. Then he donned the army cap and jacket, before stepping up to a heavy steel-barred gate. Julius tapped a six-digit code and it opened with a click, followed by a three-second buzzer.

This was the riskiest part. Julius knew an alarm would sound in the security room when the gate opened. He tried to act normal but held his stomach and pushed his head back, hoping to disguise his distinctive posture. With luck, the guard in the security room would peek up from whatever he was doing to pass time and see a soldier stepping out for a perimeter patrol or a sneaky errand.

It worked to Julius's advantage that most of the men sent from the local barracks were scruffily dressed, unarmed and barely older than he was. While Adebisi family guards and drivers provided everyday security, government soldiers were a visible insurance policy. It took a hefty bribe to the commander of the local garrison to have a couple of dishevelled teen soldiers sat in front of your home or office, but the service was backed by an understanding that the entire local garrison would go after the bad guys if you got kidnapped or robbed.

Julius walked slowly, so as not to arouse suspicion. He was in an alleyway used only by trash and delivery vehicles. Thick walls on either side marked the boundary of two compounds, each topped with electrified wire and CCTV. Besides the walls around individual compounds, there were massive outer walls enclosing the entire development. Julius had rolled through thousands of times in a car and never given the space much thought, but on foot the empty pavement, red tarmac and long blank walls felt like a surreal maze.

'Cigarette, soldier?' an overweight private sat behind a gate across the street shouted, with a strong Hausa accent. 'I'm all out and not halfway into my shift.'

'Don't smoke,' Julius said, quickening his stride.

'I've not seen you around,' the young soldier said, pressing his doughy cheeks between the bars like a bored zoo animal. 'Are you new? Where you posted? The Adebisi place?'

'Adebisi,' Julius confirmed. 'I'm in a hurry, sorry!'

'All that textile money, but the Godmother don't give no sun shade!' the soldier said, before erupting in a deep laugh.

Julius had read news articles where Bunmi got called the Godmother, but even St Gilda's thugs didn't make jabs about his mother, lest Collins or the twins found out.

As he strode briskly past a cart sweeping non-existent dirt from the gutter, Julius guiltily realised he'd never considered how the guards sat by the compound gate without shade.

Those guards must really hate me . . . They were kids who'd joined the army to escape rural poverty, watching Julius ride chauffeured limousines, or skate the compound in sneakers that cost more than an army private earned in two months.

But these thoughts were wiped when Julius saw Duke, squatting on the kerb, with his scooter leaning against a high purple wall.

'Jailbreak!' Duke said, standing up and high-fiving as both lads cracked huge smiles.

'Walk took longer than expected,' Julius said, taking a furtive glance behind, before giving Duke a hug.

Julius had been tantalised by forbidden glimpses of Duke at school and hours bouncing messages on his secret phone. Now his best friend was real. The slender limbs, wild hair and dusty skin after a long ride south.

'We should probably get out of here,' Duke said.

'How was the ride out?'

'It's the furthest I've been,' Duke replied. 'The beltway's smooth. No cops around. Biggest problem was getting through the gate into this compound. I babbled something about collecting a suit for dry cleaning.' Duke undid a buckle holding a spare helmet to the back of the bike. 'Catch!'

'Safety first!' Julius laughed, getting a whiff of old sweat as he pulled the thick foam over his head.

'Six thousand in the market,' Duke explained. 'It's beaten up, but nobody will recognise you with that on.'

Duke accelerated hard, taking Julius by surprise and almost throwing him off the back. The modern roads in the gated estate made it easy to ride fast. They buzzed up onto pavement, skimming through an open pedestrian gate next to the traffic booth. After the development's barren access road, they merged into late-morning traffic on the beltway.

Julius didn't mind the sweat slick inside his shirt, the potholes or the diesel haze as the bike cut between lines of static trucks and dilapidated buses rammed with bodies. He felt free and uncharacteristically optimistic.

Biting Collins's nose had flipped a switch. Julius's bulk and surname had always offered some protection, but damaging Collins had made St Gilda's bullies wary. It also helped Julius understand why Duke acted the way he did: it was better to be yourself and take shit than live miserably by pretending to be something you're not.

'I've not had breakfast and I know a place,' Duke said, able to speak as they caught sluggish traffic close to Akure's centre.

Transport Union officials marshalled all roads into the town centre. The scooter queued for ten minutes at a union roadblock. Duke handed three hundred naira to a fake gangsta with a black eye and gold tooth. A bored woman wrote the bike's registration on a green ticket and passed it to Duke before they crawled another half-kilometre, swerving around pedestrians with eyes on stalls selling Chinese-made clothes and cheap housewares.

Duke locked his bike to a fence with a heavy chain and was rapidly surrounded by powerfully built men.

'Five hundred to keep it safe!' the biggest one demanded.

Duke shook his head and offered two.

'Five hundred,' the thug repeated, tapping his ear as if to say *Are you deaf?*

'No man ever paid five hundred to chain a bike,' Duke spat as he took out his keys and grabbed his padlock to free the bike.

'You do not have that option!' the man shouted, forcing

himself between Duke and his scooter. 'You lock, you pay.'

An older fellow with horrendous body odour chimed in. 'We have to eat, you fancy boy!' the meaty sweat-glazed head boomed. 'He come to our corner and fix chain, he gotta pay our price, yeah?'

Five goons and a couple of hanger-on kids jeered in agreement. Julius felt useless as Duke bitterly handed over five hundred naira.

'I'll pay your five hundred,' Julius told Duke as they walked away. 'It's not worth spoiling your mood.'

'Five hundred to chain a scooter to a fence!' Duke said, shaking his head. 'It's never more than three, but all my fault for chaining up before asking. But we'll have pies to die for!'

The two teens jostled their way into a grubby concrete shopping precinct. The shops were busy and market stalls sold higher-end stuff like jewellery, sunglasses and fancy fabric.

'Pie Oven,' Duke said, pointing towards a double-fronted fast-food joint, crisply done out with white tiles and green plastic chairs. 'Always busy, but worth it.'

It was only eleven, but Pie Oven had a bum on every seat and a line down the street. As Julius and Duke shuffled forward, a bunch of well-dressed women wearing yellow sashes from the Healing Prayer Church passed along the queue, giving out leaflets.

Julius smiled as he took a leaflet with a metal lapel badge attached. There was a headshot of his uncle, followed by blurb, which Duke read aloud.

'Re-elect SJ Adebisi as Ondo State Governor – Four More Years of Decency & Excellence in Government.'

'I'm with Rotimi Rotimi,' Julius joked. 'But don't tell my mum ...'

Orisa had made breakfast, but Julius's appetite stirred as he shuffled through the door and caught a steamy whiff of spiced meat and just-baked pastry. He ordered a jerk chicken pie with gravy and rice, while Duke went for stewed beef pie and a Scotch egg. With no hope of a seat inside, they found a concrete bench at the edge of the precinct.

'Stupendous pie!' Julius said brightly.

Pigeons chased the rice Julius dropped around his feet as he shovelled with his plastic fork.

Duke tilted his clamshell food tray towards Julius and spoke with his mouth full. 'Try the Scotch egg.'

Before Julius could take the offer, a woman shrieked at the opposite side of the precinct. Careful not to spill food, the boys rose slightly and looked behind.

The women from HPC who'd been handing out leaflets were now trying to unfurl a long *Vote Adebisi* banner and tie it between two concrete posts. This had angered a group of men, some shouting *This is our area* and *You have no right to be here*, while a couple of younger, fitter men tried to tear the banner away.

'We live in a democracy,' one of the HPC women shouted as she fought to take the banner back. 'We've had banners here before.'

As Julius scoffed more pie, women who were handing out leaflets around the precinct came to reinforce the group with the banner. One had a walking stick and led with the crook end, cracking a young man over the head.

'They're only handing out leaflets,' Julius said. 'What's the biggie?'

'Do you follow politics?' Duke asked.

'Not if I can help it.'

Duke narrowed his lips in slight disapproval, before beginning to explain. 'Your mother's church campaigns heavily for your uncle, obviously. But the stalls in this precinct are controlled by the Transport Union. They're the people who gave us the green ticket to enter this part of town. The union supported your uncle in the last election, but former governor Rotimi got the union leadership back on his side by promising to use Ondo State oil revenue to give fuel subsidies to taxis and buses, and no doubt a healthy bundle in the pockets of the union's leadership.'

'I remember,' Julius said, nodding. 'Ma threw a vase when she found out.'

Thirty union men had piled into the centre of the precinct and weight of numbers had forced the church women to surrender. There were shouts of *Don't touch me* and *Keep your hands away* as the angry women were stripped of leaflets and banner and muscled out of the precinct.

But a new sound was growing from of one of the streets feeding into the precinct. A mix of shouts and footsteps.

Duke closed his food box and shot to his feet.

'We have to bounce.'

'Why?'

Before Duke could stand, sixty burly men armed with wooden clubs and black masks charged into the precinct. A man screamed as his costume jewellery stall was toppled. Merchandise flew everywhere as men used bats and crowbars to tear the wooden stall apart.

'Who is this?' Julius gasped, glancing around, not sure which way to run.

'Area boys,' Duke explained. 'Like the ones we paid five hundred to park. They still support Adebisi. My guess is, they sent the ladies into the square, knowing it would lure all the Transport Union thugs into one place.'

More masked area boys poured from another alleyway. They'd clearly been well drilled, some with orders to smash market stalls and shop windows, the remainder charging into the centre of the precinct, launching clubs and iron bars at union men while chanting, 'Adebisi, Adebisi, Adebisi!'

Julius felt sick with fear as a stall selling lamps a few metres in front of him got toppled. Its owner tried escaping with the day's takings, but an enormous area boy booted her in the back, then tore the money pouch from around her waist as another punched her brutally in the face.

Pie Oven's plate-glass frontage got caved as a mass brawl broke out between the area boys and Transport Union enforcers in the precinct's centre.

'Back to my bike,' Duke said, tossing his pie and starting to run, with Julius close behind.

They pushed their backs to a wall as union reinforcements stormed past them into the square. A woman with two screaming kids turned her ankle in a pothole as Julius heard a bang, followed by a flash of flame.

'The union have always controlled the precinct,' Duke explained breathlessly. 'If the area boys are going to try and take it, it means all-out war on the streets.'

Julius was more concerned with the injured woman than the politics. He helped her up, then grabbed the larger of her two frightened toddlers. Hundreds of shoppers were fleeing the precinct. Julius found himself funnelled into an alleyway, between market stalls, getting tilted by the crowd as owners frantically tried to pack away their stock.

There were two more bangs and an eruption of car alarms.

The kid in Julius's arms wailed as Julius looked back to make sure Duke and the boy's mother had kept pace. The first police siren wailed as Julius almost stepped on an elderly woman who'd fallen and twisted her arm.

'My bike's here,' Duke said, cutting out of the stream of bodies as they reached a fork in the road.

Julius looked behind for the mother, who mouthed thanks before taking her child back and hurrying on. Duke went down on one knee to unlock his bike.

As Duke kicked his scooter to life, Julius looked back towards the precinct. At least one large shop was ablaze. Swirls of dark grey smoke rose from smashed market stalls and the victorious area boys had made his name into a war chant.

Adebisi, Adebisi!

Victory, victory, Adebisi!

THIRTEEN

Everyone shopped at the Pegasus Centre on the edge of town. Even at Saturday lunchtime, the old High Street behind the train station was lightly populated and the family butcher where Georgia's nan got her meat had *Going out of business* in the window.

Red Parrot Books was sandwiched between a Cancer Research charity shop and the boarded frontage of a short-lived bagel place. Georgia felt wary as she pushed a door with a big *Boycott Amazon* sign in the window.

The heating inside wasn't doing much. There was a musty smell, in a space too small to be anonymous. Georgia found herself confronted by a table stacked with copies of *Socialist Worker*, *Support the Living Wage* mugs and busts of Karl Marx moulded from recycled vinyl.

The cafe was on the first floor, up stairs with a wobbly bannister and layers of peeling stickers. It had a greenhouse roof, chairs that didn't match and three toddlers rumbling over grubby beanbags where the sloped roof was too low for grown-ups.

'You found us!' Zac said brightly, catching his knee on a

table as he stood from behind a half-drunk soy cappuccino. He pulled Georgia into a tight hug. 'Sorry it's short notice. The hospital keeps changing my shifts.'

Georgia shrugged. 'I was just sat at home.'

'How are you feeling?' Zac asked.

Two weeks after her sister's death, Georgia was feeling *wrong*. She was getting up, going to school, doing homework and all the other stuff she'd always done. But where there had been goals and meaning, it now felt like endless grey days. And when Georgia was alone, she sought the meaning of existence, but only found an ache, like someone was using a handheld Dyson to suck out her insides . . . But that's not the first thing you say when you meet a pal for coffee, so she half smiled and said, 'Not bad, I guess . . . You?'

'Everything's weird,' Zac confessed. 'I looked in Sophie's wardrobe before I came out. If I throw her stuff away, it's like I'm throwing her away. But, if I don't, I'm the creepy guy in a flat full of dead-girlfriend clothes.'

'Her memorial service was amazing,' Georgia said. 'And I really like that she donated her body to science.'

Zac nodded. 'Your mum seemed less keen . . .'

'Nothing makes my mum happy,' Georgia groaned. 'If Sophie had a normal cremation, she'd have still found something to moan about.'

'Is she still staying with you?'

'No, thank God,' Georgia said, managing a smile. 'Mum had a screaming row with Dad the day after the memorial and stormed out. Apparently I always take Dad's side, so she's not talking to me either.'

'How is he?'

'Dad's working every waking hour on some presentation. It's

been great having you text and stuff. You feel like the only sane adult in my life.'

Zac gave a flattered smile, then laughed. 'I'm not that sane . . . My sleep is messed up and I've been drinking more than I should.'

Georgia looked concerned. 'Really?'

'I got a written warning at work,' Zac admitted. 'One of the paramedic bikes got in a smash and the front brake hasn't been right since it was repaired. My shift controller ordered me to go out on it and I told her where she could stick the idea . . .'

'Surely that's *dangerous*,' Georgia said sympathetically.

Zac nodded. 'Definitely no fun if your front brake locks at fifty miles an hour. An outside mechanic checked the bike. They agreed I was a hundred per cent right not to ride it. But I *still* got written up, because the hospital has a zero-tolerance policy on *aggressive and threatening behaviour*.'

'Could they sack you?'

Zac shook his head and laughed confidently. 'They're *massively* understaffed. But I've got to meet someone from human resources next week. Then I'll probably have to waste half a day doing an anger-management workshop.'

'That sucks,' Georgia said as she opened a menu. 'I haven't had lunch. Is the food here OK?'

'I think they source the bread from a Soviet gulag, so avoid the sandwiches,' Zac suggested. 'But Kamila bakes vegan muffins and brownies out back and they're pretty rock and roll.'

Georgia furrowed her brow. 'I want a latte, but it says they only do soy or oat milk.'

'Soy is better IMO,' Zac said. 'Think of the poor dairy cows, udders covered in shit and infected pus oozing into the milk . . .'

There was only one staff member working. After bringing

tea and toasties to the mums of playing toddlers, the round-faced waitress smiled fondly at Zac, then spoke with a Czech accent.

'You must be Sophie's sister,' she said brightly. 'You are so like her!'

Georgia smiled and blushed as Zac charmed the waitress.

'Georgia, meet the *wonderful* Kamila. Kamila, I've just been praising your muffins.'

'The orange is really fresh, baked this morning,' Kamila said proudly.

'I'll go for that and a soy latte,' Georgia said. 'How did you know Sophie?'

'Through SAG,' Kamila said.

'The Socialist Action Group,' Zac explained. 'This is where we have our weekly meetings.'

Georgia nodded. She'd heard of Zac going to SAG meetings, but Sophie wasn't as political as Zac and Georgia wondered if he knew she'd called it SWAG – Socialist Wankers Action Group – behind his back.

'Sophie was too busy to come regularly,' Kamila told Georgia. 'But she made an important contribution.'

'Cool,' Georgia said, stifling a smirk.

As Kamila headed behind the counter, Zac leaned across the table and cleared his throat.

'Something ominous?' Georgia asked.

Zac spoke delicately. 'I asked you to meet here because I had an idea. I just hope it doesn't seem patronising . . .'

'I'll do my best not to be offended.'

'I moved to a new school when I was a teenager in Hong Kong,' Zac began. 'I felt alone and powerless, until I started getting involved in pro-democracy meetings. At first, I was scared to go on a demonstration or speak in a meeting. But I found that I got along better with people who cared about more important stuff than shopping and video games. Instead of being a kid in a room messaging a few dumb friends, I had a connection to something that mattered.'

Georgia looked suspicious. 'You think I should get into politics?'

'Political activism,' Zac said defensively.

'I could join the Young Conservatives,' Georgia teased. 'My dad would like that.'

Zac laughed so hard he banged a knee under the table. 'Don't say that here, you might not make it out alive! But, seriously, I'd love it if you came to one of our SAG meetings. It's informal. Everyone has different opinions. We usually meet Thursdays, but we're actually meeting up at the town hall on Monday night to try and stop the council finance meeting.'

Georgia looked confused. 'That's the budget cuts, or something?'

Zac nodded as Kamila slid coffees and two orange muffins on the table between them.

'I was telling Georgia she should join us on Monday night.'

'Of course!' Kamila said brightly. 'I'll be there.'

Kamila shot off to give menus to customers who'd just come up the stairs as Zac explained.

'Everyone voted for a government that promised to end right-wing austerity. Now the left is in power, playing a different tune. Every local council in the country must approve an annual budget by the end of this month.

'Local governments are cutting back on social care, education and housing. Closing libraries and leisure centres. Old people won't get care. There will be less social workers looking after vulnerable kids. No money to repair school buildings, bigger school classes and less choice of subjects.'

Georgia could hear her dad saying, *Money doesn't grow on trees* . . . She had nothing on, but bought thinking time by checking Google Calendar on her phone.

'I'll feel like a freak,' Georgia said awkwardly.

'I'll introduce you,' Zac said. 'There's a fair few teenage activists and none of them bite.'

Georgia laughed as she broke the top off her muffin. 'Any good-looking ones?'

Zac flicked one eyebrow. 'If you don't come, you'll never find out.'

FOURTEEN

Rain hit as Duke's scooter twisted its way out of the crowd. Dust turned to coffee-brown slicks and potholes flooded. The downpour would make skating the penguin pool impossible, but the violence had left Julius too shocked to care.

He'd spent enough time around his mother and uncle to know political success depended on the loyalty of key groups. Army, police, area boys, churches, university cults and the big unions were all courted with money and favours. But knowing was different to being on the ground, watching a stallholder punched and robbed, or seeing the desperate face of the woman tangled in the fleeing crowd.

It was a ten-minute ride north to Duke's apartment block. He wheeled his bike down to a metal storage cage in his building's basement, then warned that although the electricity was currently on, they'd be stuck in the elevator for hours if it cut out.

They had a good-natured chase up thirteen flights, clothes dripping wet, and an interlude helping an elderly lady with two sacks of rice.

'Rain's come late this year,' the woman said as she unlocked the metal gate over her apartment door. 'We need it to clear the stink.'

'It was my pleasure,' Duke told the woman, refusing a ₦100 note, then giving Julius a shove and sprinting back towards the stairwell.

Julius bounded three stairs at a time to catch up. Duke smiled as he crashed into the wall on every landing, making screeching noises and giving a commentary like a kid driving Hot Wheels.

'He rounds the last corner beautifully. The gangling Julius Ade-beastie is catching up, but it's the final stretch and he's not going to make it past the six-time champion of the universe . . .'

Julius kept running, bundling Duke into the steel-plated door of apartment 6J. They gasped and laughed as Duke pulled keys chained to his belt loop, turning two deadlocks, before a regular lock let them stumble inside.

'Drink?' Duke asked, kicking off squelching canvas sneakers as he moved towards the fridge.

It was a decent size by the standard of city apartments, though the entire place would have fitted in Orisa's kitchen. There was a single bedroom and a small shower room. The main area was open-plan, with a basic kitchen at one end and a folding wooden partition separating Duke's sleeping area.

Books and file boxes made the space feel smaller. Not just shelved, but mounded on chairs and tables. Histories, biographies, stacks of yellowing newspapers, jazz CDs, VHS tapes and audio cassettes hand-labelled with the names of famous people interviewed by Duke's Uncle Remi.

As Duke poured a glass of Coke, Julius picked up a tarnished award, shaped like a TV camera on a tripod.

'Nigerian Broadcaster of the Year, 1998,' Julius read aloud, then from an award next to it that looked like a big gold testicle, 'United States Broadcasters Association, Outstanding Report by an Overseas Reporter, Remi Balogun, 2003.'

A framed photo behind the trophies showed a decades-old picture of Remi in a brightly coloured safari suit. A man of action, jumping from a helicopter a couple of metres off the ground.

'I remember when your uncle read the news,' Julius said, nodding thanks as he accepted the Coke. *'It's eighteen hundred hours, and these are the headlines from Africa's largest network...'*

'Uncle had a three-year contract, a smouldering Brazilian wife and a five-bedroom villa on Victoria Island,' Duke said. 'But he resigned when the broadcasting minister demanded that the evening bulletin have more lifestyle and entertainment news and less criticism of the president. Now, Uncle is a rebel, writing anti-corruption blogs and newspaper opinion pieces and binning angry letters about his bank overdraft and non-payment of his beloved nephew's school fees.'

'A rebel,' Julius laughed. 'That's where you get it from.'

Julius moved to get a glimpse through the sliding balcony doors. He wiped condensation with the sleeve of his army jacket, thinking he might see smoke rising out of the precinct. But the view was in the opposite direction, towards Arctic Zoo. From this distance, the zoo was a hilly green canopy. The mildewed enclosures matching the green of overgrown paths and the hulk of the revolving restaurant topping the hill like some vast, rust-streaked flower.

'I've drawn the zoo from up here,' Duke said. 'It looks eerie in the rain. And if the balcony doors are open, you can hear the tigers roar.'

Julius stared for ages. The violence at the precinct had been distressing and he tried to calm himself with deep breaths and the sight of rain pelting treetops.

'Something stronger?' Duke suggested.

Julius was startled when he turned away from the balcony. Duke had taken off his sodden shorts and polo shirt, leaving tight orange undershorts and his giant hair comically flattened by rain. The bottle on offer was Squadron dark rum.

'Since we can't skate . . .' Duke said. 'And to calm my nerves!'

Julius let his friend top his glass with rum but suddenly felt edgy. Duke was smaller but had chest and navel hair. He rarely thought about Duke being two years older, but now it felt important. For all his bulk, Julius's body remained boyish. He feared Duke would find him unattractive. And while part of Julius wished it hadn't rained and they'd gone skating, another part was thrilled by Duke's body and things that might happen in the privacy of the apartment.

'I've never been alone with a guy before,' Julius said, necking half his rum and Coke for courage.

'Same,' Duke said, closing in with a crooked, uneasy smile. 'I've read a zillion web pages though . . .'

This admission made Julius smile with recognition, remembering trawls for websites that offered upbeat advice for gay teens. They mostly had images of white boys with skinny jeans. Kids who didn't live in countries where cops fired tear gas canisters into gay clubs and sex between men was punishable by fourteen years in prison . . .

'I'd always erase the browser history afterwards,' Julius confessed. 'But I was terrified there was some way my mum or brothers would find what I'd been looking at . . .'

'In Holland, they give gay kids lube and condoms in school,' Duke said enviously.

'Gay pride, gay marriage,' Julius added, laughing as he drained his glass and planted it atop a stack of books. 'Lucky pricks...'

Duke took a slug straight from the rum bottle as Julius pulled his T-shirt over his head.

Julius had rediscovered the easy vibe they'd felt when racing up the stairs. They paused, chest to chest, no sound but breathing and rain. Then they moved together to kiss.

FIFTEEN

Seventy minutes later, Julius stood breathless in a shower cubicle, wrestling a grimy curtain that billowed and stuck to his legs. It was barely warm, and the sixth-floor water pressure feeble, but he felt full of life.

He'd already been away from home longer than planned. But if military school was the price of making love to Duke, it still felt worth it. He imagined telling his mother every detail and seeing her head burst like an egg in a microwave.

Duke had showered first. Towelling dry, then spending ages fixing his hair in the steamed-up mirror. He put on clean shorts, tidied a stack of books they'd crashed into, flipped two sofa cushions with sweat patches and buried the empty rum bottle at the base of the trash can.

'Hungry?' Duke asked as Julius ambled out, slightly drunk as he found his shorts.

'I don't want to go home,' Julius said longingly, casting an eye at his backpack with the unused skateboard poking out.

'We'll sort something,' Duke said. 'Somehow . . .'

Julius ached at the thought of how difficult that would be. 'It's rare that my ma goes on weekend business.'

'Might have to run away,' Duke joked. 'Scam one of your rich relatives and ride trains around Europe . . .'

'Sounds like a plan,' Julius said.

He stepped past the sofa, intending to put his arms around Duke, but a key sounded in the door. While Duke glanced about, chasing evidence of bad behaviour, Julius envisioned Adebisi family guards powering through the door and dragging him home for a whipping on his mother's orders.

But it was Duke's Uncle Remi. Heavier than the man Julius watched on television as a small boy. Waves of processed newsreader hair had been traded for a simple razor cut with tufts of grey, but he'd retained bleached-white teeth and studious good looks.

Remi was abuzz, zipping through the door, pirouetting a large tan briefcase onto the sofa, then rushing to the fridge to gulp from a carton of pineapple juice.

Julius anxiously kicked his towel back into the bathroom and tried to locate his T-shirt. But it wasn't unusual for boys to sit about in shorts when there was no air conditioning, and Remi's mind was on a higher plane than stray towels and rearranged cushions.

'I thought you were in Lagos till Monday,' Duke said.

'Drove back when I heard there was trouble in town,' Remi explained, draining and refilling his glass of juice. 'Have you seen?'

'Things kicked off, so we stayed indoors,' Duke said. 'This is my friend Julius, by the way.'

'Julius Caesar!' Remi said as he spun extravagantly and grabbed a little FM radio out of a cabinet above the sink. 'It's pleasing that you have company. My nephew spends too much time with a tin of pencils.

'I had Radio Tango International on as I drove into the garage,' Remi continued. 'They had people phoning in, talking about the situation across the city. Rotimis and Adebisis have been spraying election money like confetti. The Godmother must have given the area boys an absolute *fortune* to make them cocky enough to start a war with the Transport Union.'

'Casualties?' Duke asked.

'All over.' Remi nodded. 'Unconfirmed reports that three people burned to death inside a shop close to the precinct. There are brawls and smashed glass all through the city.' Remi looked frustrated as his radio stayed silent. 'Fresh batteries?' he asked, agitated, as he pulled a kitchen drawer hard and began to rummage. 'Or can you get radio from that box under the television?'

'Not Radio Tango, Uncle,' Duke said. 'It's an unlicensed station and we're out of diesel for the generator. There might be a website I can stream through my phone, but I've almost used my data allowance . . .'

'Never any batteries!' Remi complained. 'Where do they all go? They're worse than socks!'

'I've got unlimited data,' Julius said, reaching into his shorts for his phone, then realising he'd left it on a shelf in the bathroom.

But Remi's interest in the radio was fleeting. He placed his empty glass in the sink, then reached for the tattered briefcase he'd thrown on the couch as he walked in.

'From an insider at the Chinese Development Bank in Lagos,' Remi said, thumping the case like the back of an old friend. 'Audited accounts that the Chinese requested before funding projects by Ondo State government. My friend tells me these figures are way more honest than the state accounts released to the public. I'm hoping they go back far enough to show that Rotimi Rotimi and SJ Adebisi are even bigger crooks than—'

'Uncle,' Duke interrupted violently. 'This is my friend from St Gilda's, Julius *Adebisi*.'

For a second, Remi looked like he was going to inhale his tongue. Then he clutched the case to his chest as if Julius might snatch it and bolt.

'Don't upset yourself, sir,' Julius said respectfully. 'My lips are tight. I'm no fan of my mother's politics.'

Remi considered this suspiciously as he slotted the briefcase into a gap between the refrigerator and the wall. He moved closer to Julius, then eyed him over the top of his amber-tint sunglasses.

'I see resemblance to Bunmi,' Remi noted. 'Your height and posture. These are not the only copies of the documents, by the way.'

The worry in the last sentence made Julius suspect it was a lie.

'Uncle, he's not going to go running to his mum,' Duke said reassuringly. 'They don't get along.'

'But I *should* probably leave,' Julius said, feeling awkward. 'I think I saw a taxi stand when we arrived . . .'

The mention of a taxi focused Remi's brain. Bunmi Adebisi would never let one of her kids out without a car and a bodyguard close by. And now Remi studied his surroundings. He saw the towels and wet hair. Sensed the rum on both boys' breath and finger scratches on his nephew's back.

'I see now!' Remi said, wagging a finger and grinning to himself. 'This old fool walked in on something naughty!'

SIXTEEN

Maya messaged as Georgia was on the bus home from meeting Zac.

> **Maya:** Just found out there's gonna be an INSANE house party on the estate tonite! Wanna come?
>
> **Georgia:** Am I invited?
>
> **Maya:** You're so innocent! Girls who look like you are invited to EVERYTHING :-)

Georgia was wary of going to some random kid's house on the estate. But booze and boys were not without attraction, and with her dad working crazy hours, the other Saturday-night options were sitting home alone with dark thoughts, or walking to her nan's and watching *Britain's Got Talent*.

> **Georgia:** OK, count me in!

It was just before eight and Georgia was on foot, close to Isaac Newton Estate, as she felt her mobile vibrate. *Dad Calling.*

'Cookie, I just got home. Where are you?'

'Hey, Dad,' Georgia said, walking slower and feeling guilty as she lied. 'I'm going to Maya's. Just a quiet night, watching a movie or something. I left a note on the dining table and a Pyrex in the fridge with that chilli bake Nan brought round.'

'I've hardly seen you this week,' John moaned. 'I thought we might order pizza and find something on Sky Movies.'

'Tomorrow's Sunday,' Georgia said. 'I'm free all day.'

'I've got to go into the workshop tomorrow,' John replied. 'Metro Powerlines sent a bunch of detailed queries about our survey drone proposal. Things are going to get sticky if we don't win the contract, so your Uncle Phil and I are going to power through while the workshop is quiet and get back to them first thing Monday.'

'Detailed questions must mean they're taking your proposal seriously,' Georgia pointed out.

'Hopefully,' John agreed. 'If you're not coming home, I might drive round and see your nan for an hour.'

'I'm a bit late, Dad. I'd better go.'

Georgia felt anxious about the party and guilty for lying to her dad, but her mood improved as Maya answered her front door and gave her a hug.

'Georgia girl, you scrub up nice!'

The scruffy little flat had kids charging around. Maya's twelve-year-old brother kept peeking up from homework to ogle Georgia's legs as she waited in the kitchen while Maya went upstairs for her coat.

Maya came down with her neighbour Amy and her older sister Courtney, who surprised Georgia with more hugs.

'Gutted 'bout your sister,' Courtney said. 'She doctored me one time at hospital, when I busted my elbow.'

'Really?' Georgia said brightly, as Maya cuffed her brother around the head.

'Eyes on homework, Kieran,' Maya ordered.

'Heading off, Mum!' Courtney shouted into the living room, grabbing keys off the kitchen counter and smiling at Georgia as they stepped outdoors.

Georgia relaxed as the foursome headed across the estate, but the others were wearing jeans or leggings and she wondered if her black tights and skirt were overdoing it for a house party on the Isaac Newton Estate.

As Georgia had recently learned, the low-rise section of the estate was occupied by families and old folks. The homes were packed tight, but the vibe wasn't much different to the streets where richer kids like Georgia lived. When outsiders talked about Isaac Newton, they were usually thinking about a pair of nineteen-storey towers on the estate's eastern side. Apple House had been empty for years, though asbestos and government cuts had delayed the demolition. It's twin, Gravity House, where the party was taking place, had been given a cheap makeover and was used as housing of last resort. This meant refugees, the homeless, people released from prison and kids like Andre, who grew up in the care system and got the boot on their eighteenth birthday.

The lift rattled up to the eleventh floor and the four girls emerged, gagging and holding hands over their faces.

'Old sick and dog crap all mixed up,' Maya moaned, dashing to a railing and heaving fresh air.

Georgia had never been up one of the towers. The sun was getting low and her inner geek wanted to trace the rows of lights and see if she could spot her street. But the other three were charging down the balcony that ran in front of the flats, towards music booming out of an open front door.

They passed a furious barefoot Hindu man who'd just been protesting the noise. Georgia baulked when they got to the door of the party house. There was an enormous dude on the doorstep, keeping out three gobby lads who'd barely hit their teens and had the waistbands of their trackie bottoms almost down to their knees.

'If you turds try and get in again, you're goin' over that balcony!' the giant shouted. But his voice changed when he saw Courtney. 'Girls, welcome!'

'This big beast is Andre's big brother Marco,' Courtney explained. 'When'd you get out of young offenders?'

Georgia didn't hear Marco's answer because she got sucked inside, sandwiched between Maya and Amy, as they passed down a hallway pinned with posters of boxing movies and a soupy haze of marijuana smoke.

'Oy-oy!' Rolf shouted, scrambling off a chair, before giving Maya a kiss and a Peroni.

It needled Georgia that Maya had forgiven her boyfriend for the incident at the station, but there was no denying Rolf's appeal. He had cocky charm and a cynical world view that made Maya laugh, plus a great body and the social status you get dating one of the coolest boys in year twelve.

Amy spotted a bunch of pals and Georgia was living her worst party nightmare. Stripped of her friend group, overdressed and standing on the bare boards of a living room full of people she didn't know.

'Rolf said you were coming,' Georgia heard from close behind. 'I told him Georgia Pack was too straight to come to a house party on the estate.'

'Eh?' Georgia said, getting handed an absurdly yellow supermarket-brand alcopop by a tall guy in a V-neck.

He was a year-twelve or thirteen, but she knew him as one of the lifeguards who manned the leisure centre pool when she helped at the Old Ducks Aqua Club. He was Dean. Possibly Dwayne . . .

'Lifeguard,' Georgia said, remembering her mother's warnings about drinks spiked with date-rape drugs before bravely taking a sip. 'I didn't recognise you with your clothes on.'

Dean or Dwayne laughed. 'You're great with the old ladies, but I haven't seen you there for a while.'

Georgia nodded. 'It used to be me and one other girl. But it's the kind of activity that looks good on a university application. They've got so many volunteers, there's a rota now.'

'Dean, you big ponce!' a guy who looked absolutely trashed said as he stumbled past. 'Why don't you . . .'

Georgia didn't hear the end of the sentence because the loudmouth tripped on an upturned bread crate that Andre used as a coffee table and sent empty cans and bottles flying.

'Some people can't pace themselves,' Dean said, cracking a big smile. 'It's not even half-eight. So, what was I saying?'

Georgia took a gulp of her yellow drink and smiled. 'Introductory conversation, something about me not being here because I'm too straight . . .'

Dean laughed.

They talked about the leisure-centre pool being privatised, a physics teacher they both hated and found common ground discussing difficult mothers. As Georgia finished her second yellow drink, she was starting to buzz.

Then Dean made a cheesy comment that he felt he had *a connection* with Georgia and started touching her hand. And while Dean seemed nice, no part of Georgia wanted anything more than a conversation with him. She babbled something about having to ask Maya a question and bounced.

Georgia found everyone in the kitchen. Stoned people were

eating tubes of shoplifted cookie dough, Rolf had no shirt on and Courtney was kissing big Marco, who they'd met on the door.

'So, Dean-o?' Maya said, phrasing it like a question.

Georgia shook her head. 'Not my type.'

Maya shouted. 'All the cool people are here in this kitchen!'

A Metallica song came on. Georgia talked to Andre, the host, switched from yellow alcopop to sweet cider, got hit on by three guys and chased by Dean, who repeated the line about having a connection, then asked for her number.

Georgia gave her number out of pity and immediately hated the idea of having to deal with his call. He was smart and attractive, but four years older and there was no spark. But as nine o'clock and a second cider passed, Georgia noticed everyone pairing off and felt jealous when she saw Dean on the doorstep with his hand squeezing a buttock.

Maya and Rolf were entwined and Georgia found herself on the hallway floor, getting in the way of people using the bathroom and wondering about a bus home, or calling Dad to pick her up. He'd combust if he found out she was at a party in Gravity House, but she feared walking this neighbourhood alone.

She'd just joined the queue for the bathroom when a man with a beard came bundling through the front door.

'Move, move, move,' he shouted.

He was older than the partygoers, barefoot and wearing jeans soaked in blood. Georgia backed up to the wall as he shot past, clutching a Londis carrier bag and chased by two men. The one in the lead held a yellow stun gun and wore regular clothes. Georgia only realised they were cops when the second one went by, shouting into a radio.

The bloody man crashed the particle board door at the end of the hallway hard enough to leave a dent. The bedroom had a circle of kids sharing a joint and screams erupted as he raced to the back of the room.

The window had been opened to let out smoke and he flung out the carrier bag and shouted, 'Free drugs!' before jumping onto the bed.

'Hands in the air!' the cop with the Taser shouted.

Another cop swept past Georgia as the lead pair wrestled the bloody man down in the bedroom.

'What happened?' Rolf asked, scrambling out of the kitchen.

'Drugs or something,' Georgia said.

The party music had stopped. Georgia felt her ears ringing as an officer with stripes spoke into her radio by the front door.

'Suspect detained. Package, suspected narcotics, has been thrown from window on east side of Gravity House. I need bodies down there looking, before someone steals it.'

Georgia suddenly felt sober. None of the partying kids had anything to do with the drug dealer who'd burst through the front door, but everyone was drunk, there was a thick marijuana haze and Georgia was far from the only kid who hadn't told her folks they were going to a crazy party at the most dangerous address in town.

She had to get out of here fast . . .

SEVENTEEN

Julius rolled over in his bed, squinting as he caught blazing sunlight through a crack in the curtains. The day before felt like a dream. The violence. Duke's apartment. Getting the cab to drop him a few doors from home and sneaking back into the compound, unnoticed.

He had his official phone on the bedside table, but he reached for the other one, which was tucked behind his headboard, with the charging lead out of sight. He'd bounced messages with Duke before he went to sleep and was disappointed to find nothing new now. He was hungry enough for breakfast, but it was only eight and a lie-in was more tempting.

A click from the bedroom door startled him. Julius buried the illicit phone under his covers as Orisa's head came around the door. Sunday was her day off. She was dressed in a Nigeria soccer shirt that had been passed down from one of the twins and grey leggings, sweaty from a session on the cross trainer in the downstairs gym.

'May I step in?' Orisa asked. But it wasn't a question.

Julius moved his long leg out of the way as Orisa settled on the edge of his double bed. Her post-workout glow was surprisingly

125

pungent and her well-defined shoulders and biceps reminded Julius that his petite cousin often did free weights with the bodyguards.

'Where did you go yesterday?' Orisa asked.

Julius's fingers dug into the mattress. But he tried to stay cool.

'I was here,' he said, doing his best to sound unflustered.

Orisa shook her head. 'The guard ran to me when he saw you leave through the gate wearing an army cap.'

'He . . .' Julius stuttered, his chest feeling tight. 'I . . .'

'Don't choke yourself. I covered your lanky butt before he made a call to your mother.'

'Really?' Julius gasped with relief. 'What did you say?'

'I said you were visiting a school friend who lives a couple of houses up the road.'

Orisa had been running the household since the twins were born. She was part of the family, but his mother would surely fire her for such blatant disobedience.

'I owe you,' Julius said, bowing his head as Gabe ran down the hallway outside.

'You owe me an explanation,' Orisa said firmly.

'You must have figured out where I went.'

Orisa nodded. 'Duke. The one your mother expressly forbade you to see?'

Julius nodded.

A sympathetic smile broke on Orisa's face. 'The heart wants what the heart wants.'

Julius took a couple of seconds to unpick this. He'd grown up with Orisa but had rarely considered her life beyond the kitchen. She dressed traditionally when she worked or attended church, but in her free time Orisa was tomboyish, wearing jeans and the twins' outgrown football shirts. And when visiting relatives asked Orisa when she was planning to marry, her pat answer was *I need a husband like I need a hole in the back of my head*... Until he met Duke, Julius had felt like the only gay person in the world. Now he wondered if he might not be the only gay person in his house ...

But while Julius's feelings for Orisa warmed, Orisa narrowed her eyes and grasped his wrist tightly.

'I covered for you yesterday because I don't wish to see you bounced to military school. But you must be clear: it was a one-off.'

Julius felt hopeful. 'You could cover for me,' he began pleadingly. 'You run this house. If you tell a driver that I need to be somewhere, they'll do it. You could say I have a dentist appointment or an errand to run for you.'

Orisa tutted. 'You're being *ridiculous*.'

'Please,' Julius begged. 'Duke's my only friend. I *have* to see him.'

'I had crushes when I was fourteen,' Orisa said. 'Your head is in the clouds. You don't really know what you want.'

Now Julius was narked. 'Were your crushes on boys or *girls*?'

Orisa reached across the bed and slapped Julius across the face.

'Enough nonsense,' Orisa snapped as she stood up. 'I risked a lot to do you a favour and you try to turn it against me.'

The slap made Julius instinctively angry, but before he could growl back, he was shocked by tears streaking down Orisa's face.

'I'm sorry,' Julius said, his eyes welling. 'Truly.'

'Make no mention of this again,' Orisa said sharply. 'Funny business will be taken to your mother, without mercy.'

'I love Duke,' Julius choked.

Doubt crossed Orisa's face, but her tone stayed severe.

'Your mother wants you four boys at church this morning,' she said. 'Wear your new suit and be ready at ten!'

EIGHTEEN

Maya and Rolf took Georgia all the way to her front door. She heard her dad snoring as she wobbled up the stairs, kicked off her All Stars and crashed face-first on the bed.

But the alcopops were stronger than they'd tasted, and the world refused to stay still when she closed her eyes. The swaying was better when she rolled on her back, but after a couple of minutes she had a brick in her stomach. It rose up her chest and she only properly realised what was going on a moment shy of disaster.

Georgia scrambled across the hall, mouth filling, then noisily spraying egg-yolk-coloured puke into the toilet. She gasped desperately, fearing she'd wake her dad, who was only a thin partition wall away.

'Ahh, crap . . .'

She held aching stomach muscles as a second wave kicked off.

Georgia would have liked a shower, but her body felt leaden and she settled for a swoosh of Listerine and a glass of tap water. Back in her room, she tipped out her laundry basket and left it by the top of her bed as an emergency puke bowl, then lay staring at the ceiling and wanting time to fast-forward to the point where she didn't feel like this any more.

It was light when she woke. Her throat was raw from all the smoke at the party. Her brain felt like it had swollen up inside her skull and she had dried sick on her chin and pillowcase. Her sweat smelled boozy and she dry-heaved as she sat up.

'My first hangover,' she told herself, prodding around her throat and wondering how long it would last. Her instinct was to google hangover cures, but her phone wasn't on charge and she spun around frantically when she realised it didn't appear to be anywhere. 'Christ . . .'

Georgia flicked off her bedsheet, looked on the floor, behind the bedside table.

Where did I see it last?

The skirt and top she'd worn to the party didn't have pockets big enough for her phone, so she must have had it in her jacket.

But it was hot at the party. Did I take the jacket off? I can't remember wearing it on the way home. Dad will crack up if I've lost another phone . . .

Georgia needed to pee, but finding her phone felt more urgent. She shot downstairs and saw her black denim jacket on the floor below the coat rack. She was chuffed as she squatted down and felt the phone and her door keys in the pocket. The battery was down to eight per cent, but that wasn't a biggie.

'Good morning,' John said brightly. 'Beautiful day out there, isn't it?'

'Dad,' Georgia croaked, trying to fake some enthusiasm as she turned round and saw him standing in the kitchen, with his hands holding the top of the door frame. 'I thought you'd have gone to work already.'

'It's only eight,' John said. 'So, you didn't sleep over in the end?'

'Maya's got a house full of siblings,' Georgia said. 'I got in before eleven. You were snoring, so I didn't wake you up.'

'Good time?'

'Sure,' Georgia said, trying to disguise a gruff voice. 'We dragged out a board game. Sang along to a couple of lame Disney movies . . .'

'Very wholesome,' John said. 'I'm making breakfast. Liver and bacon, would you like some?'

Georgia retched at the thought of liver. 'I'm gonna shower,' she choked.

'Or I can cook eggs with runny yolks, or fry up some squid in olive oil with extra tentacles . . .'

Georgia froze at the bottom of the stairs. *He knew* . . .

John smiled. 'Or maybe you'd prefer the Alka-Seltzer and paracetamol I've put out on the kitchen cabinet.'

'So, I'm busted,' Georgia said warily.

'You'd have woken a hibernating bear with that retching in the bathroom,' John said, smirking. 'At least you made it to the bathroom. The first time Sophie came home drunk, she hurled in the umbrella stand in the hallway.'

'Really?' Georgia said, relieved that her dad was seeing the funny side, but not daring to push her luck.

'I turned you onto your front,' John said. 'You were on your back, but that's dangerous if you vomit in your sleep.'

'I don't remember,' Georgia said, touched.

'You were blotto,' John said. 'But you did tell me I was the best daddy in the world at one point.'

'*Must* have been drunk,' Georgia said, smiling cheekily as her dad stepped out of the kitchen doorway for a quick hug.

She felt like a little girl again as his big hand pressed between her shoulders.

'You get one free pass, because you're a good kid and it's been a rough few weeks. And *don't* say anything about this to your mother.'

'Love you, Dad.' Georgia smiled.

'Back at you,' John said. 'And I had an email from the organisers of Rage Classic. They said they're sorry you missed out because of your bereavement and they want to offer you direct entry to next year's final.'

Georgia's head was fuzzy, but her dad had just been super-nice and next year was way off.

'That's really cool of them,' Georgia said, then pointed up the stairs. 'Gotta pee.'

John had left for the workshop when she came back down, dressed for self-pity in a big orange hoodie, with damp hair and a ball of evil-smelling laundry. He'd left the TV at the end of the dining table on and *Sunday Politics* was showing as Georgia stuffed the washing machine.

Normally she'd have gone straight for the off switch, but Georgia was curious after her meet-up with Zac the day before.

The screen showed protestors being chased by police outside a council building, cutting to a shot of a cop being hit by a flying traffic cone, then to an enormous woman yanking a man in a suit and helmet off his bicycle and screaming, 'Dirty fascist! What about the kids and pensioners?'

'*Similar scenes were played out in Liverpool and Leicester,*' the voiceover purred. '*In Truro, the budget meeting had to be abandoned after protestors blockaded the town hall, preventing councillors from entering the building. This week, the focus turns to the south-east, with police on alert for trouble as the leaders of* twenty-six councils and all thirty-two London boroughs meet to agree budgets.

'Joining me in the studio to discuss the budget protests are Diane Mooney, our local government minister, along with Vincent Ludsthorp, a spokesperson for the National Public Service Union. Mr Ludsthorp says many of his members face job losses and pay cuts under the new budgets, and he spent the early hours of Thursday in a police cell after being arrested outside Harrogate town hall.

'Minister, I want to begin with a question for you. How can a government, elected less than eighteen months ago with promises to improve public services, bring in cuts described as the biggest in a generation? Have you betrayed the people who voted for you?'

NINETEEN

The Healing Prayer Church began in an abandoned three-hundred-seat cinema. Now its main Sunday service took place inside The Cross, a purpose-built arena that could seat four and a half thousand and beamed the service to hundreds of thousands more across West Africa.

As a kid, Julius had enjoyed the spectacle. Crowds in their best clothes carrying fancy Bibles with leather bindings and gold clasps. The services were kept short and loud, and he'd lapped up the attention that came with being the son of the founder.

Now, Julius was a teen cynic, who'd rather spend Sunday morning in bed than in a suit and tie. He thought the congregation were fools, dazzled by whiz-bang as they sang and shouted, before queuing up to pour hard-earned wages into his mother's pockets.

'Today we are truly honoured,' Preacher Pepple shouted from the circular stage as drums rolled and spotlights pulsed on all sides.

'Honoured!' four thousand people shouted back.

'The founder will speak briefly, in person!'

Julius was high up, in a ring of seats reserved for VIPs and the Church's biggest donors. Gabe glanced up from his phone as lights strobed and a fake thunderclap boomed around The Cross. The crowd were on their feet, cheering as Bunmi Adebisi stepped between the lights. Tiny on the stage, but vast on the circle of six video screens above it.

'Are we happy today?' Bunmi shouted, breaking into a huge, gawping smile.

The crowd roared in agreement.

'Are our tomorrows bright, because of the love God shares with us all?'

Nobody in the crowd disagreed, but Julius hated the power of the person who stood between himself and Duke.

'Yesterday people from this church were treated with brutality in the precinct,' Bunmi said seriously, then paused for the hissing and tuts that rustled through the crowd. 'There was rioting and disorder through the whole of Akure.

'Last night, I visited my beloved brother, our state governor, SJ Adebisi. A man I love with all my heart. A man who has done *so* many things of which I am proud. I want you to know that he is not scared by these weak-minded troublemakers. The culprits will be found and punished under the eye of God and I ask you to pray for decent elections over all of Nigeria in the months ahead.

'Now I call this service to a close, and wish peace, health and prosperity to you all. Amen!'

'Amen!' the crowd shouted back, before erupting with applause.

The lights in The Cross came up and Julius watched the crowd split. Most pouring to the exits via strategically placed donation boxes, while a sizeable minority queued at folding tables. Some tables sold books and charms, but the biggest queue was of tween girls, who wanted the handsome and hunky members of The Cross's house band to scrawl signatures on glossy pics and phone cases.

The twins had wangled their way out of church, so the bodyguards just had Julius and Gabe to marshal from the arena. Rather than fight the crowd, the brothers were led through a private door and down several flights of carpeted steps.

Bunmi was waiting for them when they exited into a gloomy concrete space, beneath The Cross's steeply raked seats.

'Hey,' Julius said warily, as Gabe put his arms around his mum's waist.

'You were good,' Gabe told her cheerfully.

Bunmi laughed. 'Thank you, Gabriel. You must be after something...'

'No,' Gabe protested, then tilted his head and grinned ridiculously. 'Though I wouldn't say no to a dirt bike...'

Julius envied Gabe's rapport with their mother, but was quickly distracted by a two-man security team dropping one of the metal collection boxes. Hundreds of tightly folded banknotes sprang out and coins rolled in all directions over the bare concrete.

'Imbeciles!' Bunmi snapped at them. 'I will dock wages if I see this again.'

Gabe charged off and started helping the bumbling security crew chase rolling coins. This left Julius facing his mother alone.

'The new suit fits well,' Bunmi said admiringly, as she took a small bunch of keys from her handbag.

Julius looked baffled. 'Who do I give these to?'

'For the meeting room upstairs.'

'Am I not going home?'

Bunmi opened her eyes wide, as if her middle son was a fool. 'You and Gabriel are attending the family lunch in support of your uncle's re-election campaign. It's at 1 p.m. You will wait in the conference room until they are ready for our entrance.'

'Are you kidding?' Julius groaned. 'That's half my Sunday. I've got homework.'

'You could have brought your homework to do in the meeting room.'

'I didn't know,' Julius whined.

'Orisa didn't tell you?'

Julius shook his head, knowing she'd not told him because she didn't want to listen to him moan about it. 'Why have I got to sit through this?'

'This is an event for *families*,' Bunmi said. 'You *will* interact and be happy. Do not skulk in some corner with your telephone or I will take the telephone away.'

Orisa hadn't told Gabe either. The ten-year-old was wily, knowing he'd get nowhere by complaining in front of his mum, but swearing as he stomped up two levels behind Julius.

A bodyguard led them along a curved hallway that ran behind the arena's seats. The conference room had a marble floor and huge wooden table with twelve seats along each side. A glass wall gave a grand view over The Cross's thousands of seats.

Julius peered down at crews of volunteers, still in church clothes, walking the empty rows, picking up litter, while in the centre the hydraulic stage had lowered and the innermost banks of seats were slowly retracting to make a space for the family banquet.

As Gabe spun himself in a plush leather chair and flipped

channels on a TV, Julius sat at the other end of the table and took out his phone. After checking his messages, he remembered that he'd been meaning to google Duke's Uncle Remi.

Typing in 'Remi Balogun' brought up a short Wikipedia entry, along with a bunch of photos and video clips from his newsreading prime. Things got more interesting when Julius added *Adebisi* to the search.

The first article in the result was from the *Lagos Times* and had been written by Remi six years earlier. It was a lengthy and well-researched exposé, describing how a London-based company had bought sixteen million pounds' worth of vaccines and medicines from Indian pharmaceutical companies, then resold them to the Ondo State healthcare system for more than forty million. Twenty-four million profit had been stolen from Ondo State's meagre public health budget, and while the article made no specific allegations for fear of being sued, Remi clearly thought the Adebisi family was behind the Lithuanian shell company that scooped the profits.

As Julius scrolled more search results, he found articles by Remi linking his mother's illegal imports to the collapse of Nigerian textile manufacture and the Adebisi family to multiple scandals. These ranged from a contract to build two gas power stations, that cost over 70 billion naira but were never completed, a soccer stadium that went eight times over the original budget, to a colossal deal with the Chinese Development Bank that involved pre-selling a quarter of Ondo State's oil production for the next thirty years, in return for a vast loan that had been used to fund the governor's mansion, and dozens of other projects from which Adebisi-owned companies stood to profit.

Julius had grown up hearing that corruption was part of the

Nigerian way and that it was so ingrained in society that you had to go along with it to have any chance of success. But if what Remi had written was true, his mother and uncle had made all the money they could ever need but kept stealing anyway.

The opening line from one of Remi's blog posts clawed at Julius's conscience: *In Ondo Province, the lights stay out and one child in three goes hungry, but a new survey of wealth in Africa shows the Adebisi family are now worth half a billion US dollars . . .*

Julius also noticed that Remi's criticism of his family and other corrupt members of Nigeria's elite had coincided with a plunge in his status. In ten years, Remi had gone from famous newsreader, to a journalist whose articles were published by prestigious newspapers, to a guy whose most recent articles only appeared on his own anti-corruption blog.

Julius heard a toilet flush and glanced up as Gabe exited the bathroom that adjoined the conference room.

'*Sooo* bored,' Gabe moaned as he flicked drips off his wet hands.

Every time Julius had read an article by Remi, or one of several other prominent anti-corruption campaigners, he'd found links to more stuff he wanted to read. He was so engrossed that it took Gabe's toilet break to make him realise he needed a pee.

The men's bathroom was ludicrously plush, with marble toilet seats, neatly folded hand towels and a chrome shelf holding toothbrushes, disposable razors and mini bottles of cologne, mouthwash and shaving foam.

Gabe had opened one of the foams and used it to make a smiley face on the mirror, secure in the knowledge that his mum wouldn't use the men's and nobody would dare complain to Bunmi about her favourite son's mischief.

Gabe had vanished when Julius stepped out, smelling of Tom Ford Noir and with a couple of mini colognes in his pocket to experiment with later. He thought about sticking his head out to check on Gabe, but there was a bodyguard outside, so his little brother couldn't cause much trouble. Julius also realised Gabe's absence might be his only chance to speak with Duke before the evening.

He sat with his back to the door, which would give him a couple of seconds to pocket his secret phone if Gabe came back. Duke answered after a couple of rings and seemed chuffed to hear Julius's voice.

'Hey, you,' Duke said, soft and cheery. 'I was thinking about you. Where you at?'

'Stuck at The Cross, waiting for some stupid buffet function to start. I've been reading articles your Uncle Remi wrote about my family.'

Duke laughed. 'I'll assume we're no longer on speaking terms...'

'I feel dumb,' Julius admitted. 'All this stuff is there online for anyone to read. There's a ton of evidence, but nothing ever sticks.'

'People hear what they want to hear,' Duke said philosophically. 'Frankly, I wish my uncle would stop being so obsessed. He thinks he's going to change the world, but his blog keeps getting trashed by hackers, he's been sued by so many people he's broke and if he's not careful he'll wind up at the side of a road with his guts hanging out.'

'My mum is *such* a cynical bitch,' Julius hissed. 'Telling me I'm breaking God's law by kissing you or being around you, but at the same time, she's ripping off millions from a vaccination programme that's supposed to save kids' lives.'

'Don't get *too* political with me,' Duke said irritably.

'What do you mean?' Julius asked. 'I'm reading all this eye-opening stuff . . .'

'I hear it from my uncle *all* the time,' Duke explained. 'I don't mean to be rude, but I'd rather talk about something else.'

'Pick a topic,' Julius said. 'Sport? Science? iOS versus Android . . .'

Duke laughed. 'Close your eyes, take a deep breath. Imagine you and I are on a golden beach. Out of our lives, a million kilometres from anywhere.'

'I like that,' Julius replied, feeling some of the tension drop out of his shoulders. 'I could kiss you as the waves wash up over us and drink salty water out of your belly button.'

'Imaginative,' Duke said, laughing. 'And what would you do to me *after* that?'

Julius paused to consider, then shot up in the air and dropped his phone as the doors of a storage unit beneath the television flew open.

'Pervert!' Gabe shouted, stumbling out of the cupboard and onto his feet. 'You're talking to that homo again. I heard *everything*.'

Gabe sounded angry, but his face was shocked and tearful.

'Gabe, he's my friend,' Julius said, looking down at the phone on the floor and wondering if Duke could hear. 'Why the hell were you hiding in a cupboard?'

'I was bored,' Gabe explained. 'I was gonna burst out and try to make you jump.'

'You don't understand,' Julius said, taking a step closer to his brother. 'There's nothing wrong with what I'm doing.'

Gabe looked like this was the craziest thing he'd ever heard.

'You were talking to a boy about kissing him. That's being homo. And don't say I'm too young to know, because I've seen videos online. You'll go to hell and I'm telling Mum.'

'Don't,' Julius said firmly, as he picked the secret phone off the carpet and saw that the call had dropped. 'You heard what Mum said. If you go to her, they'll send me away to military school.'

'Which makes you into a man,' Gabe said. 'Which is what you need to get normal.'

Gabe started a brisk walk towards the door. Julius backed up to block his path.

'Please, Gabe. You're my brother and I'm *begging* you not to tell Mum. At least let me try to explain. I've got a book about being gay that I bought in London. I can show it to you. There are millions of gay people in the world. Maybe it seems weird to you, but it's totally normal.'

Gabe shook his head. 'Why can't you like girls like everyone else?'

'Because . . .' Julius groaned. 'I don't know exactly. Some people are wired differently. Is there something you want? I've got money in my savings. You can have it. Lego, Star Wars, fancy football boots.'

'Mum buys me all that stuff,' Gabe said, eyeing the door like he was about to make a dash. 'And everyone will say I'm gay if you are.'

'Gabe . . .'

The ten-year-old made a sprint for the door. Julius tackled him, grabbing his brother under the arms and catching a kick in the head as he lifted Gabe easily, then pinned him, squirming, against the table.

'Piss off, homo,' Gabe spat.

142

Julius stared into his brother's eyes. He was angry, but not with Gabe, who was parroting stuff he'd heard from the twins, his mother and random kids at school. Nothing short of strangling Gabe would stop him from snitching and Julius couldn't bring himself to throw a punch.

'Do whatever. Ruin my life,' Julius sighed, choking up as he shoved Gabe down the table and backed up because he didn't want to catch another kick.

Gabe tugged his rumpled suit jacket and scowled defiantly. The guard outside had heard Gabe shout and was stepping in to investigate.

'I have to find Mum,' Gabe blurted, ducking under the bodyguard and starting a charge down the hallway.

TWENTY

Before Sophie died, Georgia ate school lunch quickly and went to the library to read or study. Now, she hung out with Maya, a bunch of Maya's friends and their boyfriends, who were mostly older.

Only year-twelve and thirteen kids were allowed out of school at lunchtime, but the teaching assistants on the front gate didn't know everyone, and Georgia never had a problem getting out if she was with Rolf and a couple of his burly mates.

They went to a few different places, but the most common was Denton's Gelato. It was way more expensive than the school canteen. Georgia knew her dad had money problems, so rather than press for extra cash, she'd just get a cheap filter coffee and a Twix or Kit Kat.

There were about twenty kids from Georgia's school sprawled over the cafe's tables. Maya had been yawning all morning because her youngest sibling had spent the night screaming with toothache. She sat sideways in her chair, with her head in Rolf's lap.

Georgia found Rolf irritating, but the way he cradled Maya and kept his voice low while she dozed was surprisingly tender.

In contrast, the lads at the table behind Rolf and Maya were noisy dicks, flicking sugar cubes at each other, while one tried to tell a story about a girl he'd got off with at a music festival.

'It's funny how you're *so* much better at scoring when none of us are around,' one of the pals noted.

Georgia smirked, but knew better than to give any indication that she was listening and kept eyes on her phone. Dean had sent her a long text before school, saying he was sorry if he'd come on too strong at the party and asking if she'd like to meet up for a coffee one afternoon after school.

Georgia was torn. She'd seen Dean with his hand on another girl's butt, so he was clearly the kind of guy who hit on anything in a skirt. But she envied what Maya had with Rolf and felt childish, having never snogged a guy, when Maya and her mates spoke casually about being on the pill and strings of exes . . .

The phone in Georgia's hand started to ring: *Zac Calling*.

'Hey, 'sup,' Georgia said, trying to sound cool for the sake of company, then covering one ear to shut out the idiots at the next table.

'Glad I caught you,' Zac began. 'I was hoping you'd be switched on during lunch. Are you still coming to the demo at the town hall tonight?'

'I think,' Georgia said, sure she'd caught a wary note in Zac's voice.

'Spanner in the works at my end,' Zac continued. 'One of my colleagues was in a motorbike accident.'

'Really?' Georgia gasped.

'Nothing serious. But he's in a neck brace, so I'm going to be on duty tonight.'

'Oh,' Georgia said. 'I've got mounds of homework, so it's probably for the best . . .'

'No, no,' Zac protested. 'You should go.'

Georgia squirmed. 'I won't know *anyone*.'

'I already gave Kamila a call,' Zac said. 'You remember her?'

'The waitress at the Red Parrot,' Georgia confirmed.

'Kamila will be there with her boyfriend, Gerard, and loads of other SAG people. They're meeting outside Red Parrot at ten past six. She says you're very welcome and she'll introduce you to everyone.'

Georgia didn't fancy it but didn't want to disappoint Zac either. 'I got in trouble for staying out late Saturday. I'd be pushing my luck on a weeknight . . .'

'I'll text Kamila's number,' Zac said. 'Let her know if you're going or not.'

'Right,' Georgia said weakly. She wanted to see Zac for coffee or a walk in the park, not one of his political meets.

'I'm on a fifteen-minute break and I need coffee,' Zac said hurriedly. 'I hope you get there tonight.'

'Speak soon,' Georgia agreed, and Zac hung up.

Maya grinned as she raised her head out of Rolf's lap. 'That your fancy man?'

Georgia tutted and smirked. 'Maya, Jesus!'

Maya laughed. 'You *totally* have a crush . . .'

'Maybe,' Georgia admitted. 'But he's twenty-seven, and my dead sister's ex-boyfriend . . .'

'That why you blew out Deano at the party?' Rolf asked.

Maya and Georgia both scowled at him.

'Why do you care?' Maya asked Rolf sharply.

'Dean's seen me hanging around with Maya and you,' Rolf explained. 'He's in my art class and he asked if Georgia was seeing anyone.'

'What did you say?' Georgia asked too eagerly, wincing as

she realised she'd left an opening for Rolf to have a dig.

Rolf grinned. 'I told him he'd be wasting his time, because you're not his type.'

Georgia looked offended. 'Why am I not his type?'

'Dean's a *total* player,' Rolf said admiringly, then glanced warily, fearing Maya's wrath. 'I'm not being funny, but he's a year-thirteen, and you're . . . You're innocent compared to someone like Maya.'

'Hey!' Maya said, giving Rolf a gentle slap on the knee. 'I'm a slut now?'

'Don't go all woman on me and twist it around,' Rolf pleaded, holding up his hands. 'I think Dean liked you a lot, OK, Georgia? All I'm saying is, he's eighteen. He's been around a lot of girls and he'll wanna do more than hold your hand . . .'

Georgia never knew what to expect from Rolf. One minute he was a pig, but now it was like he was looking out for her. Rolf and Maya were both staring, expecting her to speak, so she changed the subject.

'I was supposed to be meeting Zac at Red Parrot Books tonight,' Georgia babbled. 'You know the council budget cuts? There's a demo outside the town hall. I said I'd ask around and see if anyone else wants to go.'

Maya looked horrified. 'Some bunch of freak nerds, freezing their tits off and moaning about the government.'

Georgia didn't completely agree, but nodded to support her friend.

'Hold up,' Rolf said brightly. 'Is that like I saw on the news? With that enormous woman pulling the nerdy bloke off his bike and people lobbing traffic cones and shit.'

'That's the one,' Georgia said.

'There's one like that here?' Rolf asked keenly.

'Tonight,' Georgia replied.

Rolf stood and called to some pals a couple of tables down. 'Chris, Jake. You know them punch-ups that have been on the news? Georgia says there's gonna be one tonight outside our town hall.'

'I *didn't* say punch-up,' Georgia noted.

'Who said punch-up?' one of the noisy lads at the next table asked, standing up.

'I saw that,' one of Rolf's mates chirped. 'That fella in Leeds stood on the mayor's car and took a dump through the sunroof.'

'Aggro, let's have it!' another lad shouted.

Georgia gave Maya a *my god they're idiots* look but was surprised to find Maya smiling roguishly.

'Nothing ever happens on a Monday night,' Maya explained. 'It might be a laugh . . .'

TWENTY-ONE

A bodyguard came into the conference room and made Julius surrender both phones. But while the situation was the most important thing in Julius's life, it was just one item on his mother's to-do list.

At the buffet, Bunmi posed for photographs, held babies, shook hands and laughed at all the jokes. Gabe kept his distance from Julius, finding kids he knew from school, chasing around and getting yelled at when they started a water fight in one of the bathrooms.

Julius's afternoon moved slowly. He ate burgers and cake for comfort, then snapped his disposable fork and imagined driving the jutting shard of plastic into his throat. Or someone else's throat... A driver took him home on his own at five. In his room, Julius was phoneless, and anxiety made his brain mush. He decided to read some more of Remi Balogun's corruption articles, but his laptop wouldn't connect to Wi-Fi.

'Your mother told me to change the password,' Orisa explained coldly, glancing away from *Nigerian Idol* on the living-room couch. 'You are not to use the house telephone or have the new wireless password until your mother has dealt with you.'

'Fabulous . . .' Julius said.

On the skulk back to his room, he kicked a wooden stair rod, hoping to snap it. But it just sent a jarring pain up to his hip, which seemed like a perfect metaphor for his powerlessness.

It was midnight when Bunmi got home. Julius loathed her as he peeked between the curtains, a drunken sway as she stumbled out of the front passenger seat, while the bodyguard scooped Gabe, fast asleep, from the back. He heard her walk up the stairs, stopping briefly to drop a bag in her office. Julius blocked the hallway as she stepped out.

'What's going to happen?' he asked fearfully.

Bunmi looked clownish. Barefoot, squashed hat, smudged make-up and a taint of body odour.

'I am tired,' she said softly. 'My life does not revolve around your antics. You must wait until I decide what the consequences are . . .'

Julius barely slept. Monday morning had the usual routine with a weird vibe. Orisa waking him up. Uniform, teeth, books and breakfast. Gabe was gluey-eyed and irritable and the twins strangely muted as they rode the long-wheelbase Lexus to St Gilda's.

Duke sighted Julius during morning break. His lumbering walk seemed sad, but his presence was a relief, since Duke feared his friend might already be on his way to military school. But Duke had been hopeful enough to dig his uncle's prehistoric Nokia out of a drawer and buy a cheap SIM card in the market. When he got a chance, he'd press it into Julius's hand and they'd at least be able to talk.

Duke had double art after lunch. Rainy season had arrived late, but hard. The paved path was blasted by giant raindrops as he jogged towards St Gilda's art and drama block. He'd almost reached the entrance when Collins steamed towards him, with a protective cup over his surgically rebuilt nose and school shoes sploshing waterlogged grass.

'Dirty queer!' Collins shouted, emphasising his point with a vicious punch in the mouth.

A couple of kids from art class saw Duke crumple but didn't intervene. As Duke splashed down, tasting blood, Kehinde and Taiwo helped Collins drag him around the side of the building.

'On your feet, queer,' Taiwo ordered as Duke got yanked up.

The three muscular lads marched Duke through the rain to a groundsman's shed near the school perimeter. As the twins bounced Duke's face into the side of the hut, Collins produced a key and freed a padlock from the door.

'Inside,' Collins spat.

Duke got kicked with a wet shoe and clattered a shovel as he sprawled into a wooden repair bench. Two ride-on lawnmowers were parked in the back and the smell was cut grass and petrol.

'What did we tell you about going near our brother?' Kehinde demanded as he grabbed a wad of Duke's Afro and used it to tug back his head.

'How many warnings?' Taiwo added, glaring down Duke's ear. 'Are these clogged with wax?'

Collins found a three-pronged hand fork on a shelf and held it to Duke's throat. At the same time, Taiwo unzipped Duke's backpack, spilling the contents over the shed floor and bending down to retrieve Duke's phone.

'What did we tell you?' Kehinde repeated, then punched Duke fiercely in the kidneys.

But Duke was dazed from getting his head bashed, and his tongue sloshed around in blood.

'You turned my cousin into a homosexual,' Collins said nastily, pressing the fork hard enough to draw blood. 'Our family runs this town, Duke. We could end you. Nobody would bat an eye.'

The trio exchanged satisfied smiles as Duke squirmed and dribbled blood. Collins got bored holding the fork and banged the point of his elbow hard into Duke's back.

'Like that?' Collins taunted, then did it twice more.

Taiwo stepped around in front of the bench, holding Duke's phone.

'Huawei hunk of junk,' Taiwo said, knocking the screen on a corner of bench but failing to smash it. 'Open your mouth.'

Kehinde pulled Duke's hair back harder and pinched his nose shut. As Duke fought for breath, Taiwo rammed the phone deep into his gasping mouth, making his jaw crack and pinning his tongue to the back of his throat.

The fight for air gave Duke the strength to buck himself free. He inhaled, gargled, then vomited blood, phone and lunch over the bench.

Kehinde backed up to avoid splatter. Duke's shorts ripped as Collins tugged him off the bench and let him drop to the floor.

Duke's tongue felt gaps where teeth had been as he choked and coughed. Collins and Taiwo landed brutal kicks as Kehinde grabbed a petrol can and started unscrewing the cap.

'I say we burn the queer,' Kehinde suggested brightly.

'God's work,' Collins laughed. 'Those who submit to shameful lusts will be cast into eternal flame!'

Duke eyed them defiantly from the floor.

'Who asked you, homo?' Taiwo snarled, then used the bench as leverage for a vicious two-footed stamp. Duke groaned as his chest made a fleshy crunch.

'Oh, shit!' Collins said, laughing madly. 'That was his ribs!'

Taiwo was laughing as Kehinde drizzled petrol all over Duke's uniform.

'Any last words?' Taiwo taunted. 'Maybe for your boyfriend, Julius?'

'Kiss my ass,' Duke growled. 'You'll burn in hell, not me.'

'You even wink at Julius and we'll light the matches next time,' Kehinde added, letting the last stinging drips of petrol run into Duke's eyes, then flinging the empty can to the back of the shed.

TWENTY-TWO

It was still light as Kamila pulled down the metal shutters on the Red Parrot bookshop. The air was warm enough to make Georgia wonder if she could have left her coat at home.

'I told some people at school,' Georgia told Kamila warily. 'A few might turn up.'

'Young people don't care . . .' Kamila's boyfriend, Gerard, opined. 'Too busy with Pornhub, Netflix and the rest of that cock and bull.'

Gerard was a pudgy-featured giant in a waxed jacket with the sleeves too short. He had a mad professor vibe, and crumbs showered the pavement as he tore a bite from one of the Red Parrot's leftover baguettes.

'Play nice, Gerard,' Kamila warned.

She snapped the padlock on the last shutter, then gave Georgia eyes that seemed to say *Don't worry, he's not as bad as he seems.*

'I need a drink – the bread's dry,' Gerard complained.

'I'm not going back in. We're already holding up the others,' Kamila said.

*

Nine other members of SAG stood at the corner by the boarded bagel joint. The women mostly wore dark clothes with pierced everything, and apart from one black dude, the men looked like they should catch some sun. Sam was the youngest, maybe thirteen, and wearing skinny jeans with big rips and the most trashed pair of All Stars Georgia had ever seen.

'Your first demo?' Sam said, incredulously. 'I must have been to a million. Have you heard that saying about war? Ninety-nine per cent boredom, one per cent mayhem. Demos are about the same.'

Sam had a tiny smiley mouth with a missing tooth and Georgia decided she liked him as Gerard galloped ahead of the group chanting, 'Tally-ho! Smash the state!' Then Gerard spotted a newsagent. 'I'm purchasing a can of Irn-Bru.'

'Gerard's pretty wacked,' Georgia noted.

Sam laughed. 'Mental as . . . But, actually, super brainy. He got his maths degree when he was nineteen. Then he got interested in genetics and wrote a theoretical paper on Junk DNA that won a major prize. Zac always says Gerard will either win a Nobel or blow up the planet.'

Georgia smiled. 'You know Zac?'

'Zac's a total ledge.' Sam nodded. 'I've been on so many things, like demos, with him. He lends me interesting books and stuff. I've even got the idea of being a paramedic from him. I thought about becoming a doctor like your sister, but I'm a B student on my good days.'

Sam's expression dropped, like he'd stepped in dog crap.

Georgia smiled. 'It's fine – you can talk about Sophie.'

'Awesome sauce!' Sam said. 'I only met Sophie once. She seemed great though.'

'Are you here with your parents?' Georgia asked.

Sam shook his head. 'My mum, Wendy, and her wife run RNN.'

'What's that?'

'Red News Network,' Sam explained. 'It started as a newspaper, but it's all online now. Mum's in Belgium covering some anti-capitalist demo. I'm staying with their friend, Don. He's the one over there with the dodgy moustache.'

Georgia nodded. 'I shook hands with him, but it's hard to remember names when you meet everyone at once.'

Sam was taller than Georgia and had a better view as they turned a corner. 'Is this your pals?' he asked.

Georgia was surprised to see about thirty estate kids, giving off a clueless vibe. She spotted Maya and pushed through the SAG members walking ahead.

'Bloody hell, you brought loads!' Georgia told her friend.

About three quarters were boys, who she suspected were more attracted by chaos than politics.

The lively teens in branded polos and trainers were a contrast to the bohemian SAG members. Georgia had a horrible *what-have-I-done* feeling as the two groups exchanged wary hellos, then got caught off guard when Kamila snatched her into a huge hug.

'You've brought so many of your friends! This is *amazing*.'

Sam and the other SAG members were all throwing positive vibes at Georgia too.

'What now, boss?' Maya asked.

Georgia realised Maya was talking to her and glanced about feeling helpless. But Gerard had caught up from his diversion into the newsagent and took control.

'Boys and girls, town hall, that way! Quick-a-march!'

Gerard led the charge on an imaginary horse.

One of the other SAG members punched a fist in the air and shouted, 'No cuts, no budget!'

The first reply was limp, but by the third shout everyone was joining in.

Georgia felt part of something, arms linked with Kamila and Maya, and Sam behind. Their rowdy group acted like a magnet for lone protestors and smaller groups. They numbered more than a hundred when they reached the town hall, interrupted by Gerard launching a kick at McDonald's front window and screeching, 'Capitalist scum,' at a bewildered five-year-old with a Happy Meal.

Georgia had walked past the town hall hundreds of times and skated on the ice rink they put out front every Christmas, but she'd never seen it like this. The noise grew as they approached. There were several hundred people milling about, waiting for the council members to arrive for the budget meeting. Some had placards with anti-cuts and anti-government slogans. There were heaps of uni students, workers from the leisure centre whose jobs faced the axe, dustmen and street cleaners in high-viz bibs, librarians, social workers and a big group of teachers, including a couple from Georgia's school.

'Evening, Mr Hannan,' Maya shouted cheerfully. 'This is why I won't be handing in my homework tomorrow.'

Mr Hannan gave her a thumbs up. 'Off-duty, Maya. Couldn't give a toss.'

The employee and political groups mostly looked civilised, but the other element in the crowd made Georgia uncomfortable. Thuggish blokes, older and scarier than her posse of teens.

Rolf, Gerard and a lot of the lads dispersed, but Georgia stuck with Kamila, Maya and Sam as they moved through a loosely packed crowd towards the town hall entrance.

157

The building was a grotty post-war job. Eight storeys of dirty concrete with underground parking. The window frames were rusting and a tacky refurbishment with brightly coloured cladding was like lipstick on a rotten corpse.

A split ramp led down to a fountain featuring supermarket trolleys and a basement theatre that had been shuttered for longer than Georgia had been alive. The ramp going up was a single-lane road leading to the town hall's glass atrium. The small parking lot in front had spaces marked for bridal convoys and disabled.

With protests all over southern England, the cops didn't have enough officers to patrol the town hall concourse. Since the protestors' aim was to stop the council budget meeting from taking place, they'd placed a line of waist-height barriers in front of the entrance ramp. A dozen officers were spaced behind this barrier to stop the demonstrators climbing over, while a command truck and two vans filled with cops in riot gear were parked down a side street.

'Comrades,' Kamila said happily when she caught up with a big group from another branch of SAG. 'Do we have tactics?'

'The pigs are protecting the ramp, but the cars still have to cross the concourse,' a hobbit-like man with dark glasses explained. 'We've got lookouts at the side and rear in case they try to sneak the councillors in.'

It stayed calm long enough for Georgia, Maya and Sam to saunter around the square, people-watching. Everything snapped into focus when a pair of cop cars came tearing along the town-hall access road, with a red Nissan X-Trail sandwiched between them.

The crowd charged forward, blocking the road towards the upper ramp and atrium. Georgia found herself at the back of a crazed mob. People were screaming *scum, shame* and *turn back*. Free-range eggs pelted the red car with four council members inside, while others pounded on the front of the cop car that continued inching towards the barriers.

'Do not obstruct the police vehicles,' a loudspeaker inside one of the cop cars announced as Georgia found herself engulfed by shoes and elbows.

A bunch of cops had jumped out of the riot van. They formed a line and banged batons on their plastic shields as they advanced. The crowd outnumbered the officers by at least thirty to one, but the drumming was a psychological trick designed to intimidate and most of the crowd fell for it and backed off.

There was a snapping sound and a cheer as a burly young man tore the bumper off the rear police car. At the same time, three officers from behind the barriers swooped in, snatching a slender woman who'd positioned herself with both hands on the hood of a Nissan.

More eggs and paint pounded the convoy, but a second line of riot cops moved in front of the lead cop car and started a fast march that cleared a path to the police barriers.

The crowd booed and cursed as the chunky Nissan accelerated up the ramp to the town-hall entrance. Its rear screen was cracked, and the bodywork a modern-art master-piece of paint, eggs and flour. Long-range missiles flew over the barriers and the four councillors in the vehicle shielded behind a giant golf umbrella as they dashed towards the main entrance.

'Scum!' Georgia and Maya shouted, grinning at each other as the excitement drew them in.

The first councillor had just made it inside the door when a woman in a peace-symbol hoodie jumped down from a parapet over the atrium. She knocked the only female councillor to the ground, then dumped a soggy mass of custard powder and wet bread in her face.

The cops hadn't considered attack from above. Several officers panicked and ran back from their positions along the barrier. The crowd cheered and surged forward, rattling the barriers until people at the front started feeling the pressure.

'Back up! This is dangerous!' someone near Georgia was shouting desperately. 'People could get hurt.'

Up at the entrance, the hooded custard bomber had snatched one of the councillor's high-heeled shoes, before starting a heroic sprint down the ramp towards the crowd. A chubby cop tried to tackle her, but the protestor hurdled him and the officer wound up in a heap.

There were wild cheers as the custard bomber flung the councillor's fancy high-heeled shoe into the crowd, seconds before two large men lifted her over the barrier to safety.

Georgia looked up, grinning, as the custard bomber crowd-surfed over her head. But more bodies were moving in, and cries coming from people pressed against the barriers were getting serious.

'Back away, back away!' people by the barriers were shouting. 'There are kids up here!'

There was a crash of metal. The crowd stumbled forward, carrying Georgia with it. The police barriers were designed to break before a crush became life-threatening and now more than two hundred protestors started a charge up the ramp towards the atrium.

'No cuts, no budget!'
'Free tuition, free school meals!'
'Kill the pigs!'

A security guard and the three councillors who'd made it into the atrium looked about frantically, trying to lock the huge double doors. But by the time they'd spotted the floor bolts at the bottom, the protestors were too close.

Georgia paused halfway up the ramp, but Maya yanked her arm and Sam seemed high on life.

'Come on,' Maya begged. 'This is mental!'

'What about the cops?' Georgia warned.

'Fifty cops and millions of us,' Sam said exuberantly. 'They're way more scared than we are.'

Rolf, Gerard and a bunch of kids from school charged past and Georgia didn't want to be a stick-in-the-mud.

As she entered the town-hall atrium, it was total chaos. People were pulling pictures off the wall, yobs had lobbed a bust of Winston Churchill through a stained-glass window, fire extinguishers were being blasted and telephones ripped out of the wall behind the reception desk.

'Anarchy,' Sam was shouting, flailing skinny arms wildly, as the fire alarm went off. 'Kill all humans!'

Maya had vanished, so Georgia followed Sam up thickly carpeted stairs, more accustomed to brides posing for wedding photos. The floor crunched with broken glass as they cut into a long hallway. One office already had its door kicked in, and some thugs were running off with laptops and toner cartridges.

Sam grabbed a tall metal trash can and used the end to punch through the glass panel in a door.

'Christ,' Georgia said, shielding her eyes as glass splinters flew past.

But she loved the crazy freedom of it. She grabbed a bin and laughed wildly as she rammed it through the glass in another door. Then Georgia and Sam charged down the long hallway, yelling and kicking doors.

'Anarchy!' Sam shouted.

'No cuts, no budget!' Georgia added happily, as she pounded every door.

They had to halt at the far end. The hallway was blocked by two Asian guys wheeling a giant photocopier towards a staircase. There were laughs and gasps as the huge machine tilted and smashed down the stairs. Women coming the other way squealed in fright as the photocopier bouldered past and ripped open a set of double doors.

The doors led into the upper gallery of the council meeting chamber. The councillors had long vanished, but cameramen and journalists who'd come to cover a budget meeting had stuck around, recording chaos, as dozens of protestors threw seats out of windows, ripped light fixtures off the walls, tipped over the main council meeting table and sprayed graffiti.

'It's a war zone down there,' Georgia blurted.

'Riot cops are storming in from the front,' someone shouted.

Waves of people began flooding the upper gallery. There was no direct route from the gallery to the chamber below. Georgia looked down warily as protestors grabbed hold of a polished brass rail, then dangled and dropped it into the chamber below.

It was a six-metre drop. Georgia didn't fancy it, especially onto floor covered in broken glass and upturned chairs. But she didn't fancy getting Tasered by the riot squad either.

'We've got to,' Sam said firmly, yanking her arm.

The camera crews and journalists decided not to stick around as riot cops came down the stairs at the end of the hallway, drumming the backs of their shields.

Sam vaulted down fearlessly, groaning as he stumbled sideways and thumped his head on a wooden partition.

'Come on,' Sam urged, knee buckling as he stumbled up. 'It's not that high.'

'I'll catch you, pet,' a big guy with a northern accent shouted as he held out his arms.

Georgia grabbed the rail and swung her legs over. She hesitated before letting go, but she could see riot cops clambering over the trashed photocopier in the doorway and leapt into the man's arms.

'Light as a feather,' he joked, but bolted away before Georgia could say thanks.

Riot cops were now pouring into the gallery above. A young man who'd chickened out of jumping got slammed into the wall by shields. Georgia noticed a single cameraman still filming as she started running out of the back of the council chamber, but Sam was hobbling from his awkward landing.

'Just go,' he groaned, holding the wall to stay upright. 'There's no point both of us getting nabbed.'

Georgia shook her head. 'Put your arm around my back.'

Sam did what he was told, and they began a hobbling jog down a long hallway. Everyone else got further ahead, until it felt like they were the last protestors in the building.

'Eyes on two down here!' a cop shouted eagerly from behind.

Georgia's chest felt tight and Sam's weight was straining her neck.

'You can't save me,' Sam urged. 'Go!'

She looked back as a stocky riot cop abandoned her clumsy shield and broke into a sprint.

'I'll make sure the others know what happened,' Georgia told Sam as she started to run.

But the cop knew she had back-up and decided to leave Sam to someone else.

Sam tried to block the officer, but there wasn't much of him and she used her thickly padded riot gear to splatter him against the wall. Georgia could almost taste freedom as she sprinted around a corner and saw an open fire door. But the cop seemed to have a rocket motor and she rugby-tackled Georgia, sending her sprawling painfully on the tiled hallway.

'Hands up on your head,' the cop growled, quickly finding her feet. 'Are you carrying a knife or any other weapons?'

'No' Georgia shuddered as she put her hands on her head.

The cop lifted the steamed-up visor of her riot helmet, then went down on one knee as she peeled a set of plasticuffs from her belt.

'What's your name?'

'Georgia Pack.'

'Been in trouble before?' the cop asked as she patted Georgia down. 'Arms together, behind your back.'

'No,' Georgia gasped, blinking sweat out of her eyes as the plastic cuffs bit her wrists. 'Oww.'

'Well, Georgia Pack,' the cop said, giving a little laugh, 'you've got yourself in a whole lot of trouble now . . .'

TWENTY-THREE

Julius felt detached. His body spent a rainy afternoon in history and Mandarin classes, but his thoughts focused on his looming fate. He'd settled at his desk for afternoon registration, when an Ijaw kid called Nengimote came in late and slid a cardboard-backed envelope onto his desk.

'Collins asked me to give you this,' Nengimote said, a tremble in his voice hinting that Collins hadn't asked nicely.

The form tutor was droning as usual. '. . . I am delighted to say that the tardiness record of this class has improved dramatically over the latest recorded period. As a result, I shall . . .'

Julius was conscious of the noise as he ripped the paper flap. He squeezed the envelope and tilted it towards the light to see inside. The envelope lining was streaked in dark, clotted blood. Duke's blood-smeared motorbike licence slid out, followed by the tap of two bloody teeth on the desktop. One almost bounced to the floor. Julius felt sickened as he caught the tooth and dropped it back in the envelope, but the kid at the next table had seen.

At the bottom of the envelope was a lined page, torn from

one of St Gilda's custom-printed homework diaries. There were diary notes in Duke's handwriting – *History due, art club, uncle Lagos meeting* – but the big black letters inside the fold were Collins's childlike scrawl:

You did my nose.
So. I did your boyfriend.
Have a fun day!

Julius tilted his head, clenched his fists and drilled holes in the ceiling with his eyes. He imagined a hundred horrible deaths for Collins. He wondered where Duke was, and whether Collins – and the twins, who were surely involved – had done more than punch out teeth.

He stayed at the desk, glowering as classmates filed out, then stood up, trying to think where to get hold of a weapon. A fire extinguisher, a metal barbell from the school gym, a jar of acid from the science block . . . But Collins would be expecting his rage and could snap Julius in half.

What I really need is a gun. Tuck it in the back of my trousers, rip it out and blast a hole through his stupid face . . . Julius didn't have the heart of a killer, but it was satisfying to imagine the scene.

He walked to the waiting Lexus on autopilot. The twins usually came home later, after sports practice or a video game session with Collins and their crew at the governor's mansion. Gabe had arranged a playdate with two mates and Julius opened the door to find them wrestling on the back seats, amidst a pungent whiff of preadolescence.

'Shut up and seat belts!' the driver yelled into the back as Julius climbed in the front.

Rage changed to dull loathing as the car crawled through

school traffic. As Julius stared at the lights on the dashboard, he was startled by knuckles tapping on the driver's side window. A body-built Transport Union thug had his face close to the glass, while the road ahead had been blocked with rusted oil drums.

'Our cars *never* get stopped,' Gabe told his friends curiously as he leaned between the front seats.

The driver lowered his window, but instead of a rolled banknote, he confidently flicked an ID, showing he was part of Governor Adebisi's security detail. The goon looked at the card with contempt, then pounded on the metal roof. This was a signal for half a dozen union officials to swarm the car.

'Up your ass to the governor's office!' the man leaning in the window shouted furiously. 'He let the precinct be torn away from us. Now we move patrols out here and *you* pay like everyone else!'

The men outside shouted agreement and several thumped on the hood. The driver wasn't going to risk the car getting scratched or losing a door mirror for the sake of two hundred naira and handed over the money. But the man at the window pointed at Julius and wagged a finger.

'I have seen you in photographs,' he said. 'Tell your mother to dial back this aggression. People have died. For what?'

Before Julius could answer, the driver blasted his horn and rolled off, fast enough to scatter the men in front of the car.

'Don't tell your mother I paid a bribe,' the driver begged Julius. 'It will come from my own pocket.'

'I'm not the snitch in this car,' Julius said sourly, cutting a backwards glance that made Gabe freeze.

Orisa had prepared kebabs, fries and Fanta for Gabe and his friends. She still seemed sore at Julius and made no attempt to enforce Bunmi's *no food upstairs* rule as he put skewers on a plate and walked to his room.

Julius switched on his air conditioner and threw open the curtains. The sun had broken through, turning the afternoon rains into a heat haze, but he could still see the soldiers on the gate. One was the guy who'd sold Julius the army cap and jacket, and he wondered what he might charge for a revolver and a box of bullets.

His thoughts switched to Duke as he pulled off his shoes. Remi was struggling for money, and Julius imagined Duke getting his teeth looked at by one of the dubiously qualified dentists who set up in slum areas or rooms behind shops. The thought depressed Julius so much he buried himself in bedclothes and listened enviously to Gabe and his friends, bantering as they played Call of Duty in the room next door.

He'd just dozed off when his mother stormed in without knocking.

'This is childishness, with all your clothes inside the bed!' Bunmi shouted. 'I've already called your name three times – don't make me say it again. Get up now!'

'Why the hell should I?' Julius found himself shouting.

Yelling wasn't the best way to start a conversation with his mother, but feeling he had nothing more to lose made him fearless.

'I have spoken to the recruitment department at Army Boys Academy. You would already be on your way, but there is a lengthy waiting list.'

'I guess you're stuffed then,' Julius said boldly.

'You are disrespectful.' Bunmi shouted. 'If I hear anything else from that mouth—'

'Duke's my best friend. He makes me happy.'

'His kind will go to hell,' Bunmi spat. 'He is no longer a pupil of St Gilda's. Multiple allegations of homosexual behaviour were made against him. The headmaster has agreed to expel, and you will not see him again.'

'I'd rather live in a tin shack with Duke than a palace with you,' Julius said, suddenly tearful.

'Look at how he's influenced you,' Bunmi said. 'To turn a clever boy like you into someone who hates his own mother.'

'Why should I hate you?' Julius railed. 'Because *you* hate who I am? Because you care more about the family reputation than my happiness? Or how about the money you stole from the vaccine programme? Or the area boys you paid to fight the Transport Union and the three people who burned to death as a result?'

'Have you no respect?' Bunmi shouted.

Julius reared up, so angry that his mother backed up to the door. 'No,' he agreed noisily. 'I'm almost fifteen – you have *all* the power over me now. Flog me, send me to Army Boys. Punish me however you like. But as soon as I'm old enough I'm leaving here . . . and I'm never coming back.'

TWENTY-FOUR

Georgia was freaking as she got marched out of the town hall by the riot cop.

I'm the good girl. The A-student. How did I get here? What will Dad say? Mum? Nan? Zac? Maya? How serious is this? What can they prove? Was there CCTV in that hallway where I smashed the window?

The back door of a police van opened. Two plasticuffed women sat on padded benches. Georgia recognised the peace-symbol hoodie of the woman who'd custard-bombed the councillor, then the door whomped shut and the only light came through a grilled vent in the roof.

'First-timer?' Peace Hoodie asked as she shuffled up to Georgia. 'I'm Jen.'

'You can tell?' Georgia asked, then added, 'I'm Georgia.'

'You look scared to death,' Jen explained, taking her arms from behind her back and revealing her cuffs dangling off one hand. 'How old are you?'

'Fourteen.'

'Good age for a first offence.' Jen smiled. 'Kill anyone?'

'No.'

'Then you'll be OK. But keep quiet, even if you think you're talking your way out of something.'

Georgia looked confused and the middle-aged woman across the van leaned forward and explained in a posh-country-lady accent.

'Imagine saying, *I saw some chaps doing stuff in the town hall, but I wasn't involved.* That's no admission of guilt, but you are admitting to being on the scene when laws were broken. If you give the police nothing, they need a witness to put you at the scene. And one can always claim that a witness is lying.'

'First offence, fourteen years old, you're golden,' Jen reiterated, placing a hand on Georgia's back.

'My dad will flip though,' Georgia said. 'Mum will have a field day, saying Dad's not looking after me . . .'

'You think you've got regrets,' Jen began. 'I hid up on that roof for four hours. Jumped down, did my bit to that councillor and got away. I should have jumped a bus and gone home. But when I saw everyone charging up that ramp, I *had* to get stuck back in. And when the riot cops storm, who's the first person they grab?'

'The one who made them all look stupid?' Georgia guessed.

Jen laughed. 'I've got a two-year suspended hanging over me for trashing a police car,' Jen explained. 'And I haven't peed in six hours . . .'

Georgia, Jen and the older woman across the van all started laughing. Then the van door came open again and two male riot officers shoved Sam inside. He stumbled awkwardly as he found a place to sit, but smiled once he'd settled.

'Long time no see, Sam,' Jen said brightly.

'Nice work out there,' Sam said as he looked at the older woman. 'It's Rosemary, isn't it?'

The woman nodded, but sounded surprised. 'I don't think I've had the pleasure . . .'

Sam gave his gap-toothed smile. 'I've been doing a lot of growing. I was at a demonstration about rural post office closures with my mum and you gave me a sherbet lime.'

'I do love a sherbet lime,' Rosemary said brightly.

Sam looked at Georgia and sounded more serious. 'You've not been busted before, have you? Whatever you do, don't say one word to the cops.'

'We explained,' Jen said as she gave Georgia a squeeze. 'Though the poor girl still looks wrecked.'

Georgia was glad the van was too dark for anyone to see her cheeks flush red. 'Maybe you guys get arrested on a regular basis, but it's a big deal where I come from.'

'I've been done thirty-three times,' Rosemary said proudly. 'Thirty-four if you include Greenham Common, when someone opened the back of the van and we all scarpered.'

'Prison?' Sam asked.

'Several times,' Rosemary admitted. 'But judges love my accent. I never get long.'

There was more laughter as the door opened. Two uni students were herded in, giggling and smelling of booze as they squeezed beside Georgia. Up front, an officer got in the cab and a light came on as he started the engine.

'Excuse me, officer,' Rosemary said politely, knocking on a grilled flap behind the driver's seat. 'I hope you know we're campaigning against police cuts too. So, could you pop us out at the mainline station?'

'And I'll buy you all a cup of tea and a cream bun first,' the cop in the driving seat said as his passengers laughed.

Fifteen minutes later, the van doors opened to a merciful

blast of fresh air in a police station car park. They'd stopped alongside an identical van filled with men that was already being unloaded. The driver ordered everyone to wait, but Jen barged out before the officer could do anything. She'd already unbuttoned her jeans and squatted down on her haunches to pee on the tarmac.

'Best thing ever!' Jen shouted, pumping her fist.

The cop wasn't going near her while there was a risk of getting peed on. Two hoodies climbing out of the other van started wolf-whistling but got shouted down by campaigner types telling them to stop being sexist.

Jen's toilet break earned her an immediate escort inside the station. Mercifully, the back door of the van was left open to let in fresh air as two more vanloads and a car with cuffed demonstrators in the back pulled up. But suspects were only going in two at a time and each pair took ages to process.

'Have I got two juveniles, Pack and Dewar?' a female officer in plain clothes asked as she leaned into the van.

Georgia helped Sam hobble down from the van and carefully straddled Jen's puddle of urine, before wishing good luck to Rosemary and the drunk students, who were now propped against each other, fast asleep.

The scene inside the police station was mental, with arrestees penned off in a waiting area, queuing along hallways and packed into side rooms. Besides demonstrators breaking out in chants, there were drunks, a homeless guy telling non-existent dogs to stop barking, a woman who'd had her car stolen and an old lady in her dressing gown who'd wandered off from her care home.

'I'm Jennifer, the juvenile support officer,' the woman explained, holding clear bags containing Sam and Georgia's keys, wallets and phones as she led them down a hallway to a lift. 'I'd normally do stairs, but it looks like you're hurt!'

When the lift arrived, Gerard came out, sandwiched between two mountainous officers. He was stripped to the waist and sporting a fat, bloody lip.

'Virtual high five!' Gerard said brightly, raising a set of proper metal cuffs. Then Sam got a serious look. 'Have you told Georgia not to say a word?'

'On the case, baby,' Sam laughed as Gerard got marched away.

'Oggy, oggy, oggy!' Gerard shouted to a line of cuffed demonstrators.

'Kill the pigs,' a shout came back.

'Since you're both under sixteen, special custody rules apply,' Jennifer explained as they went up. 'You're to be kept separate from adult suspects and we have to call a responsible adult to be here with you.'

On the second floor, Jennifer unlocked room *C16 Juvenile Support*. It was a stuffy, carpeted space, with an office behind the glass partition down one side. There were boxes of toys, brightly coloured armchairs and a toddler-sized drawing table.

Jennifer unlocked a metal cabinet and took out a pair of garden secateurs. 'Will you do anything silly if I take those cuffs off?'

'Does anyone ever answer yes to that question?' Sam asked sarcastically.

Rather than take Sam's bait, Jennifer snipped the cuffs around Georgia's wrists. Sam held out his arms, but Jennifer gave him a *you-wish* look before putting the shears away. She came back with two forms on a clipboard.

'OK,' she began as she sat facing the two teens. 'We're

snowed under. Since you've both been arrested for minor charges of trespass and criminal damage, all I need is your full names and addresses and the contact details for an adult who can take you home.'

Georgia had feared a night in a cell or an appearance before a judge. 'Really?'

'Really,' Jennifer said, mockingly. 'The charges and evidence will be reviewed by a prosecutor. You'll receive a phone call or letter to say what will happen within a few weeks. That could be a dismissal, an invitation to admit guilt and accept a formal police warning or a notice that we intend to press charges and take you to court.'

Jennifer looked annoyed as Sam stretched into a bored yawn.

'I'll need my mobile to look up Dad's number,' Georgia said, dreading the moment when he got the call.

They filled in forms on clipboards. Sam struggled to write with cuffs but still scrawled *I hate the fuzz* at the bottom of the page. It was childish, but Georgia smirked when she saw it.

Sam put up his hands. 'Excuse me, fascist tool of state oppression, I've finished.'

'Quite the little radical,' Jennifer scoffed, eyeballing Sam as she took the two clipboards back to her office.

'No luck with your dad,' Jennifer told Georgia a few minutes later. 'I left a message on home, work and mobile numbers. Perhaps I should call your mother?'

Sam mucking around made Georgia feel less intimidated, but mentioning her mum sent stress levels back to max.

'She's a long way away,' Georgia choked. 'It's not even ten o'clock. Dad's probably driving. He'll call back any minute.'

Georgia was relieved when the phone in the office rang,

but feared a blast as Jennifer passed her the cordless handset.

'Hey,' Georgia said, squeezing her eyes shut in fear. But her dad's voice wasn't what she'd expected.

'Cookie?' he slurred. 'You're at the police station?'

'Dad, are you drinking?' Georgia queried.

'So drunk,' John agreed. 'We lost the Metro Powerlines bid. Financial due diligence. The report said we *lack the long-term financial stability to become a partner that provides mission-critical services...*'

Georgia understood. One of her dad's biggest fears was that Metro Powerlines would like his business proposal but prefer the security of working with a bigger company.

'I'm winding it up,' John said tearfully. 'The business is kaput.'

Georgia felt tears welling in her eyes. 'Dad, I'm really sorry . . . I know you've had a crap day, but can you listen? I've messed up *really* badly and I need your help.'

Georgia heard a woman say something behind her dad. Then the phone got snatched.

'Georgia, it's me,' Auntie Michelle said. 'Phil and your father just rolled up in a taxi. They're roaring drunk. Did I hear him say you're at the police station? Have you been attacked?'

'I got arrested,' Georgia said meekly.

'They arrested him?'

'No,' Georgia said. Then broke the syllables down like she was speaking to a three-year-old, 'I have been ar-res-ted. Dad must come to the po-lice sta-ti-on.'

'Really?' Michelle asked. '*You?*'

In the background, Georgia could hear her dad slur something to Uncle Phil. Phil roared something back about everyone being bastards, then her dad sounded tearful as he shouted, 'Tell Cookie I love her. Tell her I'm sorry I've ruined everything...'

'Shut up,' Michelle snapped. 'I can't hear Georgia with you two idiots in my ear.'

Then there was a big crash as Georgia's dad fell backwards from one of Auntie Michelle's dining chairs.

TWENTY-FIVE

Orisa was always up by six to prepare breakfast. Julius listened by his bedroom door until he heard her footsteps on the stairs. Once he was certain Orisa had reached the kitchen, he stepped into the hallway and crossed to the locked door of his mother's office.

It had a simple lever lock, good for stopping people bursting in while you were getting dressed, or kids from entering rooms they weren't supposed to, but easily defeated with a nail file or sturdy paperclip. Julius had learned the knack years earlier, when Kehinde and Taiwo amused themselves by locking him in dark rooms and telling him there were ghosts inside.

The bolt snapped open after a little jiggling and he took a furtive glance up and down the hallway before slipping inside.

Bunmi was a night owl, often coming home after social functions and working for two or three hours, not rising until long after her boys had left for school. The ornate desk bore evidence of this, with empty Guinness bottles, a whisky tumbler and the desk lamp glowing.

Julius went straight behind the desk and opened the second drawer in a file cabinet. He thought his mother might have moved her stash of pre-paid SIM cards after discovering one in his old phone, but she hadn't made that link and he slid two ₦10,000 SIM packs out of a stack held together with an elastic band.

He hoped to find an old phone and charger in the drawer, but had no luck. He looked in more drawers and opened a glass-fronted cabinet, yet still didn't find anything. He wondered if he might be able to find an old phone in Gabe or the twins' rooms, but before progressing with this thought he noticed a Shoprite carrier bag tucked between the office chair and the side panel of his mother's desk.

It was the bag she'd been carrying when she came home from The Cross late on Sunday night. She'd have left the driver to deal with anything unimportant, but she'd carried this bag herself and taken time to stash it in her office before going to bed.

After wheeling back the chair, Julius was delighted as he saw that the bag was filled with banknotes. Bunmi kept jewellery and money in a floor safe in her bedroom, but the money in the bag was church donations. It hadn't yet been moved to a safer place, because most of the notes had to be unravelled from the cigarette-sized tubes that people kept in their pockets for giving bribes.

Julius had already spent longer in the office than he'd meant. But money would enable him to buy a phone and other freedoms, especially if he was sent away to boarding school. He pushed his hand down the bag, and as his fingers sifted, he realised that the amounts were large. Most likely the contents of the collection box in The Cross's VIP level.

Most of the rolls comprised bundles of ₦1,000 notes. These were the highest value notes issued by the Bank of Nigeria but would still struggle to buy a cup of coffee in a cafe at the mall. To avoid carrying bricks of cash to church, larger donations had been made in US dollars. Julius noted twenties, fifties and even a tightly wound roll of hundreds. It would be quick and easy to steal the lot, but he'd be prime suspect and had no obvious place to hide a large amount.

Reasoning that his mother was busy and distracted, Julius decided he could take a fifth of the money with little chance of being detected.

He found a large padded envelope in the waste bin and started filling it with money. He picked out the roll of hundreds, but thought his mother might know about it and put it back. After plumping the bag under the desk so that it looked fuller, he headed for the door, but paused when he heard footsteps.

Nerves made him fear his mother, but she moved with the back of her sandals slapping her heels. This was the muscular gait of one of the twins. Probably Kehinde, who'd start his day with a splash in the pool if he woke early enough.

It was still before seven when Julius got back to his room. He felt miserable and vengeful over what had happened to Duke. But it was the sense of powerlessness that had quashed his spirit. He felt stronger after standing up to his mother to a point where she'd almost seemed afraid, and for stealing the SIM cards and money.

Julius locked his bathroom door and sat on the lid of his toilet, unrolling notes and counting. It added up to three hundred thousand naira and nine hundred dollars. It would be tough to get away from bodyguards and buy a phone in a shop, but someone at school was sure to have an old phone to sell. And the rest was enough for Duke to get his teeth fixed by a proper dentist – if he could find a way to get him the money.

TWENTY-SIX

Remember that time when I was fourteen and got arrested in a riot at the town hall and Dad was so drunk he puked all over Auntie Michelle's car on the way to pick me up at the police station?

They'd laugh some day, but judging by Michelle's expression when she dropped John and Georgia home at a quarter past three in the morning, it was best not mentioned in front of her for a couple of decades . . .

When Georgia woke, her world seemed broken. Once it was Mum, Dad and Sophie. Uniform ironed, breakfast on the table, Mum honking if you weren't buckled in the back seat of her Honda Jazz by eight forty. Now, Georgia was the only one awake. She checked her dad, face down on his duvet, long whistling snores and trousers bunched around the ankles.

It was already nine and it felt bizarre having nobody to make her go to school. Old Georgia wanted to scramble around and get to class in time for second lesson. New Georgia would have happily spent the day pottering about in Kermit the Frog pyjama bottoms, except she couldn't face her dad.

She could hack a telling-off, loss of pocket money, getting

grounded, or whatever. But seeing Dad all hungover and depressed about losing his company felt way worse.

Georgia didn't get many messages and didn't check her phone till she was at the kitchen table with a bowl of Crunchy Nut and News 24 showing scenes from budget demonstrations all over south-east England. There was one missed call and a voicemail. Georgia turned the TV down, so she could hear as the news ticker rolled at the bottom of the screen: *Government ministers condemn trouble – Mayor of Haringey has minor burns after being caught by exploding petrol bomb – Thirty-two arrested after shops looted in Barnet – Woolwich budget meeting disbanded after distress flare fills meeting chamber with blue smoke – Tonbridge police officer hospitalised after being hit by missiles...*

'Georgia this is your mother,' the phone crowed furiously. 'Auntie Michelle called and told me what happened. Call me back *immediately...*'

Georgia swore under her breath. Auntie Michelle calling Mum felt like a betrayal. Though, since she was fourteen and her dad was barely conscious, Georgia knew most adults would have done the same.

Then there were written messages. The oldest was a WhatsApp from Maya, *Just saw you bundled into police van. BAD GIRL! Hope you OK.*

Zac had written, *Kamila said you were arrested. SAG has good legal people. Call me when you get home.*

Then there was a short, baffling message from Rolf, who wasn't in Georgia's contacts. *It's Rolf! Will you still talk to me now you're famous?*

This message had a link at the end and Georgia's finger hesitated before she dabbed. It took her to the website for the *London Met*, a morning paper given out in London and at transport hubs in the commuter towns around it.

The headline was: *BUDGET BATTLE – Town Halls Erupt in Night of Mayhem*. Georgia was stunned to see herself in the photograph that took up the bottom two-thirds of the page. It had been taken as she jumped over the gallery rail in the wrecked council chamber, with two riot cops storming through a door behind.

She remembered feeling terrified of the drop, but the photographer had captured Georgia looking like a crazed revolutionary. She had one fist in the air, and a long lens had compressed perspective, making the riot cops far closer than they were.

The newest message was sent by Maya minutes before school started. It said *Call me when you get out of prison!* and came with another photo.

Maya stood in the middle of the picture, holding *London Met* with the photo of Georgia's leap on the front cover. Loads of kids grabbed free newspapers at the station before school. A couple of Maya's girlfriends held copies on either side, as did Rolf's year-twelve mates behind. Rolf must have taken the photo, and Maya's little brother Kieran had got in, squatting by the girls' feet with a copy in each hand.

Georgia's appetite had been replaced by a gaping mouth and a cannonball in her gut.

In shock, she blinked and saw bright lights and floaters in her field of vision. She felt like she was going to fall off her chair and grasped the pine table as she imagined walking around school with everyone staring. She felt like burrowing under her duvet and never coming out, and might have done so if she hadn't heard the toilet flush upstairs.

John was stirring and Georgia felt less like facing him than ever . . .

'Cookie, are you home? Did you go to school?' John queried from the top of the stairs.

Georgia needed a PE kit for Tuesday afternoon, but rather than go up to get it, she grabbed her bag, patted her blazer pocket for keys and bus pass, then crept out of the back door and round the side of the house.

It was twenty to ten when her bus arrived. Georgia was relieved to find she was the only person on the upper deck, then horrified to see the floor and seats littered with abandoned copies of London Met, with her fist-pumping leap on the cover.

At first, the thought of touching a newspaper made Georgia shudder. But when she did lean over and pick one off the seat in front, she saw it for the first time without the shock factor. It felt like another person, but at least it was a cool person. Nicely fitting jeans, green eyes, trails of flying hair and a distinctive button nose that gave an air of mischief.

Georgia decided the shot must have been taken by a photographer crouching in the rows of chairs on the opposite side of the gallery. They had probably snapped dozens of people jumping, but picked Georgia because she was beautiful and the timing with the riot cops had been perfect. She thought about all the creepy men in suits, looking at her face on the trains into London, but still walked around the bus, gathering three copies in good condition and dropping them inside her backpack.

'No need to ask where you've been,' Miss Stockwell said curtly when she arrived at school.

The main gate got locked when school started, and the deputy head stood behind a barred side gate. Dressed in a tweed skirt and a blouse with sausage dogs chasing beachballs, she wrote down Georgia's name and form, then glanced up and down her uniform.

'Are those canvas?' Miss Stockwell asked.

Georgia sighed as she lifted a scruffy black pump. 'Half the school wears these,' she said.

'You can wear those for gym, but school shoes must be waterproof,' Miss Stockwell said. 'Do you have a letter of excuse for your lateness?'

'No.' Georgia sighed again, wishing she'd stayed home as two year-eight girls arrived behind and started whispering.

'Can we have your autograph?' one asked sarcastically.

'You two are in enough trouble!' Miss Stockwell snapped at the year-eights. Then back at Georgia. 'That's a thirty-minute detention for lateness and a strike for uniform infraction. If you get a second strike before the end of the year, you'll get another detention.'

Georgia's phone started ringing as she headed into the school's main lobby. It was supposed to be on silent, but luckily Miss Stockwell was out of earshot. She pulled the phone, fearing *Mum* or *Dad*. Seeing *Zac* made her smile. He was the one person who'd probably make her feel better.

'I'm in school,' Georgia whispered as she dashed for cover in an alcove between two banks of lockers.

'I thought I'd be leaving a message,' Zac said. 'You met a kid called Sam last night?'

'Sure,' Georgia agreed. 'He mentioned that he knew you.'

She heard footsteps and glanced around anxiously, but it was a year-seven boy holding a sick note.

'One of Sam's mums is a woman called Wendy Dewar,' Zac explained. 'She works as a publicist, she's on the national committee of SAG and she runs the Red News Network.

She *loves* the picture on the cover of today's *Times* and she's desperate to speak to you . . .'

Georgia interrupted. 'You mean *London Met*?'

Zac laughed. 'I haven't seen *London Met*. But you're on the cover of *The Times* and *Mail*. And it's *everywhere* online.'

'My nan gets the *Mail* . . .' Georgia moaned.

'Sophie would be *so* proud of you!' Zac gushed.

'You think?' Georgia said, not convinced her big sister would approve of a window-breaking rampage . . .

'So, Sam's mum, Wendy, got in touch with me and asked for your number. I said I'd have to ask you first.'

'What does she want?'

'That photo has made you *the* face of the budget-cuts campaign. I think she wants to interview you for RNN, and try to get you interviews elsewhere to promote SAG.'

'Why interview me?' Georgia asked. 'I got carried away last night. I know dick-all about politics!'

'Wendy's really nice, but if you don't want to help the cause . . .' Zac sounded disappointed. 'She won't ask you to do anything you don't feel comfortable with.'

Georgia twisted her black pump and bit a thumbnail. 'What do you think I should do?'

'Most of us live our lives without ever impacting on anything. The photo's a fluke, but it gives you a chance to make a difference.'

'*People go through life blindly,*' Georgia said. 'That's what Sophie wrote in her suicide note . . .'

'Sophie was messed up when she was depressed,' Zac said, 'but I do agree with that.'

Georgia heard more footsteps, but this time they were heavier. She had to speak fast.

'All right, give this Wendy my number. Now I *really* have to go.'

Georgia dropped her phone into her blazer pocket as Mr Rothstein came into view. He was in his twenties. He'd taught Georgia art in years seven and eight, and while Georgia never saw the attraction, half the girls in her class crushed on him.

'Didn't see a thing,' Mr Rothstein said with a slight whiff of cigarettes as he got close.

Georgia laughed awkwardly.

'I smiled when I saw your picture on the train to work,' Mr Rothstein continued. 'I attended a protest in Golders Green last night, but it was tepid. Are you going to the big march to Parliament tomorrow?'

'I've not heard about that,' Georgia said. 'I'm probably grounded till I'm eighteen.'

Mr Rothstein laughed and nodded. 'Better not get yourself into trouble, eh? And switch that phone off.'

'Yes, sir,' Georgia said, using her obedient old-Georgia voice.

Mr Rothstein raised his right hand and they did a fist bump. And as if that wasn't weird enough, when Georgia got to French, half the class jumped up and started cheering.

TWENTY-SEVEN

When Georgia checked her phone at lunch, she had twenty-eight messages, five missed calls and two hundred new Instagram followers. She was a superstar in every lesson. Every hallway slowed by high fives and selfies, and Georgia quickly realised it was quicker to autograph the newspapers shoved in her face than to argue that she didn't want to. One cheeky year-seven even got his arm signed with a bronze Sharpie.

Georgia feared the germy contents of the spare PE kit box. Luckily, she found spare shorts in her locker and Rolf lent her one of the school's shiny red gym shirts, freshly laundered, but gigantic.

The teachers split girls into teams of five and they did twenty-minute rotations of basketball, hockey and football. Georgia preferred solo sports like running, but threw herself into the games, hoping that a sweat would take her mind off things.

Ten minutes before the end, a hockey ball flipped up and whacked Georgia on the knuckles. It wasn't bad, but she milked the injury to get an early walk to the changing room. As the rest of the girls filled the changing room with noise and BO, Georgia was already showered. And for the first time in her life, she had to screen her messages. Journalists had got her number from somewhere and she had two requests for newspaper interviews and a call from a researcher from BBC News.

There was a voice message from Georgia's nan. She had an old-person's knack for stretching a story, and as Georgia listened to a convoluted explanation of how her grandmother had seen the picture after her neighbour Joanie knocked on the kitchen door while she was upstairs doing her yoga, a fresh message from Zac popped up.

Georgia swiped down to read: *Best not to talk to any journalists. Call Wendy Dewar as soon as you get this? She's really nice and will guide you through.*

Georgia was breaking school rules by using her phone, but there was steam and bodies between herself and any teacher who stepped into the room. When she saw Wendy's number at the end of Zac's message, Georgia realised it was one of the people she'd been ignoring all day.

As Georgia pressed *call back*, a message popped up from Instagram.

Congratulations on your 1000th follower.

Georgia wondered how all these people had found her name and contact details as the call to Wendy rang in her ear.

'I was hoping you'd be willing to do some interviews later today,' Wendy explained, after hellos. 'That image of you jumping is *so* iconic. I want your voice out there, pushing the anti-budget campaign to young people who aren't involved in politics.'

Georgia cringed. 'I'm not very political.'

'That's why you're so great!' Wendy said reassuringly. 'We have dozens of stuffed shirts who can talk about the issues.

You're youth and passion. That defiant fist pump as you scrambled away from the riot cops!'

'I didn't *feel* fearless,' Georgia confessed. 'Zac said I could make a difference, but I can't see my dad letting me do this. I'm not his favourite person right now . . .'

'I spoke to your father already,' Wendy said. 'You're good to go.'

Georgia gasped. 'Pardon me?'

'I dropped into his workshop, hoping to catch him,' Wendy explained. 'He seemed subdued, but says you're old enough to make your own decisions.'

Georgia shuddered at this. Her dad wasn't perfect, but he'd always cared. From obsessing over which parent could drive her home from swimming, to paying a private dermatologist to look at the eczema she used to get behind her knee joints. Now, John had lost a wife, a business and an older daughter. A broken man who'd gone to the workshop with a hangover to tell his six employees that they were out of a job.

From wanting to avoid her dad, Georgia had a sudden urge to hunt him down for a hug. But Wendy kept rattling on in her ear.

'. . . I can pick you up as soon as you finish school. I've been trying to get you on *Hudson at Five* on the BBC News Channel, there's a few radio interviews, then I'd like to get you back to my house to record a short interview we can put on Red News Network, and we'll need to discuss your ongoing social media strategy . . .'

Georgia moved the phone away from her face to check the time. 'School ends in six minutes,' she told Wendy.

'I'm by the front gate,' Wendy answered. 'I was hoping to catch you coming out.'

'You're here!' Georgia said, backing up as a soggy towel swept by.

'It's a silver Audi A3,' Wendy explained. 'It's parked to the left of the front gate. I've also seen a photographer and a couple of journalists hovering about looking for quotes. Press are not supposed to approach you if you're under sixteen, but that doesn't always stop them.'

'Press . . .' Georgia repeated, stressed as she ran hands through damp hair. 'I've had two hours' sleep. I'm a total mess. I don't have clothes, unless I go home first.'

'Take a couple of deep breaths,' Wendy urged. 'This is my job. I can guide you through, OK?'

'OK,' Georgia said.

Georgia dug down into her bag and spent the last minutes of school brushing her hair and fixing it in a ponytail. She'd normally have met up with Maya, but she was worried about getting mobbed by journalists or more kids wanting selfies if she waited around.

She moved fast when the bell went, a heart-in-mouth skid on the puddled floor as she exited the locker room, while simultaneously texting Maya: *Gotta meet someone. Speak laters.*

Journalists would expect her to use the school's main doors, so Georgia cut down a set of fire stairs and exited through a swing door behind the year-twelve and thirteen common room. A couple of Rolf's mates said hi as Georgia cut past, up a wheelchair ramp and through a side gate.

A man outside the gate shouted from behind, 'I just dropped fifty pounds.'

Georgia's head shot around instinctively, falling into the photographer's trap.

'Beautiful, Georgia!' the photographer said, camera snapping rapidly as he closed in with a big Nikon. 'Give us another smile.'

Georgia was tempted to flip the photographer off but realised that would make a better photo. The silver Audi was parked on the yellow zigzags in front of the school gate, and the passenger door flew open.

'Hop in,' Wendy said, pressing the start button.

Georgia threw her backpack in the footwell and settled into a cream-leather racing seat.

Front tyres squealed as they pulled off, sending kids scattering. Georgia glanced back as a photographer chased the disappearing car.

'There's a baseball cap in the glovebox,' Wendy said. 'Put it on and look down until we've cleared the school traffic.'

'Why does anyone care?' Georgia said irritably. 'It's just me jumping over a brass rail.'

Wendy laughed as Georgia studied the car. She'd imagined muddy floor mats and a drab socialist at the wheel. But the car was new, with leather seats and Bang & Olufsen speakers and Wendy was also well-trimmed, in Gucci watch and pricey-looking heels.

'The fish are biting,' Wendy explained cheerfully, as she made it through a light and swung left. 'Sky wants you, the BBC wants a package about you for the main six o'clock bulletin. If we get time, we'll fit in some drive-time radio.'

'And *Hudson at Five*?' Georgia asked.

'Dumped him,' Wendy scoffed. 'His show gets a hundred thousand viewers, versus four million on the six o'clock news.'

'Can I drop home and get clothes?'

'I'd rather not,' Wendy explained. 'School uniform isn't the height of fashion, but *ordinary schoolgirl* is part of your appeal.'

Georgia knew she could say no, but while she'd hardly slept

and was worried about her dad's mental state, she also found all this exciting.

Her phone pinged three times in rapid succession as Wendy blasted down a bus lane. Georgia ignored the first two from people she didn't know, but opened the one from Maya and almost choked when she read it: *Don't forget, you have detention.*

TWENTY-EIGHT

Georgia clasped her hands together to stop them trembling. She'd seen the newsroom a thousand times, but now *she* was at the news desk with a microphone pinned to the lapel of her school blazer, wondering how many film stars and prime ministers had sat in this chair before her.

There were lights and screens around the circular set. Automated cameras swept silently on black rails. The presenter, Kirkwood Rowley, was talking to his director, getting timings and information through his earpiece, while viewers at home watched a highlight package of the previous night's violence.

Kirkwood looked to Georgia with a warm smile and said, 'Twenty seconds. Just be yourself!'

Georgia admired Kirkwood's impossibly white teeth. Her nan wanted him to win when he was on *Strictly Come Dancing*, and she found herself trying to remember the name of the famous soap actor he was married to.

Then the screens at the rear of the set turned into a huge copy of *that* picture and Kirkwood spoke in his most serious voice.

'Following last night's disturbances, Britain awoke to

newspapers and websites dominated by a striking image of a young demonstrator making a dramatic leap to escape riot police. What many of you probably didn't realise is that the protester in the photograph is just fourteen years old. Her name is Georgia Pack and I'm delighted to say she's rushed here from school to speak with us on the six o'clock news.

'Georgia, thank you for being with us. It must have been strange, waking up to see you've become the face of these protests against budget cuts.'

'A *really* odd day,' Georgia agreed, feeling like her head was in flames. 'I think I had eleven followers on Instagram yesterday. Now it's eight thousand and something.'

Kirkwood smiled. 'My understanding is you're a regular year-ten pupil and this was your first ever protest march. What made you *so* passionate about this?'

'My sister, Sophie,' Georgia said, choking up as she said the name. 'She was a junior doctor who committed suicide because she was overworked and made a tragic error. I know these budgets are for local government, not the health service, but it's the same issue: squeezing more work out of people for less money, and that has devastating consequences.'

Kirkwood hadn't been expecting an answer like this and broke from his scripted questions.

'Your sister died recently?'

'Last month,' Georgia said.

'I'm sorry to hear that,' Kirkwood said sombrely. 'But last night's protests involved a lot of disruption. Estimates put the cost of damage to vehicles and property at over ten million pounds. Much of it has to be paid from the very council budgets you are trying to save. So, aren't SAG and the other groups co-ordinating these protests going about this the wrong way?'

'I . . .' Georgia blundered. 'I'm no expert. It's a pity if things are damaged. I didn't cause any damage myself. We wanted to stop the budget meeting from taking place and I'm happy that we succeeded. Peaceful protest is great, but would I be on the six o'clock news if I'd sent an email to my MP?'

Kirkwood smiled. Georgia felt like she'd cleared a hurdle and her shoulders relaxed.

'There are going to be some protests as groups try to stop tonight's budget meetings, but I'm told the focus is switching to a larger demonstration outside the Houses of Parliament tomorrow afternoon,' Kirkwood read from his autocue. 'Many teachers, refuse workers, fire officers and other public-service employees will be walking out to join this protest. Do you think you'll be with them?'

'I haven't given it much thought,' Georgia admitted. 'It's during school time and I'm probably grounded after last night. But young people are going to be affected by these budget cuts, like everyone else. It's worth skipping a couple of lessons to stick up for something you believe in.'

'So, you would encourage your fellow pupils to walk out of school and join tomorrow's protest?'

Georgia nodded resolutely. 'Teachers are protesting, so how can they say it's wrong for pupils to do the same?'

Kirkwood looked away from Georgia and towards the camera. 'Georgia Pack, a very determined young woman, thank you for speaking to us. Now, it's over to Felicity with an update on the weather . . .'

Monitors cut to the shot from the adjacent weather studio as Kirkwood wheeled his chair over and shook Georgia's hand. At the same time, a studio assistant in slippers started unclipping the microphone on Georgia's blazer.

'Thank you for coming on,' Kirkwood told her. 'The protest at Parliament tomorrow is trending in a big way. My daughter is in year twelve and all her friends are going.'

'Really?' Georgia said, finding it ridiculous that she'd become a spokesperson for a political campaign she barely understood. 'My nan absolutely *loves* you. Would it be cheeky if I asked you to do her an autograph?'

Kirkwood seemed flattered and quickly scribbled on a yellow script note:

To Georgia's nan,
Keep an eye on that headstrong granddaughter!
Kirkwood Rowley

Wendy was waiting outside the studio's soundproof door as Kirkwood began reading the headlines.

'It's like you've been doing that your whole life!' Wendy said brightly, giving Georgia a kiss and hug before an assistant led them out of the building. 'I love the angle about Sophie! It makes you seem *so* authentic. Now we're off to Sky, and I've set you up a Twitter account . . .'

TWENTY-NINE

Tuesday third period was maths. Julius raised his hand, blurting that he'd eaten something bad and desperately needed the toilet. The teacher tutted, but Julius clutched his sides.

'Sir, I know the rules, but I *really* must go!'

Classmates divided between those jeering and saying he was faking, while others yelled *diarrhoea* and begged the teacher to ship him out before he sprayed the floor.

'Go,' the teacher snapped. 'But do not make a habit of this.'

'Sorry, sir,' Julius said, leaving his bag, because taking it would be suspicious.

He raced to his locker and grabbed another bag from inside. Then he cut into a stinking toilet block, where a slender janitor in camel-coloured overalls stood mopping. When he saw Julius, he backed into the large disabled cubicle and they spoke quietly.

'Show me the thirty thousand.'

Julius had the stack of notes folded in his school trousers. Teachers at St Gilda's earned respectable salaries, but unskilled staff were recruited from the slums behind the girls' school and thirty thousand was two weeks' wages.

The janitor gauged the amount of money by eye, before

dipping into his trouser pocket and taking out a freshly cut brass key.

'I will lose my job,' the janitor warned as he waggled the key. 'You must behave decently if you are caught?'

'I'll just say I found it,' Julius said. 'You had no problem with the shed key you got for my cousin, did you? And you know my family is powerful. There was no investigation.'

Julius then walked swiftly across soggy playing fields towards the girls' school and cut left. His exit was down a puddled path to a gate the groundskeepers used for deliveries.

The padlock was a rusty contrast to the freshly cut key and it took strength to turn the barrel. Julius stole an instinctive glance back, before stepping through the gate and reaching between metal bars to reattach the lock. The school tractor had churned the dirt track and he was wary of mosquitos as mud gobbled his school shoes.

After squelching a couple of hundred metres, the track merged with the road that Julius took every day on his way to school. It was the emptiest he'd ever seen it and he was relieved by the sight of a battered Mazda in the yellow and blue livery of a licensed Akure taxi.

The driver seemed less keen on the muddy lad striding towards his car.

'Master Julius?' he asked suspiciously. 'You cannot be in my taxi with shoes like that!'

'I have sneakers,' Julius said, patting his bag.

The driver started the meter while Julius sat on the back seat with his legs out of the door, pulling off his muddy shoes.

It was twenty minutes to Duke's apartment block. While Julius switched St Gilda's uniform for shorts and thongs, the driver blasted Cameroonian makossa music, only turning it down to deal with three checkpoints, where he paid off area boys and two sets of Transport Union officials.

'Now I must pay both sides,' the driver shouted over his music. 'Akure is a powder keg because of these shenanigans. It will go boom soon, mark my words.'

'Let's hope for peace,' Julius yelled back as they stopped close to Duke and Remi's apartment.

He tipped generously and apologised again for the muddy shoes.

'Call any time you need a ride,' the driver told him. 'You have my number. Mud wash out easy!'

Julius felt liberated, walking with no bodyguard and letting the carrier bag with his muddy school shoes swing. His appetite drew his eyes to a cart selling skewered meat, but the hope of seeing Duke was more enticing.

He was about to hit the buzzer on the lobby door when he noticed a big black suit stood in front of the doorman's desk.

Can they know I skipped school, already? Has Mum got someone tailing me?

As Julius backed up from the entrance, he noticed two more suits, and although bright sun turned the glass into a mass of reflections, one was very familiar . . . *Simeon.*

It wasn't a massive surprise. Bunmi often fired people to give them a fright, then took them back on a lower salary. But Julius doubted the men were here for him. Simeon was no fool and would have the sense to stand out of sight and position a colleague across the street to stop him getting away.

So, why are they here?

Whatever the reason, Julius cursed, acting like he'd forgotten something as he turned and backed away.

He couldn't call: Duke's phone had got smashed by Collins,

Remi's apartment didn't have a landline and he didn't know Remi's mobile number. But when he'd arrived on Duke's scooter, they'd entered via a ramp at the side of the building and wheeled the bike to a basement storage cage.

There might be a guard covering that entrance too, but Julius had come all this way and decided to chance it.

The door to the storage lockers had a numeric keypad, and while there was a buzzer, he felt certain the three goons in the lobby would have made friends with the doorman. His only choice was to sit on the kerb and hope someone else buzzed.

It was now lunchtime back at St Gilda's. Julius was almost defeated and thinking about a taxi back to school, when a contractor pulled up in a battered panel van. He buzzed the lobby and told the doorman he was delivering new bathroom fittings for Mrs Ladipo's fourth-floor apartment.

Julius generously held the door while the man trolleyed in a toilet, shower tray and washbasin. He let the door close gently so that the lock didn't click, then gave the delivery man a minute's start before chasing through. He passed the rusted storage cages, and Julius felt intense fondness when he recognised Duke's bike.

There was no obvious sign of CCTV, but Julius still feared a black suit in his path to the stairs. He prayed that Duke was home, almost tasting Duke's mouth as he bounded past the sixth-floor landing. But it was his uncle, Remi, who slid the bolts and answered the door.

'Young Julius,' Remi said, surprised and suspicious. The former newsreader wore a pressed shirt and tie, but no trousers. 'You'd better come in.'

The apartment had been crammed and messy on Julius's previous visit, but it was clear someone had rifled through.

Tossing books, throwing papers, tipping up furniture and ripping the door off the refrigerator.

'I have your mother to thank for my messy visitors,' Remi explained.

'That was nothing to do with me,' Julius said apologetically. 'What did they take?'

'They didn't steal. Just rifled through and made this mess.'

'Not even the budget papers?'

Remi smiled knowingly. 'The originals are in a safe place, and the most important pages are scanned and backed up in the cloud.'

'I'm glad,' Julius said as he peered behind the wooden partition. The floor where Duke's bed had been was a rectangle of dust and dead bugs, the bed tilted up and propped against the wall.

'He's still in hospital,' Remi said.

Julius hadn't had any news about Duke's condition and looked shocked. 'I heard he lost a couple of teeth. I didn't realise it was hospital bad.'

'Ribs smashed, internal bleeding, multiple blows to the head,' Remi said darkly, as he found his trousers over the back of a dining chair and began stepping into them.

'My god,' Julius said, eyes welling.

'The teachers told the ambulance crew that Duke had *fallen down some stairs*. When I spoke to your headmaster, he claimed Duke was beaten because he made unwanted sexual advances towards three younger boys. He all but told me Duke had got what he deserved.'

'I'm sorry,' Julius said, staring down at the mess. 'For everything, but especially my family . . . I expect my headmaster will have a fat wallet, courtesy of my mother.'

'Undoubtedly,' Remi said, smiling wryly. 'How did you pass the goons in the lobby?'

Julius only now realised the three men were here to intimidate Remi.

'Via the storage cages,' Julius explained, unzipping his backpack. 'So, how is Duke?'

'Better than before,' Remi said, upset. 'My nephew's face was a bloody pulp. He can see out of both eyes now and is eating soft things. He must leave hospital tomorrow because I can't afford it.'

'This might help a little,' Julius said, taking six hundred US dollars from the backpack. 'I took it from my mum. I had to bribe a school janitor and buy a new phone, but this is the rest. If I'd known Duke was hospitalised . . . Maybe I can help some more . . .'

Remi smiled warily as Julius put the money down on the dining table, the top bare because everything had been tipped onto the floor.

'Is this the scene where your mother has cops burst in and arrest me for handling stolen cash?' Remi asked as he reached towards the money. His tone changed when he saw the hurt on Julius's face, 'I'm sorry. I'm an old cynic.'

'I'm ashamed . . .' Julius began. 'Let me know *anything* I can do to help with your corruption investigations. Mum will send me to Army Boys Academy once a place opens up. But I'll be around in holidays and I can open the lock on my mother's office.'

Remi nodded thoughtfully as he took the money off the table. 'You can see the pressure I am under, with my home smashed and goons following my every step. You seem like a decent young man, and your support is appreciated.'

'I try,' Julius said. 'Since Duke isn't here, I'll head back to school. If I sneak into the grounds before lunchtime's over, there's a chance they won't miss me. Can I give you my new mobile number, to pass along to Duke?'

Remi saw a pen on the floor and gave it to Julius.

'Duke doesn't have a new phone, so I'll give you my details. He asks if I've heard from you every time I visit the hospital, so I'm certain he'll send a message once he gets your number.'

THIRTY

Georgia's phone was a hot potato. Nine hundred friend requests. Two hundred thousand new followers. Retweeted by politicians and celebrities. Twenty news organisations wanted interviews and a sphere filled with fancy chocolates had arrived from London's trendiest modelling agency. The handwritten message: *Let's work together!*

Sleep wasn't happening. Georgia woke at quarter to five on Wednesday morning, peeking out at journalists and a TV crew whose cars were parked to prevent easy escape. It felt oppressive, but at least the lonely widow next door had enjoyed herself, handing out tea and rock cakes and getting herself on Channel Four news, saying that Georgia was *a nice girl who'd helped plant her spring bulbs when her knees got bad.*

Georgia was surprised to see the kitchen light shining into the hallway as she came downstairs. John was at the dining table, dressed in T-shirt and trackie bottoms as he worked a spreadsheet on his laptop.

'Nobody sleeps in this house,' Georgia noted drily.

'Trying to do the decent thing,' John explained, rubbing a tired eye. 'If I juggle money around and sell off some equipment, I can hopefully give Tracy and the guys six weeks' wages . . .'

Georgia stood behind her dad.

'You need a shave, prickly boy,' she said as she opened the fridge. 'Too early for a bacon sandwich?'

'Never,' John smiled.

Georgia flicked the grill on to heat up, speared a packet with a sharp knife and started laying out rashers.

John hadn't yelled at Georgia for getting arrested. He hadn't grounded her or stopped pocket money. He'd let her do heaps of interviews and proudly told Georgia how great she'd been on BBC News. But while it made Georgia's life easier, part of her craved the properly strict dad of old.

'I googled that modelling agency,' John said. 'They're the real deal . . .'

Georgia laughed. 'From anti-government rebel to skincare ads in one week. I'd be the fastest sell-out in the west . . .'

John shrugged weakly. 'You'd make money, and there won't be much going spare if I'm out of work . . .'

'There must be a job in the drone business,' Georgia encouraged. 'You know *everyone*.'

Georgia felt shock as her dad dabbed a tear from his eye. It wasn't the first time she'd seen him cry, but this felt more desperate, because it was about his own failure, not Sophie, or Mum, or Uncle Phil's cancer scare . . .

'It'll work out,' Georgia said, standing behind her dad and giving him a kiss on the cheek. 'You're smart. It's all just a bit shit at the moment.'

As Georgia ate bacon sandwiches, polished off homework, showered and dressed for school, the TV and press gaggle grew to more than twenty. She couldn't face the news and kept her phone on silent. Her dad was in the shower when Wendy sent a message to say she'd be arriving in ten minutes.

Georgia watched the Audi pass the house and ran downstairs as Wendy used the turning circle at the end of the cul-de-sac to change direction. She grabbed her schoolbag and felt like she'd flipped into an alternate dimension when she opened the front door to shouts and chaos.

'Georgia, give us a wave!' a photographer shouted.

'Good morning, everyone,' Georgia said politely as she rubbed her arms. 'Turned chilly again, hasn't it!'

She moved swiftly down the front drive as microphones waggled in her face.

'Georgia, will you be walking out of school today?'

A woman stepped in front of her. 'Georgia, your headmaster says any pupils who skip school to attend today's protests will face serious consequences. Do you have a message for your headmaster?'

'Georgia, you're live on Sky News. Will you be attending the protest in London this afternoon? Has Daddy written an excuse note?'

More microphones swooped as Georgia was forced to stop walking. She took a deep breath, staying calm as Wendy said she must.

'I wish the organisers of today's protest every success,' Georgia stated. 'If young people wish to attend, I fully support them, if they behave respectfully and stay safe.'

'But will *you* attend the protest?' the man from Sky asked.

Georgia teased, as if she was about to nod, then said, 'No comment.'

'Has your father written an excuse note?' the same guy repeated.

'He has not,' Georgia said, pushing through the bodies. 'Now, I have to get to school.'

Georgia broke through the journalists and hopped in the front passenger seat of the Audi. Wendy gave a double honk to make sure nobody got in the way. When Georgia glanced behind, she was surprised to see Sam in the back in school uniform.

'Mental,' Sam said cheerfully, sticking his head between the front seats. 'You OK?'

'Never a dull moment,' Georgia said as she got a wave from a primary-school kid who always rode his bike up and down the street.

'There's deffo gonna be a walkout at my school,' Sam said proudly. 'My cousin goes to some poncy grammar and even *they're* all talking about leaving.'

'Have you decided?' Wendy asked Georgia. 'As your publicist, it makes my life easier if I know what you're doing.'

'You can't chicken out,' Sam added. 'You're the main man.'

'Sam, that terminology is *very* sexist,' Wendy rebuked, but her eyes kept pressuring Georgia.

'I didn't ask to be a leader of anything,' Georgia said irritably. 'If kids at my school walk out, I'll join them. I'll see what the vibe is at lunchtime.'

They were super early, so they drove out to Sam's school first. Kids reached in to shake Georgia's hand when they recognised her and a few even did selfies.

Georgia's nerves grew as she neared her school. To ensure maximum publicity, Wendy had tipped off the press about taking her time and dropping off Sam. This gave the media scrum at the house time to reposition for Georgia's arrival at school.

Besides journalists, there were fifty kids milling around outside the school and a muted cheer went up as Georgia got out of the car. A news channel was broadcasting her arrival live. Georgia could hear the correspondent talking to camera as she went through the school gates.

'. . . Pack is a young woman thrown right into the heart of this protest movement. The big question remains: how many school pupils will join today's protest? Organisers predict it will be the biggest political demonstration in Central London since protests against the Iraq War in 2003, when over a million – including thousands of secondary-school pupils – joined in . . .'

Kids gawped as Georgia got through the school gate, then scattered as Miss Stockwell charged to Georgia, accompanied by a meaty boys' PE teacher.

'My office, right now,' Miss Stockwell snapped.

Georgia felt like a prisoner, sandwiched between Stockwell and the PE teacher as she got marched through the school lobby and into a small office next to the staffroom.

'Sit,' the PE teacher barked.

'What have I done?' Georgia asked, sitting in a plastic chair.

'There are one thousand children in this school,' Stockwell began. 'The youngest are only eleven, and it is my duty as senior staff to ensure the health and safety of every one of them. Is that clear?'

'Crystal,' Georgia said, close to sarcasm.

People who taught Georgia hadn't bought into her media image as a scary rebel. But senior staff like Miss Stockwell didn't know her and were feeling pressure from parents, media and school governors.

'After some discussion with the headmaster over whether to put you in isolation, we have decided to let you join normal lessons today. However, if you take part in *any* disruptive activity, you will be placed in isolation outside my office.'

Georgia rolled her eyes.

'I don't like your attitude, young lady,' the giant PE teacher snapped, loud enough to make Georgia jump.

'If today doesn't go well, we'll need to discuss whether you have a future at this school,' Miss Stockwell added.

Georgia saw through the scare tactics. The year-eight who set fire to the Christmas panto set didn't get kicked out, and Georgia was a straight-A student who'd had one detention in four years.

'Can I go now?' she asked.

Miss Stockwell did a big theatrical thing of opening the office door and guiding Georgia out.

As Georgia made it back to the lobby, she saw a group of year-twelve boys with a big cloth banner made with two broomsticks and a white bedsheet.

No Budget, No Cuts was scrawled across in black shoe polish.

THIRTY-ONE

Julius was dressed for school. He sat on the floor propped against his bed, speaking quietly to Duke on the secret phone he'd bought off a kid in his Nigerian Lit class.

'What time did you get out of the hospital?' Julius asked quietly.

'Early morning,' Duke said. 'I was supposed to leave last night, but we had to wait for my prescription from the hospital pharmacy. Remi couldn't get a taxi. The Transport Union and area boys are causing such grief that taxi drivers are staying home.'

'Are you comfortable?'

'Pain meds make me queasy all the time. Breathing is OK, but if I cough, or sneeze, it feels like I'm gonna pass out.'

'I didn't get caught sneaking out of school yesterday,' Julius told Duke. 'It's too risky sneaking off two days running, but I have the key. I might try tomorrow, or Friday.'

'Remi has business in Lagos this weekend. My mother is coming to look after me,' Duke said.

'Is your mum cool?' Julius asked.

'For sure,' Duke said. 'But it's a small apartment. Once

211

she's around we won't have privacy.'

'I'll try tomorrow, but I'm riding my luck,' Julius said.

'I'm worth the risk though?' Duke asked.

'Always,' Julius laughed. 'I'd better go, before Orisa comes chasing.'

'OK. It has been . . .' Duke paused.

Julius heard a deep thud through the phone, before a duller version of the same flexed the glass in his bedroom window.

'What was that?' Julius asked.

'This whole building shook!' Duke said, alarmed. 'Something just went bang in a big way . . .'

Julius crawled across to his window and peeked out front. Jimoh – the bodyguard who was about to drive him to school – and the two soldiers on the front gate were having an animated conversation about what they'd heard.

'I heard it here, eight kilometres from you,' Julius told Duke.

'Can't be a good thing . . .' Duke said.

'Julius,' Orisa shouted from the bottom of the stairs. 'Everyone is ready to leave.'

'Got my marching orders,' Julius told Duke as he grabbed his backpack and school blazer. 'Speak later.'

'Give the fine folks of St Gilda's my love,' Duke joked.

As he ran downstairs, Julius wondered if he'd dare sneak out of school today. It would be tricky, because third period science had most of the kids who'd been around for his escape from maths the day before. But the look on Duke's face would be amazing . . .

Julius was startled to see his mother at the bottom of the stairs, not just awake, but dressed, made up and on the telephone.

'I heard it from here!' she was telling the person on the

other end. 'I expect accurate updates as this develops . . .'

Kehinde grabbed the front seat of the black S-Class Mercedes. Taiwo and Julius sandwiched Gabe in the back. Julius had pocketed his illicit phone hurriedly and was alarmed to see a corner protruding from the pocket of his shorts as he settled into soft Mercedes leather. He waited for Gabe to look the other way before pressing it out of sight.

Kehinde's phone pinged with a message as the soldiers opened the front gate. He whooped exuberantly as he spun round and looked at Taiwo behind. 'Collins says there's been a huge bomb at the Transport Union Office. Governor's mansion is on lockdown as a security precaution. He can't get to school.'

'Lucky him,' Gabe noted.

Julius felt left out as Gabe and Taiwo scoured their phones for info.

Jimoh asked the car to play Sunshine Star, a local radio station fuelled by phone-ins and trashy news.

'*I was in the transit park waiting for my ride and the shaking almost knocked me off my feet,*' a caller with a crackly line and background chaos was saying. '*The Transport Union offices have been annihilated. There are pieces of dead people scattered around. Because of God's blessing, I was under a metal shade that saved me from the rubble and blast.*'

'*How many do you think are killed?*' the DJ asked.

'*Many, many! Injured, all around me. Dead, I do not count, but there is multiple for sure.*'

'*For those of us trying to get to work, what is the situation with city buses?*'

'*Nothing in, nothing out,*' the caller explained. '*Transit Park West is sealed off by union officials. I am trapped inside. Many,*

many guns. Only the injured are being allowed to go.'

'What about police?'

'I hear sirens. Plenty of ambulance, but no police. No local police, or state police.'

Julius understood the significance of this. Area boys and cops were loyal to his family, while the Transport Union had switched to supporting former governor Rotimi. The bomb was another aggressive move by the area boys in their turf war with the Transport Union, and police inaction showed whose side they were on.

Another caller began speaking on radio. *'I believe there was an early-morning meeting of union officials when this bomb exploded.'*

'What makes you say that?' the DJ asked.

'My boyfriend's apartment overlooks the rear of Transport Union Headquarters. Every Wednesday morning there are always the big-man cars parked in the street behind the office for this early meeting. Lexus, Mercedes, Bentley. I can see them all from my window as I speak and they are blasted to bits...'

As this well-spoken voice came from the Mercedes's speakers, Taiwo reached around with his iPhone to show a photo someone had posted on Twitter. It was taken from across the muddy transit park and showed rows of long-distance buses, local buses and taxis, like on any other morning. But the five-storey Transport Union building on the far side had caved, its buckled steel frame looming over a mound of concrete and shattered glazing units

Taiwo laughed, slapping one knee. 'This will teach the Rotimi-loving scum to betray us!'

Gabe looked excited as he craned his neck to see the image. Julius was thinking how his mum had been up and dressed, almost as if she'd been expecting something . . .

'Rotimi's youngest son is in my class,' Gabe said, smiling. 'Last week he was all like, *The area boys making a move is desperation. Everyone knows Adebisi can't win a third term.* Now I'm gonna be like, *Where's your Transport Union buddies now, bitch?*'

While his brothers gloated, Julius considered death and carnage, but also more selfish thoughts. The city was going to erupt and there would be no way to get to Duke.

'How dumb are they?' Kehinde asked. 'Gathering for a meeting at the same time and place, every Wednesday.'

'Asking for trouble,' Taiwo agreed.

Unable to show his secret phone, Julius had to listen to more callers on the radio. Gabe turned his screen away, so Julius couldn't the see messages he was bouncing to his friends.

'Kids in my class are getting off school now,' Gabe told the car bitterly. 'Adam lives in town and he says there's fights and windows getting smashed.'

Kehinde looked at Jimoh. 'Shall I call our mum and check what she wants?'

Jimoh was an enormous barrel-chested man, who'd been guarding the Adebisi family for as long as Julius could remember.

'Call her if you wish,' he said brightly. 'But your mother usually knows what's going on before it happens, so don't bet on your chances of getting out of school.'

'That's truth,' Kehinde agreed with a laugh. 'I'll give it a shot though . . .'

There was an angry caller on the radio as they turned off the beltway at their usual exit.

'*All this power struggle makes me sick!*' she railed. '*Adebisi,*

215

Rotimi, who cares? Do they *starve? Do* they *shed blood on the city streets? One tapestry in the new governor's mansion costs more than I will earn in ten lifetimes . . .'*

'Can't get through to Mum's mobile, or the house,' Kehinde told Jimoh.

'Telephone lines are probably overwhelmed with this chaos,' Jimoh suggested, then smiled. 'But there are no buses or taxis. We're making record time!'

Julius peered out as they passed a spot that had been a Transport Union toll point since they'd lost control of the markets. But the tarps the union officer hid under when it rained had been burned black and instead of union officials collecting tolls, there were three police officers in full riot gear, peering through car windows as they waved people by.

'Transport Union is getting wiped,' Taiwo noted cheerfully. 'What a morning!'

Kehinde laughed and punched the Mercedes roof lining. 'Adebisi power!'

'Adebisi, Adebisi!' Gabe chanted, copying the punch.

Julius felt less triumphant. First, he doubted the Transport Union and the Rotimi family would roll over. This was the beginning of something, not the end. And the twins' machismo reminded him of what they'd done to Duke and how much he hated them for it.

Roads and pavements were eerily quiet as they skirted the centre of town. Gabe scrambled over Julius's lap to get a look at a badly beaten man on the kerb. His shirt was dark red with a stab wound and his leg broken in all directions.

Gabe had a sensitive side, but acted the thug when the twins were around. 'So grim,' Gabe said, as he snapped pictures on his phone.

'Why must this idiot park here?' Jimoh said furiously when they stopped at a three-way intersection.

The offence was caused by a tatty Nissan truck, its open rear deck piled with scaffold poles. The wheels on one side were parked up on the kerb, and the hazard lights were flashing.

'Ridiculous,' Jimoh railed. 'If he parked five metres along, the intersection would be clear.'

Jimoh drummed the steering wheel while two cars passed the other way. The giant driver figured it was his turn to pull out and pass the parked truck, but he had to slam the brakes as a car failed to give way and blocked him off.

'You can see I'm coming through!' Jimoh shouted, blasting his horn and gesturing at the other driver to reverse.

The driver of the car facing them looked angry, honking back and making gestures for Jimoh to do the backing up. While his driver focused on this, Julius's eye caught a large truck, making too much noise as it came up the side street.

It reared up onto a kerb, getting faster when it ought to be slowing down. Julius shielded his face. Gabe also saw what was coming and dived sideways into his brother's lap.

Julius realised at once that this was a planned attack. It wasn't just Transport Union leaders who were in the same place at the same time of day. The scaffold truck acted as a backstop when the speeding truck drove straight into the twins' side of the car.

The big Mercedes scraped sideways, two wheels lifting off the ground. Julius's neck snapped one way, but it was caught by a firework bang as airbags exploded on all sides. Gabe screamed as the truck that had hit them backed away. A man had jumped from the car that stopped them getting through. He aimed an automatic rifle at Jimoh and ordered him not to move.

Jimoh floored the accelerator, hoping to reverse. But the engine was programmed to shut down after an impact. The powdery explosive residue from the airbags fizzed up Julius's nose and his door wouldn't open because it was pinned to the scaffold truck.

'Out of the car!' men with guns shouted from outside. 'No funny business!'

Kehinde and Taiwo had got the worst of the crash. When the gunmen realised they were too dazed to get out, two rushed to the side of the Mercedes and grabbed the doors. At the front, Kehinde's door came open and a man started dragging him out.

'You listen, listen! Do as you are told!'

But brute force wasn't enough to untangle Kehinde from popped airbags and a fastened seat belt.

The rear door next to Taiwo had a damaged lock and the second guy was using all his strength to get the door open. This gave Taiwo time to reach behind Gabe, delving into the little storage compartment in the armrest and pulling a Glock pistol.

'Don't,' Julius shouted, instinctively folding himself over Gabe. 'We're surrounded!'

But while the plan to stop the car had been thought through, the attackers hadn't considered difficulties extracting occupants from a car with damaged doors.

Taiwo had a point-blank shot at the man trying to drag his twin out of the front passenger seat. As his head exploded, the gun blast added more smoke and a sound that left Julius's ears with a ringing sound that swamped everything else.

Outside, the guy trying to force Taiwo's door open stumbled back at the bang, while the one up front with the machine gun opened fire. Bullets smashed the windscreen and pelted the front of the car. Taiwo got his damaged door open, using the lever on the inside.

As Taiwo came out shooting, Jimoh grabbed a gun holstered inside his jacket and began shooting through the shattered windscreen.

Julius was deaf. His eyes streamed and he couldn't understand why none of the bullets spraying the front of the car had hit him. He dived to the floor, then felt Gabe's shoe on his balls. The ten-year-old was trying to force the sliding roof open, but Julius saw his own way out now Taiwo and some of the smoke had cleared.

He shoved Gabe, then scrambled over dead airbags towards the open rear door. Taiwo had made it out of the car. He'd caught a bullet or three in his torso, but not before fatally shooting both men who'd rushed to open the side doors.

Jimoh was sprawled across the front passenger seats, most likely dead. There was no sign of Kehinde or the guy who'd been at the front of the car. As Julius crawled out, he felt sure there would be more than three men involved in such an elaborately planned attack.

Maybe they'd run scared when gunshots came back out of the car, or maybe they were crouched around a corner, or behind the scaffold truck, ready to blast the instant they had a clear shot.

Terrified, Julius slid carefully along the rear seat until his head poked out, peering backwards and under the open door to see if anyone was around. He caught a vile smell coming from the front, where a bullet had ruptured Jimoh's bowel.

The only obvious movement outside was a civilian car, whose driver was making a frantic three-point turn to escape. Julius saw that the two assailants who'd been shot by Taiwo wore police uniforms, but the clothes fitted poorly and a lack of radios, cuffs or other cop equipment made him sure they were fakes.

Julius sighted Taiwo's Glock and picked it off the ground as he scrambled out. He'd not handled a gun in a year, but he'd been on an anti-kidnapping course and he remembered the basics.

After checking the clip and seeing four rounds, he made sure the safety was off and the barrel clear.

The street ahead was blocked by the car and the truck that had rammed them. Julius thought he could see movement on the far side. But deafness and poor sightlines meant it could be anything from concerned bystanders to Transport Union goons who wanted to finish him off.

Just before he ran, Julius remembered his little brother. Gabe had stopped fighting the sun roof and now squatted in the footwell, looking petrified. A bullet had blown a hole in the back of the driver's seat and Julius remained astonished that nothing had hit him.

'Come on, pal,' Julius said.

Both boys had been deafened by the guns going off inside the car and Gabe didn't respond until Julius tugged his school shirt.

'I think all three guys are dead,' Julius said as he yanked Gabe over the rear seat, then grabbed a spare ammunition clip from the armrest. 'But there could be back-up. I know you're scared, but we have to move.'

THIRTY-TWO

Julius's hearing started coming back, but something was affecting his balance. Usually cocky and full of himself, Gabe had shocked eyes and a clammy skin as his older brother marched him down a narrow alleyway by his hand

'Where are we going?' Gabe asked. 'I've got my phone – we should stop and call Mum.'

'We'll clear out first.'

It was the oldest part of the city. Rusty satellite dishes and sewage trickling along the gutter. The apartment buildings were old. Crude breeze-block extensions added two or three storeys to the original structures, blotting all but the most persistent sunlight.

Julius eyed the strands of laundry hung over and between balconies and stopped suddenly when he saw what he wanted.

'Piggyback,' Julius told Gabe, as he pointed up. 'Grab shirts and shorts, the big and small.'

Gabe looked baffled. 'Why?'

'You see anyone else in St Gilda's uniform around here?'

The washing was out of reach, unless you were an exception-ally tall boy balancing a surprisingly heavy ten-year-old brother on your shoulders. Gabe ripped down boys' and men's shorts, a Pokémon singlet and a fake Manchester City football shirt. As this happened, Julius spotted a bloody lump just below Gabe's knee. Wounded skin blistered over a shard of Mercedes cabin trim, but Gabe was so shocked he'd not mentioned pain.

After lowering Gabe and glancing at the balconies to make sure they hadn't been spotted, the brothers raced another hundred metres. They crossed a stretch of lightly trafficked highway that should have been gridlocked at this time of morning. Then Julius led the way down a muddy embankment behind an aluminium-sided warehouse building.

The parking lot was empty. After sploshing through a couple of deep puddles, Julius placed his gun down on the concrete. He loosened his tie and top shirt button, grabbed a handful of his undershirt and pulled everything off in a single movement.

As Gabe did the same, Julius took phone, wallet and rolled-up bills from his grey St Gilda's shorts and put them next to the gun.

'You've got another phone!' Gabe gasped as Julius pulled up his stolen shorts.

The shorts belonged to someone with a hell of a gut and Julius had to yank and knot a great length of drawstring to keep them up.

'Is my phone all you care about?' Julius said furiously. 'They shot at us. Taiwo's probably dead. I'm trying to get away and you're on about snitching on me again . . .'

'No,' Gabe said, looking wounded. 'I just . . .'

'I wish you'd grow up,' Julius told Gabe angrily, peeling off shoes and socks as Gabe pulled up his stolen shorts.

'It's nasty around here,' Gabe said, looking at Julius's bare feet.

'Not as nasty as a bullet through your head when they spot the rich brat's shiny school shoes. If we pass a store, I'll buy us sandals.'

'Shall I call Mum?'

Julius didn't answer straight away. After checking all the pockets, he pushed his and Gabe's shoes and uniform inside his still-buttoned shirt, then tied it in a ball using the sleeves and flung the whole lot onto the warehouse's flat roof.

'Now they won't know we've been here,' Julius said, feeling parking-lot grit dig into his feet and realising his soles had softened since childhood days, running barefoot with his country cousins. 'I just have a cheap calls-only SIM – do you have data on your phone?'

'Of course,' Gabe said as Julius dropped the spare clip in his pocket and tried getting the gun to sit in the elastic waistband of his new shorts.

'Use maps and get our location,' Julius said. 'No point calling unless we know where we are.'

'Right,' Gabe said, then he gave Julius a pleading look. 'Was Taiwo dead?'

'I don't know,' Julius said, then shocked himself by thinking, *I hope so . . .*

Three heavily built guys were crossing the road towards the embankment. Julius eyed them, one hand on the gun.

'Down here,' Julius ordered, keeping his back to the metal wall as he led Gabe into an alley between the warehouse and its identical neighbour. 'Is your GPS working?'

'We're here, where these two roads meet,' Gabe said, more his normal self as he let Julius see the map on screen.

'Try Orisa first,' Julius said. 'Mum's phone is likely to be busy.'

223

A battered minibus with construction equipment on the roof stopped at the top of the embankment. To Julius's relief, the three men ducked through its rear doors before setting off with plumes of grey exhaust.

Gabe was close enough for Julius to hear the calls flake out.

'I tried Mum *and* Orisa, but it says no network.'

'It gets overloaded in the city centre when something big happens and everyone tries to use their phone at once,' Julius explained, remembering the same thing happening during the violence at the precinct. 'We'll try every few minutes until we get through. Give me the phone. Let's see what's around here.'

Julius opened Maps on Gabe's phone. They were on a street he didn't know, but it appeared to be a major road radiating east from the city centre. Home was seven kilometres south, either through Akure's outer slum districts or by taking your life in your hands and walking beside speeding traffic on the beltway. The Cross was three kilometres east. The route had no obvious dangers, but would anyone be there at nine on a weekday?

But while Julius studied the map, he'd subconsciously known where he was going all along. Crossing the city centre from south to north meant going through the precinct and other dangerous areas at the heart of the battle between area boys and Transport Union. But even with Gabe limping, he could be with Duke in half an hour . . .

THIRTY-THREE

If Georgia got told off when she was a toddler, she'd sulk by wrapping her arms around her head and pretending to be invisible. She wished she had the same power now. Every wary glance from a teacher. The *Oh-my-god-it's-her* stares when she came out of a stall in the bathroom. Shouts in the corridor. Every single person in History class acting like a gun went off when she grated her chair.

'I'm not starting the revolution – I just dropped my pencil case,' she told them.

Maya saw the strain on Georgia at morning break. Instead of going to the canteen with Rolf and his loud mates, they sat under a slatted staircase, sharing a Yorkie bar.

'I honestly don't care what happens,' Georgia said. 'I want this over, so I can go back to being boring.'

'Or become a celebrity model . . .' Maya noted.

'Not in a million,' Georgia said, slowly shaking her head.

Georgia watched the nervous approach of two year-seven boys, neither of whom had experienced the growth spurt their parents expected when they bought oversized uniforms at the start of the school year.

'What?' Maya grunted, making them more scared.

'Just...' the one with sticking-out ears began. 'We wondered if you knew how long the demonstration will last?'

Maya smirked. 'You guys want to go? What are you, eight years old?'

Georgia was more sympathetic. 'Guys, I don't mean to be rude, but you're quite little. There might be scuffles with the cops and London's a long way. You could get lost...'

Sticking-out-ears looked like he was about to burst into tears and Georgia put her head in her hands as the lads retreated up the stairs.

'If some kid gets hit by a car, or abducted by paedos, I bet I'll cop the blame,' Georgia said sourly.

Maya gave her arm a squeeze. 'Don't worry. I'll visit you in prison.'

Georgia laughed. 'That's what I want to hear...'

The pips went for third lesson, but as Maya and Georgia clambered out of their spot under the stairs, Miss Stockwell came over the school PA system.

'*Will all pupils please stand quietly and listen for special instructions. All lower-school pupils please go immediately to the main hall for a special assembly. Years ten and eleven, please go to the sports hall. Years twelve and thirteen to their common room.*

'*I repeat, all pupils must now go to a special assembly. Pupils in lower-school...*'

Georgia had more eyes on her than ever as they crossed the school to the sports hall. The senior staff had planned it so that all the scariest teachers were putting on a show, barking orders to line up, shut up and sit straight.

Nobody had put chairs out and the year elevens and twelves

were rebelling against being made to sit cross-legged on the floor.

'You'll be treated like grown-ups when you can be trusted to behave like grown-ups,' a teacher yelled.

'No budget, no cuts!' a bunch of kids started chanting.

Four teachers stormed through to surround the group and make them stop. Georgia made sure she was close to a couple of teachers she knew well so that nobody could accuse her of being a ringleader.

The head of year eleven made a popular shaggy-haired lad called Enoch stand up for shouting and tried to make an example of him.

'Detention, three days!' he roared. 'Now stand outside!'

Enoch got huge cheers as he walked out backwards, bowing and making peace signs. There were several more minutes of chaos and three girls were ejected before things settled down enough for Headmaster Byrne to emerge from the PE equipment room.

The head's arrival was another scare tactic, but it got ruined by a boy shouting, 'Mr Byrne's come out of the closet!'

'We love you, Mr Byrne,' another group of girls shouted, getting a big laugh.

'Good morning,' Mr Byrne began, looking rattled. 'I have been headmaster of this school for eleven years, and this is the only time I have *ever* had to call every single pupil out of lessons for a special assembly. My deputies will be talking to other year groups, but I am speaking to you, because I believe the core troublemakers are in this room.'

Georgia stared at her toes as five hundred eyes turned on her.

'If you leave school, for a political protest or any other reason, there will be severe consequences. I have asked the police to place officers outside the school and arrest anyone who tries to leave. Furthermore, if there is significant disruption today, I will cancel proms, dances, the end-of-year field trips and activities for the *entire* school.'

Mr Byrne looked pleased with himself as a *that's-not-fair* groan crossed the room.

'That includes the year-eleven prom, for which I know many of you have already purchased dresses and made other preparations.'

Everyone was looking at Georgia again, including a lot of scowls from the kind of girls who were *really* into prom.

'Don't stare at me,' Georgia blurted, almost shocked to hear her voice shooting across the sports hall. 'I'm not in charge of anything.'

Maya saw Georgia was upset and got stuck in. 'Comrades!' she began powerfully. 'Georgia's sister died because of cuts like this! Does it really matter if you don't get to dress up and go to some lame school dance?'

A pair of teachers swooped towards Maya, but she was making her own way towards the fire doors at the back of the room.

'Hands off,' Maya told teachers as kids sitting on the floor made way. 'Anyone touches me, I'll lay you out!'

Close to three hundred kids were laughing as Maya booted open the fire doors, setting off an alarm.

'Years ten and eleven, this is not acceptable!' Mr Byrne roared.

Only the first few rows could hear his voice over the alarm, and the kids were riled up, debating the merits of prom vs protest.

'It doesn't matter for you because you get your leavers' prom *next* year,' a year-eleven girl near to Georgia was telling a bunch of younger girls. 'My mum's been paying for my dress in instalments ...'

As the noise swelled, the senior teachers up front didn't seem sure what to do. The threat had made an impression, but the emergency assembly hadn't struck fear into the kids the way they'd hoped and Maya setting off the exit alarm made it difficult to assert control.

'No cuts, no budget!' more kids than ever chanted, but at the same time a group had worked themselves into hysterics over the idea that prom might get cancelled.

Finally, a PE teacher found the key to shut off the exit alarm and heads of year ten and eleven decided the only option was to send the kids back to class and deal with them in smaller groups.

'In an orderly fashion,' they emphasised.

Georgia wondered where Maya had gone as she crossed school grounds to third period chemistry.

It seemed assemblies with the other year groups hadn't gone the way the staff hoped either. Year-nine boys were racing down hallways, banging lockers and chanting, 'Riot, riot, lunchtime riot!'

When Georgia bumped into a couple of Rolf's mates, they were fuming because they'd been told year-twelve and thirteen kids would have to stay in school at lunchtime.

The whole building had an edgy vibe. Teachers knew they were close to losing control as kids meandered back to lessons and piled into the toilets. More than half of third period was gone by the time Georgia got into her chemistry classroom, and there were still doors banging and teachers in the hallway, yelling at kids to get inside classrooms.

Two goth boys who always sat opposite Georgia in chemistry gave her a smile as she settled on her stool.

'There's twenty kids for every teacher,' one goth told his pal. 'They're not cops; they don't have weapons. They're not even allowed to *touch* us. If school kicks off when the lunchtime bell goes, what can they *actually* do?'

THIRTY-FOUR

Akure's Old Town was eerie. Wind ripped across the precinct, a sound usually blotted by motorbikes, horns and haggling stallholders. Only the birds were out, and even they seemed bewildered by the lack of humans.

Most shops were closed, but Julius noticed one with the grille over the entrance open and a rotating rack hung with canvas shoes inside. The owner came to unlock the inner door when he saw the barefoot brothers.

'Here to stop looters,' the owner said, resting his shotgun against a counter as he took a bolt off the door.

A bell tinkled as the boys stepped inside, squeezing past racks and boxes that were usually set out on the pavement.

'We weren't expecting to walk far, but we got kicked off our bus,' Julius explained. 'I want something cheap to cover our feet.'

The man was elderly, with a kind smile, but smelled like he hadn't washed in a while. 'Too much broken glass for barefoot boys,' he said sympathetically. He reached towards the bottom of a rack and pulled off a pair of Gabe-sized shoes in a bright design with pineapples on.

'Can I get plain ones?' Gabe asked.

'That design is not selling,' the man explained as he looked at Julius's giant feet. 'Your brother can have those for nothing. You are more difficult. What size are you?'

'Forty-nine,' Julius said, making the man chuckle.

'I only have sandals that big,' the shopkeeper said, forgetting his shotgun as he walked behind the counter to grab a reaching pole.

'I'll try Mum again,' Gabe said, but Julius batted his hand away from his pocket.

'What?' Gabe mouthed silently, failing to grasp that pulling a ₦300,000 iPhone wasn't the best idea when a shopkeeper was giving away shoes.

'I don't mind paying,' Julius said as the man hooked one of the mesh nets hanging from the ceiling and lowered it carefully to the counter.

The net was filled with cheap foam thongs in cellophane packs and the elderly shopkeeper rummaged until he found a set big enough for Julius.

'I must give you something,' Julius insisted, as he slipped the thongs between his toes.

'Good deeds bring me closer to God,' the man said. Then he smiled. 'And the way things go in this town, I'll meet him soon enough.'

As if to prove this, there was a crash of metal outside. Gabe looked out, seeing a woman with a bloody nose who'd just clattered the metal frame of a market stall. Clouds of birds launched as she limped towards the centre of the precinct.

As the shopkeeper hurriedly slid bolts back on his door, three women in their late teens sprinted past the window. The one in the lead caught the bloodied woman easily, grabbing her hair and sprawling her with a kick in the back.

The woman screamed as the teens set about her. After a frenzy of kicks and stamps, the burliest of the trio picked their victim off the ground and dragged her back the way they'd come, barely conscious and trailing blood across the precinct.

'The woman collected protection money for the Transport Union,' the shopkeeper explained.

Gabe looked rattled. 'Will they kill her?'

Julius put a hand on his brother's shoulder and avoided the question. 'We haven't got far to go,' he reassured.

The shopkeeper refused Julius's money again before they left.

Outside, Gabe ploughed through a deep rain puddle. He said his new shoes looked suspiciously clean, but Julius knew it was just for the hell of it.

'Where *are* we headed?' Gabe asked as his pumps squelched.

'Where do you think?' Julius asked. 'You're the one always telling me I've only got one friend.'

Gabe had suspected, but still wore a look of concern and dropped off the pace.

Julius marched ahead. 'Tell Mum whatever you like,' he snapped. 'Tell her I took you to see my homo friend. Snitch on my secret phone. She doesn't scare me any more.'

Gabe jogged a few steps to catch up.

'I don't want Mum to send you away,' Gabe said pleadingly.

Julius smiled as Gabe looked embarrassed.

'Mum's never got time,' Gabe admitted. 'The twins are mean. I'd miss your stupid face.'

Julius was touched and put an arm round Gabe's back.

'Who knows what'll happen?' Julius said softly.

'I wonder what they're doing to that lady who got beat up . . .'

Gabe said, suddenly anxious. 'Was Taiwo dead? And where did Kehinde go? He vanished while we hid in the back seats.'

Julius had no answers and let Gabe talk himself out.

They passed dozens of smashed and burned-out cars. A fearsome group of area boys stared them down but saw two scruffy kids who didn't look worth robbing.

It felt less tense as they neared Duke's building, north of the city. Shops were open, though most only raised a single shutter, enabling them to close in seconds if trouble arrived. Kids even took advantage of school closures and thin traffic by kicking a ball around in the street.

Julius worried about finding his mother's goons in the lobby. They'd offer protection and a ride home, but he was desperate to see Duke. Julius only saw a doorman as he walked briskly past the entrance. Perhaps the chaos meant his mother couldn't spare three men to intimidate a journalist, but rather than chance it Julius went round the side and hit the buzzer.

'Delivery for Lapido, fourth floor,' he said, standing close and going on tiptoes so the camera above the button only caught the logo on his stolen football shirt.

'Push,' the doorman crackled, as the door buzzed.

'Don't say anything rude or weird to Duke,' Julius warned, breathless, as they rounded the last balcony before the sixth floor.

Gabe looked fearful as Julius rang the bell.

'Who's calling?' Remi asked suspiciously.

He opened all the bolts when he recognised Julius's voice.

'Shit!' Duke croaked from behind his screen. 'Get over here. Let me see you!'

Remi had tidied the apartment. Apart from the missing fridge door, it looked better than before the goons had trashed it. Duke was tough to look at. His face was so swollen that he was barely recognisable, his fists clenching with pain when he tried to move.

Julius had imagined a kiss or hug, but all Duke could offer without hurting were his fingertips.

'Barely a scratch,' Duke joked, hoping humour would ease Julius's pained expression.

Julius furiously thought about Collins, Kehinde and Taiwo using Duke as a punchbag. And the headmaster who'd let them get away with it . . . He looked at Remi. 'Shouldn't he be in hospital?'

'His mother is coming on an overnight bus,' Remi answered. 'The Catholic hospital only takes American dollars. Six hundred a day just for the bed. The state hospital might admit him, but he has open wounds and that place is notorious for infection.'

Gabe stood awkwardly by the end of the bed, not knowing where to look.

'Hey, little guy,' Duke said, waving with the tips of his fingers. 'You must be Gabe.'

Julius vented some of his anger. 'This is what the twins were *laughing* about by the pool,' he told Gabe bitterly.

'So how come you're *both* here?' Duke asked, then gave a long groan as he tried sitting up.

Thinking how to answer made Julius realise how stressed he was.

'Long story . . .' he began as he drew up a chair beside the bed.

THIRTY-FIVE

You only notice sounds when they're different. Georgia realised this as kids poured into hallways at the start of lunch. Voices felt sharper, bodies moved faster. Fists pounded on lockers.

'Freedom!' someone shouted.

Georgia was wary. She took time zipping her books away. She was last out of class and didn't answer when a kid asked if she knew train times to London. But she was behind a hallway scrum and felt safe peeking at her phone. Her notification screen scrolled almost to infinity. Six voicemails, twenty-seven SMS, sixty Twitter messages, six hundred new followers on Instagram...

'You seen Maya?' Rolf asked, coming out of nowhere and giving Georgia a far-too-friendly thump on the back.

Rolf was with all his usual mates. Guys Georgia didn't like, but she found herself among them as they surged down the hallway, shoving younger kids.

For all the bravado after the assemblies, most pupils were doing their usual thing. Heading for lunch, dribbling a ball towards the all-weather pitch or fighting over the outdoor ping-pong tables.

But there was a scene with about eighty kids at the front gate. Rather than leave teachers exposed, the gates had been locked and left unattended. A couple of girls tried climbing over, but the narrow mesh gave no footholds, and if they got to the top, they faced jagged wire.

The strategy of letting kids burn themselves out seemed to be a good one. After a few rowdy minutes, thoughts turned to food and the crowd began peeling away.

'Total bollocks,' Rolf complained as their group watched from a few metres back.

Georgia saw wry humour in it: the bluster and bravado of youth revolt swatted by one adult with a padlock. She also liked having the responsibility taken away: she wouldn't get into trouble, but nobody could call her chicken when there was no way out.

Most kids were already heading inside when a trio of year-thirteen girls came screaming across well-trodden grass inside the school's front wall.

'It's open at the side,' they were shouting. 'Everybody! We need help keeping it open.'

'Here we go, boys and girls!' Rolf shouted jubilantly.

A year-eight kid got so excited he tripped over himself, but Georgia, Rolf and sixty others began a charge along the grass.

While most kids made noise and hoped for the best, a group of year-thirteens had used their brains. Guessing staff would lock the front gates, they'd waited by the vehicle entrance at the side of the school.

These gates were controlled from a switch in front reception, used throughout the day by part-time staff and visitors. When the gate had opened for a busload of wet-haired year-sevens returning from swimming lessons, the girls jumped out from between two parked vans and stood in the gate's path, activating a sensor that stopped it from closing.

Now there was a foot race. A caretaker and teacher were rushing towards the scene, demanding the year-thirteen girls let the gate close. A larger, noisier posse was belting along the front of the school grounds, trying to beat them.

Most kids at the front gate had been from upper school, but the noise and drama of the charge over the grass drew in swarms of littler kids. Georgia was a good runner and found herself near the front.

'There is a fast train in nineteen minutes,' a girl whose voice was not to be messed with shouted. 'It's on time, so if you're coming to London, you need to move quickly.'

Maya had escaped school after she'd kicked off in assembly and there were hasty hugs as she met up with everyone outside. Tons of younger kids had piled out of the gates, but they didn't have the bottle for a trip to London and either turned back or headed into a park that began where the school playing fields ended.

By the time they'd marched to the station, there was a core of about seventy kids, mostly years ten through to thirteen, but a few little terrors, who interrupted their walk to rob pork pies and Heineken from Tesco Metro.

There were only four ticket machines at the station. Georgia joined the queue, but was way back when the train arrived. After hesitating, she joined kids vaulting the ticket barriers and raced up steps to cross the platforms.

A couple of burly year-thirteens held the train doors as everyone piled aboard. Georgia was one of the last to make it, leaving a couple of stragglers for the stopping service four minutes behind.

Cheers broke as they moved off. Trains at this time of day were usually empty, but Georgia found herself with standing-room only. When she looked around, she saw the uniforms of kids who'd escaped schools further up the line. There was also a big group of local council workers with banners printed by their union, and folks Georgia recognised from the demo at the town hall.

She tried to hide among Rolf and his strapping mates, but once Georgia got spotted, kids from the other schools wanted selfies with her. She also took her own pic of the crowded train carriage and put it on her Twitter and Instagram with the message:

On my way.
This is gonna be BIG!
#nocutsnobudget #kidsrighttoprotest

Maya and a couple of girlfriends watched Georgia's phone in awe as her tweet popped with dozens of likes and comments.

'BBC News just retweeted you,' a girl said.

'Three hundred likes in two minutes, superstar!'

Georgia saw Wendy was trying to call her, but the train went through a tunnel before she could answer. By the time they came back into daylight, they were slowing for the next stop. There was a group of fifty young teenagers in printed yellow T-shirts at the end of the platform. They had *SOS Save our Schools* banners and adult supervision. There were clumps of random kids and people who looked like they were heading to the protest all along the platform.

When the doors behind Georgia opened, a bunch of lively old women jostled aboard.

'Oooh, look at all these handsome young men!' the first lady said as she eyed one of Rolf's mates.

'What a nice bum!'

'Stop sexually harassing the young men,' another granny added, before they all shrieked with laughter.

Rolf's crew looked mortified as Georgia and Maya laughed.

'They want to close down our keep-fit club and ballroom dancing,' one woman explained to Georgia as the train moved off. 'There'd be more of us, but a lot of us have health issues.'

More protestors crammed in at the next stop. It was the last before the train went fast through to London Euston. People had to stand in the disabled toilet and smaller kids joked around, letting year-twelves and thirteens lay them in the overhead racks.

Georgia was worried about not having a ticket when they arrived at Euston, especially when she saw transit cops at the barriers. But everyone pushed and shoved. Georgia leapt through the gate behind one of the pensioners and the ticket inspectors opened a side gate when the crush looked dangerous.

Georgia usually came to London a few times a year, for shopping, or a musical on her mum's birthday. The station was always busy, but so many people were arriving for the protest that everyone shuffled towards the Underground like penguins.

Cops looked down from the restaurant gantry as the crowd inched down the Tube station steps.

'*Passenger information,*' the station announcer said, echoing through the huge space. '*Due to overcrowding, Westminster, Leicester Square and St James's Park stations have been closed. Passengers wishing to attend the protest at the Houses of Parliament are advised to travel to Green Park or Waterloo, or take a bus from the concourse in front of the station . . .*' After a pause, the announcer added, '*No cuts, no budget!*'

The whole station erupted in wild cheers and whistles. But moods soured as protestors got closer to the Tube steps and found marshals shutting barriers at the top of the stairs to prevent overcrowding on the platforms below.

Forty minutes later, they got off a train at Piccadilly and joined a huge crowd crossing Green Park. The crowd was cheerful, but there was a hint of menace, with vanloads of riot cops and fierce-looking London gang kids hanging around. Shops and cafes were closing, because mobs were stealing anything that wasn't bolted down.

Georgia was walking up The Mall with Buckingham Palace at her back when a BBC News crew spotted her. Nobody had paid attention as she'd crossed Green Park with her schoolmates, but she caused gridlock once there was a camera on her.

'I've spotted Georgia Pack,' the breathless correspondent said, chasing Georgia as the cameraman walked backwards in front of her. 'Georgia, we're covering the protests *live* on BBC News. We're seeing huge numbers of people pouring into London, possibly the largest protest in a generation. Many thousands of younger people are probably here because of the example you set. Do you have a message for them?'

'I'm no leader,' Georgia said, pushing hair off her face as Maya and Rolf grinned over her shoulders. 'We elected this government to end austerity. They've betrayed every promise and it's time they listened.'

A huge cheer went up, though Georgia felt like she was acting. Saying what people expected Georgia-the-rebel to say, more than something she passionately believed.

'Police are urging people not to come into Central London and the Westminster area because the crowds are too big,' the correspondent stated. 'Would you agree with that?'

'I've not seen any problems,' Georgia said. 'A bit of pushing around the stations and people nicking baguettes from Pret a Manger, but it's mostly good-natured.'

'And, lastly, do you expect you'll be in a lot of trouble when you get to school tomorrow?'

Georgia tipped back her head and laughed noisily. 'All my teachers adore me,' she joked as a bunch of girls started *woo-woo*ing and waving their arms around behind her. 'But, seriously, there's thousands of kids here and I don't see why we're different. If we believe something is wrong, don't we have as much right to protest as our teachers, uni students or anyone else?'

THIRTY-SIX

Remi had learned enough first aid in the National Youth Service Corps to remove Gabe's splinter and clean the wound. While he cut a dressing for his young patient, Julius folded back the screen beside Duke's bed, picked up a coffee table and laid out a Scrabble board.

Remi didn't join the three boys in the game, because he was prepping a speech for a meeting of anti-corruption activists the following day. He kept a portable radio on, raising the volume so they could all hear the noon bulletin.

'*. . . Akure Fire Service has confirmed eighteen dead in this morning's blast at an office building near the Western Transit Hub. With at least thirty-three more unaccounted for, the elite National Rescue unit is flying from Lagos with specialist equipment and sniffer dogs.*

'*Many of the dead are thought to be high on the ladder in the Ondo State Transport Union. The union's national president, Sam Elendu, has said the bombing is symptomatic of police inaction during recent disturbances in Akure and has called on the national government in Abuja to investigate.*

'*Ondo State Governor, SJ Adebisi, gave a press conference*

in which he described the blast as a "heinous act of terror", and promised swift action to catch the perpetrators...'

Remi snorted at the last part.

'I know my family are into all kinds of shit, but how is this in their interests?' Julius asked. 'Stirring trouble? Bringing the city to a standstill?'

Remi turned away from his papers and stroked his chin. 'They thought the area boys were a rabble,' he explained. 'Adebisi gave money and encouragement, expecting them to cause trouble. The intention was to punish the Transport Union for turning their support back to Rotimi. Nobody expected an organised campaign to take control of the city centre and slaughter the leadership of the Union.'

'Can't my uncle tell them to stop?' Gabe asked.

'I fear your uncle and mother have created a monster they cannot control,' Remi said dramatically. 'Now there is a war and everyone will suffer for months, if not years.'

Edgy and confused, Gabe looked at Julius. 'Are Mum and Uncle *really* such bad guys?'

Julius had got the Scrabble out because Gabe's nerves were frazzled.

'Nobody can become rich and powerful without doing bad things,' Julius said diplomatically. 'Now it's your turn. Focus your microscopic brain on the game.'

Gabe was way behind the older boys and a sore loser, but he got offended when Julius tried to look at his letters to help out. Both brothers kept checking their phones, which were on different networks but showed *No signal*.

'Earlier the calls kept dropping,' Julius noted, chirpy after scoring fifty-two points with *jukebox*. 'Now it's like there's no cell network to connect to.'

'That is the nail on the head,' Remi said. 'When there is trouble, the police switch off phone networks so that trouble-makers cannot co-ordinate.'

'Are my mother's goons still around?' Julius asked. 'Her people carry police radios that are probably working.'

Remi shook his head. 'The Ford they were following me around in had its tyres slashed while I was in a meeting. The next day, they came in a very nice Lexus that fell victim to a mysterious petrol-tank fire while I ate lunch in a restaurant ...'

Julius laughed as he imagined Simeon explaining a burned-out Lexus to his mother.

'I have few friends left in this town,' Remi added. 'Luckily, your mother has many enemies.'

For the second Scrabble game, Gabe accepted a hundred-point start and got super-tense as it neared the end with his lead shrinking to eight. Duke was trying to make a game-winning score with his final letters when Remi's phone broke into a string of delayed text messages. Gabe's phone pinged a second later.

'NiCom is back,' Remi said, peering at his Samsung over the top of his glasses. 'Now everyone will call at once and swamp the network.'

Gabe almost toppled the Scrabble board as he snatched his phone off Duke's bed. He dialled Orisa, then froze with angst and passed his phone to Julius. 'It's ringing.'

'Gabriel?' Orisa blurted frantically.

'It's me,' Julius said. 'Gabe's here too. We're both safe.'

'God be praised!' Orisa sang. Then, away from the phone, '*Bunmi, I have the other boys* ... Are either of you injured?'

Before Julius could answer, his mother snatched the

handset. Her voice was tearful, but her accusatory tone made Julius feel unloved.

'Why did you not call sooner? I have the entire police force out looking for you.'

'Nobody has landlines any more. Mobile and data *just* came back on.'

'I feared my babies were dead,' Bunmi sobbed.

'Hi, Mum,' Gabriel said as Julius moved the phone so they could both hear. 'I got a splinter in my leg, but Remi took it out and it barely hurts.'

'Remi Balogun?' Bunmi guessed, shocked and sour. 'I might have known! But I did not think your brother would be stupid enough to cross town in riot conditions!'

Julius wanted to ask his mother why she had such a problem with him, but it wasn't the moment for a showdown.

'What about the others in the car?' Julius asked.

Bunmi wept noisily. Gabe gave Julius a fearful stare as Orisa took the phone back.

'We'll update you when you are safely home,' Orisa said.

'No,' Julius said, desperate to know, but also worried how Gabe might react.

He heard his mother's voice away from the phone, weaker than he'd ever heard it. 'They might as well know . . .'

Orisa took a breath to compose herself. 'The driver was dead in his seat. Taiwo is shot twice and in emergency surgery now. Kehinde was dragged away from the vehicle and treated very badly . . .'

Orisa paused.

'Is he alive?' Julius asked, frustrated at having to wring out every sentence.

'They slashed his throat after they'd beaten him,' Orisa

said. 'Your mother is in shock. Those bastards sent a gruesome photograph to her phone. You know how she loves those twins...'

More than me, Julius found himself thinking as he saw a tear streak down Gabe's cheek. He put an arm round his shoulder.

Bunmi took the phone again and sounded more like her fearsome self. 'I have the police chief here at the house. She has a tactical team close to your building. Be ready to leave the instant they arrive.'

Bunmi hung up without any goodbye and Gabe glanced around tearfully. At Duke's battered body, up at Julius, then at the Scrabble game that would never be finished.

'I'll pee before the cops get here,' he decided.

'Sorry about your brothers,' Duke said, unconvincingly.

The sentiment was so ludicrous that Julius broke into laughter.

'It's the randomness that disturbs me,' Julius said. 'Kehinde went one way into a mob. Me and Gabe ran the other...'

Duke finished Julius's thought. 'They'd have slashed your throats too.'

'*Everything* is shit now,' Julius growled, wanting to kick something hard. '*So* messed up...'

Gabe flushed the toilet as a thud of compressed air from a door jack was followed by Remi's steel-plated door flying dangerously into the room.

'Everyone down,' a cop shouted as three charged in, dressed in full riot gear. 'Hands on heads... Check the other rooms.'

Remi tried to move papers off his lap before getting off his chair, but a cop grabbed the back of his shirt and sprawled him face first across the floor.

'You listen when I speak!' the cop ordered, planting his foot on Remi's back and pointing a tear gas launcher at his face.

'They're looking after us!' Julius shouted. 'Why didn't you knock?'

A cop almost splattered Gabe with the bathroom door as he stepped out.

'This is T411. Apartment secured. I've got both boys,' the cop closest to Julius told his radio. 'Has the transport arrived . . . ? OK, we'll be down directly.'

'What about my door?' Remi asked furiously as the officer let him sit up.

'File a complaint, Balogun,' the cop said, his snort indicating how likely this was to succeed.

'They helped us,' Julius repeated furiously.

'Mr Adebisi, I need you to walk this way,' the cop said politely.

'Remi, I'm sorry. I'll pay for your door,' Julius said, then he stepped towards Duke, catching the corner of the Scrabble board and knocking a few letters on the floor. 'I'll see you soon. I hope your mum isn't held up by the transport problems . . .'

'Try to steer clear of Army Boys Academy,' Duke joked.

'Nice to meet you both,' Gabe said sweetly as a riot cop helped him over the smashed door.

Julius's brain was flat out as the cops led a brisk walk down six floors, hoping Duke got better, wondering what was going on in Gabe's head and if Taiwo would live. Guilty for not feeling bad that Kehinde was dead and imagining what might have happened if he'd run the other way after crawling out of the Mercedes . . .

'Careful,' the cop walking beside Julius said, grabbing the teenager after the back of his thong caught a step. 'Are you fit?'

'All good,' Julius said weakly. He was glad he'd not eaten since breakfast because there was nothing in his belly to puke.

There were four riot cops in the lobby, and more on the street protecting a three-vehicle convoy. Front and back were tatty Hyundai estate cars, the workhorses of Ondo State police. In the middle was a fearsome riot truck, with solid tyres, bulletproof windows and a snowplough-like scoop on the front designed to smash barricades.

The green uphill view from Remi's apartment had left Julius out of touch with the ground. Every shop had closed, street soccer had ended and there was a hazy, burnt smell in the air.

Gabe was curious as they climbed in the riot truck, impressed by thick bombproof glass and the clank as the airtight door shut.

Solid tyres and poor roads made a tough ride as they sped down empty streets, occasional siren blasts scaring anything that dared get in the way.

The brothers peered through the thick glass slots at endless fires, people whose eyes streamed from tear gas and flimsy barricades made by those trying to protect homes and shops from looting.

Area boys strutted in well-armed packs. The city centre now belonged to them. Small-time crooks who'd spent most of their lives protecting your parking spot, selling bags of weed, or surrounding you with muscle and politely suggesting you lighten your wallet by several hundred naira to make it to the next corner without getting your eye blackened . . .

Julius saw a dead girl on the ramp leading up to the beltway. Gabe's age, probably a kid from the slums beyond. She'd been smashed by something heavy and fast. Gabe saw her too. He kept quiet, but gripped Julius's wrist.

'She might go to heaven,' Gabe said after a while. 'Kehinde *definitely* won't.'

THIRTY-SEVEN

It was London's biggest protest since the Iraq War. Packing Parliament Square, down The Mall to Buckingham Palace and northwards, engulfing Charing Cross and Trafalgar Square.

From news helicopters, the crowds made spectacular symbols of protest. From the ground, it was no fun. People squashed against walls and shopfronts, shunted by tetchy police. Stations, shops and cafes closed. No toilets and nowhere to sit.

People were still arriving at four o'clock, but more were trying to leave. Georgia got her backpack entangled with a bewildered Aussie tourist. When she'd sorted that, Maya and everyone else from her school had vanished. The phone network couldn't handle a million handsets in a few square miles, so she couldn't call or text to get back in touch.

Georgia's calves ached after being on her feet for four hours. She faced a lonely four-kilometre walk to Euston, a crush at the station and a packed train home, so she was relieved to spot a SAG banner held by a woman she'd been introduced to outside the Red Parrot bookshop before the town hall protest. She couldn't remember her name, but then she saw Zac was there too.

Zac felt like the best thing to happen all day. He wore combat boots, ripped jeans and a torso-hugging T-shirt with the Health Workers Union logo on the front and FIGHT CUTS on the back.

'What are the odds in this crowd?' Zac asked Georgia.

He gave her a hug as Kamila, Gerard and the other SAGgers said hello.

'How's it been?' Zac asked. 'We saw your BBC interview on the big screen at Piccadilly Circus.'

Georgia looked embarrassed as Zac showed her a photo he'd taken of her face, twenty metres tall, over a sea of protestors.

'My feet hurt, and I'd give anything for a clean loo and a mug of tea,' Georgia said.

Zac laughed. 'You sound like your nan when we took her to the farmers' market.'

'I'm a bad revolutionary,' Georgia confessed.

'We're all heading up to an Ethiopian restaurant in Russell Square,' Zac said. 'It's a trek, but Kamila knows the owner and says it's great. I'm sure there's space if you're interested.'

'I didn't know Ethiopian was a thing,' Georgia said. 'All I have is twenty quid, and I need six-eighty for my ticket home . . .'

'Zac's treat,' he said. 'I *seriously* don't recommend going to the station. I've been to protests smaller than this and you still stand in a crush for three or four hours because every train is full. If you wait until ten, it's usually died off.'

'Ten!' Georgia gawped, wary of her dad's reaction, but also really wanting to hang out with Zac.

Georgia, Zac and eight other SAG members set off for Russell Square. They were led by Kamila, navigating with Google Maps, and Gerard, who was shirtless, painted orange and carrying a two-and-a-half-metre inflatable alligator.

Phones came alive once they were out of the packed protest

area. Georgia ignored the scrum of incoming messages, but called Maya, who'd left when Rolf got bored and made it onto a train before the crush.

Georgia was nervous as she dialled her dad. He answered right away, sounding subdued. He said he hadn't been able to face the guys at work. He'd been home all day and was mostly interested in locating the can opener so he could make beans on toast.

'Try the dishwasher basket,' Georgia suggested, before hanging up.

A bunch of SAG members from other branches had already arrived at the restaurant. Georgia felt cringingly out of place in school uniform. The restaurant wasn't like any she'd been to before. The floor was covered in loosely woven rugs, with big flat cushions to sit on and exotically carved tables, barely twenty centimetres high.

Georgia was spared navigating an Ethiopian menu. The early arrivals had agreed a fixed price for the whole SAG group and the staff set out stacks of finger bowls and jugs of house wine, before bringing platters of food.

'A little drop?' Zac asked.

Nobody commented on Georgia drinking wine and she pulled pumps off aching feet and chilled out. Grateful for soggy cushions and her first food since breakfast.

'No clue what I'm eating, but it's not bad,' Georgia said.

Georgia topped up her wine as someone asked a waiter to switch on a TV behind the bar. A big cheer went up from the SAGgers as the six o'clock news started with helicopter shots of the vast crowds in Central London.

'*The headlines at six . . . London grinds to a halt with an estimated eight hundred thousand protestors out on the streets.*'

Georgia felt her cheeks burn as she saw herself on the screen for a soundbite. Her caption, *Georgia Pack – SAG Activist & School Protest Organiser.*

'We elected this government to end austerity. They've betrayed every promise and it's time they listened.'

Georgia cringed, hearing her voice come out of the TV, but another huge cheer erupted in the restaurant and people reached over and patted her on the back.

'I'm not a bloody organiser and I've never even been to a SAG meeting,' Georgia protested to Zac.

'Georgia, my sons weren't interested in this,' a woman with cropped greying hair explained as she leaned back from the cushion behind. 'But when they saw the photograph of your leap, they saw it wasn't just another one of Mum's lefty causes. You made them *want* to get involved. They made banners, they were texting schoolmates. Thousands of young people came out today because of you.'

'That's good . . .' Georgia said weakly, then gave Zac a *get-me-out-of-here* look.

'You're amongst friends,' Zac soothed. 'Eat, relax, but go easy on the wine.'

There were a few cheers as the TV news cut to live scenes, with a sunset sky over Piccadilly Circus. Most protestors had gone home, but a few hundred troublemakers had stuck around to battle the cops.

As the correspondent crouched beside a burnt-out Lexus, police with riot shields faced masked protestors and a barrage of souvenir plates looted from Pride of London gift shop.

'Gerard, you're missing all the fun,' Zac joked.

All joy got sucked out of the restaurant when a woman with a stiff face and grey lampshade hair came on screen for an interview. Her caption read: *Yvonne McMahon, Minster for Communities and Local Government.*

'*This government is committed to providing excellent local services. We respect the passion of people who came out to protest, particularly the hard-working council staff, teachers and care workers. And I can assure them—*'

'Minister, your government was elected with manifesto promises to increase local government spending,' the newsreader interrupted. '*After last week's violence and today's huge protests, will there be a spending review?*'

The minister shook her head. '*There will be no spending review. In real terms, this government will be spending eight-point-four per cent more on local government services than the previous...*'

The rest of the minister's response got drowned in a restaurant full of jeers.

'This is why we need real action,' Gerard roared, pounding a fist into his palm. 'Left wing, right wing, they're all bandits! We need bombs!'

This triggered outrage and debate. A few radicals agreed with Gerard, but the majority were in the *violence-is-always-wrong* camp. Georgia was amused by the way nobody seemed to be listening to anyone but themselves, then Zac shot to his feet with the loudest voice in the room.

'There hasn't been a revolution in this country for hundreds of years,' Zac said passionately. 'The political class is *way* too comfortable. You just saw the minister brush off today's protest. Bombs might not be the way forward, but we need something more than peaceful protests.'

A few tables over, Gerard stood up and glowered at Zac.

'Something like what?' he asked.

254

THIRTY-EIGHT

The area in front of the house was full of limousines and cop cars, so the riot truck could barely get in the gate. As Julius and Gabe weaved between cars towards their home, police officers went the other way, carrying boxes out to dark blue vans.

Teddy, the soft-spoken political technologist, held the front door. Gabe shot under his arm and found his mother by the bottom of the main staircase.

She squeezed Gabe and kissed his sweaty forehead as Julius looked around. More cops were carrying boxes down the stairs. In the large living area to the right of the front door, a dozen men and one woman were deep in conversation. At the poolside, bodyguards and drivers in suits and dark glasses sat on loungers, awaiting orders.

As Gabe hugged Orisa, Julius faced his mother. Their hug was short-lived, like two boys forced to shake hands after a fight.

'What are these clothes?' Bunmi asked suspiciously.

'A washing line,' Julius said, shaking his head and tutting loudly. 'Do you think it's safe to walk through town in St Gilda's uniform?'

She accepted this grudgingly. 'You were always the clever one,' she conceded. 'I am grateful you looked after Gabriel.'

While his mother remained stiff, recent awkwardness with Orisa was forgotten as the cousins hugged.

'I was scared you were gone for good,' Orisa said, dabbing her eye. 'I prayed with my whole heart for this!'

'Where's our stuff going?' Gabe asked as he eyed his PS4 sticking out of a box.

'We will stay at the governor's mansion for a while,' Bunmi explained. 'The security there is superior.'

'Their indoor pool is the best!' Gabe said brightly, but Julius's first thought was about sharing a home with Collins.

Teddy approached warily, one spindly finger on his Breitling watch.

'I know this is a family moment,' he told Bunmi, barely above a whisper. 'But the timings for Julius are extremely tight.'

Bunmi nodded to Teddy, then glanced at Orisa. 'Are Julius's things packed?'

'Timings for what?' Julius asked, sensing a ride to military school in time for some thuggish induction.

'Come to my office,' Bunmi told Julius. 'Teddy too.'

They waited for cops with boxes to pass before Bunmi led the charge to her office.

'Shut the door,' Bunmi said. She took a tin out of a glass cabinet. 'You know what Teddy does?'

'He's your political-campaign advisor,' Julius said as Bunmi clanked the tin down on the desk.

'Your behaviour is continually scandalous,' Bunmi said. 'In a major crisis, you risk the centre of town to see this *Duke*.'

'I went to the only people I knew I could trust,' Julius blurted.

'Balogun is our enemy!' Bunmi snorted. 'Your homosexuality

is known around St Gilda's. It is only a matter of time before it causes a publicity scandal, during a finely balanced election campaign.'

Julius sighed and shook his head as his mother kept talking.

'Teddy pointed out that your behaviour could still cause scandal if I send you to Army Boys Academy, or any other Nigerian school.'

Bunmi opened the tin and Julius saw the family passports stacked inside.

'Here,' Bunmi said, flicking Julius's passport across the desk. 'Teddy has the details. Your flight leaves for Lagos at 7 p.m.'

'Tonight!' Julius blurted.

'Collins needed plastic surgery,' Bunmi said. 'That incident caused a family rift and it is not sensible for you to stay at the mansion.'

'I can stay here,' Julius said desperately.

'To sneak off and cavort with Duke?' Bunmi scoffed.

'Where am I going then?'

'Teddy has your itinerary,' Bunmi said, swiping her hand to show it wasn't important to her. 'I have many things to do before I visit Taiwo at the hospital. You will be gone before I get back.'

As Bunmi headed out of her office, Teddy shuddered from the awkwardness as he took a plastic packet from under his arm. Julius saw *London Heathrow* on the flight itinerary as Teddy set it on the desk.

'Your helicopter is waiting on the pad at the edge of this development. It will get you to Lagos Heliport in an hour. The direct flights to London are booked, so you change planes in Amsterdam—'

'London,' Julius said, gobsmacked. 'To the family house?'

257

Teddy nodded. 'A car will meet you at the airport. You'll stay at the house over the weekend. On Monday, you have an interview with Mr Craven. He's an educational placement specialist. He will discuss your school options, help you deal with any entrance exams. He thinks you can be settled into a British boarding school within weeks.'

It was a big deal, piled on top of a massive day. The one thought that rang clear was that the toughest British boarding school was a let-off compared to Army Boys Academy.

'When do I have to leave?' Julius asked.

'Right now,' Teddy said. 'It will be evening rush when the helicopter lands, and you know how the lines at Lagos Airport can be.'

'Can I at least shower and swap these stolen clothes?'

'I spent your ma's money on business class,' Teddy said, showing a touch of sympathy as he opened the door. 'There are showers and decent food in the Star Alliance lounge.'

Orisa was waiting outside, with a big wheeled suitcase and in-flight backpack.

'I can easily send anything I have forgotten,' Orisa said. 'There's eight hundred pounds and an ATM card in a zipped pouch at the bottom of the flight bag. Milena, the housekeeper, says she will fix a British phone by the time you arrive, and she will prepare your food until school starts.'

'At least give him a clean shirt,' Gabe said as he raced out of Julius's room with a striped Superdry polo. 'I'll miss you.'

'I'll call,' Julius said, swapping his shirt, then snatching Gabe off the floor so they could hug face to face. 'I'll be back in the holidays.'

Gabe was trying not to sniffle as Teddy took Julius's flight bag and led a charge downstairs. Orisa brought up the rear, the heavy case crashing on each step. A driver was waiting, with the trunk of his big BMW open.

Julius quickly hugged Orisa, shook Teddy's hand and looked back to see if Gabe had come out to wave. There was no sign of him as they reversed carefully out of the crammed driveway.

The helicopter stood on an unsold lot at the edge of the walled development. It had been chartered at short notice, a battered veteran of a thousand hops between oil platforms in the delta. The seats were dirty and there was a strong smell of jet fuel. A white-skinned, white-shirted co-pilot turned round and spoke in a South African accent.

'You good with the harness, man? Wear the ear defenders in the pocket.'

The driver loaded Julius's luggage into the spare seat and gave the pilot a thumbs up before shutting the wobbly plastic door. The jet engine went full blast, pelting dust and grit that made the driver fear for the paint on his BMW.

The ear defenders snapped Julius into a cocoon as the helicopter lifted. He saw home, with the pool and the car-packed drive. At helicopter speed, St Gilda's soccer pitches were less than three minutes away. He eyed towers of smoke from the city centre and skimmed close to the revolving restaurant above the green expanse of Arctic Zoo.

From high up, the puddled penguin pool reminded Julius of the silvery lining of a razor shell. He remembered the afternoon when things had been perfect. Riding their boards, with the tall weeds cutting them off from everything but clear blue sky.

PART THREE

Walter J. Freeman Adolescent Mental Health Unit – East Grinstead, UK

Georgia knocked but didn't get a response. The door had been propped open, so nurses could look in as they walked by, and she craned her neck into the opening.

'Hello?' Georgia said, her nose catching body spray as her sheepskin slipper took a half-step. 'Julius?'

There was something comical when she saw him sat up in bed: a cartoon bear who'd been hit on the head by a beehive. A nurse had dressed Julius in mouthwash-green disposable pyjamas while he was sedated, but they dug into his armpits and the button over the belly had pinged off.

'The ward manager, Susannah, said you were awake. She asked me to show you around and take you upstairs to breakfast . . . I'm Georgia by the way.'

Julius laughed, wagging a finger that Georgia realised was longer than her whole hand. 'I know who you are,' he said, then winced and put a hand over the eight scab-crusted stitches from his trip through the coffee table. 'It hurts if I smile,' Julius explained. 'My head is groggy from the knockout juice in my ass. So, when I wake and see Georgia Pack, I be hallucinating.'

'I'm ninety-six per cent sure I'm real,' Georgia joked.

'Matt – my boarding-school roommate – would shit!' Julius

said. 'He has ten of you taped to the walls around his bunk.'

As Georgia cringed at the thought of being a pin-up, Julius threw off a triangle of bedclothes. He whipped them back in a panic, remembering that the disposable pyjama bottoms covered him even less effectively than the top.

'Oh . . .' he babbled, embarrassed. 'Give me . . . I mean, if you step out while I put on . . .'

Julius had an unzipped wheelie case on the floor. Once he'd put on a hoodie, black Nike tracksuit bottoms and some Prada pumps, he caught up with Georgia in the hallway. New arrivals always spent a night in the observation room opposite the nurses' station, and three staff stared out of their glass cube as he emerged.

'That way is just more rooms,' Georgia explained, pointing right. 'You're not supposed to go into another patient's room, but they're not super strict.'

Georgia led off in the other direction.

'Laundry room there,' she said, as an Indesit spun. 'Powder is in the cupboard above. The machines are first come, first serve, so it gets busy in the evenings. Kitchenette over there.'

Next, they passed into a D-shaped reception. Scandinavian leather chairs and a spherical vase filled with lilies were designed to impress parents forking out a thousand a day to keep teenaged darlings safe. Two sets of toughened-glass doors separated reception from the world, the outer set only opening when the inner ones were locked.

'Escape eez impossible,' Georgia said.

She was trying to sound like a soldier in the cheesy WW2 movies her dad liked, but Julius just looked baffled.

'Through those doors are the therapy rooms, and the waiting area where you—'

'Lost my heroic struggle for freedom,' Julius joked.

Georgia liked this turn of phrase and laughed. She'd only agreed to show Julius around because Susannah would nag until she agreed. But she sensed that Julius might be OK, provided the lumbering head-in-the-clouds charm didn't vanish with the last effect of the haloperidol-lorazepam cocktail they'd shot in his rear.

'There's a gym in the basement, if that's your thing,' Georgia said, aiming a hand towards two lifts with the unit's main staircase wrapped around them. 'There's a rec room with a pool table in the general ward on the second floor. We're allowed up there, but eating disorders on three and the addiction ward on four are off limits.'

'And food?' Julius asked.

'First floor, you can join me for brekky now if you're hungry.'

'I'm queasy, but my mouth is dry,' Julius said, stroking his throat. 'I could probably go for milky coffee. Maybe yoghurt if they have some . . .'

'In little pots,' Georgia said, moving towards the stairs. 'Food here is mostly OK. But every week has the same menu, which gets repetitive after a while.'

By the time Georgia had explained this, they'd reached a first-floor hallway, lined with some of the better efforts of patients in art therapy.

'When are we allowed out?' Julius asked.

'You'll be confined until you've been assessed by your psychiatrist,' Georgia said. 'After that, most people can go out with family. But you're restricted to hospital grounds if you've been sectioned like me.'

'What's sectioned?'

'Sent here by a court,' Georgia said. 'Either because of

something you did, or because you're a suicide risk. I'm here for a pre-sentencing evaluation, before my big day in court.'

'I see,' Julius said, smirking. 'It's so weird that you're showing me around. I remember the day it happened, it was all anyone at school could talk about. And that other guy who lost his eye . . .'

'Gerard,' Georgia said.

The double doors into the dining area were wedged open. It was peak breakfast, with thirty diners, a line for hot drinks and noise worthy of a school canteen. All tables were either in use or waiting for staff to clear trays and wipe down, so Georgia was pleased to spot her friend, Alex, surrounded by empty chairs.

Georgia got chocolate-chip Weetabix and tea. She showed Julius how to use the coffee machine. He found yoghurt and also his appetite when he smelled bacon and put three rashers on a side plate.

'Alex, Julius. Julius, Alex,' Georgia introduced as she squeezed between two chairs and set her tray down.

'Julius baby, what are you in for?' Alex asked, narrowing her eyes, as she sucked a baked bean from the tip of her fork.

THIRTY-NINE

Six Months Earlier: Dormansland Hall Boarding School – Sussex, UK

The Hall – as everyone called it – had a three-hundred-year tradition of almost being one of Britain's elite boarding schools.

When Julius saw the school website, he was sold on pictures of comfortably furnished bedrooms and close to half of the kids being from overseas. He also hoped having three of seven boarding houses filled with girls would give the alpha males something other than the weird-gay-Nigerian kid to focus on.

Julius didn't read about The Hall's world-class sports coaching, or the boast that twenty former pupils had won Olympic medals. But it meant he got privacy three evenings a week, when his roommate Matt went off to practise with the UK Archery squad.

He'd seen a message from Duke as he came out of the day's final lesson, but had yet to check it because he'd been held up by three girls who wanted him to join their drama co-op.

As Julius entered his room, he skimmed his backpack across a floor speckled with dry mud from school pitches. It crashed to a halt amidst the mess of footwear and textbooks under his bed. Then he hooked his tie and blazer inside the door and closed it to keep out noise from first-form boys playing no-rules rugby in the hallway.

After swiping Matt's big V-shaped cushion, Julius propped himself on his bed, unlocked his phone and smiled when he saw a selfie Duke had taken earlier that day. He was by the polar bear cage at Arctic Zoo. Eddie, the one-eyed polar bear, stared curiously over Duke's shoulder, looking even scrawnier than when Julius had seen him in the flesh seven months earlier.

Long walk around the zoo today, Duke's message read. *Legs getting stronger. Sat drawing for ages. Maybe back on a skateboard soon!*

Julius zoomed Duke's face. It was good to see wounds mostly healed and expensively implanted teeth replacing the pair that had been knocked out. But six months' recovery at home had seen Duke's wiry body grow chubby. It wasn't better or worse, but the change reminded Julius how long they'd been apart.

Duke showed as online when Julius closed the image.

"Sup!' Duke answered brightly, after a couple of rings.

Duke's face came on Julius's screen, but the picture disintegrated if he moved.

'Same shit, different day,' Julius said cheerfully. 'Good to hear your voice!'

'Maybe back to school soon,' Duke said.

'How's that sitting?' Julius asked.

'I'm not loving the idea, but I *have* to get out of this apartment. Ma is driving me crazy, with daytime TV and insisting I'll waste away if I don't eat a two-thousand-kilo rhinoceros.'

'She there now?'

'Supermarket,' Duke said. 'It'll have to be state school, cos uncle is broke from my medical bills. And he got himself arrested.'

Julius looked worried. 'He OK?'

'He's got this Anti-Corruption League going. So, in a state where everyone is either Rotimi or Adebisi, he's made both sides hate him.'

Julius laughed. 'The last honest man in Ondo State . . .'

'Me and Ma beg him to be careful,' Duke said. 'People know his face, because he used to read the national news. He thinks that makes him too big to get into trouble.'

'Is he in jail?' Julius asked.

'One night in the cells. Bullshit charge of obstructing the highway when a crowd turned out to hear him speak. But with the election next week, and this water-poisoning scandal, the city is more volatile than ever.'

Julius sounded confused. 'Water poisoning?'

'Haven't you seen news from back here?'

'I find it depressing,' Julius admitted. 'When I speak to my mother, she's so cocky about winning the election it depresses me even more.'

'I feel that,' Duke agreed. 'Area boys have controlled the city centre since before you left. Last week, people started getting sick. Vomiting blood, diarrhoea, skin breaking out with big sores. Some even dropping clumps of hair.'

'Where you are?' Julius asked anxiously.

'City centre and some of the slums,' Duke said. 'Nobody has been ill this far north, but we're drinking bottled water in case it spreads.'

'What caused it?' Julius asked.

'Everyone assumed it was a bug. But when the water company ran tests, they found massive levels of aluminium sulphate. CCTV showed three tanker loads getting dumped in the water treatment plant that supplies the city centre. The aluminium reacts with the metal in water pipes to release sulphuric acid. It basically burns up your insides.'

Julius tutted. 'Just when you think it can't get worse . . .'

'Everyone assumes the Transport Union did it. The area boys mostly live in the town centre, so most of them got poisoned. Plus, nobody is going into town. All the restaurants and shops are closed, so even area boys who didn't get sick can't make money.'

'Are people dying?' Julius asked.

'Some, mostly little kids and old people. It's thirty-six degrees today. There's no safe drinking water in the city's biggest slum. You can get bottled, but the price has shot up and those people can't afford it.'

'Crazy,' Julius said, shaking his head.

'Every bus out of Akure has people hanging off the roof, and drivers charge crazy prices for tickets.'

'A stupid war so my stupid uncle can be governor for another four years . . .' Julius complained.

'How's life outside of the crazy?' Duke asked.

The situation back home made Julius's problems feel tiny. 'Pretty good here,' he admitted guiltily. 'I miss Gabe and Orisa, and you *obviously*. Half-term break starts tomorrow. I asked Mum if I could fly home and she was like, *No way you're here during election week*.'

'That sucks,' Duke said. 'But you said your family's house in London is massive . . .'

'Gabe and some of my country cousins came over for summer holidays. But this time it's just me and the house-keeper. I don't even think Mum wants me home for Christmas. It's like she blames me for Kehinde dying. Or feels I should have died instead . . .'

'Heavy,' Duke said. 'You've made friends at The Hall. Won't you hang with them?'

'They live all over the world,' Julius answered. 'Matt, my roommate, lives in Hampstead, North London. I'll probably go up to his place. There's a few others who live close to London, but most go off with their families. Skiing, or whatever.'

'I'm around to talk to, at least,' Duke said. Then his tone bloomed with mischief. 'You know what you should do? Big empty house in a posh part of London? Tell everyone you're having a party. I bet *heaps* of people would come.'

Julius laughed. 'They'd trash the joint!'

'Which belongs to your mother, who you hate . . .' Duke noted.

Julius's laugh turned evil. 'I *like* that. The house actually belongs to SJ, but he's my mum's bitch, so it's the same thing.'

Julius grinned as he watched Duke's pixelated fist punch the air and chant, 'Party, party, party . . .'

FORTY

'Georgia,' the interviewer said as an iPhone recorded on the glass table between them, 'it's six months since you were thrust into the limelight. A million people took to the streets of London, but in the end calls for a spending review were ignored, and every council approved a budget in line with government rules. Was the whole campaign a waste of time?'

Georgia shifted awkwardly in her chair. It was a school day, but she sat in a meeting room at a hip Soho hotel, recording her sixth and final interview of the day. She was sick of questions, but Wendy had taught her to keep answers short and upbeat.

'It's always good for people to peacefully express their opinions,' Georgia said, hoping she didn't sound as jaded as she felt. 'I wish the government had listened. SAG and other groups will keep fighting for decent homes, schools and healthcare. If the government ignores that, they'll be punished at the next election.'

The interviewer nodded sympathetically.

'Since the protests, people say you've been less involved in SAG's political campaigns and more interested with making money out of modelling and advertising. Has Georgia Pack sold out?'

'I'm here today in my role as a brand ambassador for D'Anger cosmetics,' Georgia said, faking enthusiasm. 'Being a political campaigner doesn't mean you have to walk around in a donkey jacket with scruffy hair and be serious about everything. Politics and social justice are important, but that doesn't mean you have to be boring.'

Wendy stood behind the interviewer and discreetly mouthed, 'Products,' to Georgia.

Georgia knew what she had to do. 'Can I just say, I use D'Anger's products every day,' Georgia beamed. 'They're a great British company. All their products are environmentally friendly, with bio-degradable packaging. They're manufactured using natural ingredients and the company pays employees in shops and factories the living wage.'

The journalist sensed the publicist's interference. 'Don't worry,' the journalist said, looking back at Wendy. 'We're using the photographs of Georgia with D'Anger products and I'll plug it in the article. But nobody will click through if it's a total puff piece.'

'Of course.' Wendy smiled, glancing at her watch, then telling a lie. 'But Georgia has another interview across town, so I can only give you a couple more minutes.'

The journalist coughed as she turned back to Georgia. 'You've tweeted to a million followers, saying that education is a *pointless treadmill*. Are you setting a bad example to your peers?'

Georgia made a thoughtful-pause gesture, before reeling off an answer she'd used several times before. 'I was a star pupil. I got A grades in everything. But look where the pressure to be the best at everything led my sister. Sophie spent years working *so* hard. When it went wrong, she felt like it was the end of the world and that life wasn't worth living.

'I'm not saying everyone should flunk school and become a bum. But life isn't a video game, where the only goal is to reach the next level. Think about what makes you happy and do that, instead of trudging on doing things because everyone else does them.'

'I think I have what I need,' the journalist said, as she grabbed her iPhone and stopped the voice recorder app.

'You did great,' Wendy told Georgia after the journalist had exited the meeting room.

Georgia sighed and shook her head. 'I've never spoken such crap in my life.'

'D'Anger are paying you enough to cover three years at uni,' Wendy reminded her. 'If we head straight to my car, we'll beat the worst of the rush-hour traffic.'

Georgia yawned as Wendy drove her home. She found the clumps of kids in barely different uniforms depressing. The spirit of youth, crushed by dark polyester, petty rules and pointless facts. *Pawns of the capitalist system*, as Zac would say.

But if Sophie hadn't died, I'd still be one of them...

'Drop me at the Texaco station, please,' Georgia said, when they got near her house.

'You want me to wait?'

'Nah,' Georgia said. 'If I cut through the park, it's two minutes to home.'

'I'll be in touch,' Wendy said, blowing an air kiss as Georgia got out of the Audi.

She got an *I-know-you-from-somewhere* look from a couple

of hoodies, unravelling a pack of cigarettes as they walked back to a tatty Peugeot.

Georgia put her card in the cash machine and felt proud that her balance was £21,000 as she drew out four hundred.

Inside the shop, she grabbed bread, eggs, microwave curries, chocolate bars, a chicken-mayo sandwich and a bunch of bananas, because she felt there should be at least one healthy item in the house.

Kids from her old school ignored her as she cut through the park, relishing outdoor air after stuffy buildings and cars.

'I'm home, Daddy,' Georgia sang as she pulled her key out of the front door.

She'd had a battle getting it open because a padded envelope snagged under the draught excluder. The TV in the living room showed horse racing, but John sat in the kitchen. He had food down his *I have the body of a god, it just happens to be The Buddha* T-shirt and wore the Adidas shorts he'd had on all week.

'I got your curries,' Georgia said, and she started putting food in the fridge.

John raised a half-eaten tin of mac and cheese with the lid clinging to the top. 'I had this already . . .'

'You put the metal tin in the microwave?' Georgia said, concerned. 'I'm surprised it didn't blow up.'

'Ate it cold,' John said emotionlessly. 'It's crap either way . . .'

Georgia's first instinct was to say *yum* or *nutritious*, or something else sarcastic. But her dad hitting rock bottom frightened her. Her worst nightmare was coming home and finding he'd done the same thing as Sophie . . .

'So, the interviews were good,' Georgia lied, in her most upbeat voice. 'Wendy asked how you were doing.'

John laughed. 'What did you say? *Sat around smelling like*

armpits, spooning cold mac and cheese out of a can.'

Georgia's lips tightened as she changed the subject. 'Did you fill in the job application Uncle Phil gave you?'

John sounded sour. 'I'm not working for Metro Powerlines with my little brother as my boss . . .'

'It wouldn't have to be forever,' Georgia encouraged. 'Earn some dosh, give yourself reason to get out of bed in the morning. You *always* complained about being the boss and having to keep everyone happy.'

John sighed. 'The form doesn't have to be in until the sixteenth. I'll get there . . .'

'I got cash at the Texaco. Do you need any?'

John shook his head. 'Your school called.'

'The automated, *your son or daughter is absent*?' Georgia asked.

'That one woke me up at half nine,' John said. 'Then an actual teacher called. Mr Woodinvag, or something . . .'

'Dumervil,' Georgia corrected, smirking.

'He wants me to come in and discuss your unauthorised absences,' John explained. 'I told him I couldn't fit him into my hectic schedule. Then *he* started lecturing me on the importance of your education and *I* suggested he go fornicate with a duck.'

'He'll be in a *great* mood when I get to school tomorrow,' Georgia said, halfway between laughing and groaning.

'What are you having to eat?' John asked.

Georgia reared up, because this was code for *what are you cooking me for dinner.*

'I had lunch with Wendy. I got a sandwich from the garage, and I'm going to have that before I go and meet the gang at Red Parrot.'

'Oh . . .' John said, wounded.

Georgia wanted to tell her dad to get off his arse and make his own dinner. She wanted to tell him to see a doctor and get antidepressants. Or talk through his problems with a therapist. But she'd said it all a hundred times before.

When Georgia told her dad something he didn't want to hear, he'd accuse Georgia of turning into her nagging mother. The only thing worse was when he listened with a sad-little-boy face and looked tearful. It felt hopeless, so Georgia tried to stay out as much as possible.

She scrubbed off make-up she'd worn for the interviews and tried to de-stress in the bath. She made a cup of tea, deliberately not asking her dad if he wanted one, even though he was at the kitchen table pretending to read *Drone Monthly*. Then she took the mug up to her room and had it on her bed with the chicken sandwich.

Her phone buzzed as she squashed the triangular packet and uneaten crusts into a ball.

Gerard calling.

'This is a rare honour,' Georgia answered sarcastically.

'You're coming to the Red Parrot meet tonight, aren't you?' Gerard asked.

'For sure,' Georgia said. 'What are you after?'

'How do you know I'm after something?'

Georgia laughed. 'Of all the people I've ever met, you're the least likely to call and ask how my day went.'

'How did your day go?' Gerard asked.

'What do you want?' Georgia asked back.

Gerard cracked a supervillain laugh. 'I've been tinkering with the drone I bought off your dad. Does he still have his workshop down the road?'

'Dad signed a personal guarantee,' Georgia sighed. 'We're stuck renting that workshop until someone buys the lease. And, so far, my dad has made zero effort to sell the lease, even though it's costing a thousand a month . . .'

'Serves him right for being a capitalist swine,' Gerard said, with no irony. 'I need more motors, a control board and some of the 3D-printed parts for his impeller kits.'

'Message me a list,' Georgia said. 'It's no biggie. I have a key and its five minutes from my house.'

'I also need you to give me two hundred pounds,' Gerard said.

Georgia scoffed. 'You can shove *that* idea where the sun doesn't shine . . .'

Gerard's tone darkened. 'I heard about the D'Anger deal you signed. You're minted. I need to buy different props and things. The way the drone is now, it's *impossible* to fly.'

Georgia found this unlikely. 'It's a survey drone, designed to potter around looking for corroded power lines or cracked roofing felt. Any idiot can fly them . . .'

'Wrong,' Gerard said bluntly. 'Your father's design is weak. It's probably why he lost the Metro Powerlines contract . . .'

Georgia tutted. 'If you bring it to the Red Parrot, I'll look at it.'

Gerard felt this was absurd. 'Why would you know anything I don't?

'You're a biologist with a big brain, but no common sense,' Georgia said wearily. 'I've been flying drones since infant school.'

FORTY-ONE

After an hour's study time and a splat of shepherd's pie that left him craving Orisa's pepper soup, Julius crossed the school grounds to an annex with art, drama and cookery rooms.

Pupils at The Hall had free time between dinner and bed. But staff nagged if you spent every night staring at your laptop, so Julius had signed up for twice-weekly weight training and Thursday night Cake Club.

The idea was that kids learned baking and raised money for charity selling cakes in the cafeteria at Friday morning break. Kids worked in pairs and Julius's partner, Chloe, was the type of person who was easy to get along with if you let her be boss. So, while she whipped up a carrot cake, Julius sloped off to talk to his mates.

Matt and three other lads at the back didn't take baking seriously. Gooey muffins and charred tarts were specialties and they were happiest when something was on fire.

'My T-shirt came,' Matt was saying as Julius wandered into earshot.

Matt lifted his flour-dusted apron, revealing a new tee, with the famous photo of Georgia Pack's leap off the balcony.

'What a girl,' a kid called Alexei said, grinning.

'I watched Georgia on *Late Night Live* in the summer,' Matt said, licking his lips. 'I was drooling.'

'Just your mouth?' Julius teased.

'Aren't you in the wrong conversation, Julius?' Matt shot back. 'I think those girls by the fridge are talking about cowboys.'

Julius smiled and flipped Matt off.

When he'd arrived at The Hall, Julius found out there were a few out gay kids, especially in the upper forms. It gave him the confidence to be honest about himself, and nobody made much fuss about it.

'Julius may be gay,' a titchy Israeli kid called Sacha told Matt. 'But I bet he *still* bangs a girl before you.'

The joking tailed off as Chloe came over, looking stern.

'Julius,' Chloe said curtly. 'Could you back away from the morons and pipe the passion-fruit frosting?'

The boys made whiplash sounds as Julius followed orders. He sliced the corner off an icing bag and was on his fifth muffin when a door at the back of the room burst open.

Two boys disguised with towels charged in, holding cans of shaving foam. As Matt and his three pals turned to see what was happening, they got blasted with white streaks.

'Fife House rules!' the attackers shouted.

The Hall encouraged rivalries between its seven boarding houses, with sports matches, academic quizzes and competitions to raise the most money for charity. There was also a tradition of less wholesome battles in the final days of each term.

'That is not acceptable!' cooking teacher, Mr Oxenbury, roared.

One of the attackers from Fife House exited the way he came. The other lost his footing on a streak of foam, which enabled Sacha to grasp the sleeve of his polo shirt. The Fife kid broke free, but not before Matt and his pals had blocked the back exit.

His only chance was to scramble forward, out of the main classroom door. A mixing bowl and a bag of flour hit the floor as the wiry lad ducked under a stainless-steel bench.

'Julius, get him!' Matt pleaded.

'Don't get involved,' Chloe warned.

But Julius still felt like an outsider, amongst lads who'd known each other since prep school. The feud didn't interest him but fitting in did.

As the Fife kid closed, Julius lunged, forgetting the bag of passion-fruit frosting in his hand. When he connected, the frosting did a custard-pie job. The lad's mouth had been open, and he stumbled into a bench, spluttering the icing he'd inhaled as Mr Oxenbury stormed the scene.

'No, no, no!' he roared.

Julius found himself more scared of Chloe, who gave him a two-handed shove and a pointy shoe in the shin.

'I spent ages making that,' she growled.

'Discipline bench,' Mr Oxenbury roared as he yanked the coughing Fife kid off the floor. '*And* you,' he added, tapping Julius. 'And the clown quartet at the back. I've had *more* than enough of you this term.'

Discipline bench was a row of warped gymnasium benches outside the oldest part of the school. Until 1983, any boy sent there got a thrashing. Now, the most painful aspect was being made to sit in the cold.

Since it was the last evening before half-term, The Hall was in party mood and lots of kids had found trouble. Drunk fifth-form girls were cross-legged on the floor. There were younger boys whose torn shirts suggested a fight, and two lads who'd attained god status after being caught partying in one of the girls' houses. But the majority were soldiers in the war between Fife and Brushwood.

All the lads from Fife House got called away by a pair of shouty teachers. Drunks and fighters were taken for more serious action. But Julius and the others from his house still sat in the dark when the dorm lights went out at 10 p.m.

'Maybe they forgot us,' Matt suggested. 'Should we just go to bed?'

'Last night of term,' a lanky boy explained. 'We'll be here till the teachers get kicked out of the village pub.'

FORTY-TWO

SAG gained publicity and thousands of new members after the spring protests. The branch that met in the Red Parrot's upstairs cafe now held larger meetings in a church.

But slick social media and hobnobbing with middle-class folks over ethically sourced nibbles wasn't everyone's idea of progress. Gerard got expelled from SAG when he threw wine at a man talking about how much his house was worth. Kamila and many other long-term SAGgers also felt the group had been swamped with moderates.

Georgia arrived at the Red Parrot with a Waitrose bag-for-life stuffed with drone parts. It was the second meeting of a yet-to-be-named splinter group. Some preferred Socialists Against Austerity, but New Socialist Action Group had a couple of supporters and Radical Anti-government Socialists was in the mix because it made a good acronym.

'Bus was late,' Georgia said, a touch breathless as she rounded the top of Red Parrot's tight staircase and gave everyone a wave.

The cafe was closed for the day. Zac got off his seat and gave Georgia a hug.

Georgia was less keen on Elodie, an athletic paramedic who was Zac's new housemate. She'd separated from her husband and wasn't up for anything serious, but Georgia knew they had something going on.

Kamila and three other members sat in a loose oval of chairs. Gerard was a lone wolf by the cafe counter, with a giant green smoothie and a graph pad, on which he scribbled notes and diagrams, as if nobody else was there.

'I got most of the stuff you asked for,' Georgia said as she put the bag down next to Gerard's chair.

Gerard slapped his notepad, face down so Georgia couldn't see. He was left-handed and his palm blue with ink.

'What didn't you get?' he asked intensely.

It sounded rude, but Georgia had known Gerard long enough to expect it. His intelligence was eccentric but easily dealt with once you knew what made him tick.

'No brushless motors,' Georgia explained. 'They're sixty quid a pop and I think Dad's staff pocketed the spares before they got laid off.'

'I need motors,' Gerard stated.

'I think everyone's here now,' Kamila told the room loudly. 'Shall we start?'

A couple of uni students rounded the top of the stairs, bringing the number in the room to nine.

The first item on Kamila's agenda was whether the yet-to-be-named group should have membership fees, or voluntary contributions only. Three people wanted the whole thing to be unstructured and anarchist. Kamila was a born organiser, who wanted memberships, committees, regular meetings and eventually a written constitution and elected leader.

Georgia found the discussion mind-numbing and tuned

out when they moved on to debating the group name. While Gerard yawned and went back to his scribbles, Georgia ached with jealousy as Zac edged closer to Elodie and slid his hand on top of hers.

'Georgia, NSAG or RAGS?' Kamila asked.

Everyone had been talking at once. Now it was quiet and all eyes were on Georgia.

'Eh?'

'We're tied at four votes each,' Elodie said. 'Yours is the casting vote.'

'RAGS,' Georgia decided. 'It's catchier. And saying we're the *New* SAG is catty and unoriginal.'

Zac smiled approvingly, but the student girl sat opposite tutted and shook her head.

'What's our voting age here?' she asked. 'She's only fourteen.'

'Fifteen,' Kamila corrected. 'And a member like everyone else.'

'We don't have a voting age, because we don't have a constitution,' Zac told student girl. 'How can you want a voting age, when five minutes ago you were an anarchist who didn't want an elected leader or to pay membership fees?'

'But who *can* vote?' the student girl asked. 'If I bring my seven-year-old nieces to the next meeting, do they get a say?'

'There's only nine of us,' one of the old SAG members moaned. 'If we can't agree on a name, simply draw lots and move on.'

Kamila got right in his face. 'We *did* agree on a name, Geoff. We *just* voted.'

'But is Georgia's vote valid?' Geoff asked.

Georgia was jealous of Elodie, bored with the debate and now people were telling her she was too young to matter.

'Ageist crap!' Georgia said, standing dramatically and looking around for her coat.

Zac got up and tried to calm Georgia down.

'New groups are always like this,' Zac soothed. 'Everyone wants to be the boss.'

Georgia knew she'd stop seeing Zac regularly if she walked out, so slumped back in her chair.

Across the room was another drama. Gerard had somehow offended the student girl. Her partner was less keen to walk out, but soon they were both heading downstairs.

'Utter farce,' Geoff said, checking his watch. 'I might as well get the early train . . .'

Kamila tried to persuade Geoff and another guy to stay, but by the end of the walkouts they were down to five: Kamila, Zac, Elodie, Gerard and Georgia.

'Who needs talkers?' Gerard shouted furiously, hoping the departed would hear before they exited the bookshop. Then, in an uncharacteristic display of emotional intelligence, Gerard saw that Kamila was tearful because the meeting she'd organised had collapsed and gave her a hug.

'Let's talk about my drone idea,' Gerard said importantly as he let go of Kamila and grabbed his much-scribbled pad. 'I know someone with a gig as a party intern. She can access diaries of senior politicians, and the impeller designed by Georgia's father gives us interesting possibilities.'

'What's an impeller?' Elodie asked.

After all the nonsense, Georgia jumped at a chance to contribute.

'An impeller is a pump that works by spinning,' she explained. 'My dad's company mostly sold survey drones, searching for corroded power lines and leaky roofs. But he also invented a very lightweight impeller pump.

'Quadcopters can't carry much, and liquids are heavy. My dad's impeller tried to get around weight limits by mixing liquids with air. You could use a shot of air to knock a birds' nest off a power line or blast leaves from a gutter. Or you could add liquid, like resin to fill a crack in a leaky roof, vinegar to clean an inaccessible window, that sort of thing.

'He made test impellers using 3D printers, but tooling up to put the kit in production would have cost over a hundred grand. He didn't have the money and he was scared to show the big Chinese drone manufacturers, because they're notorious for ripping off ideas.'

'You all need to see this,' Gerard said, holding out his phone.

Gerard had cued up a YouTube video, titled *Fuel Air (Thermobaric) Explosion*. The clip lasted twenty seconds, showing a fireball erupting out of a metal cylinder no bigger than a fire extinguisher. The mid-air explosion incinerated three large trees and made a shockwave that caved a metal roof like a boot on a soft-drink can.

'That's a fuel air weapon,' Gerard explained. 'Nozzles disperse a fine mist of aviation fuel into the air. The tricky part is that the mixture depends on atmospheric conditions, but if you get it right you make a huge fireball with a tiny amount of liquid. John Pack's impeller can be configured to make explosions like this.'

Kamila looked at Georgia accusingly. 'Your dad developed *that*?'

Gerard gave one of his superior snorts. 'John can't have realised his impeller could be weaponised. If he had, he'd have had defence companies queuing up to fund his research.'

Zac looked aghast. 'You're seriously talking about using one of John Pack's survey drones to create a giant fireball and blow up . . . whatever . . . ?'

'The government!' Gerard suggested cheerily. 'Well, some of it . . . The Russians add lightweight plastic flechettes to their thermobaric weapons. They can mince a person two hundred metres away . . .'

Georgia was horrified, but intrigued.

'Survey drones aren't as zippy as the racing drones I used to fly,' she thought aloud. 'But they'll do sixty kilometres per hour if you set the trim properly. If you flew to a target at top speed, you could probably blast fuel out of the nozzle before anyone shot the drone out of the sky . . .'

Elodie raised her arms in the air and sounded alarmed. 'What are we talking about here?'

'The radical in RAGS,' Gerard said determinedly.

Zac found the whole thing so mad he laughed. 'Gerard, I have *zero* desire to spend my next twenty years in prison.'

Georgia felt embarrassed by her flash of ill-considered enthusiasm. But Gerard kept rambling.

'It doesn't have to be fuel,' Gerard explained. 'There are guys at my lab in King's College working on attenuated viruses for pest control. My old lab partner wants to build a synthetic virus that stops the Killer T cells that control rodent immune systems. If they made a human version, we could load it in a drone. Wipe out a state banquet, or the entire platform at a party conference.'

Kamila put a hand on Gerard's back. 'Darling, you're getting carried away. *Radical*, yes. Mass murder, no.'

Zac used his bulk to push into the centre of the group and made calming gestures. 'We no longer believe that *any* of our mainstream political parties serve the interests of working people. We broke away from SAG because all they talk about is more marches and social media campaigns, and we saw how useless that was in April.

'We need something more effective than marches and online petitions, but less psychotic than bombs and killer viruses.'

Georgia, Elodie and Kamila nodded in agreement, but Zac and Gerard seemed to grate on each other and the women's warm response to Zac's comment left Gerard with a face like a kid who'd had his presents confiscated on Christmas morning.

'What about paint?' Georgia suggested. 'My dad programmed an impeller drone to paint a wall without any human input. You mix ordinary paint with thinner, so it comes through the impeller nozzle. Then fly the drone in and splat two litres of paint from point-blank range.'

'That could work,' Zac agreed. 'But politicians get egged and flour-bombed all the time.'

'Drone attacks are sexy,' Kamila noted.

Gerard looked reanimated. 'For serious publicity you'd have to dump a *lot* of paint on a top-level target.'

'Queen, or prime minister,' Elodie suggested, then looked at Zac. 'What would the legal repercussions be?'

'I'd need to check with my lawyer buddy,' Zac said. 'But how serious could it be? A non-lethal drone attack would get massive publicity, but from a legal standpoint I can't see how it's different to throwing an egg or a custard pie.'

'Maximum publicity, minimum risk,' Kamila said excitedly. 'Georgia's idea is *perfect.*'

'We'd have to fit high-resolution cameras to the drone to get good footage,' Georgia said, lapping up the praise. 'We could live-stream the entire attack.'

Kamila had been tearful, now she was purring. 'RAGS would

have Georgia Pack, icon and legend,' Kamila said. 'And the first time anyone hears our name will be when a drone flies over the prime minister's head and blitzes him with red paint.'

'SAG will be eating our dust if we pull this off,' Zac said keenly. 'We'll need a publicity strategy. Wendy Dewar's the best in the business.'

'Wendy's still working for SAG,' Kamila said distastefully.

'Wendy's a publicist first and a socialist second,' Zac said. 'She'll *love* this, and she can make sure our side of the story doesn't get destroyed by government spin and BBC bias.'

'We'll suspend meetings and recruitment and focus on this,' Kamila said.

'I'll need money,' Gerard interrupted. 'The impeller unit is clever, but John Pack's drone is poorly designed . . .'

Georgia felt a dent in her family pride and reared up. 'It's a survey drone designed to be flown by repair crews after half a day's training.'

'It can't fly for shit,' Gerard insisted.

'Did you bring the drone, like I asked?'

Gerard wheeled a large plastic case from behind the cafe's counter. He took out a drone, fifty centimetres across, with stilt legs that enabled cameras and tools to be slung under the body. He stood it on the counter next to the register as Georgia started laughing.

'You've fitted racing propellers,' she began contemptuously. 'You thought they'd make it faster, but they don't generate much lift. The motors have been taken out and put back without proper alignment. And I don't know *what* you've done to the control board, but the wiring looks like a bad-hair day . . .'

Georgia took a breath before spotting something else.

'*And* your carbon-fibre frame is cracked, so if by some

miracle this mess gets airborne, you'll have vibration that makes it impossible to control.'

'Can you fix it?' Zac asked as Gerard sulked.

'If I had a week to rebuild the thing from scratch,' Georgia said. 'Luckily, there are survey drones in my dad's lock-up that haven't benefited from Gerard's *improvements*.'

Gerard was excited enough by the plan to forget his humiliation.

'John Pack's impeller design is *excellent*,' Gerard said. 'I can use the lab at my university to get the paint-thinner mixture right.'

'You handle potions and Georgia handles the magic of flight,' Kamila told her boyfriend soothingly.

'What about timescale?' Zac asked.

'Every day we wait is a chance for information to leak,' Gerard said.

'Full speed ahead,' Kamila agreed.

'What's the earliest you can have a drone ready?' Zac asked.

'I need to order a box of motors, but once I have them I can prep a drone in a few hours,' Georgia said. 'Maybe a couple of practice flights over the weekend. I'll need someone to drive me out to an open space. Somewhere where I can practise flying a big drone and not get recognised.'

'About the same for me,' Gerard added. 'When Georgia does her test flight, we can test paint mixtures for rapid dispersal and nozzle clogging.'

'If we're confident on the technical side, we need to find our target quickly,' Zac said, turning to Gerard. 'How reliable is your insider?'

'It's my sister, Pippa,' Gerard confessed. 'She's a politics nut. Joined the party youth wing when she was fourteen. Finished her degree and got a job at Party Headquarters through our uncle. But Sis feels let down by everything that's happened since they got elected.'

'We should definitely use red paint,' Elodie said. 'It'll look like blood and scare the heck out of everyone!'

'Red for *true* socialism!' Zac added as he gave Georgia a smile.

FORTY-THREE

It was twenty to midnight when the master and deputy master of Brushwood House finished yelling and sent boys to bed. Six hours later, Julius found himself nudged from sleep by a man as tall as he was, but twice as wide.

'Morning, Adebisi,' Mr Apple said, with a grin Julius found unsuitable for the hour. 'My office, ten minutes.'

'Eh?' Julius murmured dopily, defending sleepy eyes from light coming through the door as Mr Apple headed out.

'I'll send flowers to your funeral,' Matt yawned as Julius pulled yesterday's shirt over his head and hopped into school trousers.

Julius was more curious than worried. Mr Apple had done Julius's induction when he'd arrived at The Hall and, despite looking like he could smash most men with a stare, the young games master seemed a good guy.

Julius's brain was woolly as he strode past a man running a floor polisher and headed for an office close to the boys' changing rooms. Steam and sweat lingered from the day before.

'Have a seat, big fella,' Mr Apple said.

It was a tiny office, with a tracksuit drying over the radiator.

'I tried to catch you during study period last night, but I was dealing with this house feud,' Mr Apple explained. 'I wanted to know how you're settling in.'

Julius yawned as he sat in a battered foam chair.

'Would it be fair to say things have been going well?' Mr Apple began.

Julius nodded. 'It's more chilled than my old school in Akure. I like having girls around and teachers who are almost human.'

Mr Apple laughed, then slapped his rock-hard stomach. 'You look fitter too. Must be the soccer and that weight training I made you sign up for.'

'Throw in weight loss from the tasteless food,' Julius added.

'I've been thinking about your soccer,' Mr Apple said. 'You won't win many foot races, but you've got height and your positioning is excellent. And for a central defender, speed is less important than being in the right place to start with.'

Julius didn't look convinced. 'It is?'

'After half-term, I'm moving you up from house team to the second squad.'

Julius was flattered, but wary. 'They train more, don't they?'

'Two sessions per week, alongside the first team.'

Julius didn't love the idea of training outdoors through an English winter. But soccer was mostly fun, and he trusted Mr Apple because he'd recommended weight training. It hadn't turned all of Julius's flab to muscle, but his arms and chest were bulkier, and a stronger core had done wonders for the stooped posture.

'I'm happy to try, sir,' Julius agreed.

'Are you flying back to Nigeria for the break?'

Julius shook his head. 'Just London.'

'Oh well, Christmas isn't far off,' Mr Apple said.

'Exactly,' Julius said, not mentioning that he probably wouldn't be flying home then, either.

Julius had two lessons after breakfast, then five forms headed into chapel for the end of term service. Helicopter landings obliterated parts of the service, and by the time pupils emerged, The Hall's driveway was choked with cars.

'See you at my place,' Matt told Julius as he walked out of their shared room with a small backpack and a roll bag crammed with dirty laundry.

A yellow chopper set the panes in Julius's bedroom window rattling as it took off with a billionaire's daughter aboard. Then he peered down at teens wheeling their luggage down the disabled ramp in front of Brushwood House.

Boys hugged parents, pretend-throttled little brothers and threw baby sisters in the air. Other interactions were more awkward. A dead-eyed scowl at an unloved stepfather in a Barbour jacket, a burly lad leaving his luggage to a pissed-off au pair and a young couple's parting snog, viewed by embarrassed parents.

But good or bad, they all had someone.

'You need to shift, fella,' a woman in a cleaner's smock snapped at Julius. 'We're stripping beds on this floor.'

Her meanness wilted when Julius glanced around, looking tearful.

'Just leaving, miss,' he said, tugging his wheelie bag off the bed and thinking about the ninety-minute taxi ride with an empty house at the end of it.

FORTY-FOUR

The townhouse was in one of the prestigious garden squares behind Chelsea's King's Road. Four floors, nine bedrooms and an underground extension with cinema, gym and four-car garage.

Julius shared the home with Polish housekeeper Milena and two of SJ's parents-in-law, who were in town for their thirtieth wedding anniversary.

It wasn't good company. Milena listened intently when Julius tried to make conversation, but her only response was to squawk *yes*, before wandering off, having clearly not understood a word. The middle-aged couple showed no interest in Julius beyond hellos in hallways. They'd leave home each morning in smart clothes, returning in a taxi stuffed with shopping bags, or late after the theatre.

Julius had come to think of the Chelsea house as a very fine prison. Days started early at Dormansland Hall, so he relished wallowing in the huge bed until noon. He'd spend at least an hour speaking to Duke about nothing and everything, then play Xbox or watch randomness on his laptop until hunger triumphed in its daily battle with sloth.

Julius could leave splashed tiles, balled socks and tangled bedding, knowing Milena would zoom in and straighten up when he left the house. Dirty clothes went to a nearby laundry, reappearing ironed and wrapped in pink tissue paper. He had to bury his ripped jeans and Nigerian army coat in a suitcase, because no amount of hand gestures and deliberately phrased English could convey to Milena that they were *supposed* to look scruffy.

A couple of times, Julius had taken a board over the river to Battersea Park. But rain had been lashing the windows all night, so he left the house at two on Wednesday, with his hoodie up and no plan, except to stay out because being home alone made him miserable.

It kept raining as he Ubered to a Nigerian cafe behind Oxford Circus station.

'Ayamase stew and rice.' The waitress grinned, as she found Julius a seat at a long counter lined with padded green bar stools. 'Right?'

'You know me too well,' Julius said cheerfully.

The place heaved with a mix of West Africans seeking comfort food and Brits in office wear, wanting more adventure than a chicken sandwich. The waiting staff were all authentically Nigerian, but it amused Julius whenever the door swung open into a kitchen filled with Asians and Eastern Europeans.

Well fed, Julius took the Underground to a Camden side street known for skate and trainer shops. He knew shopping wouldn't quell loneliness, but tried his best, dropping several hundred pounds on trainers, a limited-edition bamboo skate deck and a trio of pricy hoodies.

Bunmi had fixed Julius a debit card and monthly allowance.

But his departure for London hadn't been planned. When he first arrived, he'd been given the code for a walk-in safe in the basement and permission to take a few hundred pounds for taxi fares and school uniform. Julius had been dipping into stacks of mint £20 notes ever since.

Matt called as Julius headed back to the Underground, apologising that he'd left it until Wednesday because his dad had gifted him flying lessons for getting an excellent school report.

'Come and hang tomorrow,' Matt said. 'My family are doing a birthday dinner for my sister, which will be snores, but you can hang out. I think there's go-karting booked, but you don't have to—'

'I'm up for anything,' Julius said cheerfully. But a tick later he noticed that he – or more accurately his top-of-the-line phone and shopping bags – were getting eyed by three sturdy lads leaning on railings outside Mornington Crescent station. 'See you tomorrow, Matt. I've gotta run.'

The three dudes tailed when Julius went past. It was a quiet time of day. He didn't fancy his chances if they got in the station elevator, but not going into the station seemed just as risky. He saw salvation in the orange light on an approaching cab, but the driver saw a soggy black kid in a hoodie and kept driving.

Julius anxiously decided his best option was to cut between the traffic and call an Uber from inside McDonald's, but a second black cab pulled up to the kerb with a smiling lady driver.

'Where to, young man?'

'King's Road,' Julius said, then changed his mind. 'Actually, Leicester Square.'

The taxi windows were steamed from the warmth in the cab. As he wiped the foggy glass with his sleeve, Julius saw one of the three lads mouthing abuse. It was a scary reminder that he was alone and a long way from home.

The rain was no better when Julius got to Leicester Square, so he headed into a cinema. The movie was the latest version of the one he'd seen a hundred times, with the superhero discovering his powers, finding his nemesis, saving the world in a computer-generated action sequence that went on twenty minutes too long and ending inexplicably with a man-to-man fist fight where all their superpowers stopped working.

It was the VIP screen, with leather recliners and a waitress who brought steak nachos and chocolate milkshake an hour into the movie. His clothes were dry and the rain had paused when he stepped out into early-evening dark.

The cinema exit was at the side of the building and he accidentally walked the wrong way into Soho. He'd read about London's gay scene online and felt curious as he lugged his shopping past a bar filled with an after-work crowd.

There were guys holding hands across a rain-spattered table, shop windows with kinky leather masks and whips on display. The road was damp and neon signs reflected off the puddles as he looked through the doors of another busy bar.

Strictly 18+

ID checks in operation.

Julius was taller than most adults and thought about stepping inside. Would he get asked for ID? Would guys hit on him? And if they did, what kind? The hot Latin guy in the black muscle vest, or the seedy dandruff guy, bulging out of his suit at the bar?

The pavement was barely wide enough for two people to pass and he got scowled at by two hand-holding women who had to shuffle around him into the road. A few steps later, a bodybuilder type with a Ghanaian accent said, 'Oooh, young and fresh.' Julius thought the guy was talking to him, but when he looked behind, he realised the man was talking into a phone.

It felt exciting seeing a place where people being gay wasn't a big deal. But Julius's excitement was tempered by a sense that he didn't fit in. He might have been the tallest man in the narrow street, but he was also the youngest. He stood out, just as Matt would have done if he'd tried to pull women in their twenties and thirties after a day at the office.

Three drunk women were getting out of a cab fifty metres up the street. Julius's got this weird tight-chested feeling, like the whole world was looking at him. His shopping rattled as he charged for the parked taxi as if it was the last lifeboat on a sinking ship.

He got the usual wary look from the driver as he jumped through the open passenger door.

'St Crispin's Square, Chelsea,' Julius said, digging a couple of rolled twenties from his trouser pocket and flapping them. 'Yes, I have money.'

'We get knocked a lot by young fellas,' the driver said apologetically.

Julius tipped his head back as the taxi took a right and stopped for a busy pedestrian crossing. He felt every bit an awkward giant. Fifteen years old and seven thousand kilometres from anyone who loved him.

FORTY-FIVE

Georgia's sister was dead, her mum gave her brain ache, it was painful being in the same room as her dad, and she hardly saw Maya now they went to different schools. Georgia needed something to belong to and RAGS filled that hole.

Zac came to John Pack's workshop with a box of brushless motors he'd bought online, chatting and making coffee, while Georgia set up a survey drone.

The following evening, Georgia showed off her skills, delicately piloting the re-motored drone up the Red Parrot's narrow staircase. Kamila and Elodie hugged her. There were laughs when she used a pulse of air from the impeller to topple a wire rack stacked with vegan shortbread, before a gentle touchdown on the cafe's glass countertop.

Gerard had met with his sister and arrived during the flight demo with a copy of the prime minister's diary for the next two weeks.

'Sis wrote by hand, because they can track who sends what to the printers,' Gerard explained.

The five members of RAGS gathered around two scrunched sheets of graph paper. The writing was awful, but Gerard had already circled one section with a highlighter.

'Most stuff is indoors,' he explained. 'Meetings, lunches, parliament.'

'So what have you highlighted?' Elodie asked.

'Saturday week looks like our best shot,' Gerard answered. 'The prime minister is attending the ground-breaking ceremony for the new Banque Générale building. It's the first overseas bank to commission a new building in London for more than five years. The PM will put on a hard hat, pick up a shiny shovel and do his whole *Britain is open for business, the economy will bounce back* speech, before turning a couple of earth clods for the cameras.'

'We might splatter some fat-cat bankers too,' Zac added cheerfully.

'What about our launch point?' Georgia asked. 'Where's this building site?'

'Google Street View shows buildings that have just been demolished,' Gerard explained. 'It's in the City of London, surrounded by tall buildings.'

'Anywhere we can get a look at the site?' Kamila asked. 'A hotel or something?'

'Tower Fifty-Two,' Gerard said. 'It's an office block with a restaurant and public viewing deck up top. We should be able to survey the site and pinpoint the area laid out for the speech and ceremony.'

There was a positive vibe in the cafe as Zac gave Gerard a cheeky kiss on the cheek. The three women laughed, but Gerard hated being touched and scoured his cheek with his shirtsleeve.

'Zac and I are off-duty tomorrow,' Elodie said brightly. 'We can check out Tower Fifty-Two.'

'You can buy me lunch,' Zac teased, making Georgia ache with jealousy.

'There's another thing I'm worried about,' Gerard said, looking at Georgia. 'What if electronic countermeasures are deployed around the prime minster?'

Georgia looked thoughtful. 'Jamming the control signal for our drone?' she asked.

Gerard nodded as Zac, Elodie and Kamila looked concerned.

'Is that likely?' Zac asked.

'I'm not an electronic security expert,' Gerard said.

'We could use the drone's homing setting,' Georgia suggested. 'By default, the survey drone is programmed to pilot itself back to its launch point if it loses a control signal for more than a few seconds. But you can set the return point manually to anywhere you like . . .'

Gerard understood. 'If we know where the prime minister will be standing, the drone will still go there if our signal is jammed.'

Georgia nodded. 'There's a Java programming interface. I'm no coder, but it should be possible to write a program that makes the drone trigger the impeller before an emergency landing.'

'I did a ton of coding in my teens,' Gerard told Georgia. 'I can help you to figure it out, but we'll need the precise location where the prime minster will be making his speech.'

'Is that possible?' Zac asked. 'Without breaking in and measuring the building site.'

'With a laser measure, an altitude reading and some *very* basic maths,' Gerard said condescendingly.

'Does this mean we don't need to be at the scene?' Kamila asked. 'Can we hide the drone nearby the night before?'

Georgia shook her head. 'It's a back-up. It gives us a chance if they block my control signal. But we're *much* more likely to hit if I'm piloting, rather than guessing where the prime minister will be in advance.'

When she got home from the Red Parrot, Georgia found her dad's good Nikon camera, then fitted his longest zoom lens and put it on charge. Zac met her on the way to school the next morning, collecting the camera, then visiting Tower Fifty-Two with Elodie and taking photographs of Banque Générale's building site.

First thing Saturday, Georgia left home before her dad woke and took the short walk to the workshop. Zac and Elodie had to work, but Gerard borrowed an ancient Volvo estate car from his grandad and they loaded it with the drone, an identical back-up drone and a rolling cabinet that Georgia had packed with batteries, tools and spare parts.

There was a tangerine sunrise as Kamila drove thirty miles north to a farm owned by one of Gerard's work colleagues. Georgia had spent Friday afternoon's double-history lesson writing a test-flight program worthy of NASA, and Gerard chose to be impressed rather than snarky.

Georgia began by fitting her First-person View (FPV) goggles and getting a feel for piloting the survey drone in an open space. The operating software had so many safety features that it was virtually crash proof, but the drone could barely reach thirty-five kilometres per hour when weighed down by two 4K video cameras and an impeller loaded with 2.7 litres of liquid.

Georgia made adjustments to get the swift-but-deadly attack they'd envisaged. She connected to a laptop, switched off safety systems that impacted performance, adjusted the trim for speed and wired in a second battery pack. Extra power would burn out the motors, but John Pack had designed survey drones to last years, while RAGS only needed a two-minute bombing run.

As Georgia tuned the survey drone into a sharp-handling 90kph monster, Gerard ran ground tests with paint and impellers, and Kamila skipped around cow pats as she dragged a quartet of shop dummies into the middle of a field.

Elderly ramblers cutting through a neighbouring field stopped to watch as Georgia flew different approaches, seeking a balance between speed and noise. Kamila cheerfully told the ramblers they were film students, practising drone camerawork for a documentary. Georgia was recognisable, so she stayed in the Volvo, wearing a Star Wars bobble hat and FPV goggles.

The final stage was testing, with the impeller unit powered up. While Georgia had doubled power to the motors, Zac had souped-up the impeller so that it erupted with a crack that sent birds shooting out of trees. Within a second of Georgia hitting the trigger, the blast of paint and air turned the dummies red and snapped a polystyrene arm.

The recoil from the impeller blast flipped the drone upside down, but the automatic stability system reacted in a hundredth of a second, saving the drone from a messy landing in cow pasture.

Gerard reloaded with green paint, so they could distinguish the effect of Georgia's second attack run. A gust of wind meant only the top half of the dummies went green, but the result was still spectacular. On the downside, the shock from the impeller recoil killed one of the onboard cameras and Georgia felt horrible vibration on the return flight because a propeller had been knocked out of alignment.

'The boosted impeller blasts are trashing the drone,' Georgia told Kamila and Gerard. 'I'd like to do a couple more practice runs, but I don't want to wreck it.'

She flew two final runs with their back-up drone. The first made sure it worked the same way as the primary. Finally, Georgia simulated a jammed signal by launching the back-up, then pulling the battery out of the transmitter linked to her goggles. Gerard had written a program and the quad kept flying, before spraying the dummies and landing nearby.

Everyone met up at the Red Parrot that evening. Georgia got showered with praise as Zac, Elodie and Wendy watched in-drone test footage and the slow-motion paint splatters Kamila shot on her phone. Afterwards, they moved on to Wendy's house, where her wife was making curry.

Georgia saw Sam for the first time in ages. She drank a couple of Peronis and stayed until political talk had been replaced by Abba and bad dancing. It was past midnight when she got home, but her brain was too busy for sleep.

She stared at the ceiling above her bed, worried about the upcoming attack and doubting it would change the world. But these rational doubts mattered less than the sense that she'd made friends and belonged to something bigger than herself.

FORTY-SIX

Julius sprawled over his huge bed, next to an Alienware laptop. Its screen showed Duke walking out of his apartment, then holding his phone up to a hallway window, giving a view towards the centre of Akure.

'Can you see?' Duke asked.

'Pic's breaking up, but I recognise stuff.'

'It's Thursday morning,' Duke said. 'But it feels like 3 a.m. Everyone is scared to go out.'

'At least this bastard election will be over tomorrow,' Julius sighed. 'Is the media still predicting SJ will win?'

Duke spoke as he walked back into his apartment and snapped bolts on the door. 'So many votes are fake; I wonder why they bother campaigning for real ones. My uncle was tipped off that the ballroom at the governor's mansion is storing hundreds of ballot boxes, pre-stuffed with votes for Adebisi. Sunshine Radio says polling stations in Ondo City, where Rotimi's vote is strongest, have received no voting papers.'

'Good old-fashioned democracy,' Julius laughed as he scratched himself.

'At least I might be leaving,' Duke said.

Julius looked surprised. 'Really?'

'Remi has been offered the job of Africa correspondent for a Dutch TV station. He'd be based in Amsterdam. They can get me an education visa, and the salary and benefits are tip-top.'

'Sweet,' Julius said as he grinned and sat up. 'When did you find that out?'

'He had an interview last week,' Duke said. 'I didn't want to say until they offered him the job.'

'That would be *so* cool, Duke! Amsterdam is four hours on Eurostar. We could see each other all the time.'

'Get high in every coffee shop!' Duke said, but his tone hinted at a glitch. 'Uncle is torn. He has debts and we're close to losing this apartment. He'd have to abandon his anti-corruption campaign, and he says TV journalism is *soul-destroyingly shallow*.'

'Do you think you can persuade him?' Julius asked.

'I'm using all my moves,' Duke said. 'Imagine, Amsterdam! A cool apartment, a European school. All the art galleries. Skate parks! A million new things to draw . . .'

'Electricity that works twenty-four-seven,' Julius added.

Duke laughed. 'You forgot, *not being terrified to drink the tap water*.'

'Is that still going on?' Julius asked. 'Are people still sick?'

'Thousands,' Duke said. 'The water is fine, but the centre of town is like a horror movie. People are seriously ill and have no healthcare. All restaurants and most town-centre shops are closed and the people who fled the slums haven't come back.'

'Where did they go?' Julius asked.

'They piled into any long-distance bus with a seat,' Duke answered.

Julius checked the time in the corner of his laptop screen and saw it was close to eleven.

'I need to shift off this bed,' Julius said. 'I'm heading to Matt's place. We're going go-karting.'

'Sounds more fun than my day,' Duke said. 'Mum's taking me to a maxillofacial specialist. I'm still getting pain in my jaw. I'll probably need another procedure, but only the Lord knows where the money will come from . . .'

Julius thought about the basement safe. Besides the British pounds he'd been gently plundering, there were Euros, dollars, gold ingots, fancy watches, jewellery boxes and other stuff he'd not even looked at.

But Julius had to park these thoughts and get ready.

After a shower, and a fashion crisis, won by black jeans and one of the hoodies he'd bought the day before, Julius rode the underground to Hampstead, where he got picked up by Matt's mum in a plush Mercedes SUV.

Matt was in the front, so Julius climbed in the back with Matt's younger brother, Freddie, and his freckled pal. It was Matt's sister Abi's fourteenth birthday, and her brothers had been allowed to take one friend each.

The karting track was inside a big warehouse. Abi was a social creature, who'd overdone the make-up. Her crew played with phones and acted out teen dramas that involved lots of *Oh my God*s and girls chasing each other in and out of bathrooms.

'You got any tracks like this in Abuja?' Matt asked.

'Abuja's the capital,' Julius corrected. 'I'm from Akure. It's state election day, so today's main pursuits will be ballot rigging, followed by a riot.'

Matt laughed as he dug his mitt into a bowl of popcorn. 'Awesome hoodie, by the way.'

'Camden, yesterday,' Julius explained as nine-year-old Freddie and his freckled pal got yelled at for running over a table. Seeing the boys mess around made him miss Gabe.

Julius scoffed hot dogs, corn chips and peanut M&Ms as electric carts whooshed around the indoor track. He got nervous when it was his turn to race. The biggest size crash helmet was a squeeze and his knees splayed awkwardly either side of the steering wheel when he lowered himself into the kart.

From second on the grid, Julius was last after two corners and suspected he was the only one in the race who hadn't driven a kart before. Matt and Freddie lapped Julius as they battled for the lead on their final lap.

Julius made an old-man's groan as he climbed out, knees and ankles sore from being wedged as he crossed the floor to console himself with more junk food.

'It's a good circuit here,' Matt said, glowing from victory over his little brother. 'What did you think?'

'I think the karts are too bloody small,' Julius joked as he rubbed his knee.

Julius's second and third races were no more comfortable, but he got a feel for the kart and put in a few respectable laps.

After karting, they drove back to Matt's house. The five-bed house was big by London standards, but not in the same league as the homes Julius was used to. Abi's friends all went home after the karting and Freddie was having a sleepover at his friend's house, so dinner was a low-key spag Bol, cooked by the au pair and eaten with Matt, Abi and their parents.

It was the kind of *proper* dining-table scene that Julius's family never did. Abi had a late-delivery gift of a new smart speaker for her room, Matt spoke at painful length about his flying lessons, while his mum tried to make Julius feel welcome by asking lots of questions about life in Nigeria. Matt's dad,

Miles, tapped emails on his phone until Julius got asked what his family did.

'A bit of everything,' Julius said warily. 'My mum runs a religious ministry and a textile business. My uncle is the governor of Ondo State, though he might not be by tomorrow!'

'Governor,' Miles said, looking up from the pasta twirled around his fork. 'I set up a tax-efficient pension scheme for some chaps doing a construction project in Nigeria. State governor is big there, isn't it?'

Julius nodded. 'Especially in the states with oil. The governor gets to decide where the oil revenue goes.'

'Is Ondo an oil state?' Miles asked.

'There are offshore rigs along our coast,' Julius said, as he demonstrated smallness with a thumb and forefinger held a centimetre apart. 'But most Nigerian oil is further east, in the Niger Delta.'

Abi had googled, getting a bunch of results about the Adebisi family. 'Holy shit, Julie, you're loaded!' she blurted.

'Abi,' her mother rebuked. 'Don't be childish.'

'*Interests in construction, property and West Africa's largest textile business have made the Adebisi family one of Nigeria's richest,*' Abi read defiantly from her screen. '*Strong political and religious influence and close relationships with Chinese investors reinforce Adebisi's position, particularly in Ondo State, where—*'

'Julius showed me a pic of his family outside the governor's mansion,' Matt interrupted. 'The place is bigger than our school.'

'You're embarrassing our guest,' Matt's mum said firmly. 'Pack it in, both of you.'

Miles piped up a couple of seconds later. 'I'm a financial

consultant,' he told Julius, taking a business card out of a leather pouch and sliding it across the dining table. 'I've handled money for many Nigerian clients. So, if there's ever anything you or your family need . . .'

Matt pointed at his dad and grinned. 'Just don't google him, or you'll see how my dad got fined for setting up dodgy tax shelters for Premier League players.'

Julius laughed as he took the card. 'You never know, sir,' he told *Miles Taylor ACCA – Founder and Senior Partner.*

Abi stared down at her plate and shook her head. 'Daddy, could you be any tackier?'

'Business is all about connections,' Miles said, eyeing his daughter fiercely. 'I didn't see you complaining it was *tacky* when you opened a stack of presents this morning. Or when you spent Easter heli-skiing in Canada . . .'

Matt's mum groaned. 'Can this family eat *one* meal in peace? It's Abi's birthday, Miles. Give her a break . . .'

'It's past seven already,' Matt said. 'OK if Julius sleeps over?'

The parents looked at each other, then shrugged and smiled.

'If it's OK with Julius's family,' Matt's mum said.

'We could chill and play Xbox till whenever, without you having to get back,' Matt explained.

Julius suspected Matt had raised the sleepover to stop his family plunging into an argument, but agreed eagerly because it meant less time alone at the Chelsea house.

FORTY-SEVEN

They thought they'd planned everything.

Kamila had just called to say the prime minister's motorcade had entered the Banque Générale site. Georgia, Zac and Gerard were in a ninth-floor room of City Lodge, a three-star hotel with a hospital vibe, and no buildings to weaken a drone's signal between the east facade and the target.

'I thought you asked if the window opened,' Zac roared incredulously.

'I asked when I booked,' Gerard growled back. 'I said I had asthma and liked fresh air.'

'But you didn't check last night, when you arrived?'

Gerard and Zac were very different people, but the same in one important respect: they both liked being in charge. While they did their alpha-male thing, Georgia focused on the problem.

The window *did* open. She'd even tested it when she'd checked in the night before. But when they'd tried to open it wide enough to let the drone out, the sliding glass pane thumped into a rubber bung.

As Georgia examined a box of drone spares on the bed,

Gerard grabbed a wheeled office chair and flung it at the glass.

'Don't be an ass!' Zac shouted as the chair bounced off the glass with a plasticky boom. 'We need something sharp. Like those emergency hammers they have by train windows.'

Gerard banged his knee on a radiator as momentum sprawled him and the chair across a little desk.

'It's just a stopper,' Georgia said, hoping her deliberate calm would rub off on the guys as she held a grubby net curtain out of the way. 'If we take this out, the window will slide all the way.'

Georgia grabbed a screwdriver but strained to loosen the screw. Zac took over. The first head loosened easily, but he had a fight with the second.

Gerard's phone rang.

'Slide it now,' he ordered.

But the window stopped in the same spot.

Georgia looked up. 'There's one in the upper rail as well.'

Zac swore as he moved back in with the screwdriver. 'I can't reach. Pull the table out.'

Georgia carefully dragged away a glass-topped table, on which the drone sat, ready to launch.

'That was Kamila,' Gerard announced. 'She's outside the construction site. The PM is on stage, about to start his speech.'

'Come *on*,' Georgia urged.

Zac was at full stretch, making it hard to apply strength. The first screw dropped out of the window casing and pinged off a metal radiator. More in hope than expectation, Zac dug the head of the screwdriver under the bung and twisted. The plastic snapped away, but the screw head stayed in place.

'It might clear,' Zac said.

Georgia gave the window a hard shove. The upper frame screeched against the jutting screw, but she got a waft of fresh air as the window opened a full metre.

'Rock and roll!' Zac grinned.

'We have no idea how long this speech will be,' Gerard said urgently as he helped Zac push the drone table back to the window.

'Hold those billowing curtains out of my way,' Georgia ordered. She fitted her FPV goggles, then said sarcastically to Gerard, 'Power on now, maybe?'

Zac held the curtains as Gerard activated power switches for the drone and impeller.

'Good to launch,' Gerard said.

Georgia's world was now through goggles. The display showed full power packs, two cameras recording and the impeller online. She throttled up aggressively, knowing the anti-collision system would save her from the ceiling, then tilted to fly forward.

Gerard had calculated the journey from City Lodge's ninth floor to the podium where the PM was speaking as 783 metres. From a standing start to a top speed of 90kph, the flight would take forty-three seconds.

Georgia was used to launching from the ground and felt disorientated having eight storeys below as she settled into level flight. As the drone accelerated, Georgia skimmed close to glazed office facades, making the drone harder to spot than against open sky.

She hadn't counted on two men in a window-washer's carriage and skimmed their heads.

'They're all dressed in black,' Zac said, watching on the laptop.

'Protection officers,' Gerard confirmed. 'Snipers, most likely.'

'Let me concentrate,' Georgia commanded, knowing there was nothing she could do if someone was a good enough shot to blast the drone out of the sky.

Her mark to turn away from the building facades was a seven-storey car park, aiming towards a giant yellow pile-driving machine at the heart of the construction site. The video glitched as she crossed the threshold, throttling down to quieten the final approach.

Georgia eyed the podium, press and the seated rows of construction workers and their families. She saw the back of the prime minister's head, with the City of London mayor and the French ambassador seated either side.

The signal stayed strong as Georgia flipped a switch on top of her control box to release the paint. The kick from the impeller sent the drone and cameras spinning.

Georgia's view was blurred by a mist of paint on the camera lens, but she could see movement down by the stage.

Zac watched the view from one of the high-resolution cameras on the laptop.

'Dead on target,' he shouted happily.

Rather than bring the drone back, Georgia had programmed a hold. This would leave it hovering thirty metres over the site, recording events, until it was shot down, or the battery died.

As the drone rose, Georgia got a sense that people in the seats were scattering. Then her whole field of view flashed orange. Georgia lost video and the battery overheat light flashed.

'I think they shot me down,' Georgia blurted.

But the drone stabilised itself and the video came back. Smoke billowed and there were licks of flame.

'Fireball,' Gerard blurted.

The drone was stable. There was no more piloting necessary,

so Georgia ripped off the FPV goggles.

'Why's it on fire?' Zac shouted accusingly at Gerard.

'How should I know?'

Georgia pushed between the guys to look on the laptop. Her FPV camera showed blurs, but one of the high-resolution cameras had survived and was showing the aftermath of an explosion.

Police were approaching the stage, wary of the grey smoke. The press were breaking out of their enclosure to get closer, while the audience of site workers grabbed kids and scrambled for the exit.

Georgia felt a chill as her phone started to vibrate. She saw Wendy's name but ignored the call.

'You total psycho,' Zac roared at Gerard. 'Spraying paint is minor assault, maximum two years. Setting off a bomb is thirty . . .'

'It *was* paint,' Gerard insisted, intimidated by Zac's looming bulk.

'You showed that video at the Red Parrot,' Zac accused. 'Fuel air weapon.'

Georgia was mystified. She'd been alongside Gerard when he'd set up the impeller the night before. The red paint looked like the same stuff they'd tested a week earlier and she didn't see how Gerard could have turned the impeller from a paint sprayer to a bomb without installing something to spark the blast.

On the other hand, he was super smart and crazy enough to do anything . . .

'I don't know what happened,' Gerard shouted, close to begging as he backed away from Zac and the laptop. 'The thinned paint *was* flammable . . .'

Zac seemed angry beyond reason. 'You had no right,' he shouted.

Georgia knew Zac had thumped the guy in the pub the day after Sophie died and he'd had the written warning for shouting abuse at his boss. But Georgia had never seen Zac lose his cool and it frightened her.

'Guys, we need to get out of here *as planned*,' Georgia begged.

Wendy called again. Georgia answered and Wendy started to babble. 'I've been getting the live video feeds. What happened?'

'Nobody knows,' Georgia yelled into her phone. 'Can't talk, gotta get out of here.'

Georgia didn't hear what Gerard said next, but Zac didn't like it. The laptop crashed off the desk as Zac grabbed Gerard's shirt and thumped him against the wall. A lamp clattered off a bedside table as Gerard slid down the wall. Then Zac pulled Gerard up and slugged him in the gut.

'Stop it,' Georgia pleaded, trying to grab Zac's arm to stop him punching again.

'It's paint, paint, paint!' Gerard shouted childishly as he tried scrambling away across the bed.

'Zac, get a grip!' Georgia pleaded.

Zac punched Gerard again. Gerard was badly winded as he tried to escape over the bed. Zac grabbed his ankles and dragged Gerard back. They were both big guys, but Gerard was pudgy while Zac had muscle.

Facing a stronger opponent who seemed determined to seriously hurt him, Gerard grabbed a set of needle-nosed pliers from the toolkit and lunged at Zac's stomach. Zac defended himself, but the cost was a howl of pain and a bloody gouge up the back of his hand.

The phone beside the bed started ringing.

318

Gerard lunged again with the pliers and this time they bedded in Zac's thigh. Zac spasmed in pain, then pushed his knee down on Gerard's throat. As Gerard choked, Zac ripped the pliers out of his thigh, then plunged them into Gerard's right eye.

Georgia dry-heaved as blood sprayed the duvet.

'I'm going to prison because of you,' Zac roared.

It was horror-movie stuff, as Gerard thrashed about with pliers sticking out of his eye and Zac's jeans sopping with blood.

Georgia nearly vomited, grabbing her coat, instinctively feeling pockets for phone and house keys.

'Georgia, wait,' Zac shouted, as she opened the door into the hallway.

But she didn't.

FORTY-EIGHT

Julius's vision blurred. His uncle's third wife's mother leaned over, wearing a Hermès neckerchief over skin cracked like an overdone sponge cake.

'Lying on this floor in such mess!' she yowled. 'Get those lanky legs off the floor at once.'

Friday night hadn't been the Roman orgy Julius had plotted on the phone with Duke. But three guys and two girls from The Hall had rocked up for a fun night, involving poker, beer, truth or dare, shots of his uncle's £750-a-bottle whisky, a monster joint and a curtain rail getting pulled off the wall.

'I will call Simon Adebisi about this,' his uncle's third wife's father threatened, from out in the hallway. 'Your antics kept us awake past 3 a.m.'

The couple doddered out as Julius sat up, rubbing a gluey eye and easing off the polo shirt stuck to his back.

Milena was already cleaning up. Spray bottles and cloths stood on the coffee table and there was a trash bag filled with beer cans in the doorway. Julius's hangover was mild, but stepping on the sharp edge of a bottle opener made him yelp, hop, then crash across a leather sofa.

His phone dug into his thigh as he sat up. He fished it out and saw the battery was down to nineteen per cent. It was almost eleven, so he was surprised to see nothing from Duke. But Anya from school had messaged to ask if she'd left her jacket at his house and Matt had sent a pic of a half-dressed girl in one of the spare bedrooms and the message, *You should probably change the sheets* . . .

'I'm sorry about the mess,' Julius told Milena guiltily when he passed her in the hallway, using bleach and a dish sponge to work a stain off a chair.

His thoughts turned to the election back home as he stepped into his room. He sat on the end of his bed, opened a Nigerian news app, clicked the *State Elections* tab and scrolled. Thirty-three of thirty-six states had now declared governorship results, but Ondo wasn't one of them.

When he tapped *Ondo*, the headlines had barely changed from the day before.

Adebisi-Rotimi battle too close to call.

Second recounts demanded amidst allegations of fake ballots.

Death toll in rural polling station shoot-out rises to five.

Adebisi says, 'Result closer than anticipated,' as Rotimi supporters bullish.

Second night of violence hits Akure and Ondo City.

Julius considered messaging Duke, but they often stayed online for more than an hour, so he decided to shower first. As he moved to put his phone on a charging pad, a green *Breaking News* box rolled across the screen.

321

London: *Sensational footage as prime minister suffers burns in drone attack.*

Rather than squint at his phone, Julius grabbed a remote and flipped the wall-mounted TV to BBC News. The screen showed a looped video of the attack. Not the jerky low-latency video Georgia had flown by, but the high-def feed from the stabilised camera slung under the drone's belly. The approach looked like video-game footage as it zoomed over construction equipment and closed on the prime minister's rear. Everything spun and went red. Then orange. Then blacked out, before the eerily silent video resumed from a hover thirty metres above chaos.

Prime minister's injuries described as serious but not life-threatening scrolled across the bottom of the screen. *French ambassador serious but stable ...*

The news channel switched from drone footage to an excited correspondent at a police cordon.

'*The video of the attack has been watermarked by a group calling itself Radical Anti-Government Socialists,*' she explained. '*It's not a group I have previously heard of, but the attack clearly shows sophisticated planning and knowledge of the prime minister's schedule.*'

'*Christine, I'm going to interrupt you there,*' the newsreader in the studio said, as the director cut back to the newsroom. '*We're getting more on this fast-moving story. Reports are coming in of a bizarre incident at City Lodge Hotel, close to the Banque Générale site, and from which several eye witnesses say the drone was launched.*

'*Hotel staff say two bloodied men were taken to hospital under police escort following a stabbing incident. There has been no official police statement, but a hotel manager told a reporter from* the *Newman News Agency that she was called to the room after a guest reported hearing a disturbance. She said the window in the room had been forced open and the room contained a second drone, as well as a laptop that was still relaying a live video feed.*

'*A hotel security officer challenged a young woman fleeing the scene, but she was able to escape through a fire exit.*

'*I have also just been told we have a short statement from the City of London Police. It concerns a suspect who is a minor, but we have been cleared to release her identity, as she may present a danger to public safety.*

'*The statement says,* "An initial viewing of CCTV footage has led investigating officers to suspect that the person who fled City Lodge after assaulting a member of hotel security staff is Georgia Pack."

'*Viewers may recall, Pack was the teenage activist who adorned the front page of many newspapers when she led a series of school walkouts during anti-government protests in April. Pack is known to be an experienced drone racing pilot...*'

Julius was fascinated by the unravelling story as he stripped for his shower. When his stale-smelling polo shirt popped off his head, the TV set in the tiles over his bathtub showed a photo of a pretty girl with braces, aged about twelve. She held a small racing drone and wore a shiny nylon bowling shirt with *Drone Pack* embroidered across the front.

Georgia Pack – Suspect popped onscreen. Then the photo switched to a more famous one of Georgia's leap over the railing in the council chamber.

'*City of London Police would like members of the public to report any sightings of Georgia Pack,*' the reporter at the police cordon said excitedly. '*But urge the public not to approach her as she may be armed and dangerous...*'

FORTY-NINE

While Gerard and Georgia had practised the mechanics of the attack, Wendy had created an elaborate media plan for the aftermath of a successful, non-violent attack on the prime minister. The plan called for laptops and equipment to remain in the ninth-floor hotel room, continuing to stream live video from the drone to the internet while Zac, Georgia and Gerard walked briskly to an elevator.

After passing through the hotel lobby, they would make a two-hundred-metre walk to a VW Golf parked in a side street, with Elodie waiting in the driver's seat. She would drive the trio three miles north to an Islington house, where they'd meet up with Wendy. Kamila, who was acting as a scout at the attack site, would travel separately by Tube train and arrive a few minutes later.

The house had cameras and a backdrop ready to record interviews for Red News Network. By the time the interviews were over, two of Zac's activist lawyer friends would have arrived. Wendy would then call the media, tipping them off about a location close to where the suspects were hiding. Ten minutes later, the lawyers would call the police to tell them that

Kamila, Georgia, Gerard and Zac were prepared to surrender. Wendy would send out tweets asking activists to come and give support. If all went to plan, there would be a media scrum and maximum publicity as the police arrived, taking the four suspects and their lawyers into custody to face minor assault charges.

But that plan had literally gone up in smoke.

Georgia found herself scrambling up the steps at Farringdon Tube station, casting sly glances at CCTV and half expecting a phalanx of armed cops at the ticket barriers.

She'd ridden one stop, figuring the longer she stayed on the train, the more likely there'd be cops waiting at the exit. Her Oyster card opened the barrier and the clear November morning felt blinding as she exited, walking fast to nowhere in particular.

Georgia dreaded prison as she wondered how badly the explosion had hurt the prime minister. But it was Zac's childish behaviour that overwhelmed her. Losing his temper and squaring off with Gerard, like two kids in a school lunch line . . . Sophie used to joke about Zac's socialist pals, his week-long sulks and two-hour phone calls to his mother in Hong Kong. Zac boasted about egging prime ministers, getting arrested on demos and being wanted by the Chinese authorities. And the day Sophie died, when he turned up drunk and bloody after a fight in a pub . . .

Zac's a dick, like Rolf and all his idiot mates. How did I not see that? Why did I follow him into this?

Georgia's brisk stride was weighted by the dark heave that comes before crying. She imagined escaping consequences by jumping in front of the bus barrelling down the road. She winced when she picked out her phone and saw *Missed call – Dad*. She imagined him in his boxers, watching his daughter throw her life away on the kitchen telly.

Part of Georgia wanted to call back. Tell Dad she was sorry and that she loved him, but her practical side won out. Wendy answered breathlessly.

'Honey, where are you?'

Georgia read from the bus stop up ahead. 'Farringdon Road, towards King's Cross. Is it on the news? Is anyone dead?'

'They're saying the French ambassador has serious burns.'

'The prime minister?' Georgia asked, glancing over her shoulder at what she feared was a cop car but was just a regular white estate.

'Second-degree burns to his face and neck,' Wendy answered. 'But they arrested Zac and Gerard with stab wounds. What the hell?'

'Zac went nuts,' Georgia explained. 'He thinks Gerard swapped the paint for an explosive without telling us.'

'Did he?'

'I have my doubts,' Georgia said, lowering her voice as a holding-hands couple came the other way. 'I think there would have had to be something extra fitted on the drone to spark the explosion. But Gerard said the paint was flammable. Something could have sparked it accidentally.'

'BBC said one of the PM's bodyguards shot a stun gun at the drone as it approached.'

'That could do it,' Georgia realised, stopping by the kerb at a busy junction.

'Gerard got his bomb by accident,' Wendy said, aghast.

'And pliers rammed in his eye,' Georgia added, hurrying across as the green man popped up. 'That hotel room was like a horror movie.'

'We're all in a lot less trouble if we can prove the explosion was an accident,' Wendy said. Georgia heard a doorbell ring in the background. 'That's probably Kamila.'

'Where now?' Georgia asked, as she heard Wendy walking downstairs to answer a door. 'I could get a taxi over to you? I don't remember the address . . .'

Georgia heard a big crash down the line. Then a thud and shouts.

'Police, police, back to the wall, hands on head.'

Georgia's hand trembled as she heard a scuffle, followed by Wendy shouting, 'I know my rights. I'm a journalist.'

'On your knees,' a cop yelled back.

The phone got picked off the hallway floor and an officer confirmed, 'Sir, she's talking to Pack. The call's still live.'

'Hello?' a cop said into the phone, as another shouted, 'Who else is in this house?' in the background.

Georgia dabbed the end-call button, lungs feeling smashed as she stumbled into the glass frontage of an office building. She sat on a marble ledge. Close to vomiting, hands and knees shaking uncontrollably.

She thought about throwing her phone away because the cops were probably using it to track her. Instead, she scrolled her contacts until she found the emergency lawyer Zac had told her to call if things went wrong.

But Zac was a total idiot, so she called her dad.

FIFTY

After boozing the night before, Julius didn't have the oomph for the cinema or Battersea Park skateboarding. But he thought a walk might clear his head, so he strolled to a favourite sandwich place, near King's Road, and grabbed strong coffee and turkey and bacon on rye to go.

Out of guilt, he also bought two cream cakes for Milena. But her English was terrible and when he got home he found himself shouting, 'This is a thank you for cleaning up my mess,' several times and, 'These are for you.'

He'd grabbed a plate for his sandwich and was turning towards his room when Milena pointed to a flashing light on the answerphone. 'It came for you.'

Everyone called Julius on his mobile, so he was curious as he grabbed the cordless handset and searched for the *play message* menu. The voice was familiar but unusually rapid.

'Julius, if you are home please pick up immediately,' SJ said. 'There is an urgent matter of family business. I will try to get your mobile number, but please call at once.'

Julius figured he'd get a deserved bollocking for the party. He thought a busy state governor might forget about a teen doing minor damage to a house thousands of kilometres away, but Julius didn't like having trouble linger and called back to get it out of the way.

He expected a receptionist or assistant, but went straight to his uncle.

'Julius my boy!' SJ said, remarkably fond considering Julius had trashed his house and bitten off the tip of his son's nose. 'I hear you are at the Chelsea house this week?'

'Yes, sir,' Julius said, thrown by his uncle's tone.

'Has your mother told you about the election?'

'No.'

'It's bad,' SJ said darkly. 'The result will be announced in one hour. Rotimi is back, by the narrowest of margins.'

'Sorry to hear that,' Julius lied.

'You are my only blood family in London,' SJ said. 'There is urgent business to attend to before the new governor is sworn in on Monday. I need you to take and sign documents at the West African Development Bank on the Strand. There are bank account numbers you must write down. Is pen and paper to hand?'

'I'll give you my email, or you can text them,' Julius suggested.

'No, no!' SJ blurted. 'There must be no electronic record of these accounts. Your first step is to access the safe. It is situated at the rear of the basement near the wine cellar.'

Julius smirked. 'I think I saw that when I was younger, playing hide-and-seek.'

'Good!' SJ said. 'I will now give you the safe access code.'

'Pen poised, Uncle,' Julius said, before taking down a code he knew by heart.

Julius was surprised when his uncle told him the location of a concealed keypad and a second code, to unlock an additional compartment in the safe floor. SJ told Julius that this part of the safe contained letters, with detailed instructions for moving money from bank accounts held by the Ondo State Government into a variety of accounts held by shell corporations in Switzerland, Costa Rica and the Isle of Man.

Julius thought about the criminal implications of what he was being asked to do as he filled four sides of A5 paper with names, account numbers, amounts and passcodes. He wondered what Remi could do with this information and worried that he still hadn't heard from Duke.

'Your contact at WADB is called Eddie,' SJ said as he neared the end of the convoluted explanations. 'His fee was agreed at twenty thousand pounds. There is cash in the safe to pay him. Take a couple of thousand and buy yourself something nice for your trouble.'

'That's very kind, Uncle.'

'Call me on this number when the process is complete. No electronic messages! Not ever!'

'I will,' Julius agreed. 'Is my mother with you at the mansion?'

'She is in town, dealing with her legal situation,' SJ said.

'Legal?'

SJ coughed, then sounded irritated at having to explain. 'Rotimi has promised to go after our family for corruption and says Adebisi money funded the transport park bombing. Under the Nigerian constitution, a state governor has immunity from any crimes committed while in office. So your mother is Governor Rotimi's target and she is taking defensive steps. Meeting lawyers and such.'

Julius wasn't his mum's biggest fan, but that didn't mean he wanted her thrown in jail. 'The police are loyal to her though?'

SJ laughed. 'Rotimi will put his men in all the big police jobs.

The rank and file will follow because the state government pays their wages. I asked your mother to join you in London until the dust settles, but you know her way. Bunmi is never afraid to stand and fight . . .'

'Nobody has outsmarted her yet,' Julius observed.

'Agreed,' SJ said, laughing proudly. 'Right now our family must pull together and focus on the tasks we have been given. Yes?'

'I'll get right on it,' Julius said.

He resented this sudden call on his loyalty. He'd been exiled to a lonely existence thousands of miles from home. He was only being involved in family business out of desperation and a big part of him would have delighted in telling Uncle Simon to go screw himself. But Julius depended on his family for everything from school fees to pocket money and getting on his uncle's good side might significantly increase his chances of being allowed a visit home.

Julius called Eddie, who said the West African Development Bank's London branch didn't open on Saturday, but that he'd meet there in an hour.

Julius was gobbled by curiosity as he ran down to the basement safe, opened the heavy walk-in door, then followed SJ's explanation, lifting out three metal shelves that braced a panel concealing the second keypad. After a whirr of bolts, a hook fitted into a porthole to raise a heavy panel in the safe floor. The area below was the size of a child's mattress.

Document wallets were difficult to fish through the small opening, even with Julius's gangly arms. He carefully ticked off his checklist of bank documents, bond certificates and an opaque plastic folder labelled *Emergency Instructions*.

After closing the floor compartment, Julius counted out

Eddie's £1,000 bundles, and decided he deserved five for himself.

SJ's in-laws had arrived back from lunch. They glowered at Julius as he jogged outside with twenty thousand and a stack of documents in a backpack. He decided an Uber straight to the bank was safest, but then spent forty awkward minutes seeing muggers everywhere as he waited outside the shuttered bank.

'So sorry,' Eddie said, in a polite Ivorian accent as he stepped off a hire bike and shook Julius's hand. 'It was difficult finding a sitter to look after my daughters.'

After pushing up the bank's metal shutter and unlocking a door, Eddie led Julius into a musty space with burst foam sofas, peeling carpet and missing ceiling tiles.

'This branch does little business,' Eddie explained. 'It is mostly here so WADB can have a UK banking licence.'

Eddie switched on a dusty Dell and offered a hot drink as Julius settled into an office chair. While the antique PC booted up, Eddie fetched two coffees and a filing trolley.

'How long will this take?' Julius asked.

'Two to three hours,' Eddie guessed as he unzipped the emergency instructions wallet and licked his finger before flipping a page.

After a moment's browsing and a few marks with a highlighter, Eddie handed Julius a letter signed by his uncle, then a chewed biro and sheets of blank paper.

'I will need the governor's authorisation on various cheques and documents,' Eddie explained. 'You can practise his signature while I work through the electronic transfers.'

FIFTY-ONE

John Pack had spent weeks in his dark place. No shower, shave or haircut and he'd dropped seven kilos because food didn't matter. But a daughter – the only one left – on the end of a phone and in trouble snapped his mind into focus.

He told Georgia to wipe her face, find a cafe, order a coffee and sit somewhere out of sight. He told her not to resist if the police tried to arrest her, then he hung up and dialled the solicitor who'd done contracts for his drone business, unsure if he'd pick up on a Saturday.

'You want Megan Seebag at Buick-Seebag,' the lawyer said. 'She'll cost, but she's the best.'

John found Buick-Seebag's twenty-four-hour number, explained that he was the father of the girl who'd piloted the drone that set the prime minister's head on fire, and was halfway into a pair of trousers when Megan returned the call.

'You called the right person,' Megan said confidently. 'I'm going to explain *exactly* what your next steps should be. Do you have a pen?'

When Georgia's phone rang, she was in the basement of a Pret a Manger, too sick to drink the flat white cupped in her hands.

'Megan said it's important to show you are co-operating at every stage,' John explained. Georgia noticed how he sounded like his old self. 'When I hang up, call 999 and tell them where you are. Megan says they'll take you to the anti-terrorist unit at Holborn police station. Be polite, but say *nothing* about the attack until Megan gets there.'

'OK,' Georgia sniffed.

'Megan will be at Holborn in forty minutes. I'll drive down, but with Saturday shopping traffic it might take a while.'

'OK,' Georgia choked.

'Do it straight away,' John said. 'Love you.'

'Love you,' Georgia said tearfully.

Tapping 999 into her dialler app felt monumental.

'Which service, please?'

'Police,' Georgia said.

FIFTY-TWO

'Turns out I'm pretty good at forging the governor's signature,' Julius laughed.

Duke sat on the sofa in his uncle's apartment, watching Julius on an HP laptop.

'I photographed everything that looked important before I put the documents back in the safe,' Julius explained. 'It didn't seem sophisticated. Just taking a ton of cash from Ondo government accounts and putting it in shell companies owned by my uncle.'

'How much?' Duke asked.

'It was all different currencies, but I'd guess tens of millions of US dollars. And it was coming out of stuff like Ondo State Food Programme and the Police Department.'

Duke tutted. 'That's *literally* stealing food from starving kids . . .'

'Maybe I shouldn't have helped,' Julius said guiltily. 'But I'd be going against my whole family, and I'm already the awkward one they sent into exile . . .'

'You kept records,' Duke said. 'Your uncle would have just got someone else to do it . . .'

'I took five thousand for myself,' Julius said. 'I was thinking I could send a Western Union transfer, to help with your medical bills.'

'We might not need it,' Duke said, his voice perking up. 'My uncle got attacked in the street yesterday. Just scratches. But last night he was ranting about how he's sick of this city and wants to get out.'

'Amsterdam?' Julius asked.

'I'm hoping.'

Julius cracked a grin. 'Are things better now the result is in?'

'They didn't release the vote count,' Duke said. 'But my uncle got hold of the figures. There are 1.9 million adults registered to vote in Ondo State. Rotimi got 1.25 million votes, Adebisi 1.22 million.'

'That's a *lot* of forged ballot papers,' Julius gasped. 'And on the streets?'

'The worst,' Duke said bluntly. 'My mother is afraid to walk to the market, and the cops hardly leave their precincts.'

Julius shook his head as he saw Duke's mum move in the edge of the frame. 'Hello there, Miss Balogun!'

'Good day,' Duke's mother said, a touch sour as she stepped between Duke and the laptop on the coffee table.

'You're blocking,' Duke protested.

'Do not use that tone with me!' Duke's mum said. 'Are you going to sit on your behind all day? I asked you to take that stinking rubbish bag out one hour ago.'

'Got my orders,' Duke told Julius wearily as his mother walked away. 'I'll call tonight, if you're not out partying with all your new friends.'

'No chance,' Julius said. 'I'm back to The Hall first thing Monday, and I've hardly touched the half-term homework.'

'Good times!' Duke said, glancing around to make sure his mother wasn't looking before blowing Julius a kiss.

Duke's hip crunched painfully as he leaned forward to close the laptop lid. He took a couple of mouthfuls of warm cola from a glass on the table, slid his feet into a set of thongs and grabbed the knotted rubbish bag in front of the fridge.

'Your loyal slave will now commence his mighty task,' Duke said.

'You can pour me gin and give me a foot massage when you get back,' his mother laughed. Then seriously, 'Take the mailbox key – nobody has checked today.'

The electricity was on, but even with his sore hip, Duke didn't chance the elevator.

'Be careful out there,' an elderly man warned as he came up with groceries.

Duke didn't know the guy's name, but they always swapped a few words when they met. 'Just taking the rubbish down.'

'My son was knocked off his bike and robbed on the way to work,' the man said breathlessly. 'Every time you think it can't get worse ...'

'Very sorry to hear that,' Duke said.

Duke doubted there would be post while the city was erupting, but it wasn't worth arguing when it only took a few seconds to check. He pushed through a door and looked at the rows of numbered boxes alongside the building's reception desk.

The doorman hadn't come to work and Duke felt a jolt when he saw three young toughs just inside the main door. Luckily, all three had eyes on their phones, and Duke stared at his feet and crept back through the door, without checking the mailbox.

The basement was near-dark and puddled. The daily garbage run hadn't happened in a week and a huge rat slunk between overstuffed containers as Duke flung his load towards a heap of split, maggoty bags.

Unusually, the electricity had been steady all morning. Seven floors would punish his aching hip and he was wondering if he should risk the elevator when a shaft of light broke from the top of the stairs.

'Balogun?' a man asked.

Duke almost inhaled his tongue. Fear muted the pain in his hip as he jumped a puddle and charged for the basement exit.

'Where you going, homo?' the man demanded as the three heavy bodies rushed down the stairs.

Duke's thong skidded as he made it to the door, palming a green button to release the lock.

'We just want to ask where Uncle Remi is,' the man shouted. 'It's best if you don't upset me . . .'

Duke's eyes were shocked by sunlight as he stepped out onto the concourse behind the apartment block. He couldn't see himself winning a foot race with three fit men, but he knew a gap in the wire fence. The drop into the neighbouring lot would be brutal on the bad hip, but making the gap before they saw where he went seemed his only realistic chance.

But a muscular figure shot out from against the back wall, barging Duke into a concrete pillar and doubling him with a massive fist in the gut.

'Old friend!' Collins said cheerily, as the other three men burst out of the door. 'I thought you might come this way . . .'

Duke slid down the post onto his bum. He saw Collins in all his nightmares and now he was living it. The heavy-built seventeen-year-old looked like he'd been on the rampage, in black boots, and camouflage trousers with a big holstered knife. His eyes were wild, like he was high on something. His vest was soaked in sweat and his nose mangled, despite the efforts of Lagos's best plastic surgeons.

'Where's your uncle?' Collins demanded.

'I don't know,' Duke said. 'He keeps his work close to his chest.'

Duke trembled as one of the thugs crouched, feeling his pockets for a phone or wallet.

'I was just taking the rubbish down,' Duke said.

'We lost because of scum like your uncle, writing lies,' Collins growled.

'Didn't know you could read,' Duke spat.

'Comedian,' Collins snorted, then grabbed a handful of Duke's Afro and knocked his head against the post.

Duke flinched as Collins lined up his fist. But Collins pulled back.

'Look at how scared he is,' Collins boasted to his pals, then touched his nose. 'This is what his boyfriend did to me.'

Duke felt piss trickle down his leg as Collins pulled a phone. He opened the camera app and switched to video before passing it to a pal.

'Record this,' Collins told him. 'A special message for cousin Julius.'

The guy looked confused, and Collins leaned over and tutted.

'It starts when you press the red circle.'

Duke glanced left and right. He wondered if he should scream or try to run.

'Good afternoon, my cousin,' Collins said cheerfully as the other guy filmed. 'I hope that British weather isn't getting you down. Perhaps you've got yourself a skinny white boyfriend for your sickening needs.'

Duke's mouth gaped as Collins popped the leather strap over his holstered knife.

'We should do this inside by the cages,' one of the goons warned. 'The blood's gonna spray.'

'Come on,' Duke said, making a praying gesture as the huge blade caught the sunlight. 'What have I ever done to you?'

Then Collins plunged the knife into his heart.

FIFTY-THREE

The low-slung building, with circular windows and silver-grey cladding, looked more like a leisure centre than Britain's highest-security court. It was noon, but no case had begun in the twelve courtrooms, because lawyers, court staff and jurors were trapped on the wrong side of four thousand rowdy protestors.

Some banners referred to the *Bank Seven*: Zac, Elodie, Wendy, Georgia, Kamila, Gerard and his sister Pippa, who'd leaked the prime minister's confidential schedule. But it was the fifteen-year-old drone pilot who'd captured the public's imagination and the majority simply said *FREE GEORGIA*.

A beautiful girl setting the prime minister's head on fire was a global story. Twenty satellite vans and support trucks clogged the car park of the prison across the street. Sky and BBC had brought truck-mounted mini studios. Their open backs overlooked the crowd blocking the court's main gate, and teams of production assistants battled protestors, who kept running up and thumping fists and banners on the glass.

The newsreader in Sky's mini studio was helping a sixteen-year-old clip a microphone to her school blazer, while a protester behind swayed a banner that read: *Give Pack a Medal, Not a Prison Sentence.*

The news director counted the seconds for the noon headlines to end, and silently mouthed *Go*, as the newsreader finished sorting the girl's microphone and settled back into his seat.

'This is the news, live from our mobile studio outside Woolwich Crown Court, where what has been described as Georgia-mania is in full swing . . .'

The newsreader broke off as a half-drunk Fanta bottle hit the glass behind his head.

'We understand the preliminary hearing for the so-called Bank Seven, which was scheduled for ten thirty, has been delayed because lawyers for some of the accused have been unable to get inside the building. Georgia Pack and the other suspects *are* waiting in the court, after they were transferred via tunnel from the adjacent Belmarsh Prison.

'Now, I'm joined in the studio by two young protestors, Maya and Rolf. My first question is, are you missing school to be here in Woolwich?'

'Yes,' Rolf said bluntly, before Maya took over.

'This is really important,' Maya said. 'Young people deserve a voice, like everyone else.'

The newsreader nodded. 'I understand you're a close friend of Georgia Pack.'

'We're mates,' Maya confirmed. 'We both got expelled from school, so we don't see each other every day now. But we message all the time and do socials.'

'What type of person is Georgia?'

'Ordinary messed-up teen, like the rest of us,' Maya laughed. 'She's *really* clever. She was like, class super-swot until her sister died. That's what made her stop and think about how the world works.'

'A lot of people won't be happy, seeing someone who attacked a democratically elected prime minister celebrated as some kind of folk hero,' the newsreader suggested. 'Isn't it simply an act of terrorism?'

'I don't for one second believe she's a violent person,' Maya said. 'Georgia resonates because everyone is *mad* frustrated. We gave one useless government the boot. Then a new lot comes in, saying everything's gonna be better, but works out just as crummy. And like, with a two-party system, we keep the idiots we've got or bring back the idiots we kicked out. How is that a democracy?'

'Exactly,' Rolf agreed, desperate to get a word in.

The newsreader paused for a message coming through his earpiece. 'I've just heard from inside the court that the key people are now in place and that the preliminary hearing has been scheduled to start at ten minutes past twelve ...'

FIFTY-FOUR

Because Georgia was charged with terrorist offences, she'd done nine days in a maximum-security cell, rather than a young offenders' unit. She'd spent most of that time in hoodies and trackie bottoms, but John brought a blouse, skirt and black tights for her court appearance.

A chill went down Georgia's back as the tiny tank-like Megan Seebag led her into court number one. The space was designed for big jury trials and the raised seating gallery was eerily like the council chamber where she'd made her famous leap.

I'd be in school if that photographer hadn't clicked the shutter...

'Georgia!' someone shouted from a public gallery that was in the process of being cleared. Since she was under eighteen, the hearing would be in private.

Georgia glanced warily at the empty judge's platform. Her dad smiled, her mum made her feel uncomfortable, then she looked to her fellow suspects in the dock.

Gerard was at the far left, delivered from the prison hospital with a mesh patch over one eye and a cannula in his hand. Zac sat in a wheelchair to the right of the dock. He looked handsome in his dark brown suit, but Georgia could hardly bear to look at him.

'All rise for Judge Malum,' a clerk announced.

As everyone stood and the judge entered through a door directly behind her bench, Georgia was led to the jury area. She'd expected to stand with the others and guessed it was another rule related to being under eighteen.

'We *finally* made it,' the judge began, smiling as she poured a glass of water from a plastic jug. 'Let's get this moving. Lots of suspects to get through, so do keep it brief.'

The proceeding began with all the suspects saying they were present and naming the lawyers representing them. Then the judge began taking pleas, starting with Pippa, who faced the least serious charges: three breaches of the Official Secrets Act and conspiracy to commit an act of terrorism.

Pippa pled guilty to the secrecy charge but denied terrorism. Georgia listened intently as Pippa's lawyer pleaded for her to be released on bail, on the grounds she was only twenty, had no previous convictions and that a complex trial with seven defendants could be more than a year away.

'Given the serious and highly public nature of the offences, I feel the suspect should remain in custody while awaiting trial,' Judge Malum said.

Georgia dry-heaved. *If Pippa's not getting out, I'm screwed...*

Wendy pleaded not-guilty to a charge of assisting of plotters. Zac, Kamila and Elodie all pleaded not-guilty to three terrorist offences and conspiracy to commit murder. All four were denied bail.

When the judge moved to Gerard, he told the judge he did not recognise a court run by fascist oppressors, then raised his fist in the air and shouted, 'Lenin!' to each of nine charges, including several related to building the drone.

The judge looked unimpressed as she told the court clerk to enter *no plea* before sending him back to hospital.

'Georgia Pack.'

Georgia wavered as she stood. Megan Seebag was steely, charging out of her seat to approach the judge's bench with a wad of paperwork.

Megan told a great story. Georgia was a vulnerable girl. A straight-A student who'd fallen under the influence of *a bad crowd* after the shocking death of her sister. She said it was *wildly inappropriate* to have held Georgia in an adult prison for almost two weeks. She said Georgia should have a separate judge and be tried in juvenile court, because she'd been manipulated by the other suspects and was scared to speak out in front of them.

The solicitor from the Crown Prosecution Service rebutted, saying there was plenty of evidence that Georgia was emotionally stable and knew what she was involved with. He wasn't pleased when the judge took Megan's side and sent Georgia's case to juvenile court. This burdened the prosecutors with two complex trials instead of one. It also meant Georgia didn't have to enter a plea in the court.

Judge Malum smiled at Megan Seebag. 'I assume you have ideas about where Georgia should spend her time awaiting trial?'

'If it pleases you, Your Honour,' Megan said humbly. 'Out of respect for the seriousness of the charges made, I feel it inappropriate to send Georgia home on bail. I would like to suggest Georgia be released into the custody of her mother and father, on condition that she spends the pre-trial period undergoing psychiatric evaluation at the Freeman Adolescent Mental Health Unit.'

The judge glanced across to the prosecutor, who acted like this was the most outrageous thing he'd ever heard.

'Your Honour, young offenders' units are *perfectly* capable of assessing the mental state of inmates and have a level of security more suited to such a high-profile defendant.'

Megan interrupted. 'Given the number of suicides in young offenders' institutions, I hardly—'

The judge raised her hand. 'Miss Seebag, this is a pre-trial hearing, not a debate on the merits of the youth justice system.'

The prosecutor smiled. Georgia held her stomach as she noticed her dad's white knuckles, gripping the arm of his seat.

'Very well, Miss Seebag,' the judge said, letting Georgia breathe while the prosecuting solicitor slumped into his seat. 'I will have Georgia's conditional release document drawn up and signed in my chambers. And that brings this proceeding to a close.'

'All rise,' the court clerk shouted.

As the judge headed back to her chambers, Megan evil-grinned at the prosecutor.

'See you in juvenile court,' Megan taunted, before the prosecutor mouthed something foul back at her.

Lawyers and relatives began leaving the court. Georgia couldn't watch as prison officers began cuffing her co-defendants.

As Megan went into the judge's chambers to sort paperwork, Georgia found herself in the empty court with her parents and a single clerk picking up litter. She stepped out of the jury box and gave her dad a hug.

'We have the *best* lawyer,' John said brightly.

Her mum looked less impressed. 'Twelve thousand already for that lawyer,' she grumbled. 'Eight hundred a night for this psychiatric hospital and the trial might be a year away.'

'Megan says it'll be faster if the prosecution drops the conspiracy to murder charge,' Georgia said. 'I can plead guilty to all the others and go straight to sentencing.'

'Conspiracy to murder is a scare tactic,' John said. 'They don't want to admit it was a police stun gun that sparked the explosion.'

'Hundreds of thousands of pounds,' Rachel went on. 'The agreement was, we sold the house and split proceeds when Georgia left for university . . .'

'I have my D'Anger money,' Georgia said.

'This isn't the place to argue over money,' John told his ex-wife furiously.

Georgia knew this was her fault and almost wished she had been sent to young offenders. She'd had *way* more involvement in the drone plot than Wendy and Pippa, who were heading to jail. And while her mum liked to moan, she would do the right thing and pay her share. Helping a daughter who could barely stand being in a room with her . . .

'You need to get Georgia to the Freeman Unit by midnight,' Megan said as they headed out of the courtroom with the signed paperwork. 'You're entitled to stop and have a meal, or go home to pack . . .'

The court had metal detectors and pat-downs for people entering. The security line gawped as Georgia pushed through a turnstile and out into drizzle.

She knew her case had been delayed by protestors, but Georgia wasn't expecting a mob that stretched from the court's anti-terrorist fence to a line of broadcast vans over a hundred metres away.

The hearing had been private, so nobody in the crowd knew Georgia had been released. She gripped her dad's arm as protestors nearest the fence realised who it was.

'Georgia's free!' someone shouted.

But as the news burst and the crowd started to cheer, she'd never felt more trapped.

PART FOUR

FIFTY-FIVE

Walter J. Freeman Adolescent Mental Health Unit – East Grinstead, UK

It was warm for late April and the air con in Therapy Room B chugged, forcing Julius to raise his voice.

'I got the video from this anonymous message,' Julius said, as a tear welled in his eye. 'They'd blurred Collins, but it was obvious to me . . . And there were sick photos online after Duke died . . .'

Julius paused, and Georgia's friend Alex held out a box of tissues.

'Thanks,' Julius said as he dabbed his eyes. 'Sorry . . .'

'There's nothing to be sorry for. It's good to see you opening up,' Tanvi the therapist said soothingly. 'Take your time.'

Georgia, Alex and the three others in the group all nodded or *oohed* supportively, before Julius choked up.

'I really loved Duke,' Julius stated.

He started crying harder, until the therapist interrupted gently.

'How did you feel immediately after you found out?'

'I . . .' Julius wiped his eyes again. 'I found out he'd been murdered on the Sunday. It was the end of half-term and I had a taxi booked for six thirty next morning to take me back to school. And I carried on . . .'

Julius took a deep breath and tried to get some strength back in his voice.

'It's hard to explain,' he began. 'It was like I had two lives. One good, one bad. The Hall was good. I was playing soccer and working out. Doing OK in lessons and I'd made friends who had no problem with who I was. At boarding school, it's easy to keep busy, from early-morning swims to evening cinema club. I signed up for everything, to keep my mind occupied.'

'That's interesting,' Tanvi said. 'Most of you were in yesterday's group, where we listed the differences between healthy behaviour and distracting behaviour.'

'Then there was my bad life, back in Nigeria,' Julius continued. 'Duke was dead. My mum was arrested. Held in prison awaiting trial after Governor Rotimi took office. My little brother Gabe kept calling in tears because he was scared. Just thinking about home made me shake. I could have flown back for Christmas. I wanted to see Gabe, but I couldn't face everything else, so I stayed in London and spent Christmas on my own.'

'Did you talk to anyone about Duke?' Georgia asked.

'Nobody,' Julius admitted. 'My roommate, Matt, is a good guy. He asked, how come I don't Skype Duke any more. Part of me wanted to tell, but I knew I'd break down and I didn't want my good life at school mixing with my bad life. I didn't want people feeling sorry for me, or asking questions about stuff back home.'

'You built a wall,' Alex suggested.

'A wall,' Julius agreed. 'Now I realise it was building up to a crisis. You can't run two separate lives in your head.

354

'About six weeks back, things started going *really* wrong back home,' Julius explained. 'My phone died, because the bill hadn't been paid. I called my cousin, Orisa, who lived with us. She was saying the state government had got an order freezing all my mum's bank accounts. Mum was the mastermind of everything our family does. But my uncle, SJ, was running the show now she was in prison. He refused to give Orisa money to run the house, or even answer her calls.

'I got my UK phone going by paying cash in a Vodafone shop. But then I got called into the school finance office and told eight grand of school fees hadn't been paid for the new term. I got through to SJ on a special number I was given for something else. He said money was tight. He promised to sort me out, but he didn't. And the school was gentle, but they made it clear I could only stay until the end of summer term if nobody was paying my bill.'

'Major stress,' Georgia said empathetically.

'A bit!' Julius said. 'I'm staying in the UK on an education visa, so if I get kicked out of school I have to go home to all the shit. And my brother Gabe has been telling me stuff, like my other brother Taiwo's medical bills weren't paid, and my mum was beaten up in prison . . .'

'Is your uncle broke?' Alex asked.

'My uncle's wife posted pictures of a massive wedding for my oldest cousin, Luke. Collins's Instagram has pics of a Mercedes he got for his eighteenth birthday. I think SJ wants to make it clear he's the big man now Mum is in prison. We're no different to the rest of the extended family, begging for his scraps.

'The day I ended up here, I was in soccer practice. I'd barely slept in three nights. I'd had a crap morning, because I'd studied the wrong module for a geography test and got an F.

We were playing two defenders on two attackers and this kid, Rob, was needling me. He's a striker, probably the best player in our school. I'm purely a positional defender. Rob's running rings around me, and taking the mickey. There's always banter when you play, but this was different. Then I went down on my ass and he called me a homo...'

An *ahh* went around the therapy circle.

Julius played it down. 'If you play soccer, people wind you up, hoping you'll lash out and get sent off.

'But when Rob called me *homo* my brain detonated. I elbowed him so hard, it mashed his nose. He went down and I jumped on top and started punching the shit out of him.

'It took a teacher and three big guys to pull me off. Rob's nose was a mess, blood everywhere. That triggered thoughts of Duke getting beaten up and I felt ashamed, because I *hate* violence.

'Then I started crying. All the worries about home and the bottled-up feelings about Duke. They put me in the school counsellor's office. I sat on the floor and sobbed. It hurt *so* much. Like my brain had blown a fuse.'

Alex nodded with recognition. 'You're not alone, mate. I'm usually the one locked in the cupboard, waiting for the men to come take me to the nuthouse...'

Ross was nodding too. 'The first time I had a breakdown, I was *so* shocked. It was like my brain had been rebooted on different software.'

'Depression is the worst,' Laura, who rarely spoke, agreed.

'Had you felt anything like that before?' Tanvi asked.

'I'd been sad,' Julius admitted. 'I'd cried about Duke. But this was a bomb in my head. The next thing I knew, I was waking up here, in the observation room. I've heard how I wound up in the lounge, with needles in my bare ass and a splinter of a coffee table through my cheek, but that's a blur . . .'

'Julius just gave a textbook example of why it is so unhealthy to keep powerful feelings bottled up,' Tanvi told the group. 'I'd like to compliment Julius, because he's only been with us for a few days. This is the first time he's had the confidence to open up about his feelings in group. Didn't he do well?'

'Really great.' Georgia smiled, putting a hand on Julius's knee as the others in the circle nodded.

FIFTY-SIX

Georgia wore Nike trainers and silver-grey leggings as she stepped into the Freeman Unit's basement gym. There was a group of lads by a chest-press machine, but the five treadmills up back were free, apart from Julius.

'Hey, you,' Georgia said fondly. She hung a microfibre towel over the side rail and planted her water bottle in a slot.

Julius jogged at a respectable 12.5kph, but his long legs made it look slow. Most of his casual clothes were at the house in London, so he wore the grass-stained shirt and shorts from his school kit.

'Didn't know you ran,' Julius said.

'Not allowed out,' Georgia explained. 'I can walk in the grounds, but only with an adult.'

'Bad girl,' Julius teased as Georgia pressed a 5K pre-set on the console and started building speed from walking pace.

'I've got fitter since I came here, at least,' Georgia said. 'Some nights I come down and run for an hour. I like when it hurts. It stops you thinking about everything else.'

Julius glanced over as he saw Georgia's treadmill speed up to 15kph. He raised a cheeky eyebrow and pushed his to 15.1.

'Are we racing?' Georgia said, smiling as she beeped her treadmill up to sixteen. 'I know we're not supposed to talk about things in group, but you were *awesome* this morning.'

Julius pushed up to sixteen, but running faster meant lengthening his stride. His sneaker hit the metal plate in front of the belt. There was a squeal of rubber and a gasp. For an instant, Georgia thought Julius was going to fly off the end like some YouTube clip, but he grabbed the side rails and lifted his feet. Sensing that he'd stopped running, the treadmill slowed to a crawl.

Once Georgia was sure he was OK, she gave Julius a smug grin and pushed her speed up to seventeen.

'I'm too gangly,' Julius explained, as he looked in the mirrored wall and saw all the guys by the chest press laughing at him.

'The male urge to compete can be highly amusing,' Georgia noted smugly.

Julius felt embarrassed as he stepped back on the belt and reverted to his comfortable 12.5. Georgia was soon breathing too hard to keep talking, and Julius thought about how envious Matt would be if he knew he was close enough to see sweat run down Georgia Pack's neck.

Georgia kept going when Julius headed for a shower. They reunited with damp hair and fresh clothes outside Therapy Room B. Georgia felt comfortable settling into the therapy circle, with Alex on her left and Julius to the right.

Their moods dipped when Henry bounded in, showing his teeth to Ross and Laura. 'Just got back from London,' he said cheerily. 'Got them laser whitened, and had killer burgers with this girl from my old school.'

'How did you swing that?' Ross asked as Tanvi dumped an armful of yellow binders and apologised for being late.

'My psychiatrist says I act out because I have low self-esteem,' Henry explained. 'Teeth whitening is *vital* for my emotional well-being.'

'This place is a joke,' Alex growled, scowling at Henry. 'Low self-esteem? You have an ego bigger than Texas.'

Henry sniffed blood. 'You should get *your* nicotine-stained pegs done, Alex. People might start mistaking you for a human.'

Alex was about to bite back, but Tanvi jumped in. 'Henry, *sit*,' she said firmly. 'Alex, that hand gesture is not appropriate . . .'

Tanvi allowed a moment for everyone to settle into chairs, before starting the session with a reminder of the group rules: no abusive comments, no food or drink apart from water, always stay seated and everything said in group was confidential.

'Everyone except Henry was in the morning session, where we made excellent progress with Julius,' Tanvi said. 'If Julius wants to explore things further, I'll make time later. But I'd like to begin with Georgia, who has a big day tomorrow.'

Georgia squirmed in her chair as the six others in the circle looked her way.

'How are you feeling about going to London for sentencing?' Tanvi asked.

'Scared off my *arse*,' Georgia said, smiling like it was a joke, while her eyes betrayed that it wasn't.

'Would you explain, for people like Laura who weren't here when you last spoke about your situation?'

'Tomorrow is my sentencing,' Georgia explained. 'I pleaded guilty to a bunch of terrorist offences. They've accepted that the explosion was an accident, so stuff like conspiracy to murder was dropped. But attacking the PM and burning the French ambassador is still *kinda* serious . . .'

An uneasy laugh went around the group.

'What kind of sentence could you get?' Ross asked.

'If you're a fifteen-year-old car thief or mugger, there are sentencing guidelines. You almost know what you'll get before you step into court,' Georgia explained. 'But there's no precedent for someone aged fifteen being convicted of . . . what I did . . .

'I pleaded guilty in juvenile court, but I'm being sent back to Woolwich so that everyone in the drone plot is sentenced consistently. Megan, my lawyer, will request I be released under a supervision order, based on the report from my psychiatrist here. But if you watch TV, or read comments on any website, you can see the pressure on Judge Malum to come down hard.'

'What's the worst?' Ross asked.

'Under-eighteens can be given indeterminate sentences for serious crimes,' Georgia explained. 'That means I stay in prison until the home secretary decides I'm fit to be released.'

Henry laughed noisily. 'Isn't the home secretary part of the government? Good pals with the PM, who you painted red and set on fire?'

'That *can't* be right . . .' Ross added.

Georgia nodded. 'Adults convicted of non-lethal terrorist offences get seven to twelve years, and a person under eighteen should always get less than an adult. But even five years means I'd be locked up till I was twenty . . .'

Henry grinned. 'Drop by my room later. It could be your last chance . . .'

'I'd sooner rub my face in a cow pat,' Georgia spat back.

'I don't know much about the British justice system,' Julius said. 'Is young offenders much different to here?'

'Young offenders is *brutal*,' Alex warned. 'I only did twenty-eight days. But imagine there's two hundred kids in your year at school and the worst one ends up in young offenders. Now imagine you're locked up with two hundred versions of that kid.'

Georgia turned to Alex, slightly aghast. 'Cheer me up, why don't you?'

Alex shrugged. 'No point sugar-coating ...'

'I'm more worried about the other people whose lives I messed up,' Georgia admitted. 'I'll have to face people like Kamila and Zac, who could get *really* long sentences. My mum and nan will be in court. Being on this unit for six months has cost my dad a hundred and fifty thousand, and there's tens of thousands in legal bills and psychiatrist fees on top.'

'Can't you make money though?' Ross asked. 'I read you'd been offered half a million to write a book.'

'I've been offered money to write a book – or, rather, have someone else write a book with my name and picture on the cover – but the amount is way less than what people are saying, and my lawyer says I can't publish anything until after I get released from prison ...'

'There's no chance you'll be here after tomorrow?' Julius asked disappointedly.

'Can't afford it,' Georgia explained. 'If the judge swallows the psychiatrist report, I'll live at home and travel back here a couple of times a week to see my therapist or do group work in the aftercare unit.

'But if the cards don't fall my way, this time tomorrow my life will basically be over ...'

FIFTY-SEVEN

Tears streaked Alex's face as she wheeled one of Georgia's bags out to the waiting Ford. The two girls hugged as Julius came out with Georgia's main bag and shook hands with John.

'I've only known you a few days, but you've made being here a lot nicer,' Julius told Georgia. 'I'll miss you in group.'

'I hope your crap gets sorted,' Georgia said. 'Hopefully we'll catch up somewhere down the line . . .'

'Visit Akure any time,' Julius joked. 'It's a delight.'

Alex held up crossed fingers. 'Twenty quid says you'll be sleeping in your own bed tonight.'

Georgia smiled as she opened the car door. 'Any time you see Henry leaning over, feel free to kick him in the nuts for me. And there's a big Toblerone on my bed – you two can race for it!'

Alex and Julius looked sad as John Pack drove his daughter down the Freeman Unit's driveway.

By lunchtime, Georgia had become a different person. Instead of sitting across the table eating egg salad, she was on the wall-mounted TV. At least her name was, as the news channel showed a helicopter shot of a crowd swamping the perimeter of Woolwich Crown Court and a big title: BANK SEVEN – SENTENCED TODAY.

Julius was scoffing a pot of chocolate mousse when he got surprised by Mr Apple from school. The giant PE teacher had swapped his usual trackies for jacket and chinos. One of the therapy assistants guided him between cafeteria tables.

'Hello, sir,' Julius said, awkwardly aware that the last time he'd seen Mr Apple, he'd been throwing punches and flipping out like a loon.

'You look calmer,' Mr Apple said. 'I'd like to talk in private, if that's possible.'

'I can leave,' Alex said, standing up. 'Group starts in ten and I need a dump.'

Mr Apple took a seat as Alex headed off in her holed New Balance and rarely washed Newcastle shirt.

'I'll take these out of your way and leave you to it,' the assistant told Mr Apple as she grabbed two lunch trays and backed off. 'Help yourself to tea or coffee.'

'How's Rob?' Julius asked, once the nurse was out of earshot.

'Not fantastic,' Mr Apple said, sighing. 'Our star striker has a broken nose, obviously. Black eyes, concussion. His parents wanted the police involved, but they backed off when we told them you were here.'

Julius tried to find words, but just shook his head and felt ashamed.

'I've coached a lot of rough lads,' Mr Apple said. 'I never saw that violence in you. You were always off with your head in the clouds.'

'I hate violence,' Julius said strongly.

Mr Apple tried to break the tension with a joke. 'Mr Ng's filing cabinet isn't doing great either . . .'

Julius smiled slightly. 'Did you want a drink, sir?'

'Well hydrated, thank you, Julius. The senior staff asked me to visit, because we need to discuss your next steps.'

'Am I expelled?' Julius asked.

'Since your fees weren't paid for this term, you're what's known as a *pupil on credit*. We're not formally expelling you, but we won't be letting you back.'

'I can hardly complain after what I did,' Julius said solemnly.

'It's a shame,' Mr Apple said. 'I don't understand everything that's been going on in your life, but I sensed the school suited you well.'

'I liked it,' Julius agreed. 'I'm sorry I messed up . . .'

'Have you been in touch with your family?'

'Nobody who matters,' Julius said. Then joked, 'It's good to feel loved and wanted.'

Mr Apple gave a shifty look, like he didn't want to say what was coming next.

'The Freeman Unit is a few miles from Dormansland Hall, so we've sent troubled pupils here before. But parents are expected to pay for treatment, just like any other extra.

'Unfortunately, the school feels they are unlikely be repaid and is only willing to fund your stay here for three more days.'

'I didn't want to come here, but group therapy has started helping me get my head around things.'

Mr Apple nodded sympathetically. 'The school has to notify UK Immigration when a student on an education visa leaves. Do you have family here?'

'Not permanently,' Julius said.

'I'm no immigration lawyer, but if your mother is in prison and your family have cut you off, you might be able to claim refugee status. Otherwise, you'll have two weeks to get your affairs in order and fly home. Is there a responsible adult who'll take care of you in London? If there isn't, I'll have to notify social services.'

Julius didn't like the sound of social services, or immigration.

'I'll be well looked after in Chelsea,' Julius lied. 'And I have money for my flight.'

'I guess you'll head home then,' Mr Apple said. 'I brought a big bag with the rest of your things from school. The big Irish nurse said she has to search all luggage for contraband. She'll bring it to your room later.'

'Right,' Julius said.

'Well,' Mr Apple said, glancing at a wrist with no watch on it. 'I need to get back to set up inter-house hockey.'

The teacher gave Julius a clammy handshake, then bashed his leg on the next table as he walked away.

FIFTY-EIGHT

This time, the authorities had anticipated the crowd. John Pack met a police escort when he peeled off the M23, and two cars led him to a secure entrance at the rear of Belmarsh Prison.

Georgia saw no inmates, but caught whiffs of disinfectant, drains and catering-on-a-budget as she was escorted through a long passageway, with a guard ahead to unlock barred gates and another behind to lock when they'd passed through.

'It'll be OK,' John said softly.

Georgia couldn't stop wondering if the next years of her life would be bars, keys and toughened glass as a lift took them two storeys below ground to the peach-walled tunnel linking the maximum-security prison to the bomb-proof court across the street.

Megan was waiting in a hallway with one of her legal clerks. She gave Georgia a hug, but nobody was hanging around. The Bank Seven would be dealt with swiftly so that the crowds cleared and the court could get on with routine business.

It had become absurd trying to protect Georgia's anonymity when there were thousands of people outside, holding up her photo and chanting her name. Megan hadn't contested Judge

Malum's decision to waive privacy, so public and press galleries were rammed and Georgia felt every eye in the room as she entered the court.

Her parents sat with Megan at the front. Georgia spotted her nan upstairs and gave a wave as she crossed to the dock. Since her previous visit, Court One had been reconfigured for a complex espionage trial. The jury area had been fitted with monitors for computer-based evidence, the dock had been extended and the witness box was behind bulletproof glass.

Kamila, Wendy, Elodie and Pippa had already arrived from the Bronzefield maximum security women's prison in Surrey. Georgia felt wary as she joined them in the dock.

The other six defendants were being represented by a joint legal team. But if any resentment had been caused by John's decision to employ Megan Seebag, or by Georgia spending six months in the Freeman Unit while the others went to prison, there was no sign as Kamila began a line-up of hugs.

'You've grown,' Wendy said fondly as she pecked Georgia on both cheeks. 'Have you met Pippa before?'

'Not properly,' Georgia said.

'Circumstances could have been better,' Pippa joked, her accent and posture eerily like big brother Gerard.

Zac and Gerard came into the court together. They might be sharing lawyers, but body language suggested they hadn't kissed and made up after their fight. The prison officers placed Zac at one end of the dock and Gerard at the other, next to his sister.

Gerard leaned forward and narrowed his remaining eye on Georgia. 'Hopefully your fancy lawyer will get this little problem out of your way, so you can get back to town for your *Vogue* photo shoot . . .'

Georgia tried to think of a retort, but Pippa stepped in.

'She's fifteen, Gerard. Stop being a twat.'

Gerard tried to shuffle past to stand next to his girlfriend, Kamila, but a prison guard put a hand on his shoulder and barked, 'Put you there for a reason, sonny Jim.'

Georgia glanced the other way at Zac and got scrambled feelings. She no longer adored him, but he'd helped make her life bearable after Sophie died, and six months had cooled the rage she'd felt when he childishly lost his cool with Gerard.

'All rise,' a court clerk ordered.

Always the organiser, Kamila got the seven defendants holding hands as Judge Malum stepped through her door at the rear of her bench. Pippa held Georgia's right hand, Wendy the left.

'This kangaroo court is run by wankers!' Gerard shouted to the gallery.

He got cheered as Judge Malum sat down, ignoring the fuss.

Georgia felt weird, knowing there was someone in the room who knew her fate. Judge Malum's preamble was going to be torture.

'In considering these sentences, there are complex factors to consider,' the judge read from notes. 'The balance between serving the public interest and seeing that the defendants are treated fairly. The fact that the intent of the attack was largely mischievous, but the outcome severe. I must also account for the ages, needs and criminal histories of each individual defendant, and that the guilty pleas entered by all defendants have avoided the cost of a complex criminal trial.

'The one thing I wish everyone to be clear on is that the laws of the United Kingdom make no distinction based upon a victim's social status, or lack thereof. In the eyes of the law, an attack on a prime minister is no different to an attack on an ordinary citizen. I would ask the press to bear that in mind when they report on the sentences I am about to give.'

Georgia hoped this meant the press might not be happy with the severity of the sentences. Wendy looked towards Georgia and quietly mouthed, 'Looks good,' while Pippa was trembling so badly she was making Georgia shake too.

'Beginning with the most serious adult offences. A pattern of increasingly serious criminal behaviour, and the fact that he is the only defendant who clearly understood that the thinned paint was flammable and could cause an explosion, obliges me to sentence Gerard Michael Flynn to twelve years in prison, with a recommendation that a minimum of eight be served before any consideration of parole.'

Gerard put his arms up triumphantly as a mix of boos and cheers erupted from the gallery. The judge paused while it settled down.

'Zeitung Kam Li – commonly known as Zac – Kamila Julia Kowalski and Elodie May Springer face identical charges. Apart from minor infractions, none has any previous criminal history and they are each sentenced to seven years in prison with no minimum imposed.'

The judge paused for a sip of water and flipped to her next sheet of notes.

'Philippa Annie Flynn – commonly known as Pippa – you are sentenced to three years in prison for breach of the Official Secrets Act.

'Wendy Lane Maxime Dewar. While you were not involved in plotting the attack, or in the attack itself, your elaborate plans to seek maximum publicity, and failure to notify authorities when you knew of the attack, is worthy of a prison sentence.

Given that you have already served six months on remand, I have chosen to align your sentence with the time you have already served.'

Wendy was free. She temporarily broke her hold on Georgia, smiling with relief as Kamila gave her a kiss.

'Georgia Pack . . .' Judge Malum began.

Wendy gripped Georgia's hand again as she felt a dry heave up her throat.

'. . . This is one of the most complex sentencing decisions I have ever had to make. As the drone pilot, you face charges more serious than your co-conspirators. But as a juvenile I must work with different sentencing guidelines, and take into consideration the excellent and thorough psychiatric evaluation provided by Dr Holden at the Freeman Unit . . .'

Every word felt like it was taking five minutes to come out.

'I therefore sentence Georgia Pack to five years in custody . . .'

Georgia gasped as her dad's head swivelled towards her and several people in the gallery shouted, 'No!'

'. . . However, this sentence will be suspended in its entirety, subject to good behaviour and the following conditions being met. The defendant must continue to receive regular psychiatric treatment at the Freeman Unit for a minimum of one year . . .'

Georgia grinned at her dad as about twenty people in the gallery shot up and started chanting her name. It kept going for almost a minute as a court clerk repeatedly yelled, 'Silence in court,' and only yielded when three burly court officers stepped into the upstairs gallery with handcuffs in hand.

'The defendant will also be asked to wear an electronic bracelet,' Judge Malum continued. 'And accept a twelve-month supervision order, with an 8 p.m. to 6 a.m. curfew and no taking part in any public gathering involving five or more persons.'

Georgia and Wendy were going home, but their relief was dampened by the presence of the five who weren't. Pippa was sobbing and hugging her brother, while Elodie pulled Zac close and kissed him until prison guards forced them apart.

'Court adjourned. All rise,' a clerk shouted.

Zac was being led out, but Georgia bumped fists with Elodie and Kamila before they got taken back into custody. Georgia hugged her parents as Wendy hugged her wife, Jane, and son, Sam, who'd grown ten centimetres and had his hair chopped short since Georgia last saw him.

'You can see outside from the back of the public gallery,' Sam excitedly told anyone who'd listen. 'There's twice as many people as last time.'

'Great . . .' Georgia sighed.

'Can I get a selfie?' Sam asked.

Georgia didn't love the idea, but she was fond of Sam.

Wendy had taken all of a minute to switch from suspect to publicist. 'I need a phone to start making calls,' she told her wife. 'Georgia, you're going to be colossal! Newspaper exclusives, talk shows, modelling. Not just in the UK – this trial has made you *international*.'

As Sam posted the selfie *#GEORGIAISFREE*, Georgia backed into the rows of seats and signalled for her dad to follow.

'You OK, Cookie?' he asked.

'Could have gone worse,' Georgia said, keeping her voice low so nobody else could hear. 'But I don't want a circus. I want to go home. Take a long bath, put on pyjamas, watch junk TV and fall asleep in my own bed . . .'

John wore the face that told her Santa didn't exist.

'What?'

'I didn't want to say till this was over,' John explained. 'I've moved in with your nan. Your mother and I agreed to sell the house to pay for the Freeman Unit and your legal bills.'

FIFTY-NINE

The wallet was gone.

Julius threw everything out of the bag onto his bed and frantically checked again, starting with the pocket of his Supreme hoodie, where the wallet was supposed to be, then going through every other pocket, shaking out schoolbooks, turning socks inside out and pushing his hand under the board lining at the base of his wheeled bag.

Who could have swiped it? Matt and Mr Apple seemed unlikely, but a whole chain of people had handled his stuff since he'd left The Hall. From whoever packed up his room, to the receptionist on the Freeman Unit's front desk and the nurse who'd searched his bags for contraband.

With no wallet, all Julius had was a few pounds from the blazer he'd arrived in. The frustration made him thump his mattress, then kick scrunched clothes that had dropped to the floor.

You weren't supposed to go into other patients' rooms, so Julius made sure the nurses were out of sight before hopping across the hallway. Alex lay on her bed, with the TV on and Georgia's big Toblerone mostly gone.

'You want some?' Alex asked guiltily.

Julius saw the TV. It was a recording from an hour earlier. Megan Seebag stood in a press room at Woolwich Crown Court with Georgia alongside, her parents behind and a million cameras clicking.

'This has been a long and difficult journey for Georgia and her family. Over the coming days, I must ask that the media treat the Pack family with respect and allow them privacy...'

'So cool that she got off,' Alex smiled, as a triangle of chocolate stretched her cheek.

'Only just realised,' Julius said, stepping over grubby clothes, paperbacks, towels and half-eaten food. 'I'm distracted. And some dickhead ripped off my wallet.'

'How much?'

'A couple of hundred, and my debit card ...'

'That sucks. Toblerone?'

Julius fancied a bite of chocolate, but Alex's chewed scabby nails put him off.

'Is there a way to bust out of here?' he asked.

'Doing a runner?' Alex smirked.

'I have things I need to look into before I leave the country,' Julius explained. 'My school is funding this place for three more days, but they're also about to notify the immigration authorities. Immigration are supposed to give you fourteen days to stick around, but one of my cousins got rounded up, right after his graduation ceremony.'

'How come?' Alex asked.

'Immigration can detain you if they suspect you're going to disappear,' Julius explained. 'I have no idea how likely that is, but I don't intend to stick around and find out.'

'You can't walk out the front door,' Alex said, 'but this is no prison. When I was first here, this guy, Prakash, jumped off the smoking patio, smashed his girlfriend in her car and strode back through the main door like nothing had happened.'

'Really,' Julius said.

'Don't get too cocky,' Alex said. 'In case you haven't noticed, we're in the arse end of nowhere and you don't have a car waiting.'

'My old school's about three miles from here. They used to torture us with these bloody awful night hikes. I never thought they'd prove useful, but I almost know my way cross-country to Dormans station from here.'

'So, both my pals abandon me on the same day?' Alex said grumpily.

'Money's the snag,' Julius said. 'Without my wallet, I don't even have train fare.'

'I'd lend you, but my dad only brings ciggies and chocolates. He knows I'd use money to buy booze and get trashed. You could rob Henry's room. He's always in the rec room and the au pair just brought a new iPad Pro.'

'Hopefully I can get money at my family's house in Chelsea,' Julius explained. 'I need short-term cash, not an iPad.'

Julius looked behind as the TV showed a live shot of Georgia getting out of her dad's Ford. She jogged up the driveway of a house, followed by a cloud of shouting media.

'Georgia, can you stop for a welcome-home photo?'

'Georgia, when will you be going back to school?'

'Georgia, now the court case is over, will you issue an apology to your victims?'

SIXTY

Julius's escape window was between the sun dropping at eight thirty and nine, when staff locked the doors onto the smokers' patio. Alex checked the hallway was clear, but there was no way up to the first floor without passing the nurses' station, so Julius hid a small backpack in a laundry basket and carried it with his sweaty running gear balled on top.

The smokers' patio was directly above the first-floor dining room, though the unit was built on a slope, so it was only one-and-a-bit storeys to the ground. It was a grim space, with mildewing plastic chairs and grey streaks where rain had flushed the ashtrays.

Julius hoped the area would be empty, but half-eight was a nicotine addict's last chance before morning and a dozen teenaged patients sat chatting, or leaned on metal railings, releasing plumes of smoke into a dramatic orange sky.

'There's a ledge at the end,' Alex explained, pointing past an anorexic girl in a wheelchair. 'It's not much of a drop with your height. The vehicle gate is controlled from inside, but shift change is nine thirty, so staff will be coming and going in their cars.'

'Is there a camera covering the gate?' Julius asked as he stepped past the girl in the wheelchair and sized up the drop.

'Almost certainly,' Alex said. 'But it's not like that receptionist stares at the monitors the whole time. The staff always have a battle clearing smokers off the patio by nine, so they'll be out here any minute. If I were you, I'd drop now. Squat in the bushes, then sneak out the first time the gate opens after proper dark.'

Julius felt his foot touch the ledge over a window and scraped rust as his hands slid down the metal bars. He'd hoped to dangle and drop from the ledge, but there was nothing to grab, so he had to jump.

Pain shot up one ankle as Julius landed in grass, soft enough to give way and soggy enough to feel water seep through the knee of his jeans. He spun around and saw a dining-room window level with his shoulder. A cleaner mopped inside, but the salad bar screened Julius as he edged around and squatted behind prickly holly bushes.

The sunset had gone grey, but it still wasn't dark. Alex had suggested he wait, but at least five people had seen him drop, and with half the kids in the Freeman Unit off their head on psych meds, there was a chance someone would blurt.

The short stretch of grass between the building and vehicle gate hadn't been mowed through the winter. It squelched and tangled as Julius sprinted over, then stumbled on the root of a huge tree that made a perfect hiding spot close to the gate.

After a three-minute wait, he darted from behind the trunk as a cleaning contractor's van drove through the electronic gate. He was almost through when he had to dive into the wet grass. A second car was going fast, trying to catch the gate before it closed.

Julius kept low as he scrambled through after the second car.

He ran the first hundred metres, then squatted in a roadside ditch as a car filled with night staff clattered towards him. He'd tried to remember the route but checked Google Maps to be sure.

He went right where the unit's driveway forked. Then it was a half-mile jog along a country road, and three miles' brisk walk on an easily lost track to Dormansland Hall.

Once he was off-road, Julius dialled Matt. But the signal was hopeless. By the time Julius found a signal, the school and surrounding boarding houses pierced darkness, while his Nikes carried thick mud.

Julius waited by the padlocked gate at the rear of The Hall's playing fields, known as the hiking gate. It was hard listening to youthful shouts coming from a place where he'd felt looked after and happy. The wait was long enough to make him wonder if something had gone wrong, but Matt arrived with a squelch of hiking boots and a flash of torchlight.

'Old Khan was bawling out second-formers in the lobby,' Matt explained. 'I had to get a boost out the window of the toilets behind our common room.'

There was no easy way through the padlocked gate. Matt thought about lobbing the tatty Tesco bag over the two-metre barrier, before realising there was a big gap at the bottom.

'There's fifty quid and some change in a pencil case,' Matt said. 'Two bottles of water, a torch and two Topic bars in case you get hungry. I wasn't sure if you'd checked the trains from Dormans. I doubt you'll make the ten sixteen, but there's another at ten forty-six.'

'I hadn't,' Julius admitted, wondering what other obvious things he'd not thought of as he looked inside the bag. 'This all looks great. Here's a little something to pay you back.'

Julius had muddy hands, so he wiped them on his jeans before taking out a newspaper with Georgia on the front page.

Matt looked made up as he read black marker pen:

To Matt,
Any friend of Julius's is a friend of mine!
Georgia XXX

'Awesome sauce,' Matt said. 'I can't believe you met her, let alone made friends. Plus, it'll annoy my new roommate, Theo. He's pro-government and he never stops humming. It's enough to make me miss finding your pit hairs all over my roll-on . . .'

'One time, by *accident*,' Julius protested lightly, before turning serious. 'You always joke that your dad's dodgy. But do you think I might be able to ask him for help?'

Matt peered through the fence, confused. 'You're in the market for financial management? Didn't I just sub you fifty quid because you're broke?'

'I have some questions about my mum's finances. I don't understand what's going on with her money and the family businesses . . .'

'Call him, I guess,' Matt said. 'He's my dad, I've obviously never done business with him, but he's got some famous clients. I think we'd hear if he ran off with their money . . .'

'I'm racking my brains for options,' Julius explained. 'My nightmare is winding up back in Akure, with Mum in prison, no money, and my only choice to beg an uncle who hates me for biting his son's nose off . . .'

Matt smiled as Julius glugged from one of the bottles of water. 'I *so* can't see you doing something like that!'

'Better shift,' Julius said as he screwed the cap on the half-drunk water and unzipped his backpack to fit in the stuff Matt had brought. 'I should have plenty of time to make the ten-forty-six train, but it's easy to lose the footpath in the dark, so better safe than sorry.'

'I really hope shit works out for you,' Matt said as he put his fist up to the wire mesh so they could bump. 'Stay in touch, wherever you end up.'

'Thanks for the money,' Julius said. 'You're a true friend.'

A single-track road went most of the way from Dormansland Hall to Dormans station. But Julius didn't want to risk being spotted by staff from his old school and took a less direct route across farmland.

The clock on Dormans station was about to hit ten thirty as Julius approached. The red-brick station building was shut for the night. Platform access was through a side gate and the only other passengers were a middle-aged couple, bickering noisily over very little.

They looked wary as Julius hulked past. So after buying a single to London and using the station toilet, he moved to the far end, set his bag on a bench and scraped his Nikes on the platform edge to shed as much mud as possible.

Julius was surprised as the four-carriage train rolled past to stop way down the platform. After forgetting his pack and doubling back in a panic, he caught the rear of the train as it crept to a stop. But there was another shock as the doors opened.

The first person off the train was a Dormansland second-former, dressed in school tracksuit with a hockey stick poking from the end of her kitbag. She was followed by PE teachers and tracksuited hockey squads from each of the school's five forms.

'Stick together! Line up along the platform,' an Aussie PE teacher shouted as Julius scrambled back the way he'd come, grateful for sketchy platform lighting. 'First-, second- and third-form teams ride on the first minibuses. Fourth and fifth form wait for the drivers to come back.'

As the fourth and fifth form groaned, Julius thought about a dash for the train's last door. But being six and a half foot tall meant he'd need to hide more than his face.

The train doors beeped and closed as Julius took shelter in the fragrant confines of the men's toilet. He'd been breathing the stench of a clogged bowl for fifteen minutes, when the Dormansland Hall bus returned to take the older girls back to their dorms.

Julius hadn't been able to get a data signal in the toilet, but after trains at 22:16 and 22:46, he hoped a 23:16 would be along shortly.

He got a bad feeling when he stepped back onto the platform and saw that all lights, apart from a pair of green emergency exit signs, had switched themselves off. The arrivals board flickered with random dots, while the one on the platform opposite had an unhelpful *Welcome to Southern Railways*.

'Are you kidding?' Julius groaned as he pulled Matt's torch out of a pocket.

He shone it along the back of the platform and found timetable boards. His finger ran to the end of *Departures to London*, showing that the last train was the 22:46. Then he aimed the torch up and saw that the next wasn't until 05:57.

SIXTY-ONE

Georgia awoke to musty pink bedding in her nan's spare room. She rolled, resenting the electronic bracelet on her ankle as she burrowed under the strap and scratched. She'd longed to get out of the Freeman Unit, but part of her craved the routine. Walking upstairs for breakfast with Alex and two hours in the therapy circle . . . Now she was out, she had no school, no house, no clear plan and a giant wall of guilt because she'd cost her parents their home.

How can I hate a mother that spent her life savings on me?

How can I be free, when Zac and the others are behind bars?

Her nan's bathroom had an old-lady smell and bars of soap instead of handwash. She peeked out of the window before sitting down to pee and saw that the press hadn't budged. She ran the shower hot to clear her mind, but the ankle bracelet broke the calm with a beep.

She had fifteen minutes to call in, but the amber light would strobe until she did. She found it infuriating as she towelled off and skipped back to her room, in a quilted robe that had belonged to her granddad.

The system was automated. *Press one to respond to bracelet*

activation. Press two to report a problem with your bracelet . . .
Georgia pressed one. *Please enter your six-digit bracelet number followed by the hash key . . .* By the time she'd entered her PIN and recorded a message stating her time and location, the strap was itching again.

Georgia randomly opened her Instagram and saw that the picture with Sam in the courtroom had 73,441 likes. She took a photo of her ankle bracelet and bare foot, then wrote: *This damned thing itches like CRAZY!!!*

She hadn't been allowed social media at the Freeman Unit, so this was her first post in seven months. Within seconds, there were fifty comments.

Welcome home Georgia!

Big love. Fight the power!

Thought you'd quit Insta! Good 2CU back.

Cute toes, I want to lick them!

Georgia was sick of stuff she'd worn over and over at the Freeman Unit and rummaged excitedly through a vinyl bag brought to the house by her dad. She went for a flower-print dress she'd forgotten she owned, but there was no sign of the white pumps she thought would go with it.

'Georgia, boiled eggs,' her nan shouted up the stairs.

'Look at you,' John said proudly, lowering a newspaper as Georgia stepped barefoot into her nan's kitchen. It was sunny outside, but the blinds were down because of the press. 'It's months since I've seen you in anything but a hoodie.'

Georgia gave her dad a kiss. 'Any idea where my white pumps ended up?'

'I grabbed one bag of stuff,' John explained. 'I haven't shifted the lease on the drone workshop, so I put our furniture and stuff in there, sooner than pay for storage.'

Georgia got a blast of nostalgia as her nan served up toast cut into soldiers and two soft-boiled in Peter Rabbit egg cups.

'You used to use these when you looked after me in school holidays,' Georgia said fondly as she tapped the shell.

The TV news was on, with the volume turned down, but the Bank Seven had been knocked out by an earthquake and a dead actress.

'What's the plan for today?' Georgia's nan asked, pouring her granddaughter tea from a pot. 'I'll need someone to drive me to Sainsbury's.'

'I wondered about a private tutor,' John said, nodding at Georgia. 'You've missed a ton of school, but you're bright enough to catch up and take some of your GCSEs in the autumn . . .

'That won't be cheap,' Georgia pointed out, resenting reality's intrusion into breakfast nostalgia. 'I'm going to take that meeting Jane set up with the publisher.'

'Jane who?' Georgia's nan asked suspiciously.

'Wendy's wife,' Georgia explained, then urgently gobbled an egg soldier that was about to drip on her dress. 'Wendy and her wife, Jane, run Socialist News Network and their publicity business together. But Jane's been in charge, with Wendy in prison.'

'I'd rather you made a clean break with *those people*,' John said.

Georgia tutted. 'What does *those people* mean?'

'Lefties,' John snorted. 'People who turned my daughter into a terrorist . . .'

Georgia didn't want a breakfast row and kept calm.

'As a matter of fact, me and Zac brought Wendy into the

drone plot. If it wasn't for me, she wouldn't have just spent six months in prison.'

'Wendy's an adult,' John growled. 'She made a bundle from her cut of the D'Anger deal. If she had a shred of decency, she wouldn't have created a publicity masterplan. She'd have talked to *me*, so I could put a stop to the whole thing. Do you think she'd have let Sam risk prison?'

'Come to the publisher with me and hear them out,' Georgia said pleadingly. 'I'd love to vanish into a black hole, or go back to who I was two years ago, but that's not going to happen. There's a chance for me to publish my story and make a lot of money. You and Mum are broke, and I want to pay you back.'

John leaned across the table and sounded serious. 'First, we're not broke. The equity in our house was more than your legal bills, and your mother and I will both get back on our feet. Second, you don't owe me a penny. You're my daughter – you get what you need.'

'You're fifty-six and you're back living with your mum,' Georgia pointed out.

'I love having company,' Nan interrupted. 'You can stay as long as you like.'

Georgia looked at her dad. 'Why not come to this meeting and listen?'

'Because I have my own meeting,' John said proudly.

'What meeting?'

'A job offer.'

Georgia's face lit up. 'Serious?'

'You'll hate it,' John smirked. 'It's an evil American defence corporation. They like my drone impeller system.'

'They want to make a fuel air weapon, I suppose?' Georgia said, carefully keeping disapproval out of her voice.

John smiled. 'You and your RAGS buddies gave the defence industry an excellent proof of concept. If I don't do the job, someone else will. It's a three-year consultancy contract, plus cash payment for my patents and the rights to use my impeller design. The offer's been on the table for a couple of weeks, but I told them you were my priority until your court case was over.'

Georgia didn't love that it was a defence company, but could live with anything that reduced the risk of her dad falling back into depression.

'To evil corporations and their fat pay cheques!' Georgia said, raising her mug of tea.

'Cheers,' John laughed as he chinked his orange juice. Then he cracked a huge smile. 'I really missed having you around, Georgia.'

She looked down and smudged a tear forming in her right eye.

SIXTY-TWO

Julius wondered if he'd been reported missing. Even if he had, he doubted he was important enough for a manhunt, but with his old school less than three miles away, a seven-hour wait on Dormans station seemed risky. Luckily, it was a temperate April night and he knew where to go.

Dormansland Hall owned farmland adjoining the school grounds. There were plans for a sports complex and an extra boarding house, but until money was raised, a roofless barn and dilapidated farmhouse remained. Teen couples sneaking out of school earned it the nickname Shag Shack.

Julius searched the Shag Shack, with his torch catching the graffitied walls. He settled on a battered couch, pulled up an armchair for his feet, took off soggy shoes and socks and set the alarm on his phone for 5:30.

He only managed a couple of naps and bought fruit, toast and coffee in the station cafe, before boarding the 5:56. His ticket didn't open the automatic barrier at London Victoria and a wiry inspector explained that it was valid for the previous day. He tried to fine Julius twenty pounds, but lost heart after Julius pulled his Nigerian passport for ID and gave a home address in Akure.

Rush hour was getting underway as Julius stood for a packed Underground ride to Sloane Square. He did a quick refuel with a double-egg McMuffin and imagined black-suit-and-sunglasses immigration officers bursting from the flower delivery van parked across the street as he turned his key in the smart black door of the Chelsea house.

The door clattered against something, and his nose caught cooking that reminded him of home. There was luggage stacked in the entry hall, coats piled in a chair, juju music blasting from an upstairs bedroom and a girls vs boys football match in the passageway leading to the dining room.

'Hello,' Julius told the kids warily.

They didn't seem fazed by a stranger.

He glanced into the living room, which was scattered with plates and beer cans, then darted upstairs, fearing for the state of his room.

But it wasn't his room any more. An obese, shirtless man sat on the super-king bed, with his hand down a bag of Cool Wave Doritos. The two chests of drawers were topped with travel cribs, and a tiny twin slept in each one.

'Cousin Julius,' the flabby thirty-something man said, smiling broadly, but keeping his voice down for the sleeping babies. 'Too long! It has been too long!'

People tended to remember Julius because of his size. He wouldn't have placed this cousin amongst a hundred others, except Orisa had mentioned visiting her brother's new-born twins.

'Kenny?'

'Always Ken,' he corrected. 'You must have been on a farm. No offence, but I know cow shit when I smell it.'

Julius must have got used to the smell. He realised the

stares he'd been getting on the Tube and in McDonald's weren't just because of his height . . .

'Cross-country, in the dark,' Julius explained, smiling at his tiny baby cousins. 'What's going on? Why are so many people here?'

'It's the mass Adebisi exodus,' Ken explained. 'Rotimi Rotimi wants a big pay-off from the Adebisi family now he is governor, but SJ is being pig-headed and stubborn. And SJ is immune from prosecution, so it is everyone but him who suffers.

'Your mother fixed me an excellent job as head of vehicle licencing. After the election, I was replaced by one of Rotimi's men, as expected. Then I was tipped off by a friend in the police that I was about to be arrested and charged with accepting bribes and negligence in a government post. With two babies just born, we crossed the border to Cameroon. My neighbour says we missed a police raid by less than two hours.'

'How many others are here?' Julius asked.

'Eighteen? Maybe twenty in the house. Others have passed through after a night or two. The ones who made enough money to look after themselves . . .'

Julius nodded. 'I was using this room. I had things in the wardrobe . . .'

Ken ignored this. 'SJ is so bloody inflexible, I have heard that Rotimi regrets putting your mother in prison. The transition of power would have been mature and amicable with her in control.'

'That's interesting,' Julius said as he looked down at the dried mud stiffening the bottom of his jeans. 'It's good to catch up, but I need clean clothes and a shower.'

'I'm sorry,' Ken said, making a praying gesture. 'This was the biggest room, and with twins it was ideal for us. My wife,

Gladys, put your clothes in plastic bags, but I don't know where she put them. She is with her gang of friends, in the kitchen.'

Julius passed more kids running on the stairs. Gladys sat in the kitchen, sharing a huge cappuccino cheesecake with five other women. He only knew them vaguely, but three offered hugs and they all wanted to know how his mother was doing.

Julius limply answered, 'OK, I think,' before Gladys confirmed that his clothes were in the basement, outside the wine cellar.

The lock on the basement door had been crowbarred off, then wedged with a broom for the sake of kids who slept on foam mattresses spread at the bottom of the stairs. The gym looked pristine, but fancy AV amplifiers had been stripped from racks in the cinema room and bare wires hung in a hole where there had once been a £20,000 video projector.

Julius was relieved to find his clothes in giant white bin liners outside the wine cellar. Helpfully, each had been marked, *Clothes. Do NOT trash.*

Two skateboards and a Bose speaker stuck out of one bag. There was nothing obviously missing, but it bugged Julius how his stuff had just been thrown in. Ironed shirts wrapped around their hangers. Clean underwear mixed with dirty shoes. It would have taken two minutes extra to bag it up neatly.

Julius felt a jangle of nerves as he stepped into the wine cellar. It was no surprise to find most of SJ's fine wine had been drunk or sold, while dust-free spots were all that remained of whisky and cognac.

The LED on the safe door flashed *ERROR09*. Julius checked an instruction sticker and read:

ERROR09 – After three unsuccessful attempts to open the main door, system will deactivate and safe cannot be opened for 24 hours. Press CANCEL to see remaining deactivation time.

Julius guessed kids had tapped random numbers into the keypad until the system locked them out. He hit *cancel* and was pleased to see a row of zeros on the countdown. He prayed the code hadn't been changed as he closed the wine-cellar door and tapped six numbers into the lock.

There was a beep and a satisfying whirr of bolts. The door clanked as Julius lifted the lever and he was massively relieved to see everything as he'd left it: euros, dollars, men's watches, jewellery boxes and the movable shelf that hid the second control panel for the slot in the floor.

It was an empowering sight. The country cousins could sleep in Julius's bed, steal the vintage Bordeaux and let their kids drag crayons along the walls, but he was still the son of the woman who'd made the Adebisi name count for something, and the only guy with the code for the big safe.

Julius lifted two £1,000 wraps of mint twenties, then shut the door quickly.

SIXTY-THREE

Wendy and Georgia sat on fashionably dilapidated leather, beneath exposed steel beams in Walrus Books' swanky reception area. The wall behind them had a display of the publisher's Nobel Prize-winning authors, while the *Book of the Month* cabinet was piled with the autobiography of a bagpipe-playing nun who'd won a TV talent show.

'Book editors are usually late to their own funerals,' Wendy said, keeping her voice low so the intern on the reception desk didn't overhear. 'I liked your bracelet tweet, by the way. Nice and intimate, nothing controversial.'

'Three hundred thousand likes for my itchy ankle,' Georgia said, shaking her head to show how ridiculous she found it. 'It even got a story on the BBC website, *Pack Breaks Social Media Silence*...'

'I assumed your dad would be here,' Wendy noted. 'Is he OK about this?'

'Dad stopped telling me what to do when he was depressed,' Georgia said. 'I thought he might go back to a *you'll do as I say* territory now he's feeling better. But he's been mellow so far.'

'I'm glad he's feeling better,' Wendy said.

'I thought you might send Jane, since she set up this meeting and you only got out of prison yesterday.'

'I've spent enough time cooped up, and I want people to know I'm back,' Wendy said. 'For you, the big advantage of doing a book is that it gives you breathing space. The publisher will want the book out in time for Christmas, and they'll want all your big revelations held back until the weekend before the book comes out.'

'But I won't have to write it?' Georgia asked.

'God no,' Wendy said, laughing. 'Publishers *hate* it when celebrities want to write their own books. Writing is a hard skill to master and they want a decently crafted book that's delivered on time. You'll meet the ghost writer and do lots of interviews. Hopefully they'll find someone you like.'

Georgia nodded. 'Speaking about publicity, I met this really interesting guy at the Freeman Unit.'

'First boyfriend,' Wendy smiled. 'That would make a great chapter . . .'

'No,' Georgia cringed. 'Julius is gay, and I still haven't got anywhere in the relationship department . . .'

'Boys *adore* you,' Wendy said. 'Half of Sam's mates have crushes, and he gets *so* much cred because he knows you.'

'It's creepy,' Georgia said, shuddering at the thought of Sam's geeky mates lusting after her. 'Julius was telling me about the election in his home state. The story is mental. One side blew up a building, killing thirty union leaders. The other side poisoned the water in the town centre. And when they counted the result, there was so much ballot stuffing they ended up with more votes than registered voters.'

Wendy looked intrigued. 'Where is your friend from?'

'A place called Akure, in Nigeria.'

'Ah, trying to get publicity would be *impossible*.' Wendy shrugged. 'A big aid agency like Oxfam can claim that ten thousand children have been killed in a war, or a million are at risk of starvation, and the story gets nowhere. What chance do you think I'd have with a story about Africans drinking poisoned water in a place nobody's ever heard of?'

'That's so racist,' Georgia complained.

'The way the media works *is* so racist,' Wendy said. 'Tell me about a pretty, blonde American backpacker getting poisoned while on holiday in Nigeria and you'd have a story I could work with.'

'I j-j-just thought . . .' Georgia stuttered as she grabbed her phone. 'It seems like something the world should know more about.'

Georgia scrolled up to some pictures of a late-night messenger conversation she'd had with Julius. 'This is Julius with his boyfriend. Duke got murdered, which is basically why Julius cracked up and got sent to the Freeman Unit.'

'I hate the way the media works,' Wendy explained. 'But if you know the rules of the game, you can make it work in your favour. Like with you.'

'What do you mean?' Georgia asked.

Wendy laughed. 'Do you really think your balcony leap would have made the front page of every newspaper if you were twenty kilos overweight and had spots?'

Georgia knew her looks were a factor in everything that had happened. But Wendy holding it up to her face, and the contrast with nobody caring about what had been happening in Akure, made her feel awkward and angry. She felt like storming out of the publisher's office and telling the entire world to bugger off, but Wendy's eye caught one of the photos in Georgia's messenger conversation.

'What's that?'

'That's Duke,' Georgia said. 'I showed Julius old pics of me with Sophie, and he sent me some of Duke, and his brother Gabe.'

Wendy waved her hand. '*Behind* Duke, in the cage.'

'Oh,' Georgia said. 'It's this weird thing in Akure called Arctic Zoo. It's falling down, and most of the animals died or got sold. But there's a one-eyed polar bear called Eddie that nobody wants.'

Wendy laughed. 'If you want people to take an interest in Akure, a one-eyed polar bear that nobody wants *is* definitely a story.'

'Julius said the other bears got sold to a zoo in Japan, or something. They didn't want Eddie, because his manky eye socket scares kids.'

'That's *golden*,' Wendy said brightly. 'Tweet the one-eyed bear. Don't make a statement. Give your message a hook, so people have something to chew over.'

'What's a hook?'

Wendy shrugged. 'Something like, *My heart goes out to my good friend J and the long-suffering people of Akure, Nigeria. Especially Eddie, the one-eyed polar bear who nobody wants.* Chuck in a few broken-heart and crying-face emojis and everyone will be desperate to know what you're on about.'

'Say that line again,' Georgia said as she opened her keyboard and started to type, *My heart goes out* . . .

She'd just finished editing the photo when a tall woman with dangly yellow earrings rushed out and introduced herself.

'Sorry to keep you both waiting – my last meeting dragged,'

she gasped, as she leaned in to kiss Wendy. 'I'm Verity Starling-Cole, editorial director for non-fiction. The rest of the gang is in the conference room, and, Georgia, everyone on the Walrus Books team is *soooooo* thrilled to meet you . . .'

SIXTY-FOUR

Walrus Books was offering £600,000 for a ghost-written autobiography and another £200,000 for a Georgia Pack Christmas Annual and a guidebook aimed at teen readers, to be called *Georgia Pack's Guide to Revolution*. There was also the possibility of a Georgia Pack calendar and diary. The whole *package* would be publicised with a newspaper serialisation, a Georgia Pack YouTube channel, TV interviews and a nationwide book tour.

Everyone in the meeting kept telling Georgia about her *potential*, and how she would *set the Christmas book market ablaze*. But Georgia felt grumpy as she rode home in Wendy's Audi, staring at the offer sheet.

'Not keen?' Wendy asked as she pulled up at a set of lights, behind a double-decker bus.

'I have to do it,' Georgia said, shrugging. 'It'll pay my legal bills. Set me up for university. Help my dad buy a house and get his business going, instead of working for some weapons company. But the idea of having my picture taken for a calendar, going on TV and making stupid YouTube videos . . .'

'I could get them to tone it down,' Wendy said. 'Drop the

calendar and videos. We'll meet with other publishers, who might have different ideas. And that's an opening offer. There's no way we're signing your deal for less than seven figures . . .'

'And what am I putting in this autobiography?' Georgia asked as the car moved off. 'I'm a total phoney. I'm supposed to be this inspirational, political revolutionary, whatever. But I've never studied politics. I only see the news if my dad has it on in the kitchen. And I only got into SAG and RAGS because I was a lonely kid with a huge dumb crush on Zac.'

'The crush is a *great* story,' Wendy noted.

Georgia shrivelled in her seat. 'I don't want *everyone* knowing about Zac . . .'

Wendy let go of the steering wheel and drew a headline with her hand.

'You've got it all!' Wendy laughed. 'Family tragedy, hopeless romance, hi-tech explosions and a pretty face. So, do you fancy an early lunch, or straight back home?'

'Since you gave my press entourage the slip, could you drop me at my dad's old workshop? I'm sick of the clothes I had at Freeman and the bag Dad brought to my nan's is *hopeless.*'

'No problemo,' Wendy said. 'How's your picture of Eddie the polar bear doing?'

The publisher meeting had made Georgia forget she'd even posted.

'How many likes?' Wendy asked, as Georgia checked her phone

'Three hundred thousand,' Georgia said, hiding that she was quite proud of this. 'Loads of people are asking how they can help Eddie.'

'Good for Eddie,' Wendy said cheerfully as the car swung right.

John Pack's former workshop was a few minutes' walk from Georgia's old house, and less than fifteen from her nan's. When Georgia was little, the Victorian workshops had overalled men building staircases or fixing cars, but over time glass, grease and dirt with oak boards and white emulsion got replaced by roll-up doors.

'I'll drum up more publisher meetings when I get home,' Wendy said as Georgia got out.

'Fab-a-roo,' Georgia said, a wry smile making clear it was anything but.

As Wendy reversed back down the alleyway, Georgia got the horrible feeling she'd taken the workshop key off her ring. She smiled when she saw it and got a *Don't I know you from somewhere?* look from a lad passing with a tray of coffees for the market research company two doors along.

The workshop's ventilation hadn't been on in months and Georgia was hit by dead air and nostalgia as she stepped inside. She remembered the workshop being light, with drones hand-built at two long workbenches, while Uncle Phil and her dad worked on a mezzanine floor at the rear.

Police had searched the warehouse after the attack on the PM and nobody had taken down strands of EVIDENCE – DO NOT TOUCH tape.

While the front of the building was part of a Victorian stable block, the rear extension was an aluminium-sided cube. Georgia wasn't sure if the electricity was connected, so the light coming on was a bonus.

The rear had been used for storing components and a huge 3D printer. Now, the clean space looked like a modern art gallery, the main exhibit a pair of Ikea sofas that looked smaller and tattier than Georgia's memory of them.

Her old bed was tipped on end. Her wardrobe was nearby, but only a few stickers from early childhood were inside. Luckily, John had done a decent job labelling up cardboard moving boxes with a label printer that had belonged to his company.

John had enlivened the tedium of labelling dozens of boxes with humour. Georgia laughed at *Georgia's overpriced Japanese stationery* and *Stupid Kitchen Gadgets (Never Used)*. She had to slide boxes marked *Nasty Ikea China* and *Beach Towels/ Swimwear* to get to *Cookie's clothes* I, II and III.

She needed a knife to cut the thick packing tape and was wondering where to get one when her phone rang: *Julius calling.*

"Sup,' Georgia said brightly, as she propped herself on a sofa arm. 'I was wondering how you were getting on.'

'So-so,' Julius said. 'Ankle itching?'

'You saw my post,' Georgia laughed. 'It certainly itches when someone reminds me. Where are you?'

'Just ordered lunch in a restaurant on King's Road. The family house is a zoo. So I've spent one sleepless night getting bitten by fleas in a run-down farmhouse, followed by a night on a tiny kid's mattress in the third-floor study. Bad news is, I've got a crick in my neck. The good is, I've got money and some other stuff I need.'

'Need for what?' Georgia asked.

'Not sure,' Julius admitted. 'The thing is, there's no room in the house and it's the first place Immigration will come knocking. I wondered if you knew anywhere I could stay until I'm ready to fly home.'

'I'm staying with my nan,' Georgia said, then briefly paused to study her surroundings. 'I'm at my dad's workshop right now. I suppose you'd survive here for a couple of nights. There's a bed and a toilet. There's no shower or bath, but the electric's on, so there's hot water to wash down . . .'

'Beggars can't be choosers,' Julius said brightly. 'Will your dad mind?'

'What he doesn't know can't hurt him,' Georgia said. 'And once you've set the prime minster on fire, everything else seems like small beer . . .'

Julius laughed. 'I'll eat, then grab stuff from the house. How far are you from London?'

'It's half an hour on the train from Euston, then ten minutes in a taxi. I'll send directions, but I can't wait around here for hours.'

'Can I pick up the key at your house? Or nearby, if you don't want your dad to see me.'

'You could if there weren't twenty journalists camped outside my house tracking my every move. It took my publicist half an hour to shake them all off this morning. I'll have to hide the key . . . I'll think about a good spot and let you know.'

'You're a lifesaver,' Julius said cheerfully.

After hanging up, Georgia checked out front and saw a pair of hanging baskets ideal for hiding a key. She sent Julius instructions while it was all fresh in her mind, after which she froze in place, wondering if she'd done something stupid.

Why risk upsetting Dad when he's been so brilliant about everything?

Didn't you learn your lesson blindly following Zac?

You don't know Julius that well. What if he doesn't leave after a couple of days like he's promised?

Georgia fretted as she found a roll of bin liners under the sink and started picking things out. She'd never owned a ton of clothes and a lot of the stuff was old, small, or school uniform.

Georgia realised she'd have been better off asking Wendy to drop her outside Zara at the Pegasus Centre.

It was a fifteen-minute walk from the workshop. She'd have called a cab if she'd suspected rain, but was halfway to her nan's by the time the sky turned ominous.

Georgia quickened her pace, but was still minutes from home when thunder clapped and huge drops started blasting the pavement. She'd gone out in the flower-print dress and lightweight linen jacket, assuming she'd be going everywhere by car. With a big bag of clothes in each hand, she couldn't move faster than a jog, or even wipe the rain streaming down her brow.

The doorstep journalists had dropped from fifty to less than ten, but the photographers knew they had a story when Georgia dashed around the corner with straggled hair and her sodden dress clinging to her skin.

'Georgia, what happened?' a photographer asked, abandoning his umbrella on a neighbour's front lawn, then taking shots as he ran backwards. 'Can I have a smile?'

The photographer was joined by several journalists.

'Georgia, who is J?' one of them asked. 'Is he a boyfriend?'

The others were more interested in Eddie. 'Georgia, is it true you're launching a Save Eddie Appeal? Is there somewhere your fans can send money?'

'How old is Eddie?' another asked. 'Do you think he should be reunited with his brother and sisters in Abu Dhabi?'

Georgia stopped when she reached her nan's front gate. She put down the dripping bin bags, pushed soggy hair off her face and tried not to sound annoyed.

'Maybe you should all take the time to read my post,' Georgia suggested. 'It's not about the polar bear, or whether or not I have a boyfriend. It's about thousands of people who've been poisoned by a corrupt politician.'

'So, you're not interested in saving Eddie?' one of the journalists asked.

'Is the boy called James?' another interrupted. 'Or Joseph, or Jeremy?'

'Justin?' another added hopefully.

'Judas? Joshua?'

Georgia knew stamping her foot and screaming would be exactly what the soggy journalists were after and checked her emotions.

'Cheers,' she said brightly. 'I'm going inside to dry off now.'

Georgia fumbled her key in the front door, then smiled as she kicked it shut and saw her nan coming down the stairs holding a towel.

'Look at you, drowned rat!' her nan said. 'I saw you on the doorstep, so I grabbed this.'

Georgia felt loved as her nan picked the dripping bags off her hallway carpet and took them into the kitchen.

'Get yourself a hot shower and dry clothes,' her nan said. 'I'll sort these wet bags out and make a nice hot chocolate for you.'

SIXTY-FIVE

Georgia's phone went off at 5 a.m. the next morning. She almost let the call ring out, but grabbed it because only important people had her latest number.

'I know it's early, but I saw you were online,' Wendy began.

'I feel like I've got bluebottles fizzing around in my head,' Georgia explained tiredly. 'Everything's weird . . .'

'Can't sleep either,' Wendy admitted. 'Have you seen the newspapers?'

'What have I done now?'

'Nothing much. I'm sending a picture message.'

Georgia's phone made a *whoosh* sound. She put the phone on speaker and saw the picture she'd expected in the right-hand column of a tabloid front page: stressed and soggy with two bags of clothes and the clingy dress. *Soggy Pack* was the best the headline the writer had been able to come up with.

'How is *that* front-page news?' Georgia sighed.

'Slow news day,' Wendy explained.

'I want to run away and live in the woods until everyone forgets who I am . . .'

'There's an article about Eddie the Bear on page three,'

Wendy said. 'Animal Action have set up a *Rescue Eddie* fund and they've already raised thirty thousand pounds. They sent me an email, asking if you'd be prepared to act as a spokesperson for their campaign?'

Georgia tutted. 'Anything about the corrupt election, the terrorist bomb, or the thousands of poison victims puking blood and losing clumps of hair?'

'I told you that was never going to happen,' Wendy said. 'And remember, you'll be able to buy a very nice cabin in the woods with the money you'll make from your book.'

Georgia faked a laugh before Wendy ended the call.

As she put her phone back on the bedside table, Georgia realised she had more chance of being nominated for a medal by the prime minister than of settling back to sleep. A peek from the bathroom window showed more lurking journalists than the day before, but she also noted the low wall around her nan's garden. Behind the house, it met a back garden in the next street. Georgia felt confident she'd be able to climb over without the journalists out front seeing.

And she *really* needed to escape.

Georgia hadn't been allowed out of the Freeman Unit and now she was trapped by the press. She made instant coffee and grabbed a mandarin yoghurt from her nan's fridge. She ate in her room as she dug leggings and a sports bra out of her clothes pile, all the while listening out for her nan, who often woke early and might spoil the plan.

It was one minute past her 6 a.m. curfew and getting light as Georgia stepped through the sliding door in her nan's dining room. After three deep breaths and a set of calf stretches, Georgia jogged across her nan's lawn and was careful not to snag her electronic bracelet as she threw a leg over the back wall.

She felt bad, crunching hyacinths and kicking the neighbour's gnome. There was a gate at the side of the house, but it opened with a latch on the inside and she crept out into a street of average cars and shaggy front lawns.

The rush of air was freeing, but Georgia had adapted to months of indoor running. The pavement felt hard compared to the cushioned treadmill belt. Kerbs, corners and gradients strained joints in ways they weren't used to.

It was a Saturday, so the streets were dead. The sports ground was muddier than she'd expected. Seeing her old house was sad, with strange cars on the drive and a play fort out back, but St Jude's primary had barely changed. The Old Bulldog pub was being converted into flats and she was tempted to spring an early visit on Maya when she reached the edge of the Isaac Newton Estate.

But Maya hadn't visited the Freeman Unit, sent two-word replies to messages and her social media was full of pictures with a new boyfriend from her new school. So Georgia ran on. And while she'd taken a circuitous route, she'd subconsciously known where she'd been going all along.

'You awake?' Georgia asked, peering through the letter box and rapping on the metal shutter.

She was about to rattle again when Julius opened the side door, wearing socks, shorts and a back-to-front tee.

'It's early,' he noted, rubbing his eyes as Georgia stepped in and peeled off muddy Nikes. 'How's it going?'

SIXTY-SIX

Julius had only arrived the previous evening and Georgia was impressed by the mess he'd made in such a short time.

He'd dragged John's double mattress from amidst the stacked furniture and it laid on the floor. There were clothes and pizza boxes scattered around. More intriguingly, Julius had spread papers over a draughtsman's table and drawn a diagram with arrows and weird names on the whiteboard that spanned one wall.

'This is mysterious,' Georgia noted as she eyed bank statements, sets of company accounts and a stack of unused chequebooks.

'It's doing my head in,' Julius said. 'The day my uncle lost the election, he called in a panic and asked me to go to a bank. He was moving millions from Ondo government accounts to all these private companies with weird names, in weird countries like Liechtenstein and the Cayman Islands.

'Before coming here, I grabbed the rest of the cash from the family safe, plus expensive watches and a suitcase full of financial documents. Now, I'm trying to work out what's been going on.'

'What have you got so far?' Georgia asked.

'Mostly clueless,' Julius admitted. 'But I have to figure out what SJ is up to. He won't play nice with the new state governor. My mum is in prison and the rest of my family is getting screwed over, while SJ stashes millions in overseas accounts and won't help anyone.'

'How could he help if he's not governor any more?' Georgia asked.

Julius laughed. 'In my town, you can bribe your way out of anything. My cousin Ken says the new governor ran up big debts fighting the election campaign. Our family is the richest in Ondo State, so he wants cash and a cut of some fat contracts SJ awarded to Adebisi family companies while he was governor. Then all our legal problems will go away.'

'Surely SJ is in trouble too?'

Julius shook his head. 'Senior Nigerian politicians are immune from prosecution after they leave office.'

'Convenient,' Georgia snorted. 'And he left all these papers lying around the house?'

'They were in a safe,' Julius explained. 'SJ wasn't expecting to lose the election. I was the only one in London to do his dirty work and go to the bank when it happened.'

'So what are you trying to do?' Georgia asked.

Julius looked unsure. 'I already forged my uncle's signature a bunch of times. I'm wondering if I could write myself a big cheque? Or I could blackmail my uncle into helping the family, because I've got heaps of evidence about the money he stole . . .'

'You said he had immunity,' Georgia pointed out.

'That would stop them sending him to prison in Nigeria,' Julius said. 'But they could take the money back.'

'Do you want me to have a go at sorting these papers?' Georgia asked.

'If you wish,' Julius said. 'I've called Matt's dad. He's a financial advisor. He's got an early meeting, but he said he'll come by at eleven and look at what I've got. I haven't had breakfast or coffee. I might go get something.'

Georgia was thirsty from her run. 'The hipster coffee place on the corner does good smoothies. I don't have cash on me though...'

Julius unzipped a battered wheelie bag. 'If you're short, there's about a hundred grand in here.'

'Flash!' Georgia grinned, staring at neat bundles of new £20 notes, plus euros, dollars, fancy watches and a necklace set with huge diamonds.

'Rent money,' Julius joked, flipping Georgia a £1,000 bundle.

'I can't take that,' Georgia said, but she couldn't resist sniffing the centimetre-thick pack and flicking the pristine notes with her thumbnail.

'Promise not to leg it with my cash while I get your smoothie?' Julius joked.

'I'm less guilty about you paying,' Georgia noted as she dropped the twenties back in the wheelie bag and zipped it shut. 'And I demand a blueberry muffin.'

As Julius put his T-shirt back on the right way around and pulled on jeans and hoodie, Georgia looked at the mass of random financial papers on the desk, plus a full suitcase under the table, and realised she was going to need pens, Post-its and plastic file wallets.

When Julius got back with breakfast, Georgia had found her stationery and was happily ordering papers into piles, based on which company or bank account they related to.

She scrubbed Julius's messy scribbles off her dad's giant whiteboard and began a new chart in neater writing, showing the balance in each bank account, along with arrows indicating where money in each account had come from.

The exercise appealed to Georgia's perfectionist side. The part that wanted an A in every exam and felt off when her shoes weren't lined up under the bed. She looked irritated when Julius tried to help and groaned when her ankle bracelet bleeped and she had to call the monitoring centre.

By nine thirty, Georgia had a large, four-colour diagram on the whiteboard and stacks of paperwork in labelled folders. Her head turned and heart quickened when she heard a key rattle in the door.

'Why bother telling me where you're going?' John said as he stepped in. 'It's not as if I worry about you or anything...'

John narrowed his eyes on Julius and the double mattress, then at stacks of neat paperwork and his whiteboard filled with things like £3,294,016: *Ondo Department of Education*, surrounded by a spider of arrows showing where stolen money went.

'You've only been home *two* days,' John said, sounding unexpectedly cheerful. 'Can't you just get pregnant or do drugs like a normal teenager?'

SIXTY-SEVEN

Matt's dad, Miles Taylor, parked his McLaren in front of the workshop, emerged in a hoodie and sunglasses and peered up and down the street like he was expecting special forces to abseil down the buildings and put him under arrest.

'I wasn't expecting anyone but you,' Miles told Julius warily as he stepped into the workshop seeing Georgia and John.

'My son owns many pictures of you,' Miles told Georgia, then looked at John.

'I'm Georgia's father and this is my workshop,' John explained. 'No offence, but Julius is a kid. I stuck around because I'd hate to see him ripped off.'

'Fair,' Miles said thoughtfully. He shook John's hand, tucked his sunglasses into his collar and whistled as he stared at the whiteboard. 'There's some big numbers up there. Who made this?'

Georgia raised a nervous hand. 'And I've sorted the paperwork as best I can.'

'I wish the admins at my office were this efficient,' Miles said. 'If you ever want an internship at a financial firm . . .'

'Take her,' John said keenly. 'Keep her out of bloody mischief.

She can work seven days a week for free.'

Georgia rolled her eyes. 'Easy on the jokes, Dad. You wouldn't want us being rushed to hospital because we laughed too hard.'

Miles smiled at John. 'Remember when our kids just wanted to cuddle and build Lego?'

John nodded. 'A *very* long time ago . . .'

Miles sat at the table and started flicking papers and making notes. Julius, John and Georgia stood behind, staring.

'There's five thousand bits of paper here,' Miles told them. 'This is gonna take a few hours, so a latte and a cheese roll would be *great*.'

The hipster coffee place didn't do sandwiches, so Julius and Georgia took a fifteen-minute stroll to the high street. She got asked for two selfies while they queued in a baker's and a guy on the street asked Julius if he was Georgia's bodyguard.

She worried that someone would tip off the press, but they made it back to the workshop without getting tailed.

Miles barely acknowledged the arrival of lunch and let his latte get cold, as he flicked more documents and made more notes. As the others killed time, eating lunch and playing with phones, Miles called his office and told someone to cover his one-thirty meeting.

'Who's this Eddie?' Miles asked.

'The polar bear?' John asked, which made Georgia laugh.

'Yes, Dad, with the ice caps melting, polar bears are increasingly turning to careers in financial services . . .'

'Eddie's the guy I met at the West African Development Bank,' Julius explained, more helpfully, as he walked towards Miles at the desk.

'These are broken-ended transactions,' Miles explained admiringly. 'They're the holy grail of money laundering.

Virtually impossible to detect and the banking industry's dirty secret.'

'What's one of them then?' Georgia asked.

Miles turned his office chair to face his audience. 'When you have money in a bank, it's just a number stored in a computer,' he began. 'So what stops the bank from saying your hundred-pound deposit is really fifty pounds? Or a thousand pounds? Or a million?

'Banks would have us believe their systems are flawless. They'll never admit billions of transactions per day are handled by aged mainframe computers, running code written by dead guys, in languages modern programmers don't understand.

'Transaction dates get scrambled, interest is wrongly calculated. Money pops out of thin air, or vanishes into accounts that don't exist. If you know where the bugs are, a guy like Eddie can transfer money to another bank without leaving a trace.'

'If it's untraceable, how come you worked it out?' Julius asked.

Miles rattled two pieces of paper. 'Because you gave me papers showing both ends of the transaction. This piece shows money being transferred from an account at West African Development Bank into an account that doesn't exist. The other shows money arriving at a bank in the Cayman Islands.'

Miles fanned himself to show how exciting this was.

'I haven't added up every transfer, but we're looking at between forty and fifty-five million pounds that have been transferred from Ondo State to companies owned by SJ Adebisi.'

'Just my uncle?' Julius asked. 'SJ is the politician. My mum deals with business and money.'

'Your mother is nowhere in these transactions,' Miles said.

'Your uncle wanted his own nest egg,' John suggested.

Georgia butted in. 'But if SJ had a secret plan to steal money and hide it from the rest of Julius's family, why the hell did he get Julius to go to the bank?'

'Losing the election was a surprise,' Julius said. 'SJ had to grab the money while he was still in power. Eddie and the paperwork were in London. He had to risk using me, or not get the money at all.'

Miles nodded. 'If I asked Matt to go to the bank, I'd expect him to moan and ask for twenty quid, not launch a detailed investigation into my finances. SJ underestimated Julius, which gives us the upper hand.'

'The upper hand to do what?' John asked suspiciously.

Miles smirked. 'If we want to be good citizens, we box up this paperwork. I'll call the Serious Fraud Office. They'll freeze every bank account on this whiteboard and take the money away. Eventually, most will find its way back to Ondo State Government.'

'A lump of unexpected cash for the Rotimi clan to steal,' Julius scoffed. 'What's the other option?'

'SJ lost the election six months ago,' Miles began. 'We can't be certain the money hasn't been spent or transferred, but since SJ hasn't sent anyone to London to pick up documents and chequebooks I'm guessing it hasn't been touched.'

'Can we get at the money with the paperwork we have here?' Julius asked.

Miles nodded. 'An accountant, such as myself, can get power of attorney. This enables me to manage a person's finances, look at their account statements, purchase shares, move money, pay taxes and so on. To get power of attorney for SJ, I need financial documentation for all his accounts, which I have here. Along with SJ Adebisi's signature on a set of forms.'

'I faked his signature for all those transfers,' Julius said, then realised Miles had already worked this out.

'Once I get power of attorney – I won't use my own name or company, obviously – I can set up bank accounts in Julius's name and transfer SJ's money to him. If we move fast, Julius will have control over the money before SJ knows what we're up to. And he can't go running to the cops, because he stole the money in the first place . . .'

'Neat,' Georgia purred.

John looked more cynical. 'What's your cut?'

'Twenty-five per cent is normal,' Miles said. 'But since the amounts are large and Julius is a family friend, I'll do it for fifteen.'

'That's seven and a half million quid,' John said.

Miles looked slightly ticked off. 'John, if this goes wrong, it'll be me that goes to prison, not the kid. So yeah, I'll make a *lot* of money, but *my* nuts are on the chopping block.'

'Fifteen per cent sounds fair,' Julius said. 'How long will it take?'

Miles thought for a few seconds. 'I'll start making calls. I can have the paperwork ready by this evening. It'll take five working days to lodge the power of attorney, and I can set up Julius's bank accounts while we're waiting. Once we have the power, we'll need to move fast, in case your uncle gets tipped off by a bank letter or a bounced payment. If all goes well, you'll have your uncle's money in two weeks. Two and a half, tops.'

'I was planning to fly home sooner than that,' Julius said. 'Immigration might be after me.'

'I'll fix you up,' Miles said. 'I know a golf resort that's quiet out of season, and it's the last place anyone would look.'

'Makes sense,' Julius said, smiling.

'I like the idea of the hotel,' Georgia said longingly. 'Somewhere nobody will come looking.'

'Come with,' Julius grinned. 'You've got all that book money coming.'

To Georgia's surprise, her dad was nodding too. 'It's not a bad idea. At least until the press are off our backs . . .'

SIXTY-EIGHT

Georgia had spent thirteen nights in a room at Rushton Lodge, a luxurious golf resort and spa close to Cheltenham. She regularly played snooker with Julius in the hotel's deserted lounge and currently led the all-time score twenty-eight frames to nine.

She'd eaten nice food, chilled in the infinity pool, baked in the sauna, developed a taste for hot-stone massage and done the first two interviews with the journalist who'd been picked to write her life story in time for the Christmas gift market. And when the pampering got too much, Georgia pushed herself on long, muddy runs through the surrounding countryside.

But Julius and Georgia knew their lives were only on pause.

Over a late breakfast in the dining room, Julius took a call from Miles to say he'd be visiting with final paperwork. When Georgia got back to her room, someone from the front desk had set a package on the bottom of the bed.

She sliced parcel tape with the resort-branded letter opener and got an overpowering whiff of plastic from the air that had been trapped inside. When she tipped the box, cellophane-wrapped packs slid across the bed and crushed her soul.

A striped tie, white school blouses, black skirts, black tights, a shiny PE shirt with a school logo. The nylon blazer and pleated tartan skirts were stuck in the bottom and needed a thump before they dropped out, speckled with packing peanuts held by static.

'Ugh,' Georgia moaned.

She'd be sixteen in a month. Georgia didn't mind the idea of starting college in September, even though her time at the Freeman Unit meant she'd end up taking her exams a year late. The annoying part was the bit before summer holidays. The law said Georgia had to go to school. Her dad made lots of phone calls and the only school willing to take on the notorious Georgia Pack was St Thomas's Catholic Girls' school. It was an hour's bus ride from her nan's, and after five weeks and all the hassle of settling in, she'd be sent home on study leave for exams she was too late to enter . . .

'Are you decent?' Julius asked as he leaned in from his interconnecting room, holding a laptop. 'Your uniform arrived?'

'Come through,' Georgia sighed.

'Booked my flight home,' Julius said, and he sat on Georgia's bed and showed her his laptop.

Georgia choked up when she read the screen:

KL981 23:10 – Click to check in now.

'That's tonight,' Georgia noted.

'I've got a four-hour layover in Amsterdam, then an 06:30 flight to Lagos,' Julius explained. 'I paid for extra legroom.'

Georgia smiled. 'Very wise . . . Will someone meet you when you get there?'

'I've thought about that a lot,' Julius said. 'I'd rather the family doesn't know I'm coming, in case SJ gets tipped off.'

'I'm worried about you,' Georgia said.

'I'm worried about me,' Julius answered.

'You said the guys who killed Duke are still on the loose,' Georgia pointed out. 'What if they come after you? And how will you feel when you see all the places you went with Duke?'

The reminder of Duke derailed Julius's train of thought. But after a long breath, he spoke determinedly.

'My mother is in prison. My UK education visa expired three days ago, and I don't want to live on the run. I must fix this mess with my family.'

'I'll miss you,' Georgia said, pulling Julius into a hug, and was distracted by the odd realisation that his hair smelled of the same hotel shampoo as her own.

Georgia had loathed herself in all the different combinations of school uniform and was watching a trashy daytime talk show on Julius's bed when Miles arrived. He entered Julius's room in a tailored three-piece suit, carrying a double-width briefcase that hit Julius's bed with a whomp.

'Everything's here,' Miles said, opening the case to reveal stacks of paper.

Georgia moved around the bed to be nosy, and the newness of the chequebooks, bank statements and company formation documents gave her the same thrill as a fresh box of stationery.

'It's pretty self-explanatory,' Miles said. 'It's easier to hide money in a company than under a person's name, so I've purchased two ready-made companies and split your money between them. One in Bermuda, one in the Cayman Islands. I've also opened a personal bank account for you in Nigeria and typed up instructions for securely transferring money from the companies when you need to spend it. I currently know all your passwords, PINs and security questions, but you can change them if you wish. There are also prepaid Visa cards for an emergency.'

'How does that work?' Julius asked.

Miles pulled a padded envelope from behind nylon mesh in the briefcase lid. It contained twenty cellophane wallets and he ripped one open, revealing a Visa card and a sheet with a silver panel like a Lotto scratch card.

'These are pre-paid cards, each loaded with five thousand pounds,' Miles explained. 'The pin is under the scratch panel. They're registered under a mix of false names, so the best way to use them is to draw cash from an ATM. I thought it would be good for you to have access to emergency funds when you arrive in Nigeria.'

'How much did I get?' Julius asked.

'The total amount I was able to pull from SJ's accounts was forty-two million. Minus my fifteen per cent, you get to keep £35,750,000. That's a little less than I was hoping, but I couldn't touch one account, because your uncle is actively using it to set up a new life.'

Julius looked intrigued. 'New life?'

Miles looked pleased with himself as he slid out a green wallet halfway down the briefcase and showed Julius a bank statement. There were lots of transactions in UAE dollars for designer furniture, Ikea, a Dubai Lexus dealer and a high-end jewellery store.

'Your uncle has a girlfriend,' Miles explained. He tapped a woman's name below *Simon J Adebisi* at the top of the statement. 'Nanna Holm. Google says she's a Norwegian software developer, who recently worked in the IT department at the Port Harcourt branch of the West African Development Bank.'

'SJ has four wives and nine kids,' Julius said disbelievingly. 'Maybe eleven. I've lost count.'

'If I had four wives and eleven kids, *I'd* want to run away,' Miles pointed out. 'Besides buying jewellery and furniture, your uncle paid six million US dollars for a villa on Dubai Creek and has a four-hundred-thousand-dollar powerboat on order.'

'I wouldn't have guessed,' Julius said. 'But he's never liked living under my mum's thumb. And he's protective towards his kids, but his wives are hellcats.'

'How can you have four wives?' Georgia asked.

'Yórùbas are traditionally polygamous,' Julius explained. 'It's less common now, because Christian ministries disapprove and women won't stand for it. But a few rich men still take more than one wife. My grandpa had seven over the course of his life, which is why I have a trillion cousins . . .'

'Planning to run off explains why he's not bothered about your family,' Georgia noted. 'And if Nanna worked at WADB, it must be her who put him in touch with Eddie.'

Julius nodded. 'It also explains why SJ wants my mum in prison. She has contacts *everywhere*. If she was in the wild, she'd sniff out the truth and come down on my uncle like a hammer.'

'So why is SJ still in Nigeria?' Georgia asked. 'He had a villa, fifty million and a hot Danish girlfriend.'

'I've heard estimates my family is worth close to a billion dollars,' Julius noted. 'Most of that is in my mum's companies. SJ probably wants to get his mitts on some of that before he skips town.'

'Does this change your plan?' Georgia asked, hoping Julius might stay longer.

He thought for a few seconds. 'This information fills in a lot of blanks,' Julius said. 'But as nice as this resort is, I'm going crazy waiting for the rest of my life to start.'

SIXTY-NINE

Georgia felt like running to clear her head, but Julius was going home, she had to go back to her nan's to start school and this was their last day to hang out.

Julius had two suitcases packed and ready to roll. A smaller third case and the thick briefcase Miles had left behind lay on the end of his bed.

'I'm taking the details for my Nigerian bank account and six of the prepaid Visa cards,' Julius explained. 'The rest of my documents are in this briefcase and I want you to look after it for me. If I phone or message and I call you Georgia, that means everything is fine. If I call you Miss Pack, that means I'm probably being tortured for bank account details by one of my uncle's thugs and you should ignore any instructions I give you.'

Georgia looked anxious. 'You really think your uncle might hurt you?'

'I'll do my best to avoid that,' Julius said, trying to smile reassuringly. 'SJ won't be happy when he finds I've stolen his nest egg, but I have extra leverage now I know he's planning to leave his wives and run away. And he can't take my money if all the documents are here with you.'

'You trust me?' Georgia asked.

Julius half-smiled, then shrugged. 'I have to trust someone. If I disappear, wait a year, then contact Miles and tell him to donate the money to charity.'

'Just stay here,' Georgia pleaded. 'You could probably claim asylum since your mum's in prison. Or live under the radar.'

Julius shook his head. 'I don't want my mother rotting in jail. And who looks out for Gabe and all my country cousins?'

'Your mum exiled you for being gay,' Georgia pointed out forcefully. 'Your cousin murdered Duke.'

'Nobody's perfect,' Julius joked, then unzipped a wheelie case. The interior was half-filled with twenty-pound notes.

'I've kept the dollars,' Julius explained. 'But that's a hundred and twenty thousand pounds. It should cover your legal bills and part of your stay at the Freeman Unit. There's even room for most of your new clothes.'

'I can't take it,' Georgia gawped, but found herself thrilled by the packs of mint twenties. There was also a red ostrich-leather jewellery box.

'It's the pendant my mum bought when she met Barack Obama,' Julius explained. 'You can wear it to prom.'

The hinge creaked as Georgia opened the box. The gold necklace had a simple clasp that held three pear-cut diamonds, two the size of currants, with an insanely sparkly grape in the middle.

'If you don't like it, sell it,' Julius said. 'Must be worth a few quid . . .'

Georgia shook her head. 'I'm getting almost a million for my book deal. *I'm* paying my parents back. I can't take this.'

'I've got way more currency than I'm legally allowed to

bring into Nigeria,' Julius said. 'The last thing I need is to have customs arrest me when I land.'

'I'll keep it safe for you,' Georgia said. 'With the chequebooks and everything else.'

Julius had other things on his mind and Georgia felt like her friend was already moving away as he sat at a desk and started googling options for buses from Lagos to Akure.

John Pack got to Rushton Lodge an hour later, dressed in a suit. He'd spent ten nights a few rooms down from his daughter. But he'd gone back to his mum's, because he had several meetings in London for his new job with the defence contractor.

There was time for a late lunch in the hotel restaurant before John and Julius carried all the luggage down to his Ford. The Focus wasn't huge and Julius had to put the front passenger seat all the way back to accommodate his legs. Georgia had an uncomfortable ride, cramped behind her dad with luggage sliding on the seat beside her.

Julius felt nervous as they parked up and rode an elevator down to Heathrow Terminal Four. He kept it together as he left John and Georgia with his flight bag and wheeled his luggage to the KLM bag drop.

'No point you guys standing around,' Julius said rigidly, when he came back with his boarding pass and luggage receipts tucked into his passport. 'And you never know how long it'll take to clear security.'

'Keep safe, mate,' Georgia said tearfully. She went on tiptoes for a goodbye hug, but found herself too low, until Julius dropped down on one knee. 'Message me every day.'

'You, Matt and Alex are my only friends in the world,' Julius noted, smudging tears away. 'You'll be sick of my messages.'

Georgia tried to say, *I won't*, but it came out as a big sob.

John didn't feel close to Julius, but the emotion was contagious, and his eyes glazed as he hugged Julius goodbye.

'I might never see him again,' Georgia's voice wobbled as Julius got eaten by an automatic door.

'Course you will,' John said, sliding an arm around his daughter's back and giving her a squeeze and a kiss on the cheek. 'This has been a long day! I need coffee before we drive back to your nan's . . .'

SEVENTY

Julius had the right accent and his skin was the same colour as everyone else's, but Nigeria no longer felt like home. The sun seemed too bright, tropical air sapped his strength and the six-hour bus ride to Akure was a hell of loud voices, potholes and body odour.

He could have afforded one of the black cars lined up outside International Arrivals, but the drivers were controlled by the Lagos Transport Union and notorious for taking passengers a few kilometres before robbing them at gunpoint.

The bus stopped in Ibadan and Ife, where driver and conductor climbed on the shabby roof to retrieve luggage. Julius peered out nervously, making sure nobody tried to make off with his airline-tagged Samsonite bags that would surely catch the eye of every crook who saw them.

A handsome preacher boarded in Ife and acted sore when Julius refused to buy a Bible with a 3D Jesus on the cover. Julius craved the code of silence on the London Underground as the preacher squatted in the aisle at the back of the bus and started singing hymns with the four large women squashed in the back row, occasionally breaking rhythm when the bus jarred their spines.

Twenty-one hours after saying goodbye to Georgia, the bus clattered into Akure's transit park. It hadn't rained all day and evening sun made an orange haze, with the windowless hulk of the bombed Transport Union building silhouetted and the sickly smell of diesel from local buses that were too unreliable for drivers to cut their engines.

The arrival of a long-distance bus drew beggars, boy porters, women selling soft drinks from wheeled coolers and unlicensed taxi drivers. Julius hadn't peed in six hours, but while less-burdened passengers charged the breeze-block toilets, he didn't dare take eyes off his luggage.

'Young sir, may I help with your bags?' a man half Julius's height asked.

'I have a good Toyota,' a competitor blurted. 'Local driver. Back streets, no traffic!'

Julius glanced about warily as the conductor walked around the roof, unhooking a rope net and passing down cases.

Accepting smart Samsonite bags with airline tags sent wannabe porters and taxi drivers into a frenzy. Julius doubted himself as he batted a hand grabbing his case. How could he sort complex family problems when he didn't have the street smarts to scuff up his luggage?

'You need a hotel?' a girl asked excitedly.

Julius baulked when he looked at her. Barely older than himself, she was all bones and sharp angles, with pop-out eyes and random tufts of hair. She matched all the symptoms of water poisoning, but the bags made him vulnerable, and if he gave the pitiful girl money he'd have beggars coming from every direction.

'Julius, Julius!' Remi Balogun hailed.

The greying journalist stopped dead, clutching his ribs as Julius took his final bag from the conductor.

'I thought you'd forgotten,' Julius said, sweeping his brow with relief.

'I am *so* sorry,' Remi said. 'I was waiting in the wrong place. How were your flights?'

'I survived,' Julius said, one eye on the toilet block. 'Can you watch my bags?'

After one of the best pees of Julius's life, Remi took the smallest of the three cases and led the way through the bustle to a double-cab Isuzu pick-up.

'New wheels,' Julius noted, slamming the passenger door after they'd locked his bags in the back.

'It belongs to TV Nederland,' Remi explained.

'How's that working out?' Julius asked, dust coming off the tyres as they rolled out of a dirt lot at the rear of the transit park.

Remi didn't answer until he'd rolled down his window and paid four hundred naira to a Transport Union flunkey.

'I'm a dog chasing my own tail,' Remi said. 'My heart wants to fight corruption here in Akure. My head says stick with the salary, car and expense account.'

Julius looked curious. 'If you had money, would you campaign full-time?'

'If!' Remi said sharply. 'You can only make money in Ondo State by being corrupt. So who funds the man who fights corruption?'

'I'm so sorry about what happened,' Julius said, after a pause.

'You loved Duke as much as I did,' Remi noted as they turned into clogged traffic.

'It's partly my fault,' Julius said guiltily. 'Collins took a special interest in Duke, because of me...'

Remi shook his head. 'Duke might be alive if you hadn't been his best friend. Duke might be alive if I'd sent him home to his mother, instead of bringing his mother to Akure. One thing you must learn is not to waste your life picking apart decisions you cannot change.'

'I know,' Julius said weakly.

'I'll take you to my apartment,' Remi said. 'Are you certain you wouldn't prefer a hotel?'

'There are only two decent hotels,' Julius said. 'My mum always got tipped off when someone interesting arrived in town. I want my family knowing I'm here when *I* want them to know I'm here.'

'Unfortunately, I must leave tonight to film a report in Mali,' Remi said. 'A Dutch fashion chain has announced it will only use organic cotton in children's clothes.'

'How does that take you to Mali?' Julius asked.

'Organic is *very* bad for cotton farmers, because fields cannot be sprayed with chemicals that stop malaria.'

'And you can get that story on Dutch news?' Julius asked.

'The story has a good hook,' Remi explained. 'Poor Malian children working in cotton fields die of malaria so that rich European children can wear organic.'

'That sucks,' Julius said, shaking his head as he glanced out the window at a huddle of hairless beggar kids.

'I've asked discreetly on your behalf,' Remi said. 'SJ's behaviour since he lost the election has baffled everyone. My source at the governor's mansion says Rotimi is keen to settle with SJ. He's asked for a lump sum to clear his election debts, a cut of your mother's profitable contract to supply Nigerian

431

army uniforms and assurance that no member of the Adebisi family will stand against Rotimi's son in the next election.'

'Why his son?' Julius asked. 'Rotimi's not even sixty.'

'There is a three-term limit for state governors,' Remi explained. 'Rotimi can't stand again.'

'If Rotimi gets his money, my mum goes free?'

Remi nodded. 'And the harassment of the Adebisi family ends. Rumour is, SJ wants the governor's job back. He's not fussed about money, but he won't agree a deal that stops him campaigning again in three years.'

Julius knew his uncle didn't want the governor's job back, but although Remi was being a big help, he was a journalist with no love for the Adebisi family. Julius reckoned it safest to keep SJ's secrets to himself, for now.

Rush hour meant the seven kilometres from Transit Park West to Remi's apartment in the north took an hour. Since Remi had to leave for Mali, they ate suya from a street stand before heading up six floors. Even if they'd wanted to risk the elevator, the electricity was out and Julius was a sweaty wreck after two trips to the sixth floor with luggage.

As he rolled his second bag through Remi's new front door, Julius noticed the wooden screen that once divided the room flat to the wall and Duke's bed replaced by a boldly striped sofa.

'I couldn't face seeing his bed every time I came home,' Remi explained. 'The new couch pulls out for you to sleep on. My aunt stayed a few nights. She said it was reasonably comfortable.'

No electricity meant no air conditioning, and as Remi slid the balcony doors open for a breeze, Julius realised photos of Remi's glory days as a correspondent for NTA had been swapped for some of Duke's best drawings.

'He was *so* talented,' Julius said as he studied a large drawing.

Duke's pencils had captured a St Gilda's classroom, down to tiny details like the trapped dirt where floor met skirting board and the speckled pattern of the ceiling tiles. Breaking from realism, the uniformed kids at the desks had the heads of wolves, devils and fork-tongued lizards.

'I have a poster tube for you,' Remi said. 'Some beautiful sketches Duke made of you.'

'Thank you,' Julius said, peeling his soggy shirt from his skin. 'I stink. Can I use the shower?'

'Naturally,' Remi agreed, checking the time as he pulled his passport from a kitchen drawer. 'It's impossible to get diesel in the city right now. My back-up generator is dry, and the power grid hasn't been on enough to stop food going bad in the fridge.'

'A cold shower will do,' Julius said.

He undid his belt and started emptying pockets onto a tabletop. It was fully dark now and as Julius stood by the balcony door to catch a breeze, he noticed a huge white hangar, glowing in the midst of Arctic Zoo.

'What's happening up there?' he asked.

Remi's brow furrowed with contempt. 'That's for Siberian tigers and the bloody polar bear,' he explained. 'They can't get a licence to move Eddie to his new home until his infected skin clears up. So they've built him an oxygen chamber and put him on a special diet. They've got brand new Jeeps that buzz in and out, day and night. The vets and zookeepers have taken over the executive floor at the Palace Hotel.'

'My friend's tweet raised a million pounds,' Julius noted.

He realised his phone was down to seven per cent as stepped out onto the balcony, hoping there was enough light to get a decent pic for Georgia.

'Georgia hoped the picture of Eddie would raise awareness of other stuff in Akure, like the water poisoning.'

'Westerners who dabble piss me off,' Remi said bitterly as Julius stepped back in from the balcony. 'They get it wrong so often, I can honestly say I prefer the ones who don't give a damn.'

'Georgia's cool,' Julius said defensively.

'Eddie gets fresh fish delivered by helicopter,' Remi said. 'But the local zookeepers got kicked out and threatened with arrest for breeding animals without a licence. Once the last animals are gone, the city will sell the land. I bought this apartment because I liked the view over the trees, but in five years, all you will see is high-rise blocks.'

Julius stumbled tiredly as he unzipped his biggest case and fished out boxers, T-shirt and toothbrush. Apart from a nap on the flight to Lagos, he'd been awake for forty hours and his body had hit a wall.

'Shower and sleep,' Julius said as he stretched into a big yawn. 'I will solve all the world's problems tomorrow...'

SEVENTY-ONE

Georgia: Sooo, how's Akure?

Julius: Hot, dusty. Sinuses bunged-up from the long flight and massive bruise where the woman on the bus kept digging her elbow.

Georgia: Chucking rain here. Sucks you being so far away. What you got planned for today?

Julius: Gotta pick up stuff from my old house. Then find a way to deal with SJ without getting my ass kicked.

Georgia: And I'm worried about an induction meeting at a Catholic girls' school. Guess mine is more of a first-world problem . . .

Julius: I need to get out of bed.

Georgia: I'm very fond of you. Try not to get your dumb ass killed.

Julius: I promise nothing :-) . . .

GEORGIA PACK HAS LOGGED OUT

The springs on the sofa bed strained as Julius stood up, rubbing his back. The mattress wasn't bad, but even when he lay at a diagonal, bits of him dangled off all sides. He cold-showered, dressed inconspicuously in shorts, sunglasses and grubby canvas Vans, and drank lukewarm juice from a fridge that hadn't seen electricity in hours.

Remi said Adebisi thugs hadn't been near the building since Duke's murder, but Julius stayed cautious as he crossed the lobby, then a modestly busy street, to an ATM in the front of a grocery store.

There were three people in line and Julius felt he was being watched when he put one of his pre-paid Visa cards in the slot. It was a minor triumph as the machine spurted a wad of ₦1,000 notes.

He bought Lipton tea, iced water and yam porridge in a cafe. The manager grumpily agreed to change a couple of ₦1,000s for the two-hundreds he'd need to pay bribes.

The peppery mashed yam felt more like home than anything else since Julius had landed. He smiled to himself, remembering how he'd taken porridge on his first morning at boarding school and found it was a white slush, reminiscent of baby sick.

But if breakfast had bolstered Julius's spirits, they crashed as he crossed back to the apartment building and down to the basement storage cages. Taxis weren't practical if he got in a situation where he needed to get away, and the closest Julius had come to driving a car was a tractor in a field, not a car in city traffic. But he'd ridden scooters around his family village as soon as his feet were able to reach the pedals.

The basement was lit by slit windows that cast long shadows into the mesh storage cages. Duke had died here and he imagined Collins's crew laughing as they posed with his corpse.

Julius turned the key in Remi's storage cage. He'd forgotten to ask about Duke's scooter before Remi left, and for all Julius knew it had been sold.

The cage had a battery-powered light that worked on a motion sensor. It showed an old bedsheet over the scooter as it flickered on. The petrol tank was two-thirds full. Julius remembered a seat with a split big enough to fit your hand in, but Duke had replaced it for a better one before he died.

He wheeled the scooter out of the cage and down a short hallway. Out in sun, the engine had a debate before starting, and since Julius hadn't ridden in two years, he decided to practise, riding figure-eights around the concourse. The sun dazzled, but over several circuits, Julius noticed how concrete around one of the pillars was cleaner than everywhere else.

Where they scrubbed Duke's blood...

Julius couldn't look once he'd seen it. He throttled up angrily and blasted on to the street. He was a wary rider. Taking it slow, getting the feel for steering and earning honks from more experienced riders when he stopped rather than brave narrow gaps in traffic.

A roadblock took a couple of the two-hundreds he'd rolled up while eating breakfast. A tiny paper ticket gave him a pass for the rest of day, provided he didn't lose it.

Pedestrians didn't look, and truck drivers seemed to target scooters for sport, but Julius's major fear was cops. Traffic police rarely wasted bribe-earning time arresting people, but they'd clean out his wallet for riding without a licence.

Julius tensed as he took the ramp on to the beltway, but while some cars moved scarily fast, he soon realised the straight road was less stressful than city traffic.

'Young Julius,' the guard on the development's main gate said brightly. 'Very long time! And taller than ever.'

Julius had worried about being let in. Now he'd been recognised, he worried the guard might tip someone off. After public roads, the deserted streets of the gated development felt like carpet. Unsure what he'd find at his former home, he buzzed past slowly.

The perimeter wall was unchanged, but there were no soldiers on the front gate. Between the heavy bars, he saw a dust-coated Lexus that couldn't have moved in weeks and a battered VW minivan.

Julius stopped at the dust-blown lot where he'd jumped in the helicopter at the start of his exile. He decided to park the scooter behind a faded *For Sale* sign and walk back to the house.

He'd never had a key, because there were always guards to let you in. After a wary glance at the security cameras, Julius stayed close to the wall as he jogged down the alleyway to the service gate at the rear.

He'd seen no sign of life from the front. Through the rear gate, he realised there was no sound or exhaust coming from the generator building, and while he couldn't see every roof-mounted air-conditioning unit, the ones he could were clogged with dust.

Julius looked at the brushed-steel keypad on the gate pillar and cursed himself for being unable to remember the code.

The numbers wouldn't come, but muscle memory saved him. Moving his finger from the one to seven felt wrong. It was one, three, seven. There was definitely an eight . . . *Unless they've changed the code . . .*

There was a satisfying click, followed by a squealing hinge as Julius pushed.

Flies fizzed around the big waste container behind the generator building. Julius lifted the lid, enough to catch a stench and see fresh vegetable shavings.

The door at the back of the kitchen was locked, so Julius

cut around the front. The Lexus looked dustier from close up, but the scuffed VW van had its sliding side door open. Its interior had a hydraulic ramp and a metal frame to stabilise a wheelchair.

The front door was locked too. Julius had almost reached the point where he'd decided to ring the front doorbell and hope someone friendly answered, when he saw a gap in the sliding doors on the pool deck.

He remembered the twins out on the tiles, playing music and acting like bullying dicks if he wanted to swim. The pool filter gurgled, and the water was chlorinated.

The living room had lights and a ceiling fan turning. Julius recalled that on a bright day the solar roof panels were enough to run Orisa's kitchen and keep his mother comfortably cool in her office.

The furniture looked the same, though there were crumbs on the carpet and a wheeled table, designed for a wheelchair to park underneath. Julius knew Taiwo had been paralysed since the Mercedes ambush, but the plate with food cut small and a two-handled drinking cup made it real.

Julius thought he heard someone in the kitchen. It was most likely Orisa and part of him wanted to say hello. But he couldn't be certain, and Orisa liked to think she was the boss when Bunmi wasn't around. Julius didn't want a grilling about why he'd come home and what his plans were.

The elegant bannister on the main stairs had been replaced by guide rails for a wheelchair lift. When Julius reached the first floor, he swept past his mother's office and five bedrooms before stepping into a plant room.

Along with cleaning stuff, there were flashing internet routers, fuse boxes and master switches for everything from the fountain by the front gate to the solar panels on the roof. At the centre of it all were two screens, each split into nine pictures from the CCTV system.

The family rooms weren't monitored, but there was a camera in the security booth that overlooked the front gate. Julius was sure he'd have been spotted if there was a guard on duty, but it was still good to see the booth empty, while several dead cameras suggested nobody had monitored the system in a while.

As Julius backed out, he heard a soap on the TV in Taiwo's room. He tried imagining what he'd feel when he saw his brother in a wheelchair.

Focus, focus, focus . . .

Julius stepped into his own room. The air felt ancient, but the cleaning staff had done their job before the money ran out. Objects stirred memories of his old life. Graphic novels, skateboard parts and St Gilda's uniform. Most cringeworthy were the girls he'd pinned to the wall to throw people off the scent.

Duke and Georgia would die *laughing if they saw . . .*

Julius reached deep under his mattress and was relieved to touch the gun and ammunition clip he'd grabbed on the day of the ambush. He found his old school pack in the bottom of his wardrobe. After tossing schoolbooks that simultaneously felt very familiar and like ancient relics, Julius dropped the gun in the bottom.

He added a couple of polo shirts so the shape of the gun wasn't obvious, then grabbed a folding knife from the drawer of his desk, checked that his little LED torch had a battery and dropped both in the bag.

Satisfied with his haul, Julius headed quietly back to the

stairs. His next stop would be the garage, where the security staff used to keep a good stock of stuff like extendable batons, ammunition, tactical vests and pepper spray to deal with armed thieves or a kidnap attempt.

But Julius only made five steps before his mother's office opened behind him. He glanced back to see a spiky-haired woman leap into the hallway and before he reached the stairs she'd shot a metal barb into his thigh and zapped him with 50,000 volts.

SEVENTY-TWO

Julius used every swear word he knew as he spasmed into the wall, knocked down his mother's African Businesswoman of the Year award and collapsed to the floor with his leg twitching violently.

Orisa came rushing up from the kitchen.

'Burglar,' the woman shouted anxiously. 'I thought I heard something while I was putting Taiwo's washing away . . .'

'Don't,' Orisa gasped, waving her arms frantically to stop a second zapping. 'It's Julius.'

Julius's legs were jelly as he noticed Taiwo wheeling himself out for a look.

'Why are you sneaking around?' Orisa steamed. 'When did you get back?'

'Who the hell is she?' Julius asked, furiously pointing at the spiky-haired woman and feeling queasy as blood oozed into his shorts.

'My friend Delilah,' Orisa explained. 'She helps me with Taiwo. I can't look after him twenty-four/seven.'

Taiwo was arriving in a powered chair. The mashed food had made Julius imagine some tortured golem, but he didn't look

442

that different – dressed in a tracksuit, with patterns shaved in his hair. The only sign Taiwo couldn't get up and walk was a dead left hand and a droop at one side of his mouth.

'What's the queer doing here?' Taiwo asked, slightly slurred.

'Nice to see you too, bro,' Julius said.

'Go back to your TV,' Delilah told Taiwo.

Julius had never met Delilah, but knew the name of the woman Orisa met up with on her day off. He'd spent his boyhood imagining lunches and shopping trips.

'Why's he here?' Taiwo repeated sourly. 'Nobody tells me what's going on.'

As Delilah stewarded Taiwo back to his room, Julius shuffled so that his back was against the wall.

Orisa crouched and looked at the barb, which was still attached to the zapper by two fine lengths of conducting wire.

'Taiwo's still a dick,' Julius said, shaking his head. 'Your girlfriend's cute though . . .'

Orisa soured, before realising Julius was on her side and cracking a slight smile. She snapped the fine wires, then inspected the oval of blood growing in Julius's shorts.

'Does it hurt?' Orisa asked, wiggling the barb slightly.

Julius yowled. 'It does when you do that.'

'Such a baby,' Orisa said, giving the barb a contemptuous tug.

'Oww, oww, oww, oww!'

Julius imagined a geyser of blood, but it just stung as he undid the top button of his shorts and peeled them down to inspect a wound no bigger than a fly.

'Lunch?' Orisa asked as she handed Julius a tissue. 'I assume you'll survive the walk . . .'

Julius limped down with a dead leg and settled on the living room couch with a foot on the coffee table. Delilah came in with clean shorts from Julius's room and a plaster for the wound.

'Not my best introduction,' Delilah apologised. 'I have heard much about you.'

Orisa was coming through with a bowl of pepper soup on a tray.

'Don't be sorry,' Orisa told her girlfriend. 'What can he expect, creeping about the place?'

'I missed your cooking!' Julius said brightly as he sniffed the bowl.

'It's just microwaved,' Orisa said. Then, more stiffly, 'So why sneaking around? I do not recall us falling out.'

'I didn't know who'd be here,' Julius said, then blew to cool his first spoon of soup. 'I'm not the most popular member of this family, in case you haven't noticed.'

Orisa nodded. 'You saw my little brother in London?'

'Ken's good,' Julius said. 'The twins are super cute.'

'When did you get back?'

'Yesterday,' Julius said, then added a lie. 'I stayed at a hotel.'

'Do you need money?' Orisa asked. 'We've not got much, but we muddle through.'

'It's weird seeing this house run-down,' Julius noted. 'I heard the court froze all Mum's bank accounts. Is SJ giving you an allowance or something?'

'Not since the start of the year,' Orisa said. 'We've lived by selling your mother's jewellery.'

'Have you seen her in prison?' Julius asked as he took a wallet from the back of his shorts.

Orisa nodded. 'It's a nasty place. I took Gabe with me the first time and he cried all the way home.'

'Is Gabe OK?'

'So popular at school,' Orisa said. 'Friends and parties, and an excellent soccer player. But he's subdued around the house.'

'He worries,' Delilah added.

Julius reached across and handed Orisa a pre-paid Visa card. 'That's loaded with five thousand UK,' he explained. 'Minus twenty thousand naira that I took out of an ATM this morning. The PIN is 3301.'

Orisa exchanged a wary glance with Delilah as she took it. 'Is this all of your money?'

'There's more – don't worry,' Julius said. 'I'm gonna speak to SJ and sort things out.'

Orisa shook her head. 'He won't see you. I've called twenty times to ask for help and you just get his assistant. I've been up to his new apartment. The first time, I waited in the lobby for four and a half hours, before Luke came out and ordered me to leave. The second time, I wasn't even allowed in the elevator.'

Julius nodded. 'Everyone at the house in London said SJ was ignoring them. But I can be persuasive.'

'You're a boy,' Orisa scorned. 'We can look after you here. Things are bad, but family must stick together.'

Julius shook his head. 'I'm sixteen. The same age my mother was when she started her textile business.'

'What's the masterplan?' Delilah asked.

Julius didn't answer.

'I need some things from the garage,' he said as he grabbed the clean shorts. 'Then I have to get to St Gilda's before school kicks out.'

SEVENTY-THREE

Julius's height made it tough to hide, so he didn't try. If anyone asked, he'd say he was planning to surprise Gabe when he got out of school.

St Gilda's main parking lot had the usual mums and bodyguards waiting to pick up kids. Julius walked through the lot, then round the side to a single line of cars parked up against the senior school building.

St Gilda's had no bays for top-form kids who'd earned driving licences, but some teachers sold their parking stickers. The senior school day was a few minutes from ending when Julius recognised the Mercedes that Collins received for his eighteenth birthday.

For his plan to work, Julius needed to get in the car alongside his cousin, without witnesses or fuss. If Collins arrived with mates or a friend to drop off, Julius would have to think up another plan, or try again the next day.

As the school bell trilled, Julius sat against a giant palm. A couple of guys from his old class stopped for *Hi, why are you here?* type conversations, but he acted stand-offish and kept a wary eye on the Mercedes.

He watched the senior year's richest kids ride off in butch pick-ups, Japanese coupes and American muscle cars. By four, the lot was two-thirds empty and Collins's Mercedes stood out amidst humbler cars owned by teachers.

Collins either had detention or training. The wait frayed Julius's nerves, but the upside was a lot less people around than at school kick-out time.

It was closer to five when Collins showed, but signs were bad. He was with a line of guys, their football boots scraping the tarmac. Collins had always been more feared than liked and was a brooding, shirtless figure at the back. He had socks pushed down so you could see his shin pads and his training shirt wound around his hand.

A teacher got into a tatty Subaru across the lot as three players kept walking towards the main lot. One player jumped into a Mitsubishi pick-up, while another stopped to admire Collins's car.

'Nice wheels,' the kid said.

Collins glowered wordlessly, making the younger boy scuttle off. Julius felt he only had seconds before Collins got in his car, but it was a huge risk with four soccer players and a teacher nearby.

But while the Subaru drove out and the players got further away, Collins walked around to drop a kitbag in his trunk. He threw Reebok pool sandals down by the back wheel, then leaned against the car to strip off his football boots.

As his cousin balanced on one leg, Julius stepped from behind the big palm. The Mitsubishi was leaving and the soccer players about to turn into the main lot as he made eight long strides. Julius had a hand on the passenger door before Collins even noticed him.

'Don't touch my car,' Collins roared. 'Hey!'

He ran to the passenger side as Julius slid into a bucket seat.

'I'll rip your arms off,' Collins yelled, tugging the door. 'Get out!'

'Need to talk, cuz,' Julius said as he slid the gun out of the backpack between his legs. 'If you run, or yell, I'll shoot ten holes through this fancy car.'

Collins bunched fists and the tendons in his huge neck went rigid. 'Do you think you'll get away with this?'

Julius ignored the question. Guns were lethal and noisy, so he kept one hand close to a stun stick hooked to his belt.

'Take a deep breath,' Julius urged. 'Walk around the front and get in.'

There was a smell of armpits as Collins's torso hit the driver's seat.

'Close the door, start the engine.'

'If I don't?' Collins sneered.

'I loved Duke,' Julius said coldly. 'You think I won't shoot you?'

Julius imagined blasting his cousin's brains over the Bengal-red leather. It was a satisfying mental image, but he had a job to do.

'There's too many people around here,' he said. 'I've found a spot a few blocks from here.'

There was a blast of rap music as Collins pushed the engine start button. He was impulsive and not very smart, so Julius saw short odds on Collins trying something rash as they rolled out of the school grounds.

It was the lull between school traffic and rush hour. Roads were clear as they drove a kilometre to a row of empty spaces behind a dental surgery that had moved to bigger premises. Duke's scooter was locked to a sign advertising tooth whitening.

448

'Now what?' Collins asked. 'If you kill me, my dad will hunt you down.'

'SJ won't let anyone in to see him,' Julius explained. 'He's stopped taking my calls, so I need you to phone him.'

Collins's iPhone was linked to the coupe's Bluetooth. Julius watched him use buttons on the steering wheel to dial his dad.

'Uncle?' Julius said, gesturing for Collins to keep quiet as the call got answered.

'Who is speaking?' SJ asked suspiciously. 'What are you doing with my son's phone?'

'Collins is here,' Julius said.

'Who is this?' SJ repeated.

'Your favourite nephew, Julius. I'm sat in a *very* nice Mercedes with a gun pointed at Collins. Say hello, Collins.'

'Dad, he made me drive,' Collins blurted. 'I'm at—'

Julius jabbed his cousin with the stun stick.

'Oh, God, God, God,' Collins yelled frantically. 'Dad, send all your guys to Smile Kleen Dental on—'

Julius squeezed the orange trigger, delivering another 250,000-volt spark.

'Shut your mouth,' Julius ordered. Then to his uncle, 'I'll be gone before anyone gets here. But your future will be a lot brighter if you listen to me for two minutes, right now.'

'Is this about your school fees?' SJ asked. 'I told my girl to fix that. It must be a mix-up . . .'

It amused Julius that his uncle thought him stupid enough to stage a dangerous kidnapping for a few thousand pounds in school fees.

'This is about your Norwegian friend Nanna,' Julius explained. 'And the 3.75-million-dollar apartment at 615 Crest View, Dubai Marina.'

449

SJ made a weird grunt.

'Does Collins know your plans?' Julius teased, keeping the stun stick poised in case his cousin moved.

'Whatever you are trying, it will come to nothing,' SJ said firmly.

'It already came to something,' Julius said. 'Check your bank balances. Apart from the joint account you set up with Nanna, the money I helped you move on your last day as governor has been transferred to me.'

SJ didn't know what to say next and Collins looked subdued. He'd clearly had no idea that his dad was planning to do a runner.

'Make the deal that Rotimi put on the table,' Julius ordered. 'Get my mum out of jail. Once that's sorted, you can piss off to Dubai. You won't starve. There's a couple of million in the account Nanna has been using, and the Chelsea house is worth millions.'

'Why would I be frightened of a lanky schoolboy?' SJ snorted. 'You take my money? I'll make you give it back. And your mother will rot until *I* say.'

'Here's what happens if you don't make a deal with Rotimi,' Julius said, sounding cooler than he felt. 'In one week, I'll inform your four wives that you're planning to swan off to Dubai with Nanna. I'll also send out evidence of the money. They can't send you to prison for stuff you did while you were governor, but the British authorities can charge you with money laundering. They'll seize your new pad in Dubai and the house in Chelsea.'

'A Rotimi deal is not as simple as you make it sound,' SJ interrupted. 'You and I need to meet . . .'

'This is the *only* conversation we are going to have,' Julius said. 'And in case you're thinking about sending thugs after me,

I've set things up so that only my friends back in England have the security details for the money I stole. If anything happens to me, the money goes to charity and the evidence will be posted to your wives, the British police and Governor Rotimi's office. They also have instructions not to move money or release any other information until they see me *personally*.'

'You are unreasonable, just like your mother,' SJ grumbled.

Julius decided to take it as a compliment.

'Uncle, I'm being generous.'

'I need to think,' SJ spluttered.

'About what?' Julius asked bluntly. 'If you don't make a deal with Rotimi, I'll approach his people and pay for my mother's release. But I'll make sure terms are *much* less favourable to you.'

'I can make a few calls to see what I can do to help your mother,' SJ said. 'Please. Let us meet and discuss this in a civilised fashion.'

'Not happening, Uncle,' Julius said, almost laughing.

SJ lost his cool. 'You think you are a big man?' he shouted. 'You think I have no choice? Let me tell you, boy. Few things are more dangerous than an animal backed into a corner.'

Julius felt the threat, but it meant his uncle was rattled and he kept his voice level.

'I'm leaving Akure shortly. I won't be back until you have arranged my mother's release,' Julius said. 'I'll text you a number so you can let me know how things are progressing. And you'll need to call an ambulance to the Smile Kleen Centre. Collins won't be playing soccer any time soon . . .'

Collins had been cowed by the stun stick and the revelations about his father. As Julius raised the gun, Collins scrambled to open his door.

'Please,' he whined.

Julius enjoyed hearing his cousin beg and felt no hesitation as he shot Collins through the back of his right kneecap. There was a long scream and sprays of blood as Julius threw the passenger door open.

SJ was still on the speaker. 'What was that?' he demanded. 'You'll pay, Julius! Pay one hundred-fold!'

'That was for Duke,' Julius said.

Then he tucked the gun into his shorts and hurried towards the scooter.

EPILOGUE

The British Museum – London, UK

Georgia's conditional release didn't allow her to leave the UK, while Julius's stay beyond the expiration of his education visa made it tough to get back in. They cracked huge smiles across the sprawling museum cafe when they laid eyes on each other for the first time in almost four years.

Julius had just turned twenty. He'd stopped growing at six-feet-nine. His shoulders had broadened and he'd grown a goatee.

Nineteen-year-old Georgia had short, dyed, scruffy hair, paint-spattered jeans and a plaid shirt with rolled sleeves. Her face had barely changed, but she'd done everything short of cosmetic surgery to stop randoms walking up and saying, *Hey, aren't you . . . ?*

'Way too long!' Julius said as he pulled Georgia into a hug. 'Sorry I'm late. This place is a maze and my Uber dropped me at some weird side entrance . . .'

'All good,' Georgia said, smiling as she sat back at the table.

The table was up against a railing. As Julius settled in, facing Georgia, he glanced down into an area where kids from different schools were eating packed lunch.

453

'We can move if they're too noisy,' Georgia said as a kid crashed backwards off her chair.

'So, you're an art-school girl,' Julius said cheerfully. 'With the paint under your nails and *everything*.'

Georgia buried her hands. 'I picked art because I'm determined not to turn into Sophie. But I'm a geek at heart and I'm thinking of packing it in to do Physics. How about you? How's Switzerland?'

'Mountains and cuckoo clocks,' Julius joked.

'Your Artificial Intelligence course?'

'The social side is a blast and the work's easier now my French has improved. Basically, *anything* that keeps me out of Akure is good.'

'I thought you were doing good deeds there,' Georgia said.

Julius shrugged. 'I was the biggest donor to Remi Balogun's governorship campaign, but he still got his ass kicked by Rotimi Rotimi Jr. I had better luck turning the Arctic Zoo penguin pool into a skate park.

'It's actually funny, because they've built fancy new apartments all over the old zoo site, but in the middle of it all, there's my park full of graffiti and shady kids. It's only the second skate park in Nigeria, so yeah, I'm proud.'

'Pretty special,' Georgia agreed. 'And the family?'

'Gabe's at The Hall and seems to be sticking his dick in *everything*. I'm gonna visit him while I'm over. Mum's richer and dodgier than ever. Rotimi thought he was on to a good thing, getting a cut of my mum's textile business, but it took her about six months to turn tables and sink hooks into him.'

'How is she with you?'

'Split,' Julius said, smiling awkwardly. 'On one hand, I'm the brainy one. I got her out of jail when SJ almost had her beat and she says she wants me to take over the business some day. But she won't accept that I'm gay . . . How are your lot?'

'Dad's off all over the world, running one of the top teams in the World Drone Racing league. He's happy. Wants me to try out as a pilot, but I didn't delete all my social media and spend three years keeping out of the limelight to do something that will create headlines.'

'I was sorry to hear about your nan,' Julius said.

'Thanks,' Georgia said, shaking her head. 'At least she didn't suffer.'

Georgia tried to catch the eye of a waiter, but he sailed by.

'Did you bring my book?' Julius asked.

Georgia looked embarrassed as she grabbed a paperback out of the canvas bag hooked on the back of her seat.

The cover said *No.1 Bestseller – Now in Paperback. The Last Word, Georgia Pack*, while the picture had Georgia in a fake police mugshot.

'*A riveting insight into the mind of an ordinary teenager in extraordinary circumstances*, the Sunday Times,' Julius said, reading the quote on the back as Georgia shielded the book in fear that someone would spot it and recognise her.

'I thought you'd read it,' Georgia noted as she hunted for a pen.

'Twice,' Julius said. 'But I still want the signed copy you promised me.'

'OK,' Georgia sighed, writing a message inside the front cover as a waitress arrived.

Georgia got coffee and cake, Julius a pot of tea and a tuna melt.

'And how's the love life?' Julius asked, once the waitress was out of earshot.

'Ugh,' Georgia said, sighing as she slid the just-signed book across the table. 'I never seem to get a handle on that . . .'

'Same as,' Julius laughed. He spun the book around and opened it to read Georgia's message.

'It's cheesy,' she warned.

But Julius smiled when he read it:

It's not easy to change the world.
But you gotta keep trying, right?
Georgia Pack.
xxx

Discover more books and sign up to the Robert Muchamore mailing list at muchamore.com

muchamore

muchamorerobert

@robertmuchamore

Have you read *KILLER T*?

Read on for a taster . . .

1 SLASHED RUBBER

Deion Powell was the king of high school. Stubbled and swaggering. *Powell 03* on the back of his practice jersey and a splayed walk imposed by monstrous thighs. An amber late slip flapped in his hand as the starting quarterback bowled the empty hallway, crunching in desert grit trailed from the parking lot.

'Whatcha staring at?' Deion snapped instinctively as a skinny ninth grader came out of an empty classroom. He had to hook the door with his sneaker because there was a set of textbooks stacked to his chin.

The kid jolted. Catching the door frame with his shoulder, almost spilling *Algebra 2*s, before Deion's bunched fist set him off in a rodent scuttle.

But there was too much in Powell's head to enjoy the humiliation. There'd been a tussle in the locker room after Monday night practice. A minor miracle that the coaches hadn't found out. And that morning, Deion's kid sister bounced for the school bus, but doubled back before clearing the driveway. Uptight and wide-eyed, the nine-year-old blurted that the front tires on his truck had been knifed.

So, the quarterback took a city bus and fifteen-minute jog, missing first period and catching a lecture from a tattooed school clerk, who'd heard too many excuses to care if they were true or not. *Third late arrival since summer recess. Can't come and go as you please, making like you're above the rules.*

Stress bulged Deion's veins. Sweat glazed his oak-brown skin. *Should have taken a picture of my tires to show I'm no liar. Five hundred bucks for new ones. Must have been JJ. Will everything kick off again? What if we bump JJ's crew in the hallway? And no way to avoid it in the locker room ...*

Deion's locker had been decorated by the rally team. *Powell 03*, sprayed through a stencil. *Rock Spring Rockets* stickers and nylon rosettes fixed on with sticky pads. An invite to *Aisha's 18th – Foam Partaaay* poked out of the door. He tried fitting a face to Aisha's name as he turned the locker dial.

Eighteen, six, twenty-two.

There was a grunt of realisation as Deion let his backpack drop off his shoulder. He usually left football gear in his truck on the school lot. The locker was crammed. Books, baseball cleats, protein shake pouches and a Bluetooth boom box he'd tried selling to a teammate who'd never come through with the money.

Maybe it was easiest to keep hold of the stuff. *Dump it in Terence's VW at recess.* But this made the walk to the locker another waste of time, on a day when everything was going bad.

Calm down. Think straight. Don't let stuff get to you.

'This sucks,' Deion raged, smashing his palm on his locker, and kicking the one below with his size thirteen.

His thoughts had been balled too tight to hear the girl who'd turned into the hallway behind. Pink cotton pumps, a *Rock Spring High* gym shirt and milky, vein-pencilled legs. He'd startled her and was about to apologise when . . .

Noise ripped. So loud it hurt inside both ears. Blazing light. Heat. The girl screaming. The yellow locker door, unhinged and smashing Deion in the face. Stumbling. Blood. Tripping on something. A mouthful of dust, and ceiling tiles falling like oversized confetti.

2 NOT HARRY POTTER

The klaxon yowled as twenty-four hundred high-schoolers bustled out into sun-blasted gravel and hundred-degree heat. Out of fire doors and down clanking metal stair treads. A few straddled first-floor windows. Smoke plumed from the Zone C annexe as emergency sirens wailed.

The clueless school security guard kept a wary hand on his taser. Teens from the dance studio felt scorching sidewalk on bare soles and a math teacher rolled a kid in a wheelchair past the cholla cacti at Rock Spring High's main entrance.

'This is *not* a fire drill,' a deputy principal yelled, pit stains showing as he waved students away. 'Do not gather at the assembly points. Just get as far from the building as possible.'

'Is there a shooter?' someone asked, almost colliding with a kid who walked backwards, videoing the smoke.

'Heard shots for sure,' another body close to Harry Smirnov said. 'Five or six.'

Harry followed the crowd away from school on a paved path, his jog slowing as bodies funnelled through mesh gates. He was a ninth grader. Fourteen, slender limbs, floppy black bangs, still more boy than man. He'd only been in Las Vegas eight months since moving from the UK with his aunt.

In the run-up to leaving London, Harry's two best mates joked darkly about American high-school shootings. One even wrote *mind the bullets* in his leaving card and drew a stick man letting rip with an Uzi. Now the joke seemed thin.

'Smoke's from over by the wood shop,' someone behind Harry noted as a guidance counsellor urged teens not to shove at the gate. 'My dad's a carpenter. One place he worked, there was a spark in the dust extraction and the whole joint went boom.'

'Where you going, Harry Potter?' Lupita from Harry's homeroom spat, as he cut off the path. 'Ain't no other gate up there.'

First name Harry, a black mop and an English accent made the nickname inevitable. Even his home-room teacher used it.

Vegas didn't get a lot of rain, but baked-hard ground meant flash floods when a storm hit. The mesh fence around Rock Spring's perimeter ran parallel to a concrete drainage channel, eight feet wide and half as deep. Harry stepped down into the basin, brushing weeds growing through cracks as he started a crouched jog towards the smoke.

He glanced back, but fellow evacuees saw nothing past backs of heads and shuffling limbs. The drain's sides were graffitied, the base littered with occasional pyres made from melted nylon backpacks and black-edged textbooks. These had been squirted with lighter fuel and burnt up by college-bound seniors before summer break.

Harry ducked instinctively as an ambulance skimmed the access road across the fence, lights flashing but siren off. It turned through a set of vehicle gates eighty yards ahead. The storm drain went under this access road, but the thought of snakes in the dark sent a chill down Harry's spine, so instead of charging through he lay against the gently angled wall, checking the scene as the sun cooked the back of his neck.

Smoke had been tamped by a fire crew, and puddled hose water was evaporating into a rainbow haze. This part of the school was single-storey classrooms, with a taller main assembly hall and lunch room behind. Shatterproof panes had twisted out from their frames, and aluminium roof sheets jutted into the air.

But Harry sensed calm. Two relaxed cops guarded the school's service entrance as a lunch lady in kitchen whites led a fire officer round the edge of the building, seeking a shut-off valve. Harry cupped one ear and listened to a police lieutenant briefing the freshly arrived ambulance crew.

'Some kind of explosive. Got the area cleared out and locked down, but don't hang around inside. We can't be certain it's the only device until there's been a full search.'

Harry's mum had been a photographer and journalist. She'd taken a bullet in the Ukraine and won awards for her vlogs from Brazzaville during the Third Congo War. After living in war zones, her death was ironic: wiped out by an undiagnosed heart defect as she jogged in London's Hyde Park.

Harry had been seven. His mother's death had left him with a mortal fear that his heart could explode, a fascination with news websites and an urge to follow her path.

He read biographies of famous correspondents and photo-journalists. He liked war documentaries and obsessed over films like *Spotlight* and *All the President's Men* where journalists kicked butt. A swanky Nikon camera topped Harry's Christmas wish list, back when his mates were still into *Star Wars* Lego and console games.

Until now, the fourteen-year-old's journalistic experience comprised an Under 12s Photography Prize, rugby and cricket reports for his old school in London and a Rock Spring Neighbourhood News blog that he set up at Digital Arts summer camp. But here was proper news, and Harry had the first camera on the scene.

His fancy Nikon was at home, so his phone would have to do. Harry unlocked with an iris scan and flipped to *advanced camera* mode. Sunlight bleached the screen, so he had to click and hope for the best as he shot the little rainbow and buckled roof.

There was a chance the cops at the door would see Harry dash between the storm drain and the side of the building. He was no rule breaker, but he'd waited half his life for a story. Every crunch of gravel felt like a sonic boom, but Harry timed it well and cracked an exhilarated smile as his back hit the wall by an open window.

What if there are more bombs? What if some nut jumps out of a storeroom with a machine gun? This is such a buzz ... This is why Mum loved it so much.

HOT KEY BOOKS

Thank you for choosing a Hot Key book.

If you want to know more about our authors
and what we publish, you can find us online.

You can start at our website

www.hotkeybooks.com

And you can also find us on:

We hope to see you soon!